Cut Short

A DCI Liam Doyle Thriller
Book 1

B.D. Spargo

Published by

Howfen Press

CUT SHORT

Published Worldwide by Howfen Press

This edition published in 2024

Copyright © 2024 BD Spargo

ISBN: 978-1-7385516-0-6

Howfen Press

bdspargo.com

To Chrissy,

I hope you enjoy it!
Best Wishes

Ben
ps. sorry about the British
spelling

For my Dad - Ted

Prologue

June 1996

The garden gate gave the faintest of low-pitched creaks as it opened. But that was enough. The cat flap rattled, and a barking ball of fur covered the twenty feet between the boy and the back door in seconds. He had been expecting this, and had come prepared. Before the mutt could sink its teeth into his ankles, the wire rope ligature was around its neck. The sudden lack of oxygen stifled the yelp before it was out of the Yorkshire terrier's mouth. The boy ducked back into the shadows, lifting the dog into the air, its legs flailing like a cartoon dog running over a cliff. With one gloved hand over the looped end, he pulled the wire hard with the other, locking eyes with the beast as its tongue popped out. It stared back, confused, perhaps pleading for its life. The boy smiled, his arms outstretched so the dog's stream of urine didn't soak his trainers. The dog's eyes bulged, then rolled back in its head.

The dog wasn't the reason he was there; it was just an obstacle to be overcome, though a pleasing one. When he was certain the creature would never bark again, he set it down and removed two petrol cans from his bag. He could smell an unfamiliar putrid smell, and it was coming from the shed where he knew the pigeons were housed. A loft, she'd said it was called. He didn't know how many birds were in there, and he didn't care. What mattered was that they were their owner's pride and joy.

He splashed the petrol all over the timber shack from top to bottom, working quickly, taking care not to spatter his clothes. The shed was attached to the rear of the house, and he threw some petrol over the back door for good measure. He took the box of Swan Vestas from his pocket. He struck a match then put it back in the box to light the others. He threw the flaming matchbox at the petrol-soaked shed, which went up with a *whoosh*.

He stood, transfixed, for a second. Then he was running, back along the ginnel, dead dog in one hand, bag in the other. He stopped briefly to throw Toto into a dustbin, and shoved its carcass down beneath some food waste.

The boy was nearly back at his accommodation when he heard the sirens. It would have been a rush to stay and watch, but he knew it was far too risky. He hoped she would appreciate it. Other boys tried to win her over with showing off and lewd gestures. None of them knew her or really cared about her, beyond wanting her. She would see that he had done this for her. Football might be coming home this summer, but those homing pigeons had made their last trip back to Fleetwood.

入 入 入

His good mood was lifted further when he saw Michelle sitting in her usual spot in the utility room. The sun was already up, and even the overgrown garden with its missing fence panels looked inviting. The rest of the house was at peace too. He didn't imagine that would last long. She smiled at him, flicking her long dark hair off her face, giving him a better view of her big brown eyes.

'Hey, Jay. Where did you get to last night?'

Even her voice did something to him. And she had noticed his absence!

'Had something I needed to do. Did any of the staff notice I wasn't here?'

'I covered for you. It wasn't any of the regulars on. A couple of bank staff. They couldn't give a fuck, anyway. Probably pissed off they were working when everyone else was watching the football and getting wasted.'

Her scent caught Jay's nose as he walked past the stool she perched on: its rich citrus tones briefly blocked the smoke and gasoline mix rising from the pile of clothes in his hands. If she noticed, she didn't comment, just casually flicked through *Cosmopolitan* as she sipped her tea. She was used to seeing him do his washing at this time of day. That was how they'd got to know each other. At least today his laundry wasn't wet sheets and pyjama bottoms, hurriedly stuffed in the machine before any of the other boys in the home could see. That would give them further ammunition. She never said anything about that either. She must have noticed, but she was kind, not tainted with the cruelty all the other kids seemed to have.

'I've got something to show you,' Jay said, tipping powder into the machine's drawer.

'Well, go on, then, let's see it.' She turned to face him expectantly.

'Not here. Come for a walk with me?'

'Can we smoke this on the way?' She pulled a long joint from the pocket of her Kappa tracksuit top.

'Even better.' Jay's reply was interrupted by a boy entering the room, polluting the atmosphere.

'Did you see Gazza's goal yesterday? That shut the Jocks up.'

He lunged at Jay and punched his arm. Jay felt his bicep start to deaden.

'You don't want to hang around with that little queer, Michelle. Come over to the old docks with me and we can smoke that – and then you can suck on this.' The boy grabbed the crotch of his jeans with one hand and pouted.

'Fuck off, Screech. I wouldn't go near your rancid thing. Are you coming, Jay?'

Screech punched Jay again, this time in his side, as Jay followed Michelle out of the room.

'Oh yeah, I forgot you only like sucking on your daddy's cock.'

Michelle flinched, almost imperceptibly, as the taunt hit home.

Chapter 1

Day 1: Tuesday 13th June 2023

'For fuck's sake,' Doyle said in what he thought was a whisper as the brown puddle flowed over the top of his size twelve brogues. Now, not only were his smart shoes muddy, but his socks were also wet, and dirty water had splashed up his suit trousers.

'Is that French, sir?' Anna Morgan enquired as she got out of the driver's side of the Peugeot hatchback.

'Something like that,' Doyle said. He was silently berating himself for leaving his bag containing more substantial footwear and other useful bits of kit at the self-storage unit. He was keen not to come across as an amateur or a policeman not used to operating outside big cities. He noticed that Morgan's footwear, in keeping with the rest of her casually smart appearance, was much more suited to the task ahead.

It was a beautiful summer's day. Shafts of light penetrated through the tree canopy that shaded the gravel car park. They had pulled up alongside a blue van marked 'Crime Scene Investigation'. The car park also contained an ambulance, a police van and what Doyle presumed was an unmarked police car. This almost certainly belonged to the man in a shirt and tie standing by the entrance to a footpath. There was another man chatting to the CID officer. From his short shorts and dayglo T-shirt, Doyle guessed he was not part of the police contingent. The man appeared restless and was bouncing up and down on the balls of his feet. What was missing from the car park was the Vauxhall Astra that the two detective constables from his new team had set off in a couple of minutes before Doyle and Morgan had left Force HQ.

'Blimey, size of you, d'you play rugby league?' Shorts man asked Doyle as he walked over.

'DCI Doyle and DS Morgan, Major Investigation Team.'

'Are you a cockney?' Shorts asked Doyle.

'DS Cooper, Chorley CID,' the man in the shirt said.

'What have we got?' Doyle asked.

'It was called in by this gentleman…'

'Dave Kirby,' Shorts interrupted, holding out a hand, which Doyle reluctantly shook.

'You found him, then?' Doyle asked, directly addressing Shorts for the first time.

'No, it were Trevor.'

'Is Trevor still here?' Doyle asked.

'He's in car. Down by reservoir.'

'OK, one of us will need to speak to him, get a full statement.'

'That will be a bit tricky,' Shorts said. 'Trevor's my dog.'

Doyle tried to keep the irritation off his face. 'In that case, Mr Kirby, we will need to speak to you. Now, why don't you go and wait in the car with Trevor? Someone will be along to see you soon.'

'Oh, OK, no problem.' Shorts turned and with some reluctance set off down the hill away from the car park.

Doyle waited until he was out of earshot before continuing. 'We've been told that you've got the body of a dead boy, and the death looks suspicious?'

'Not quite. The victim is a young woman. Dave Kirby thought it was a teenage boy who had fallen or jumped from the cliffs when he called 999. He didn't get too close. In fact, he wouldn't have seen the body at all if his dog hadn't run off through the fence and then barked at the body.'

'He didn't check if they were alive, or try to give first aid?' Morgan enquired.

'I think he just assumed they were dead, and was too squeamish to look further. He seems pretty shaken up by it. We've already got his details and taken a brief statement.'

'What makes you think it's not accidental or suicide?' Doyle asked.

'The paramedics. They say if the person was alive when they dropped, there'd be loads more blood.'

Doyle had seen a few falls from height in his time, including a defenestration from a tower block in Southwark. They certainly weren't pretty.

'What made Mr Kirby think it was a teenage boy, not a young woman?' Morgan asked.

'Well, like I said, he didn't get too close. But she's wearing a black tracksuit and trainers, and I guess you could say she looks boyish. You know – short hair and that.' The CID man blushed as he looked at the obviously female short-haired detective sergeant.

'It's about a five-minute walk up that way. You'll see the forensics lot when you get there,' Cooper said, indicating the footpath leading into the woods.

Doyle followed Morgan through the metal gateway past a sign welcoming them to the West Pennine Moors. The arrow on the map told him he was in a place called Anglezarke. He was pleased to find that the path was well maintained; despite his inappropriate footwear, he was able to avoid most of the puddles along the route. The track took them through woodland, where large rocks nestled between the trees as if they had been thrown there by giants long ago. Moss grew on rocks and tree trunks, giving the impression that everything was covered in a green fur. At the edge of the trees to their right, a rock face jutted up. Its top was above the treeline, hidden from view. It would have been a pleasant summer walk, Doyle thought, if they weren't going to view the body of some unfortunate soul who had met a premature and tragic end.

'What is this place? Doyle asked.

'I believe it was once a quarry. They cut the stone out of the side of the hill. Above us is moorland stretching out for miles. If you want to know more and you've got a spare hour, DC Nelson will be able to give you chapter and verse on the history of the place.'

'Thanks. Your abridged version will do for now.'

A uniformed constable greeted them at the crime scene tape and pointed at a box containing forensic scene suits, overshoes and nitrile gloves. The constable took their details for the log as Doyle set about wrestling his giant frame into the forensic suit. A task, he noticed, that Morgan completed effortlessly. Doyle was grateful for the PPE: the route off the path looked a good bit muddier and was lined with suit-shredding brambles. A car bumper and other detritus littered the undergrowth: Doyle presumed these had also been thrown from the cliff, the top of which was still obscured by trees. He opted to climb over the two-bar fence that separated the foliage from the path, following Morgan, who had squeezed her slender figure between the two rails. The pair picked their way over the aluminium stepping plates, laid down by the scene of crime officers, towards the ghostly white tent. This was perched on top of a ledge that jutted out from the base of the rock face, several feet above the ground.

Doyle was impressed they had managed to get the tent set up there, but not surprised. It generally took a lot to put SOCOs off their game. A figure sporting a disposable white suit and holding a camera complete with flash gun emerged from the tent. Doyle briefly looked up. From this angle, the quarried-out cliff face looked imposing. If the victim had been alive when she went over the top, there was no way she would have been after she landed. He could understand why Dave Kirby hadn't seen the need to get closer and try to give first aid.

'Jen, this is DCI Doyle.' Anna Morgan brought his gaze back down. 'Sir, this is Jen Knight, Crime Scene Manager.'

'Liam. Pleased to meet you, Jen. What's it looking like?'

'Appears she was dead when she was thrown from the top. The pathologist is on her way – she will confirm. Victim's on her back – I assume she landed that way. I'm thinking she must have been dropped there sometime before yesterday evening, as we had that big thunderstorm then. Her clothes are damp, but the ground underneath her appears dry. We will know more when we move her. The clothes are a bit odd – a cheap black tracksuit and trainers, both too big for her. Looks like they were brand new. The trainers have certainly never been walked in.'

'Dressed after death, you think?' Doyle was racking his brain for other possibilities.

'That's what occurred to me. I was able to check the pockets as she was on her back. Nothing at all, I'm afraid.'

'What's up top? How easy is it to access?' Doyle enquired.

'If it's where I'm thinking, there is a car park and a viewing spot. Wouldn't be difficult to park up there at night and launch her over the cliff,' Morgan answered.

'You're right – that's where it is,' replied Knight. 'I've a colleague up there now, and we're treating that as a crime scene too.'

'Good. We'll take a look after we've finished here.'

'I'm not sure we'll get much from this level from a forensics perspective. We'll have a good look in case anything useful, like a handbag or phone, was thrown over as well. I'm hoping to have some more bodies here soon to help, but we're a bit stretched at the moment. Half the team are looking at an arson from Sunday night in Limbrick.'

'Thanks, Jen. Shall we?' Doyle gestured to the tent before gingerly climbing onto the ledge. 'Normally I would suggest ladies first, but it doesn't seem so gentlemanly in the circumstances.'

'It's OK, boss. I'll take age before beauty on this occasion.'

In these situations, Doyle always had a fleeting moment when he was filled with dread at what he was about to see. This familiar sensation had to be overcome as swiftly as possible. He peeled back the fabric and entered the shelter, banishing the fear until the next time.

She would have been pretty, he thought. Her eyes were open and unseeing, the whites blood-spotted. Her limbs stuck out at unnatural angles, distorted by the fall. How old was she? Doyle wondered. Twenty? Twenty-Five? A bit older, maybe. She was slim, with dark hair. Someone's daughter, sister, lover – maybe even mother. He hoped not the last one. Her tracksuit top was zipped up so her neck could not be seen. With a gloved hand Doyle reached across and very gently unzipped it to just below her collarbones. And there it was: the unmistakable mark of a ligature. About the thickness of Doyle's little finger, halfway down her neck. This was strangulation, not hanging, Doyle knew. He'd seen similar marks with suicides, and even accidental strangulations, but the victims seldom removed the ligature then threw themselves over a cliff.

'Poor girl.' Morgan's words hung in the air.

Doyle studied the imprint on the woman's skin. He could see a faint pattern – not a weave or a twist that you would get with a wire or a corded rope, but straight lines going across it from side to side. There was something familiar about it, but he couldn't place it. He took out his phone and photographed the marks. Forensics and pathology would do this, of course, for evidential purposes, but it might be useful to have the image before the PM. He also took a picture of her face: the first thing they needed to do was find out who she was. Then Morgan drew his attention to the victim's midriff. A strip of pale white skin was exposed above her waistband where the tracksuit top had ridden up. On her left side, the green edge of a tattoo was visible – it looked like a stem, with thorns. With a delicate hand Doyle pulled the tracksuit top further up, revealing the rest of a red rose tattooed on her lower abdomen. He clicked off another pic.

Chapter 2

Back at the car park, Doyle noted that a blue Vauxhall Astra had arrived. He would have mistaken its occupants for a grandfather and his teenage grandson had he not been formally introduced to them the day before. The older man had a neatly trimmed white beard and a bald pate that reflected the sunlight. He was Detective Constable Derrick Nelson. The younger man was almost certainly not a teenager, but he couldn't have been older than mid-twenties. He was Detective Constable Zach Washington. He was dressed in skinny trousers that stopped several inches short of his ankle and flat-soled plimsolls with no socks. His upper half was clad in a short-sleeved shirt, revealing toned biceps – the result of hours in the gym rather than any meaningful use, Doyle guessed.

The DCs were walking back from the ambulance. Zach Washington had a notebook out, so Doyle assumed he had been asking the medics for some details.

'Do you think they stopped off for a bacon and egg McMuffin on the way?' he asked Morgan.

'You've not been in a car with DC Nelson driving yet, boss. It's like going out for a Sunday afternoon drive with your nan.'

That was in contrast with their own journey to the crime scene: Morgan had guided the little Peugeot at breakneck speed past everything in its path, blues and twos on. Doyle appreciated that; the early hours of an investigation were precious. This had, of course, meant that he'd not had the opportunity to get to know his new detective sergeant. He'd preferred to let her concentrate on the road.

'Boss, Sarge,' Nelson greeted them. 'We've got all the details from paramedics, who were first on scene after it got called in. The ambulance are crazy busy this morning, so we've let them get on their way. They've agreed to give formal statements when their shifts are finished.'

'That's fine,' Doyle said.

'There's a man called Dave Kirby waiting in his car by the reservoir...' Morgan said.

'Wearing short shorts?' Nelson asked.

'That's him,' said Doyle.

'He was doing press-ups on the pavement as we drove in.'

Morgan rolled her eyes. 'He found the body while he was walking his dog. Can you and Gadget get a statement from him? We're going to have a look up top, where she was thrown over.'

'You might find you get more sense out of the dog,' Doyle added.

'It will probably turn out to be a waste of time,' Nelson said. 'Mile and a half that way and you're out of Lancashire and into Greater Manchester's patch. More than likely, that's where our lass will turn out to be from.'

'You may be right, Derrick. But until we know otherwise, she's our body and our victim, and we'll do all we can to find out what happened to her.'

As they walked back to Morgan's car, she deviated across the car park, gesturing for Doyle to follow. She headed towards a parked BMW estate. A woman sat in the open boot, pulling on a pair of Wellingtons.

'DCI Doyle, I would like you to meet Dr Gupta, Home Office Forensic Pathologist,' Morgan said.

'Very pleased to meet you, Dr Gupta,' Doyle said to the

pathologist, who looked at least a decade older than his own forty-four years. 'I'm Liam.'

Boots on, the pathologist stood up. Well, she stood, but there wasn't much upward direction to the movement. Doyle judged she must be shy of five feet, even wearing the boots.

'Pleased to meet you too, Liam. I'm Vedhika. I understand you have a young lady in need of my services?'

'I'm afraid so. Looks like she's been dropped from the top of the cliff after being strangled.'

'Oh, maybe you don't need my services then, Detective Chief Inspector, if you've worked all that out already?'

Doyle detected a teasing note in her Indian accent. 'I was kind of hoping you might be able to tell us a little more than that, Doctor.'

'I'll certainly do my best. As soon as I have her at the mortuary, I will start the post-mortem. Would you like me to give you a call before I get going, so you can be there?'

'Yes, thanks.' Doyle took out one of his new business cards and gave it to the doctor. 'Oh, and don't send anything to that email address just for now – it's not working yet.' He grimaced.

'I feel your pain, Liam. IT problems drive me potty.'

⚔ ⚔ ⚔

Morgan drove out of the car park and turned left. The road headed more upwards than onwards.

'Bloody hell, that's steep.'

'You should try cycling up it,' Morgan said. 'Then you really feel the burn in your lungs and your legs.'

'You cycle here?'

'I do. But it gets less steep as you go up.'

'Well, rather you than me. I'd get breathless driving up here.'

As she changed gear, Doyle registered that she wore an engagement ring, but no wedding band. Morgan was clearly on the way up, in both her personal life and her career. Doyle's own ring finger had a pale white strip, lighter than the skin around it, where his own ring used to be. There was a hint of an accent in Morgan's voice that he couldn't place – it wasn't Lancashire or Yorkshire, but somewhere close.

He glimpsed the car park low and to his left as they continued to climb, and saw Nelson and Washington walking down the hill to meet the restless dog walker. Then the car penetrated the treeline and came out on the open moor, revealing rugged moorland going up and away to their right. Morgan pulled in to the car park and viewing area and parked next to the crime scene tape. The pair again put on protective gear.

Doyle could see why this had been chosen as a viewing point. The vista stretched out for miles. The sun was behind his left shoulder. Doyle checked his watch. Nine forty-five: he must be facing west. Below the treeline was the reservoir, its still water shimmering in the reflected sunlight. Behind that, patchwork fields of green divided by drystone walls filled the landscape, with the M61 slicing through the middle of them. Ahead and to his right was the town of Chorley. Beyond, the landscape flattened out. Blackpool was somewhere in that direction, though Doyle couldn't make out the tower.

This was his new patch – or, more accurately, about a quarter of it. It was very different to his old turf in south London. Much bigger, for a start, and far less densely populated. He had certainly stepped out of his comfort zone, but there was no turning back now. Still, there was the familiarity of a dead body and a murder investigation to conduct; comfort could be found in strange places.

The scene ahead of him was only spoilt by the amount of litter that surrounded his plastic-covered feet. That, and the police tape and the two white-suited men combing the area for clues. And of course, the fact that a dead body lay at the bottom of the cliff twenty feet in front of him. Doyle wondered why people came to a beauty spot and left behind their rubbish. Was that what this poor woman was to her killer – something that had served its purpose and could now be discarded?

Doyle followed Morgan over a two-bar timber fence to the edge of the cliff. He didn't trust himself to go too close. Not because he had any real fear of heights, but the ground was slippery and his shoes with their plastic covers had no grip. He had no desire to be remembered as the DCI who had tumbled to his death on his second day in the force. He saw the top half of the tent below and Dr Gupta entering it; she hadn't needed to duck, as he had.

'Is this place normally busy during the day?' he asked Morgan.

'There have always been several cars parked here whenever I've passed, even on weekdays.'

'Then it's likely the killer came here at night to drop the body. That takes confidence. I wouldn't fancy getting too close to the edge of that cliff in the dark.'

'It was a clear night on Sunday – not a full moon, but not far off. The night before was cloudy. Maybe he waited for a clear night.'

It was certainly possible, Doyle thought. Whoever the body was, she was pretty fresh; the killer hadn't waited long.

'You called Washington Gadget?'

'Just a nickname, boss.'

'I didn't think it was on his birth certificate.' Mind you, Doyle didn't recall any Zachs in his year at school either. 'But why that nickname?'

'He's a whizz with anything electronic – comes in handy at times.'

'Maybe he can sort out my email for me.'

'I doubt it. I can't see IT giving a DC the DCI's password. You might have to ask the super.'

'Detective Superintendent Croucher, you mean? What's his nickname?'

'I don't think he's got one, boss.'

'You're not a very good liar, Morgan. I bet I get it in three guesses.'

Chapter 3

It had, in fact, only taken Doyle two guesses on the drive back to Force HQ in Hutton to find out that Detective Superintendent Clifford Croucher was referred to – behind his back only – as Mr Burns. It was an obvious nickname for a man with a hairline that had receded to the back of his head, a sharp nose and skeletal frame. His resemblance to the *Simpsons* cartoon character was uncanny. Doyle wondered if the moniker could also be attributed to the head of the Major Investigation Team not being well liked by his subordinates. He had annoyed Doyle within an hour of him starting work in the team. In the 'little welcome pep talk', as Croucher had termed it, Croucher had told Doyle that he liked everything to be done by the book, and added 'I won't tolerate any of your shady Met police ways up here.' Doyle wasn't averse to going by the book, but sometimes he'd found it necessary to operate in the subtext between the lines.

When he entered his section's office, Doyle was dismayed to see Croucher. The super had his own office on the floor above, and Doyle had hoped his visits downstairs would be infrequent. It might have been his imagination, a bit of paranoia even, but when Croucher saw Doyle, he seemed to turn away conspiratorially. The man he was talking to was one rank down from Doyle – Detective Inspector Geoff Hales. He was the second in command of Doyle's section. Doyle had met the compact, stocky-framed man while he was waiting to be interviewed for the job. Hales had also been interviewed for the post, and had been acting up since the last DCI retired eight months previously. It wouldn't be surprising if Hales felt some animosity towards Doyle.

In the car on the way back from the crime scene, Doyle had also been able to find out from Morgan Hales' nickname: the Pearl or just Pearl. The detective inspector had not been given that name because of any beads of wisdom that he dispensed; he had been given it because his head, with thick pewter hair and a weathered, wrinkly face, sat directly on top of his shoulders. For all intents and purposes, the man was neckless.

Hales did at least acknowledge Doyle entering, with a nod in his direction. Doyle saw that the DI already had damp patches under the arms of his shirt and, unsurprisingly, he wasn't wearing a tie.

Morgan had driven the DCI back to base via a different route so that Doyle could see some of the potential routes whoever had dumped the body might have taken to the viewing area. It was possible that the victim may have been alive at the time. She might even have travelled to the spot by herself, though this looked less likely, as there was no abandoned vehicle at the car park. The post-mortem would be able to provide a rough time of death, which would help them piece some of these things together.

'Boss, Sarge,' a young woman in a hijab said, peering round her computer monitor. This was Shaima Asif, the section's intelligence analyst. 'I've checked all missing persons reports for the last week and there doesn't seem to be anyone matching our victim. I'm currently running the pics you sent through in some reverse imaging software, but no luck so far.'

'Keep going back. Our best chance of a positive ID is that tattoo,' Doyle said.

'I've also put an alert out on the system, so we will be contacted with any new misper reports matching her description.'

'Good work, Shaima.'

There must have been another twenty desks in the office, but they were all unoccupied. Doyle decided it was time he walked over to join Croucher and Hales. As he did, a desk phone began to ring. Morgan answered it.

'I hear you have a dead woman, not a dead boy,' Croucher said to Doyle.

'That's right, sir, and she has a ligature mark on her neck. She didn't fall over the cliff accidentally.'

'Any idea who she is?' Hales asked.

'Not yet, Geoff,' Doyle, said turning to the DI. 'Her pockets were empty and there was no handbag close by. She did have a distinctive tattoo of a rose just here.' Doyle pointed to his own abdomen.

'Shouldn't be too difficult to positive ID when someone does report her missing.'

'Exactly, sir,' Doyle said, turning back to face Croucher. 'We'll need a few more bodies on the team. Now we know it's a murder, we've got to be properly resourced.' Doyle thought he caught Hales wincing out of the corner of his eye.

'It might well be a murder investigation, but it isn't necessarily *our* murder investigation. Where she was found, there's more chance she belongs to Greater Manchester. Get her IDed and pass her on. There's enough of you to do that.'

'Boss?' Morgan said.

All three men turned towards Morgan, who stood with the phone in her hand. 'I've just had a PC Bowen on the line from Chorley. They've had a misper report this morning from a headteacher at a local primary. A young staff member hasn't been to work the last two days, and hasn't contacted them. They have made several attempts to get hold of her, and contacted her parents too. Description fits our victim.'

'Tattoo?' Doyle asked.

'The headteacher didn't know, apparently.'

'What's her name?' Asif asked, bobbing up from behind her screen.

'Chloe Kennedy. She's twenty-six. A teacher at Devonshire Road primary school, Chorley.'

Asif turned away and began to tap at her keyboard. After a minute or so, she looked up. 'She's got all the privacy settings maxed up on her Facebook – I'm only getting a thumbnail pic with her face obscured.'

'Check the school website. There might be a photo on there,' Doyle said.

'PC Bowen is emailing the full report. He doesn't have a pic yet, but the school is sending him one.'

'I think this might be her,' Asif said, staring at her screen. 'Her hair's longer, but the face looks the same.'

'The description taken by PC Bowen said she had short hair. She may have had it cut since that photo was taken.'

'That's her,' Doyle said, standing behind Asif and looking at her screen. He couldn't help being impressed by how quickly the intelligence analyst worked.

'I agree,' said Morgan, leaning across the desk to see.

'Did she live locally?' Croucher asked Morgan.

'Adlington.'

'Definitely ours, then,' Hales said. 'That's just south of Chorley.'

Doyle was grateful for the clarification, as he was still not familiar with the geography of the area.

'And only a couple of miles from where she was found,' Morgan added.

Croucher left the office just before DCs Nelson and Washington entered.

'Right,' Doyle said. 'Morgan, can you take Gadget, get to the school and see the headteacher and anyone who knows Chloe well? Be discreet about who you tell until we've spoken to her parents, but we need to get as much background as we can.'

'On it, boss,' Morgan said, making for the door with DC Washington in tow.

'Geoff, can you get things up and running in Chorley? Looks like we will need to set up an incident room there.' *And out of the way of Croucher,* Doyle felt like adding. 'Birdseye, you're coming with me.'

'Want me to drive, boss?' Nelson asked.

'No, I don't,' came Doyle's curt reply.

Chapter 4

When they arrived at the red-brick Victorian primary school, they were told by the receptionist that the headteacher was busy, and were asked to take a seat outside her office. Gadget slumped down straight away, and Morgan found herself wondering how long it had been since the detective constable had left school. It was the new DCI who had put the thoughts in her head, commenting on how young Gadget looked. She had been apprehensive about Doyle – and not because of what had happened. She had read the press reports and, as far as she was concerned, he had done what he'd had to do. The IOPC had taken the same view, and this was enough to convince her. The Independent Office for Police Conduct would have had no qualms about destroying Doyle's career – and life – if they had felt he had a case to answer. What had worried Morgan about Doyle was where he came from. The Met! It had built up quite a reputation over recent years for misogyny, and Morgan had no desire to be working in a real-life *Life on Mars*. She hadn't got those vibes from Doyle, though, and was starting to think that he might turn out to be just what her career, and the department, needed. Steve 'the Smurf' Murphy, the old DCI, had retired just a month after she'd joined the unit. As a result, their section had been trimmed back, and as soon as a case looked like it was getting too juicy it was handed to one of the other DCIs in the MIT, and their team took it over. What Morgan had hoped would be a good career move, investigating serious and complex crime, had so far turned out to be a frustrating experience doing lots of donkey work for others. She couldn't see Doyle putting up with that for long. After all, he probably had more experience in major investigations than anyone else in the team.

'Mrs Edwards will see you now.' The receptionist interrupted Morgan's thoughts.

A door opened, and a forlorn boy exited, followed by his frowning mother. Everything about the woman who then emerged said 'headteacher'. She introduced herself as Mrs Edwards, not Patricia Edwards, as was written on the sign outside the school. Morgan doubted that anyone ever got away with calling her Pat. Even though she was now thirty-three and a detective sergeant in Lancashire Constabulary, Morgan couldn't help feeling she had just been caught playing truant.

'Take a seat,' Edwards commanded the police officers, who duly obliged. The head sat at the other side of her large desk. 'I assume you are here about Ms Kennedy. I hope we are not wasting your time. She's normally quite diligent. I don't know what could have got into her. But her parents are worried sick, and I promised them I would call you.'

'When was she last at the school, Mrs Edwards?' Morgan asked.

'Last Friday, as normal. Yesterday she just didn't show up – no message or anything. That's unlike her. You just don't do that; everyone always leaves a message so that cover can be arranged.'

'Mrs Edwards, can I ask you, had Chloe cut her hair recently? We saw a photo of her on the school website with long hair,' Morgan said.

'Yes, she had. The admin staff were trying to find a more recent photo – one taken since the haircut – to send to the officer I spoke to.'

Morgan shared a look with Gadget. Any slim chance that Chloe was not the victim had pretty much vanished.

'If you know that, does that mean you've found her?'

'I'm afraid I think we have. The body of a young woman was found at Anglezarke this morning, and she bears a striking resemblance to the picture of Chloe I saw on your website.'

The older woman sank down in her chair, as if she was inflatable and someone had let out half the air. 'My good lord. Oh, my goodness. Poor Chloe. Her poor parents. Do you know how? Was it an accident?'

'I'm very sorry to say that we're treating her death as suspicious.'

The headteacher rested her elbows on the desk and put her face in her hands. She took a moment to compose herself then sat up, blinking back tears. 'I'm sorry, I really wasn't expecting this. I don't know what to say.'

'It's OK.' Morgan leaned in so she could talk in a softer voice. 'But we're going to need your help. Help us so that we can find out what happened, and why.'

'Of course. Anything! Anything I or any of us can do, just say.' Tears were rolling down Mrs Edwards' cheeks.

'We need to find out all we can about Chloe's life. All her recent movements. Are there any staff members she is particularly close to?'

'There's one person. A classroom assistant called Dani Wheeler.'

'Sorry,' Gadget, who was taking notes, interrupted. 'Is that Dani with an i or Danny with a y?'

'It's Ms Dani Wheeler, with an i. They have never taught the same class, but seemed natural that they formed a friendship. They are about the same age. I often saw them chatting at breaktimes. I think they met up socially at times too, but I'm not sure how often.'

'Is there somewhere we can speak to Dani, in private?' Morgan asked.

'Of course. I will send someone to get her and find you a room.'

'Just a couple more things for now, Mrs Edwards. We are going to have to keep this strictly confidential, just for today. We need to speak to Chloe's family and anyone who was close to Chloe, and conduct some initial enquiries before her death becomes common knowledge.'

'Of course, and the other thing?'

'Does Chloe have a locker or anywhere that she might keep any of her own items at the school?'

'Not as such. We try not to encourage that. Teachers tend to keep coats and bags in the staffroom and take them home at the end of each day. Valuables and small items, they sometimes lock in their desk drawers in their classrooms. Chloe's class have PE after lunch. I can get the caretaker to get the master key and unlock her drawer for you. You can take anything that might be useful.'

⋏ ⋏ ⋏

The medical room turned out to be the only available private space for Morgan and Gadget to speak with Dani Wheeler. Morgan hoped they wouldn't be disturbed by a kid with a playground injury. She made Gadget sit on one of the child-sized chairs so that there was an adult one available for the teaching assistant when they broke the news about her friend.

Dani had been keen to meet with the officers, and had bowled through the door asking, 'Is this about Chloe? Is there any news?' She now sat drying her tears with a handy box of tissues, presumably left in the room for that exact purpose.

Dani was a bit younger than Chloe, twenty-four and attractive. Stunning, in fact – a fact that didn't seem to have gone unnoticed by Gadget, Morgan noted. She wondered if the detective constable had also noticed the double Venus symbol tattooed on Dani's left ankle. She suspected not.

'When did you last see Chloe?' Morgan enquired gently.

'It were Friday night. We'd been at the Manhattan Project – it's a bar in town. We left together when it closed at one o'clock and waited outside for cabs. I live in Leyland, and she lives— sorry, lived.' Dani swallowed. 'She lived in Adlington, in the opposite direction.'

'Did you see her get into the cab?' Morgan asked.

'No, mine came first. We booked them through the same company on the app. Hers was due two minutes later.'

'And did you hear from her after that?'

'Yes, I sent her a WhatsApp on Saturday and she replied on the Sunday.'

'Was it normal for her to leave it a day before replying?'

'Not really, but I didn't think it was especially strange. She's had a lot going on in her life recently.'

'What did the message say?'

'I can show you.' Dani took out her phone, pulled up the message and handed it to Morgan.

Morgan looked at the screen. On Saturday Dani had sent to Chloe:

Good night last night. My head feels shit today. Hope you're OK hun xx.

Chloe had replied on Sunday:

Was a good night! Felt shit yday too though. See you tomorrow xx.

On Monday, Dani had sent:

Where are you? Edwards is doing her nut. Hope you're OK, let me know asap. Will try to cover for you if I can. Get in touch xx

Then later:

Really worried about you, Chloe. Please let me know if you are OK, call me if you need to, phone is always on xxx

Then this morning at 8.55 a.m.:

Chloe, please let me know you're safe. I'm thinking of going to the police xxx

Morgan scrolled up to check there wasn't anything suspicious on any of their previous messages, but they just seemed like normal girly chat.

'Do you mind if DC Washington screenshots the messages, Dani?'

'No, sure.' She sobbed again. 'I still can't believe it.'

'You mentioned that Chloe had a lot going on recently. What did you mean by that?'

'Maybe "going on" wasn't the right phrase. She'd been having a difficult time. She split up with her boyfriend about six weeks ago, and he didn't take it too well.'

'In what way?'

'He just didn't want to accept it were over. Kept pestering her, promising things would change if she took him back. It were a bit full on. He kept turning up at places where she was. Like he was checking up on her. A bit stalkerish, really.'

Morgan exchanged a look with Gadget. 'How long had this been going on?'

'About a month after they split up. She told me it had stopped in the last couple of weeks, and she was hopeful he had got the message it was over.'

'Any idea why it might have stopped?'

'The messages he were sending were getting worse. At first, they were all "I'm sorry. Please take me back" kind of thing, then they got nastier, and he threatened her. She told him if he didn't stop, she was going to report him to you lot.'

'I don't suppose she forwarded the messages to you?' Morgan asked, looking at Dani's phone, which Gadget had just handed back to Dani.

'No, but she showed me some of them. After she cut her hair short, he sent one calling her a filthy dyke and saying she'd better watch her back from now on.'

'I'm sorry, Dani, but I have to ask this. What was the nature of your relationship with her? Were you ever more than friends?'

Dani sniffed and chuckled a little at the thought. 'No, Chloe were straight, she had no interest in girls like that. She wanted another man at some point – just not a total arsehole like the last one.'

'And what is the arsehole's name?'

'Ryan Johnson. I only met him a couple of times. I know his last name as he friended me on Facebook. I unfriended him when he started being nasty to Chloe.'

'And what about other friends? Is there anyone else Chloe was close to who might be able to give us some more information?'

'She had a friend she'd known since they were kids – Stacy Vickers. It might be worth chatting to her.'

⋏ ⋏ ⋏

Mrs Edwards had introduced the two detectives to Elliot Parker, the school caretaker. Despite appearing to Morgan not far short of fifty, he dressed like a much younger man. It wasn't just the skinny jeans and floral-patterned shirt; his hair had too much product in it, presumably to hold it in a certain way that he wrongly assumed masked the fact that he was thinning on top. She didn't know how much school caretakers earned, but Morgan strongly suspected it wasn't enough to afford a Porsche. Parker, it seemed, was exhibiting his midlife crisis through his dress sense. He was friendly enough, and keen to help, though a bit too inquisitive for Morgan's liking. It didn't take him long to locate the correct key on a very large bunch – in fact, the first one he chose opened the lock on the desk drawer.

Morgan pulled on a pair of nitrile gloves, which seemed to surprise Parker and shake his cheery demeanour.

'Oh,' he said, standing back up. 'You think something's happened to her?'

'She's been reported missing, Mr Parker. We're following procedure.' They had decided that the caretaker didn't need to know any more at this stage. The press had already cottoned on to the fact that a body had been found at Anglezarke that morning. It would only take one indiscreet post on social media and the identity of the victim would be known. This would come out soon enough, but for now Morgan wanted to get some enquiries made discreetly, before the whole thing was in the public eye. A murdered young primary school teacher would attract a media circus, not just local hacks.

The contents of Chloe Kennedy's desk drawer consisted of a packet of Top Trumps cards, a superhero-type figure whose identity was a mystery to Morgan, although she suspected at least one of the men in the room would be able to name it, and a pot of a substance labelled 'slime' that, despite wearing gloves, she did not want to open. In addition to these treasures, there was a selection of stationery items, many of which also looked like confiscated contraband. The only items that appeared to belong to the class teacher were some throat lozenges and an A5 diary. There was also a remote control. Morgan removed the diary and put it in an evidence bag. Gadget dutifully labelled it.

'You wouldn't happen to know what the remote control is for, would you, Mr Parker?' Morgan asked.

'Yes, it's for the screen on the wall behind. We are all state-of-the-art and interactive now. We had them installed about six weeks ago.'

'I see. You can lock that again now.'

'Oh yes, right, sorry. I hope she's OK, and you find her soon.'

Morgan tried not to wince, knowing that Chloe most definitely was not OK.

'She's a nice girl – good laugh, you know.'

'Did you know her socially? Away from school, I mean?'

'Not really. We bumped into each other from time to time. Nothing more than that.'

Chapter 5

Oswaldtwistle sounded to Doyle like the villain in an Agatha Christie novel rather than a town nestled between Blackburn and Accrington.

'It's pronounced Ozzeltwizzle,' Derrick 'Birdseye' Nelson had corrected him on the drive over. 'Though most people just call it Ossy.'

Morgan had informed Doyle earlier that, before he grew his white beard, Birdseye had been nicknamed Horatio.

'A man called James Hargreaves came from there. He invented the spinning jenny. Funny thing was, his invention put so many folk out of work that he had to leave the area in fear for his life.'

Doyle couldn't recall exactly what a spinning jenny was, though he had a vague idea that it was something to do with cotton or weaving. The drive over had been quite pleasant, despite what they were going to do. The sun was still shining, and the Lancashire countryside was resplendent under the blue skies. He had spent months travelling back and forth from London, and he couldn't remember a journey when it hadn't been raining on the drive north of Manchester.

The pool car he had been given suited Doyle too. It was a big Skoda SUV with plenty of leg room. The mechanic who had signed it out the day before had apologised that it wasn't a BMW or Volvo. Doyle couldn't care less about the badge on the bonnet. The fact it had been valeted, however, was a massive bonus. It had taken him two weeks to determine the origin of a putrid smell in the last car he had got from the Met. The previous owner had discarded half a cheeseburger between the front seat and the console...

Doyle pulled up alongside a modest cottage with an immaculate front garden and hanging baskets on either side of the door. The two detectives walked in silence up the path. Doyle rang the bell, which played a couple of high-pitched cheery notes. The lady who answered looked to be in her mid-sixties.

'Mrs Kennedy?' Doyle said, holding up his warrant card. 'I'm Detective Chief Inspector Liam Doyle and this is Detective Constable Derrick Nelson. Would you mind if we came in?'

'Yes, yes, of course. Is it about Chloe? We've been worried sick since the school called. My husband's in the garden. I'll fetch him.' She retreated to the back of the house, allowing them to enter. 'Robert, Robert, dear, the police are here!' she shouted into the garden.

Considering the cream shag-pile carpet and his walk in the woods that morning, Doyle decided to remove his shoes. He had used a damp cloth before they left to try to get the worst mud splashes off his suit trousers. It would have to do for now, but he made a mental note to swing by the self-storage unit to pick up his other suit.

Mrs Kennedy reappeared in the hall, followed by her husband, and ushered the police officers into a tidy living room. She directed them to sit on a cream sofa that looked like it had arrived from the showroom that morning.

'You're a chief inspector,' Robert said, addressing Nelson.

'Not me, Mr Kennedy,' the DC replied. 'This is the boss.' He indicated Doyle, sitting next to him. 'I'm just a humble detective constable, I'm afraid.'

'Well, there is nothing wrong with that. I made it to deputy head, but I can't say I enjoyed that side of things much. Please call me Robert, and this is Jean. I assume you are here about

Chloe?'

'Yes, we are,' Doyle said.

'I'm sorry, where are my manners? I'm all flustered today. Can I get you some tea or something else?' Jean interrupted.

'It's OK, we're fine, thank you, Mrs Kenn— Jean.' He was about to turn their world upside down, but he knew he had to get to the point quickly, for their sake. 'I'm afraid we've got some very bad news. The body of a young woman was found near Anglezarke Moor this morning, and we believe it to be Chloe.'

Jean gasped, and Robert's face contorted, trying to work out how to respond.

'You believe it to be Chloe, Chief Inspector? And what makes you think that?' Robert's challenge was not unexpected. Doyle had to be a little ambiguous at this stage.

'The picture over there.' Doyle gestured to the sideboard, on top of which was a framed graduation photograph of a young woman. 'That strongly resembles the woman I saw this morning. Is that Chloe?'

Jean nodded in reply.

'Could you tell me, does Chloe have any tattoos?' He deliberately used the present tense.

'She's got one of a rose. Robert went mad when she had it done.'

'A red rose on her midriff just here?'

Another nod from Jean.

'Well, I'm afraid it is Chloe who was found. I'm very sorry.'

'Oh, good lord no.' Robert's face creased with distress, and his wife put an arm across his shoulder as she mopped her tears with her other hand. 'How? How has this happened?' Robert's tone was pleading.

Doyle heard the faint sound of a kettle boiling, and it was only then that he realised Birdseye had left the room. 'There's no easy way to say this, I'm afraid. But we believe someone killed her.'

'No.' Jean put her hand over her mouth.

'Do you think it was him? That useless bastard of an ex-boyfriend of hers?'

'Robert, please.'

Doyle didn't know if it was the accusation or the swear word that Jean had scolded her husband for. 'I'm afraid we don't know yet. But it is my job to find out, and that's exactly what I intend to do.'

Birdseye reappeared, holding a tray with a teapot, four cups and saucers and a jug containing milk. 'Forgive me,' he said to the couple 'But I thought you could use a pot of tea.'

'Thank you,' Jean mouthed at Birdseye, and Robert gave him a nod of approval.

'I wasn't really cross with her for getting the tattoo. It's just, she was only seventeen. The tattooist shouldn't have done it. I didn't want her spoiling her body.'

'You didn't want her growing up,' his wife interjected.

'At least it was the red rose of Lancashire she got,' Birdseye said, pouring the tea.

'That's very true – she's always been proud of her roots.'

'She was our only child,' Jean said, overcome by another bout of sobbing. 'She was an IVF baby, our third attempt. She was our entire world.'

And there won't be any grandchildren coming now either, Doyle thought, feeling guilty for having sentenced the couple to a retirement of grieving.

人　人　人

'How did it go?' Morgan asked Doyle as he was getting out of the car.

'As painfully as always, but it had to be done.'

Morgan and Gadget were wearing stab vests over their clothes. Although it was possible that Chloe's killer could be holed up in her flat, Doyle didn't think this was likely.

'Where's Birdseye?' Gadget asked.

'I left him there for now, until a family liaison officer is assigned. For some strange reason, the Kennedys seem to like him.'

'Did you pick up anything useful while you were there?' Morgan said.

'Similar to what you got from the school. The parents don't like Ryan Johnson any more than her friend does. Geoff and Shaima are going to dig up all they can on him once the incident room is set up at Chorley nick.'

'Shall I get the big red key out of the car, boss?' Gadget asked.

'No need,' Doyle said, fishing in his trouser pocket. The 'big red key' was the battering ram used for forcing entry. 'I got these little silver keys from her parents.' Doyle thought he could detect disappointment in the younger man's face. He was still at the age where he would still relish any action, no matter how small.

They'd parked round the corner from Chloe Kennedy's house, where a couple of uniformed constables had been assigned to discreetly watch the front and back entrances. The one who stood on the corner watching the front was short and rather rotund. He wasn't a young man either, though he clearly had joined the police since the minimum height requirement had been abolished.

'Any sign of movement?' Doyle asked without bothering to introduce himself.

'Nothing so far,' the PC replied. 'And I've been standing here for over an hour and a half.'

Doyle didn't consider standing on a warm summer's day watching a door any significant hardship. If the officer was hoping for sympathy, he was going to be disappointed. 'Shall we take a look inside, then?'

'Do you not want to put on a stab vest, guv?' Gadget asked.

'I think I'll take my chances,' Doyle said, pulling on gloves. 'I very much doubt that our killer's holed up in there waiting for us, but we'd better check before forensics go in.'

The curtains were closed at the front of the two-up, two-down terraced house. As he put the key in the lock, Doyle heard a familiar clicking sound, and turned to see Gadget holding a fully extended telescopic baton. 'For fuck's sake,' he muttered, turning back to the lock.

'Police! Stay where you are!' came Gadget's shouted warning as they entered the property.

He had probably watched some cop show where they did the same, Doyle thought. The front room was unoccupied, and Doyle made his way to the back while his colleagues checked upstairs.

'Don't move. Stay where you are!' a voice screamed from the garden as Doyle entered the kitchen diner.

The person who had screamed was a uniformed police officer who stood outside the closed French doors, his baton poised, ready to strike. Doyle suspected that the PC was hoping to cut a more threatening image than he had managed. The man was tall enough, but he couldn't be more than nine stone soaking wet. Doyle didn't think he would have much problem getting past him, if that had been his intention. He decided instead it was time for an introduction.

'Detective Chief Inspector Doyle,' he said, holding up his warrant card. 'I don't believe we've met before.'

The uniformed officer's pale skin flushed. 'Sorry, sir. PC Bowen, sir.'

'No problem. Didn't your mate out front radio to say we were coming in?'

'No, sir. And he's not my mate.'

'Clear upstairs, boss,' Gadget said.

Morgan turned on the lights, revealing a neat, tidy room. There wasn't any sign that a struggle or anything untoward had taken place there.

'What's it like upstairs?' Doyle asked.

'Much the same,' replied Morgan. 'Bed's made, all tidy, nothing odd at all.'

'The bed's made and the curtains are closed. What does that tell us?'

Morgan contemplated the question as Doyle wandered into the kitchen area.

'That if it was Chloe who was last here, she was either planning on coming back after dark or staying out overnight?'

'Exactly what I was thinking,' Doyle said, closing the fridge door. 'Not much food in.' He went over to the sink. There was only one piece of washing-up there. A glass containing half an inch of what looked like it had once been orange juice. The top had started to fur up with mould. 'I think this might have been here since before Sunday,' Doyle said. 'We'll have a quick look through. See if we can find anything useful. Then we'll let forensics give the place a proper going-over. It doesn't look like she was killed here to me.' Doyle's phone was ringing. 'Oh, and do us a favour – can you get Dumb and Dumber out there to start knocking on the neighbours' doors? Find out when they last saw Chloe, and if anyone has noticed anything suspicious.'

'Will do,' Morgan said.

'DCI Doyle.' He answered the phone while poking around in a fruit bowl. 'Hello, Dr Gupta, thanks for calling.' Doyle found a car key. 'OK.' Doyle looked at his watch. 'That's great, I'll see you then.' He ended the call then threw the car key to Gadget.

'What's this?'

'I'm guessing Ms Kennedy has a Fiat. If it's parked outside, get forensics to recover it. If not, get on to the DVLA and find out the details.'

Chapter 6

Dr Gupta had told Doyle on the phone that she would carry out a CT scan of the victim's body before starting the post-mortem proper. This gave the detective a small window of opportunity to visit the self-storage unit that now housed most of his possessions. He had, after all, practically driven past it en route to the Royal Blackburn Hospital, where the Home Office Mortuary was based.

It hadn't taken long to find his other suit, which thankfully he had hung in its bag next to his guitar case on an old-fashioned clothes rail. He hoped that had kept the suit crease-free. How long had it been since he'd played the guitar? He used to spend at least half an hour a day, no matter what life and work threw at him, strumming some chords, shaking the stress out through his fingers. Looking at his guitar hanging there, abandoned, in the storage unit almost made him feel guilty.

It had been nearly midnight on Sunday when he had finally managed to cram the last of the contents of the hire van into the twelve-foot-square unit. That had been after the second trip north he had made from London that day. Just before closing and padlocking the door, he had thrown his large duffel bag on top of a stack of cardboard boxes. Doyle had instantly regretted that decision, realising he would need the bag's contents at some point. And now he did. He stood staring at the cardboard mountain, wondering how he could retrieve the bag without unloading most of the boxes.

He had been issued with all the standard kit, including extendable baton, airways radio and handcuffs, the day before. But the bag he was after contained the bits of kit they didn't issue. All the things he had collected over the years as a murder squad detective and, before that, in the flying squad. The bag normally lived in the boot of his work car, ready for when he needed it.

'Fuck it,' Doyle addressed his mountain of belongings. 'Only one thing for it.' He removed his jacket. It was time to climb. For the second time that day, he contemplated the horror of accidentally ending his life in a slightly comedic fashion. Cardboard boxes were not known for their load-bearing properties, and they had certainly not been designed with the intention of taking a man's weight. Especially, Doyle thought, the weight of a man his size.

He began the ascent, taking care to place his weight on the corners of the boxes, where they were strongest, pushing off other items with his arms to keep himself balanced. Looking over the top of the cardboard mountain, he cursed. In his eagerness to check into his hotel on Sunday night, Doyle had launched the duffel bag over the top of the boxes with such gusto that it sat, out of reach, close to the back wall of the unit. Some of the boxes contained soft items such as towels, bed linen and cushions. If these collapsed with him lying across them, it wouldn't be a problem. On the other hand, some contained kitchen utensils, glasses and knives. If these gave way with him on top, Dr Gupta might end up having to do another post-mortem. He hoped she would see the funny side.

Using a bedside cabinet stacked on top of a chest of drawers for purchase, he flung himself over the top and onto the mound. It moved and sagged a bit, but bore his weight. For now. Prone, he moved forward like a sniper crawling through the undergrowth, using his elbows. A bit more movement beneath him, but nothing ominous. Then there was a ringing sound. It wasn't coming from his work phone, which was in his jacket, but his personal mobile, which was in his trouser pocket. He could not answer; they'd leave a message. But it might be important – the school, maybe, about Harry. With a bit of twisting, he fished the phone from his trousers. He answered without being able to look at the screen.

'Liam. Is this an OK time to call?' The Liverpudlian accent was familiar, but it took him a moment to place her.

'Yes, course, sorry. How are you? Any news?'

'Not good news, I'm afraid. Your vendors have run into a problem with the house they're buying.'

'Shit. Do you think they will get it resolved?'

'Honestly, I'm not sure. It looks like they've been gazumped. Might be just a ploy, of course, to try and get more money out of them.'

'Surely the fact that we were due to exchange next week must count for something? They'd have to go back to the start with a new buyer.'

'Hopefully they'll see sense. You are in a very strong position.'

Doyle considered his current situation on top of a mountain of boxes straining to take his weight. 'I am?'

'You're a cash buyer and can move quickly.'

Doyle couldn't recall ever being in a position where he was less equipped to move quickly.

'When are you moving up here?'

'I'm up here now. I started work yesterday. I'm in a Premier Inn and my stuff is in storage. It's costing a fortune. If it carries on for too long, I won't be a cash buyer any more.'

'Oh, shit – sorry, I didn't realise. I thought you weren't planning on moving for another couple of months.'

'So did I, but those above had other ideas.' That had really rankled with Doyle. He had accepted the new job, expecting to work out his three months' notice period in the Met, giving him time to organise the move north. But as soon as the top brass found out he was transferring, they couldn't wait to get him off their books. No need for the usual notice period.

'They're desperate for someone up in Lancashire,' the section commander had told him without making eye contact. 'So we're letting you go early.'

That had been just over a week ago. Twenty years' good service. Although his name had been cleared, it was still mud in certain circles. He had been the highest-ranked officer at his leaving drinks on Friday. No doubt those above didn't fancy the prospect of a drunk and angry Liam Doyle – either that, or they were too busy climbing greasy poles to attend.

'I'll find out more today, I'm sure.' The estate agent's voice broke into Doyle's thoughts. 'I wanted to give you a heads-up straight away. I'll call tomorrow with an update. In the meantime, I suggest you make the most of those Premier Inn breakfasts.'

'Thanks, Bea. Will do. Speak to you tomorrow then. Fuck!' Doyle shouted when the call ended. That was all he needed. He decided to try to put the matter out of his mind and focus on the things that he *could* do something about, starting with retrieving the bag and then finding out who had murdered Chloe Kennedy. One more precarious movement forward, and he was just able to reach out and grab the bag. He checked inside and was relieved to find, among the contents, the large cable ties he was after. Fastening the bag, he tossed it onto the floor behind him. Doyle shuffled back so he was balanced, his torso on the boxes and his lower half in mid-air. He considered his options. A careful, dignified climb-down was obviously ideal, but he couldn't work out how to achieve this without bringing an avalanche of boxes down on top of him. Doyle went for option two: jump and hope. He turned as he went, and to his relief hit the concrete floor on both feet. His triumph was short-lived, however, as he looked up to see a dislodged box hurtling towards him. Doyle didn't have time to move, but he had time to contemplate what the carton might contain before it hit him squarely in the face then sprang open, spilling its wares on the floor. It turned out that even a cardboard box full of Lego could hurt when dropped from height. But not as much as seeing the Lego itself. Harry was the reason he had transferred up here: his son had moved north with his mum last September. With things happening so quickly, he hadn't had a chance to tell Harry that he had now moved. He hoped he'd be able to see him tonight after work and surprise him – calling ahead, of course, to warn his ex-wife Fiona. Fat chance of that happening now he was leading a murder investigation. He doubted he would finish work before the boy was in bed.

人 人 人

During her time in the police, Morgan had come across many reasons why people had not wanted to let her into their homes. This ranged from the air being thick with the distinct aroma of cannabis to there being a body on the kitchen floor, a knife sticking out of it. Stacy Vickers, she suspected, had a much more mundane reason for not wanting to admit the detective sergeant and Gadget into her flat: the sheer state of the place. It wasn't that it was particularly dirty – sure, it could probably have done with a good hoover and dust, and if Morgan had ventured into the kitchen, she would have bet money on finding several pieces of washing-up in the sink. The real problem was, it was so full of stuff. There was barely a surface or patch of floor that wasn't hidden beneath a child's toy, magazine or discarded item of clothing. An excess of mismatched furniture added to the chaos.

It had not taken Morgan long to find out where Chloe's childhood friend lived, despite Dani Wheeler only knowing her name. The electoral roll had led them to the tower block in Preston. After several minutes of persuading Ms Vickers that what they needed to talk to her about was best not done on the doorstep, she let them in. It had taken some rearranging to get Stacy seated on the sofa, with Morgan settling for the arm of an armchair and Gadget forced to stand, before Morgan was able to break the news of the death of her best friend to her.

This took two attempts, as the first one was interrupted by the wailing of Stacy's toddler, whose tower of foam bricks had just come tumbling down.

'Are you taking the piss?' had been Stacy's reply when Morgan had finally told her, followed by disbelief before reality dawned on her. 'I need a fag,' Stacy said, getting up and walking to the balcony doors, seemingly oblivious to the detritus she was treading on.

Morgan followed, picking her way through empty patches of carpet as though she was navigating her way around rock pools.

'When did you last see Chloe?' Morgan asked as Stacy lit a cigarette, taking in a long draw of smoke.

'It were just over a week ago. Sunday. We went out Saturday night and I stayed over at hers.'

'When did you last hear from her?'

'That were this weekend, Sunday. Bit odd, that.' Stacy took another lungful of smoke.

'In what way odd?'

'I messaged her a few times on Saturday and got nothing back, which isn't like her, and then on Sunday afternoon I got a message saying sorry, she had been busy. I wasn't sure if she was pissed off with me.'

'Why might she have been pissed off with you, Stacy?'

'Because I blew her out Saturday night. We were meant to be going out. My mum was going to babysit but then she was sick, so she couldn't.'

'Did you go out with her most Saturday nights, then?'

'We had been, but only recently, over the last couple of months. Since she split up with Ryan. We hadn't been on a night out together for years before that; he didn't like it. We used to meet in the school holidays, when she was off work – go out for lunch and that. Oh my God – Megan! What am I going to tell her?'

'Who's Megan?' Morgan asked, pretty certain that the toddler she could see through the balcony window, rebuilding a tower with Gadget's help, was of the boy variety.

'My eldest. She adores Chloe, she's her— she *was* her godmother.' Stacy glanced at the time on her phone. 'She'll be at my mum's now. She has after-school club on a Tuesday. My mum picks her up and gives her tea. What am I going to say to her?' Stacy let out a gasp, then began to sob.

Morgan placed what she hoped was a consoling arm across her shoulders. Stacy sniffed up her sobs and tears and stubbed out her cigarette in an overflowing ashtray on a decidedly rickety table, before lighting up another. 'D'you think Ryan did it?'

'I don't know. Why do you say that?'

Stacy gave the question some thought as she took another lungful of smoke. 'I mean, he were proper horrible to her, not just like when people split up and they argue and say stuff, but, like, really nasty.'

'In what way?'

'Well, it went on for weeks after they split. Not surprising, I guess; he was really controlling when they were together, then he just couldn't accept it when she dumped him. He was abusive, if you ask me.'

'What do you mean?'

'He didn't hit her or owt like that – not that I know of, anyway. But he was threatening to her and didn't want her to have a life away from him. Some of what he said was creepy too – like he had been watching her after she kicked him out. She changed all her passwords on Facebook and that, as she thought he might be hacking her account.'

'Must have been difficult kicking him out, if he was like that.'

'It were. She did it on a Saturday morning, got a friend from the school round, and they even got the school caretaker to help in case Ryan didn't get the message, but he left and she got her keys back off him.'

'Had Chloe started seeing anyone else?'

'No.' Stacy chuckled. 'I told her she should. You know, go out and shag someone, get Ryan out of her system. But she wanted a break from men.'

'A break from men,' Morgan repeated 'What about women?'

'What? Oh God, no. I think Ryan might have thought that, though, after she cut her hair – he sent her some really nasty messages then.'

'Why did she cut her hair short?'

'Honestly? I think just because she could. If she'd done that when she was with Ryan, he would've gone mental. I think it was a bit of a "fuck you, I've moved on".' Stacy looked at the time again, then wiped more tears from her eyes. 'I'm not being funny, but I need to give Charlie his tea and then get over to my mum's to get Megan.'

'It's OK, Stacy, I understand. Do you think you might be able to stay with your mum tonight, have someone to talk to? Other than the children, I mean.'

'Yeah, maybe. Have you got kids?'

'No,' Morgan replied. She did want children at some point, but she was thirty-three now and wondered when, if ever, would feel like the right time.

Chapter 7

Mortuaries all had a distinctive smell. It wasn't the smell of death or decay as such, and definitely wasn't the smell that confronted you when you entered a property where a body had lain undiscovered for a while. This was more a mixture of chemicals and cleaning products. Not exactly unpleasant, but Doyle associated it with a life extinguished, with just one final task: to reveal its secrets to the pathologist.

'Come through, Liam.' Dr Gupta greeted Doyle in a low voice, as though in a library or place of worship. There were two people standing a respectful distance from the mortuary table, wearing the same disposable aprons that Doyle himself had put on in the anteroom. He recognised one of them as Jen Knight, the crime scene manager. The other offered his hand as Doyle walked over.

'Eddie Scott from the coroner's office.'

'DCI Liam Doyle,' he said, shaking the hand. The man was in his late fifties, Doyle guessed. He would be prepared to bet a month's wages that he was a retired police officer. There were two other people in the room who, like Dr Gupta, were dressed in surgical scrubs, masks, heavy aprons and white wellies. They were busy laying out tools and instruments on stainless steel trolleys.

It was only after acknowledging the other occupants that Doyle allowed himself to take in the long table and the unmistakable shape of a person lying on it, covered from head to toe in a white sheet.

Dr Gupta stood opposite Doyle, on the other side of the slab. She had a headset over her surgical cap so she could record all her findings as she went along, ensuring nothing was left out of her report.

'OK, I think we're ready.' The pathologist's voice was pitched at just the right level: all could hear her, but her voice was still respectfully low. 'As you all know, we have done a full CT scan prior to this. The scan told us that she had a number of fractures, including skull, both clavicles, several ribs and her left ulna and radius.' Dr Gupta helpfully indicated her own collarbones and lower arm bones, in case anyone was in any doubt. 'I can say with a good degree of certainty that all these injuries were sustained post-mortem and are consistent with what you might expect from a fall from height. The consultant radiologist will be doing a full report of the scan, and I will share that as soon as it's done.'

The pathologist took a step forward until she was right up against the table. In a very low voice, she spoke to her patient. 'I'm sorry, my dear. I just need to pull this back to show our guests.' She folded the sheet down to just below the woman's shoulders.

'Her name's Chloe Kennedy,' Doyle said. 'She was a primary school teacher.'

'Chloe.' The pathologist repeated the name.

'I'll write up a new set of ID tags,' Eddie Scott said. It was the coroner's office that was responsible for the body and had authorised the post-mortem before the identity could be confirmed, time being of the essence in a murder investigation.

'I'm afraid you were right, Liam; poor Chloe was strangled with some kind of ligature. I'll come back to that in a moment,' Dr Gupta said. She moved to the foot end of the table and folded the sheet up, revealing the victim's feet and ankles. They were discoloured, with dark purple patches that contrasted with her pale complexion 'Do you recognise what this is?'

'Livor mortis?' Doyle suggested, having seen before the way that blood pooled in a body after the heart had ceased to beat.

'Exactly, and do you know what this level of lividity in her feet suggests?' the pathologist probed, as if prompting a medical student.

'That she was upright after she died. But she wasn't hanged – the ligature mark is in the wrong place for that.'

'Correct. Look here.' Gupta indicated the tops of Chloe's toes. They were whiter, in keeping with the rest of her skin. 'Her toes were resting on the ground. Livor mortis doesn't appear on areas exposed to pressure.' Gupta folded the sheet up further, exposing the lower thighs. 'See, there is lividity here too, on the front of her knees – they must have been slightly bent, with the toes dragging on the floor.' Gupta folded the sheet again, to the top of Chloe's thighs, so they could see her hands. 'Here…' Dr Gupta indicated her left wrist. The bruising there was similar to the ligature mark on her neck, defined and indented. 'It's the same on the other wrist. It suggests to me that she was hanging, with her arms above her head, at the time of death and for some time afterwards.'

'Do you think it could be some sort of auto-erotic strangulation game that went wrong?' Eddie Scott asked.

'It may well have been auto-erotic, but poor Chloe was not a willing participant in it. The force used on the ligature round her neck was ultimately quite considerable. Her windpipe was partially crushed.'

'You said ultimately?' Doyle said.

'Yes.' She went back to the head end of the table. 'I'm sorry, my dear.' Gupta beckoned to one of the technicians, and together they gently lifted Chloe's shoulders to afford Doyle a better look at the back of her neck. 'See here?' she said, pointing to three wider marks at different points on the strangulation bruising. 'This would appear to be where the ligature was tightened. Three separate times, at least, where it was moved slightly. I think this was drawn out. Possibly over some time. I'm going to get a neuropathologist to examine her brain – they may be able to determine further.'

'Dr Gupta,' Doyle said, producing the coiled item he had retrieved from his bag in the storage unit. 'Do you think the ligature could have been something like this?' He handed her an oversized cable tie.

'Did you find this near the scene?'

'No, I had it already. We sometimes used to restrain people with them.'

The pathologist compared the plastic cable tie to the markings on Chloe's neck, then fastened the ratchet to test the resistance in her hands. 'I think, Liam, that is exactly the type of thing that was used to kill her.' She handed the cable tie to Jen Knight, who also examined it.

'Joe and Matt here,' the pathologist continued, nodding towards her technicians, 'did all the external swabs and photos before the scan was done. There are a couple of things to note. First, a chemical residue was found all over her body. We think it is some kind of cleaning agent – of the type you might find on some disposable wipes.'

'The killer trying to remove all possible traces of himself from the body?' Doyle asked.

'I think that's most likely,' Gupta said.

'I have the swabs. We'll analyse them, and hopefully be able to confirm soon, and maybe even find out what brand was used,' Knight said.

'There was also evidence of rape, although there doesn't appear to be any semen. Tests will confirm, of course. There appeared to be traces of the type of lubricant used on condoms on the vaginal swabs. Again, we will get that tested. I'm so sorry, Chloe,' Gupta said to her patient before removing the sheet, completely exposing her naked body.

It occurred to Doyle there were a lot of doctors who worked with living patients who could learn a lot from the pathologist's bedside manner.

'See here?' Gupta indicated the upper inner thigh. 'These bruises look like finger marks to me, and were made when Chloe was still alive. It appears that even with her hands restrained above her head the poor girl tried to clamp her legs closed to resist her attacker. And here.' Dr Gupta indicated Chloe's left breast, which was considerably more discoloured than the right one. 'Her attacker was molesting her with great force. It seems likely he was standing behind her while he raped her, his right hand tightening the ligature and his left on her breast.'

'Would she have had enough breath to scream?' Eddie Scott asked.

'She might have done at first. But look.' She indicated a faint red strip across Chloe's lips and lower jaw. 'We found traces of material in her mouth. The killer stuffed a rag or similar in there and taped it in place.'

This was organised, Doyle thought. The attack itself might have been sexual and violent, but this was planned, not a chance encounter.

'The clothes she was found in were put on her after death. She wasn't wearing anything underneath the tracksuit. I doubt they were her own; they were much too big for her.'

'And the time of death, Dr Gupta? Any idea?' Doyle pressed.

'It is hard to be absolutely certain but, judging by the deep colour of the livor mortis, she was kept in that position for some time after death. We know her body must have been thrown from the cliff on Sunday night. I think she died some time on Saturday.'

'Saturday? Are you sure, Dr Gupta? It couldn't have been later than that?'

'Very early Sunday morning, at a push. But the markings and the breakdown of tissue strongly suggest Saturday as the latest to me.'

'Thank you, Dr Gupta. That is all very useful.' It hadn't been Chloe who had sent those texts to her mum and friends on Sunday afternoon, Doyle realised. The killer must have had access to her phone and known the passcode.

'Please call me Vedhika. Now, I'm afraid we must start the internal examination.'

One of the technicians – Doyle wasn't sure which was Joe and which was Matt – pushed the trolley of instruments up to the table. Doyle would stay, as he always did, and watch the post-mortem. Every organ would be removed, examined and weighed. The stomach, bowel and bladder drained of their contents. Every observation of an anomaly, whether through disease or trauma, would be carefully recorded and included in the pathologist's report. Doyle would leave before they started sewing her back together, the technicians taking great care in their work to ensure that when Mr and Mrs Kennedy came to identify their daughter, she would look peaceful and at rest.

Chapter 8

The Alpha Cabs offices were not situated in Chorley town centre but in a small industrial unit on the northern fringe of the town. Morgan didn't suppose location mattered too much these days, with everyone booking cabs by phone or via an app. Doyle had called her after the post-mortem with the revelation that Chloe had been killed at some point on Saturday, which meant their top priority was to speak to the cab driver who dropped Chloe off in the early hours of that morning.

Morgan had chosen not to park in the car park, which was full of minicabs, all parked at jaunty angles. The detective sergeant did not fancy getting boxed in and then hunting for drivers so they could move their vehicles. Morgan was just about to reach for the office door handle when the door opened towards her, forcing her to step back. A man emerged and immediately exhaled a cloud of watermelon-infused vape into her and Gadget's faces before walking past them, oblivious to their presence. She watched the man, laptop bag across one shoulder, disappear out of the car park just as a white Toyota Prius rolled in and pulled up in front of two other cabs.

The reception area of the office was not the most salubrious that Morgan had ever visited, but was very much in keeping with what she'd expected. A woman at the other end of the room, separated from them by a counter and Perspex screen, was talking into a headset. She acknowledged their presence with a raised hand and a mouthed 'be with you in a minute' before continuing her conversation and tapping information into a keyboard. Gadget sat down on a sofa that would not have looked out of place in a skip. Morgan remained standing, not enticed by the sofa or by how close she'd be to the junior officer if they both sat on the two-seater. After her experiences in CID before she transferred to the MIT eight months ago, she had decided to maintain strict professional boundaries with her new colleagues and keep her social life and work separate. Her first posting in CID had been in Burnley. Keen to make a good impression, Morgan had attended every work night out and social event. Several of these had ended in colleagues making drunken advances towards her, and one time, when she had punched a DS who wouldn't take no for an answer, she'd been accused of overreacting.

She wondered whether the screen was to keep any customers who had ventured into the premises out of the office, or the drivers. The peeling walls were decorated with an assortment of notices: some laminated, others sheets of paper curling up at the edges. They were mostly reminders to the drivers of various expectations and requirements. Morgan doubted they had much effect. Judging by the smell and the yellowed ceiling, the 'no smoking' sign wasn't rigorously adhered to. The young man who had been driving the Prius came into the office. He nodded to Morgan and Gadget and headed through a door marked 'toilets'.

'Yes, lovies, what can I do for you?' the woman who had been talking on the headset asked.

Morgan showed her warrant card. 'I'm DS Morgan, this is DC Washington. Can we speak with whoever is in charge, please?'

'The owner's not here right now, but I'm the manager. Dawn, can I help?'

Morgan noticed that on seeing the warrant card Dawn's accent had become less pronounced and she now addressed them in what Morgan guessed was her telephone voice.

'Is there somewhere we can talk in private?'

'I can let you through here, but I'm on my own so I'll have to answer the phones.'

The mini cab driver emerged from the door behind the two detectives.

'Oh wait. Amir. Do us a favour, lovie?'

'What's that, Dawn?'

'Mind the phones and the office for us while I chat with these two. Won't be for long and we're quiet now.'

'Alright, but the next airport booking that comes in is mine.'

'You got it, but don't tell the others. They don't like favouritism.'

A sly smile played across the cab driver's face. 'I am your favourite though, aren't I, Dawn?'

'Course you are, darling.' She gave the driver – who Morgan guessed was at least fifteen years younger than her – a seductive wink.

The manager's office was not an upgrade on the rest of the premises. If it wasn't for the computer and modern phone, Morgan might have thought she had been teleported back to the 1970s. Dark brown tongue-and-groove panelling lined the walls, and alongside the modern items on the desk sat a large glass ashtray that was half full.

Dawn took a seat behind the desk and gestured for the officers to sit on the other side, before realising that there was only one other chair.

'Amir,' she bellowed, remaining seated. 'Bring another chair in for our guests, will you, lovie?'

Morgan sat down, deciding that it was Gadget's turn to remain standing.

'I'm guessing you're not here to rap my knuckles about smoking in a work premises. What can I help you with?'

'You guess correctly,' Morgan replied as Amir pushed an office chair through the door then left. 'We are from the Major Investigation Team. We're trying to track the last movements of a woman who was found dead this morning.'

'Not that one in the woods by Anglezarke? That was on the radio. Didn't say it were a woman, though. Did someone do her in, then?'

'It's too early to say. So far, the last confirmed sighting of her alive was early Saturday morning just after 1 a.m. She and a friend ordered cabs from here to take them home. We need to speak to the driver.'

Dawn began to tap on the computer keyboard – presumably logging in, Morgan thought.

'Right, what's her name?'

'Chloe Kennedy. But please keep that strictly confidential for now.'

Dawn mouthed zipping her mouth shut. 'You sure it was our firm she used?'

Gadget checked his notepad while Morgan had a brief moment of panic that they had gone to the wrong company.

'She used us early Friday evening from her house into town. But she has no booking on the system after that.'

'This is Alpha Cars?' Gadget asked.

'It is, lovie, you're in the right place. What was her mate's name? Maybe they shared a car?'

'Dani Wheeler,' Morgan said. Something was not right. Dani had said they had booked separate cabs from the same firm.

'Got her – the friend, that is. She booked a cab at 1.09 a.m. Saturday morning, pick-up point on Cunliffe Street just off Market Street. Drop-off, private address in Leyland.'

'Who was the driver that drove Dani home?'

'One second … Amir Hussain.'

'Is that Amir outside?' Morgan asked.

'Amir?' Dawn boomed. 'Get your arse in here now.'

It only took a moment before the driver appeared in the room.

'These two people are from the police. They need to get some details about a fare you picked up on Friday night.'

'OK, which one?'

Dawn turned the monitor 90 degrees so that they could all see it.

'OK, yeah, I remember. She's a regular. I've driven her and her mate home quite a few times in the past few weeks.'

'Was it just her you drove home Friday night?' Morgan asked.

'Yeah, her mate lives in the opposite direction. Adlington way.'

'Can you remember if her friend was with her when you got there?'

'Yeah, I offered to wait until her friend's car turned up. But she said not to worry, that it was only two minutes away. What's happened? They're not in trouble, are they? They aren't the type. They're nice girls, not like some we get.'

'No, it's nothing like that. Mr Hussain, would you happen to have a dashcam that would have been recording when you made that pick-up?'

'Yes, sure. Want to take a look? The car's just outside.'

'Perhaps DC Washington could go and look. Are you OK if he takes a copy of the footage, Mr Hussain?'

'Yes, sure. Call me Amir.'

'Thanks, Amir.'

Gadget got up and followed the cab driver out of the office.

'He's a good lad him – can't do enough for you. Some of the other drivers are right miserable bastards, moan about everything.'

Morgan studied the screen. As well as details of the driver, customer, destination and price, it showed a small map indicating the pick-up point.

'If they spent the last part of the evening here,' Morgan said, using a pen to point on the screen, 'in the Manhattan Project on Market Street, why would Dani Wheeler have booked a cab to pick her up on Cunliffe Street?'

'She wouldn't've,' Dawn replied. 'It's 'cause she booked it through the app. The app tells the customer and driver where the pick-up point is for that address. The idea is, it finds a place where the driver can easily stop, to avoid pedestrianised streets and one-way systems an' all that. You'd be surprised, the places drunk people decide to wait for their cabs.'

'It doesn't seem particularly safe telling vulnerable people to wait in quiet side roads where there are less people about.'

'That's not up to us.'

'Then who decides where the pick-up point is?'

'The app – uses algorithms or something. We have no control over that. We have had a couple of times where the suggested pick-up point wasn't much use, so we had to get on to the app people to get that altered.'

'Is it possible that Chloe Kennedy did book a minicab for that time, but it has somehow dropped off the system?'

'Can't see how. It shows up in the driver's app what jobs they have done and how much money they're due. If one had dropped off the system from Friday night, by now I would have had an irate driver wanting to know who was going to pay for the fare.'

'Something is not making sense here,' Morgan said, thinking out loud more than addressing the cab firm manager.

'It's possible that she cancelled the booking, either deliberately or accidentally,' Dawn said. 'We have had a bit of that recently – people phoning up because their booking got cancelled on the app and their cab doesn't show up.'

'How can that happen? Could it be the driver cancelling it, or someone at the office?'

'No, then it would still show up on the system. If the driver cancelled for some reason, like they needed fuel, they'd broken down or something, the job would get reallocated to another driver. If we had cancelled it back here, we would have to put a reason why, and it would still show up. That would typically only be for a customer who had been abusive in the past or something like that.'

'So, you're saying Chloe must have cancelled the cab herself?'

'Well, yes, but she might have done it by accident. We thought there might be a glitch in the system. We had a technician from the app company come out and check everything. You just missed him, actually. He said it was nothing to do with the software, and the most likely cause was touchscreens on phones – people accidentally cancelling when putting them back in their pockets or bags. They're going to look at adding another step, so when you press "cancel" it takes you to another screen to confirm that you want to cancel.'

'Do you think that could have happened to Chloe?'

'Your guess is as good as mine, lovie. I was working Friday night and she didn't phone and rebook. Mind you, it was quite a nice evening for once. She might have decided to walk home, or been picked up by someone she knew.'

⋏ ⋏ ⋏

Doyle had easily found Chorley police station. The incident room was just as he had expected, and Doyle was pleased to see that DI Hales and Shaima Asif were well on the way to setting it up for running a major investigation. A large map of the area adorned the far wall. Next to it was a pinboard displaying the blown-up images Doyle had taken that morning of Chloe Kennedy. There were also a couple of photos of her taken while she was still full of life: one with long, flowing hair and one with her more recent style – a pixie cut, Morgan had informed him on their way back from the woods.

There were also several pictures of a man Doyle guessed was Ryan Johnson. He could see from across the room his big, muscled arms and bodybuilder's physique. Doyle suspected the 'tough man' expression might be wiped off Johnson's face after he'd had a little chat with him.

Doyle recognised one of the two uniformed officers typing up notes in a corner of the room as the PC who had shouted at him from Chloe's back garden. No doubt they were entering the details from the door-to-door.

'Hello, sir,' Asif said. The others in the room looked up.

'Hi.' He returned her smile before addressing the room in general. 'Has anyone taken any calls for me from IT?' There were headshakes all round. Doyle looked at his watch before muttering, 'For fuck's sake' under his breath.

'Can I grab you for a minute?' Hales asked, limping over.

'Of course, Geoff. Have you hurt your leg?'

'No, it's bloody gout. I'm on tablets, but it still flares up from time to time.' He indicated a room off the incident room. 'We've set up an office for you in there, got your laptop and bits from HQ. Me and Morgan will be in the one next door.'

Doyle strode towards his new office with Geoff 'the Pearl' Hales hobbling behind. He had hung his jacket on the back of the chair and was sitting by the time his second-in-command came in, shutting the door behind him.

'What can I do for you, Geoff?'

'I just wanted to give you an update, sir.'

'Good. Well, don't stand on ceremony. I mean, really – don't stand on ceremony. Sit down and take the weight off that leg. And there's no need for the "sir" either – you're my DI. Call me Liam, or whatever nickname you've dreamed up for me.'

'We're still working on that,' Hales said without the trace of a smile. 'Uniform didn't get too much back from the door-to-door with Chloe's neighbours. It seems no one had seen her since Friday evening, when she left for her night out. Neighbour opposite swears the curtains have not been opened all weekend and her car had not moved from outside.'

'Have Morgan and Washington got back from the cab place yet? We really need to know where she was dropped off.'

'No, but I don't think they'll be too long. I've done the usual requesting of all Chloe's bank statements, phone records, etc. I imagine they will all start to flow in tomorrow. I did speak to the bank on the phone, and they told me the last transaction on her account was at the Manhattan Project early on Saturday morning, but they don't necessarily come out in order.'

'Good, and what have we got on Johnson?'

'He's an electrician. The last address we could find for him was Chloe's house, but then it wasn't that long ago he moved out. We think he's on pay-as-you-go, as his contract with O2 ended in January.'

'Any previous?'

'He's got a conviction for possession of Class A when he was nineteen. That MMD thingy.'

'MDMA?'

'That's the one.'

'Right, well, it hardly makes him Jack the Ripper.'

'True, but he seems to have taken the break-up badly. According to both the friends we interviewed, he was pretty much stalking her. That would give a motive.'

'Agreed, and her dad was none too keen on him either. Speaking of which, is DC Nelson back yet?'

'On his way now. There's a family liaison officer in place.'

'And what about beefing up the team? How have you got on?'

The Pearl sucked in air. Doyle couldn't tell if this was because of the pain in his leg or what he was about to tell him.

'We've only been able to grab a couple each shift from Chorley CID. Some of them are still following up on that arson attack from Sunday night. Uniform have given us a couple. Those two out there, PCs Bowen and Price, were on the early shift but seem keen to lap up the overtime.'

'And what about other detectives from the MIT?'

'Croucher's replied to my email saying there's no one available yet. He copied you in.'

'Fuck's sake, this is a murder investigation. I've seen more resources allocated to catch a guy selling knock-off DVDs.'

Hales lifted his arms, as if in surrender 'Hey, don't shoot the messenger.'

'Sorry, Geoff. I *still* can't get into my email, as those pricks in IT haven't seen fit to give me my password yet.'

'Oh yeah, they're pretty useless. That's one reason we kept hold of Gadget after he finished his detective training. We don't have to bother with IT for most things now.' He looked up at the clock on the wall. 'It's still not yet six. If you give them a call, you might catch them.'

'Thanks, I will. Can you do us a favour and get everyone rounded up? As soon as Morgan's back we'll have a briefing.'

'Will do.'

Doyle had found the number for IT by the time the Pearl had limped back out of the office – leaving the door open, to Doyle's frustration. Predictably, the IT department's recorded message played once again in Doyle's ear before he was given his cue to speak by the beep.

'This is DCI Doyle. I've have tried several times to contact you, but you have failed to reply. I can't email you, as your recorded message suggests, as I'm calling because you haven't given me my fucking email login details. I am currently investigating the murder of a young woman and haven't got time to fuck about chasing you lot around. I need my email up and working so I can get on with my job. I suggest one of you useless twats resolves this straight away.'

It was only as the DCI slammed the receiver down that he noticed everyone in the outer office had stopped what they were doing and were staring at him. When he looked up, their eyes darted straight back to their computer screens. Derrick 'Birdseye' Nelson had chosen that exact moment to enter the incident room and stood frozen, cup of tea in hand, like a rabbit caught in the headlights.

'Detective Constable. Just in time,' Doyle said.

'For what, sir?' Birdseye asked, as though it was some kind of trap.

'Getting me a cup of coffee.'

'Right-oh. How d'you take it, sir?'

'Just like me. Strong, white and very sweet.'

Chapter 9

There was a hubbub in the incident room. Doyle was pleased to see that, although there were only half as many officers present as he would have liked, Hales had at least been successful in seconding a further two from both uniform and CID.

A man wearing the epaulettes of an inspector approached and offered his hand to shake. 'You must be DCI Doyle. I'm Phil Regan, running the back shift here this evening. Anything you need, just say.'

'Thanks, Phil. Can you stay for the briefing, so you're up to speed?'

'Will do. Sorry I can't spare any more bodies, but I'll make sure you get the same again from uniform and CID from the night shift.'

'Cheers. Right,' said Doyle, raising his voice above the chatter. 'Let's get started.' He made his way over to the board and indicated one of the photos. 'This is, or rather was, Chloe Kennedy. Twenty-six years old. She was a primary school teacher at Devonshire Road and lived in Adlington. Her body was found in the woods at the bottom of the cliffs in Anglezarke this morning. We believe she was thrown from the viewing point above, some time on Sunday night, but she was killed on Saturday. DS Morgan, can you fill everyone in on her last known movements?'

Morgan came to stand at the front. 'Chloe went out on Friday evening with a friend from work, Dani Wheeler. That's her.' She indicated a photo of Dani that had been pinned up on the far side of the board.

'Nice,' said a uniformed officer, which earned him a scowl from Inspector Regan. It was PC Price, the short round officer who had been watching the front of Chloe's house.

'They had a few drinks in the Red Lion on Union Street before ending up in the Manhattan Project on Market Street, where they stayed until it closed at 1 a.m.'

'Is that the new gay bar that opened just before Christmas last year?' a detective from CID asked.

'That's right.'

'You weren't in there Friday night, were you, Jim?' PC Price quipped, and Doyle watched PC Bowen flush for the second time that day. He made a mental note that next time it was pissing down with rain and he needed a crime scene guarding, this prick Price would get the job.

'Do we think she was gay?' another detective asked.

'Not according to Dani, who is gay, and another friend of Chloe's, Stacy Vickers. That's her.' Morgan indicated another photo on the board. 'I expect they chose to drink there to avoid the attention of Neanderthals like PC Price.'

Doyle smiled as the cocky constable looked down at the floor.

'According to Dani, both women booked taxis from Alpha Cars using the app, but Alpha Cars has no record of Chloe's booking.'

'Is Dani lying – or the minicab office?' asked a female detective.

'It looks like they're both telling the truth. Gadget, do you want to do the honours?'

DC Washington moved to the front and plugged his laptop into a large flat-screen TV that had been set up next to the pinboard.

'We got this dashcam footage from Amir Hussain, the minicab driver who took Dani home,' Gadget said.

All watched in silence as the video played on the monitor. They saw the view from the windscreen as the cab turned off Market Street onto Cunliffe Street.

Gadget paused the recording. 'You can now see Dani and Chloe waiting up the road here.' He indicated on the screen with his pen.

'Why are they so far up the road?' The CID woman asked.

'Apparently the pick-up point is determined by the app,' Morgan said.

Gadget rolled the footage on, stopping just as the cab pulled up in front of both women. 'That's Chloe there,' he said.

She was slightly shorter than Dani, Doyle noticed, though they were both wearing heels. She had on a short dress and a denim jacket, and a small cross-body handbag. Both women held mobile phones.

'It's hard to see the colours in this footage, but that is a red dress and blue jacket.' Gadget ran the clip on as the cab went past the women, taking them out of view, and stopped.

'Right,' Doyle said, getting back to his feet. 'That is the last known sighting of Chloe Kennedy alive. We need to know where she went from here. It looks like she didn't return home, and she either didn't book a taxi with Alpha Cars or she cancelled it before it turned up. Dani booked her cab at 1.09 and it arrived at 1.21. Chloe told Dani and Amir that her cab was due to arrive two minutes later.'

'Sorry,' the female CID officer interjected. 'But that's crazy. The app has directed them to wait for their car away from Market Street, where there's CCTV coverage and plenty of people around, to down a quiet side street. It might be more convenient for the driver, but it's much less safe for vulnerable women.'

'I mentioned this to the manager of the cab firm. She said that was out of their control; it's decided by an algorithm on the app,' Morgan replied.

'OK, moving on,' said Doyle. 'The full report from the PM will be on the system as soon as we get it, but the headlines for now are: Chloe was strangled with a ligature, which we think was a thick cable tie of the type we use to restrain people. This was a prolonged attack, and Chloe was suspended upright by her wrists.'

'Was she raped?' another CID man asked.

'It looks very likely. There was no semen found in or on her body, but the pathologist thinks her attacker used a condom. She has taken swabs to test for spermicides and lubricants,' Doyle replied. 'There was also bruising on Chloe's upper thighs and left breast.'

'Could it be an auto-erotic thing that went wrong?' Birdseye asked.

'The pathologist felt not; the level of force used to tighten the ligature was enough to partially crush Chloe's windpipe and oesophagus. She doesn't think there is any way someone could do that and expect the other person to live. Whoever did this is forensically aware. The body was cleaned from head to toe with some kind of wipe, and all Chloe's clothing was removed. She was found dressed in the black tracksuit and trainers you can see in the pictures. So far, they haven't found any trace of the killer on the body or at the site where Chloe was dumped. This isn't an accidental killing or the result of a violent row that got out of hand. This is a pre-planned sadistic murder: poor Chloe Kennedy was subjected to a sexual assault and strangulation that lasted, the pathologist thinks, several hours.'

The room was hushed as the DCI's words began to sink in.

'We'll move on to suspects and persons of interest,' Doyle continued. 'DI Hales, can you bring everyone up to speed, please?'

Hales stood with obvious discomfort. 'Ryan Johnson,' he said, pointing to the board with a nicotine-stained finger. 'He's Chloe's ex-boyfriend and, according to her friends and parents, saying that he didn't take their break-up well is an understatement. They split six weeks ago, and he had been harassing her until it got so bad that, according to Dani, Chloe was going to report it.'

'That tallies with what her dad told me. He said Johnson had been controlling towards Chloe since the start of their relationship,' Birdseye added. 'They were both invited to her parents' for Christmas, but he didn't want to go and wouldn't let Chloe go. Didn't like her going out and seeing friends either.'

'We don't know much more about Johnson at this stage. He's got a record, but only for possession, from six years ago. Nothing since,' Hales said. 'He's an electrician, but we don't know who he works for yet.'

'If he is an electrician, he would have a ready supply of cable ties,' one of the CID men said. This earned him several nods from around the room. Doyle could tell that opinions were already being formed about Ryan Johnson. He would have to be careful to make sure these did not start to obscure the facts.

'His last known address is Chloe's house in Adlington, but we know he moved out when they split up. He's the registered keeper of a black Audi A3, according to the DVLA. We're running an ANPR check to see his recent movements. We haven't yet got phone records for him either, or even a number at this stage, but we're working on that.'

'Are we thinking he's our guy?' the female CID officer asked

'We're not making any assumptions at this stage,' Doyle said. 'But he certainly appears to have a potential motive. However, whether he has the ability to carry out such a calculated attack and do such a good job of concealing evidence is yet to be determined.'

'His face seems familiar,' PC Bowen said. 'But I can't place where from.'

'You probably don't recognise him with clothes on,' PC Price said.

Doyle let the comment slide, for now, making a mental note to speak to Inspector Regan about Price's attitude. 'Well, have a think. Priority for tonight is tracking him down. On top of that, we've got to start working out what happened to Chloe after Dani left her early Saturday morning, and we need to find where she was killed, her clothes, her phone and her handbag. One more thing: whoever killed her replied to messages from her friends and family on Sunday afternoon, after Chloe was dead.'

'Definitely sounds like the ex, then,' a detective said. 'He would likely know her passcodes.'

'Maybe,' Doyle conceded. 'But we're not going to rule anything in or out just yet. I'll be leading on this as SIO, and DI Hales will be office manager. If you haven't done so already, get your tasks from him. And remember, anything, and I do mean anything, you come up with must be reported back to him.'

Chapter 10

Police Constable Francis Bowen had been at work since six that morning. He was on the early shift and had been due to knock off at two in the afternoon, which was about the time he had come running into Chloe Kennedy's back garden, shouting at the giant of a man who turned out to be the new DCI on the MIT. He shuddered when he recalled the memory. That arsehole Jonathon Price could have warned him on the radio that the detectives were entering the property.

Bowen had happily agreed to stay on and do the back shift when Inspector Regan asked him. The overtime would come in handy, but more than that the chance to work on a major investigation didn't come round every day. Doing the subsequent door-to-door with Price wasn't exactly glamorous, but it was a start. A step in the right direction.

He stood in front of the incident board, staring at the face which he now knew was Ryan Johnson. Where had he seen him? He knew he had, and more than just once. He looked familiar. He was good-looking, but it wasn't that. He didn't think he knew him from off the telly, though he wouldn't look out of place on *Love Island*. Bowen felt uneasy about the man, a dislike for some reason, but why?

And then he realised.

'Sir,' Bowen said, approaching the DCI. 'I've remembered where I know him from. Ryan Johnson. He goes to the same gym as me.'

'You go to the gym? You want to ask for your money back,' Price said.

'Shut up.' Doyle cut Price down. 'Good work. It's Jim, isn't it?'

'Actually, it's Francis, but everyone here calls me Jim because of Jim Bowen who was on the TV years ago, apparently.'

'*Bullseye.* I used to love that programme,' Birdseye said. 'Me and my wife applied to go on it in the eighties but didn't make the cut.'

Hales joined in. 'Were you going to be throwing the darts or answering the questions?'

'Throwing the darts. The wife would be answering the questions. She would've been good at it, an' all. She knows bloody everything.'

The DC and DI laughed.

'Fuck me, Derrick, you're full of surprises. Now, does anyone object if we get back to the task of actually trying to catch a murderer?' Doyle said. 'Which gym do you go to and where is it?'

'It's called the Iron Works. It's here in Coppull.' Bowen indicated the location on the large map on the wall. 'I joined because it's local and was cheap.'

'And Johnson – does he go there a lot? When did you last see him there?'

'I tend to go either about this time of day if I'm on earlies or nights and in the morning when I'm on lates,' Bowen said. 'I've only seen him in the evenings, which I guess makes sense if he works during the day. He wasn't there last night, and I didn't go on Sunday. I'm pretty sure he was there Saturday.'

'What time was that?' Doyle asked.

'A bit earlier, as I was going out Saturday night. Must've been about half four. You can check with the records at the gym. They've got an electronic system where you tap in with your card.'

'And have you had any dealings with him? Do you know what he's like?'

'To be honest, sir, he's always in there with another couple of guys hogging the free weights. Bodybuilder types. They're a bit intimidating. I try to stay out of their way.'

'Boss?' Asif called from behind her computer on the other side of the room. 'A fixed ANPR camera has just picked up Johnson's Audi on the A49 heading north out of Standish.'

'Where's that?' Doyle asked.

Bowen showed him on the map.

'So, he could be heading for the gym now?'

'Looks possible,' Hales said.

'Right, Francis. Have you got any gym kit here?'

'Yeah, my bag's in my car. I was going to go after work before all this came up.'

'Good, well get into it pronto and meet us in the car park. Morgan, Gadget. I need a quick word in private,' Doyle said.

PC Bowen didn't need telling twice. He practically sprinted down the steps to get changed.

Chapter 11

Bowen could feel his heart rate accelerating as DC Washington, who everyone in the MIT seemed to call Gadget, brought the unmarked police car to a stop just up the road from the gym.

'You OK?' Gadget asked him.

Gadget was younger than him by a good few years, and Bowen couldn't help wondering how the detective had got such a plum posting at his age. 'Sure. I'm actually quite excited.' He didn't know whether it was really excitement or nerves.

'Remember, go in there completely normal, as you would every time you go to the gym. Put your bag in the locker, but keep your phone on you. Have you got headphones?'

'Yes.'

'Good. When you know if he is in there or not, text me. Make it look like you're selecting a playlist. Make sure it isn't obvious you're looking around.'

'Will do – I mean, won't do. Oh, you know what I mean.'

'After texting me, carry on with your workout as normal. I'll give it five minutes then call you. Make out something urgent has come up and you have to leave, but don't rush out of there like it's some big emergency and draw attention to yourself, and don't forget to grab your bag out of the locker.'

'OK, no problem.'

'While you're in there, I'm going to have a scout around outside. See if I can see his car. If you notice him leaving, call me straight away.'

'Got it.'

Bowen felt like he had already done a workout by the time he got into the gym. Must be the adrenaline. He had noticed that the two cars containing the CID officers were discreetly positioned, ready to follow the suspect if required. He had to remind himself to calm down. There was nothing difficult about what he was going to do.

The changing rooms were empty apart from someone in one of the toilet cubicles. It could be Ryan Johnson, Bowen thought, but checking further would risk blowing his cover or making him look like a pervert. He sat down on one of the benches and took his time taking off his jacket and retying his shoelaces. The toilet flushed and a middle-aged man walked straight out without washing his hands. Dirty bastard, Bowen thought, making a mental note not to use any piece of equipment after the man had used it.

'You OK, hun?'

Bowen nearly jumped out of his skin as the staff member greeted him while he was stashing his bag in a foyer locker.

'Great, thanks. You?' he almost stammered.

'Can't complain, I suppose.'

Christ, pull yourself together, Francis, he silently chided himself.

The free weights area was not immediately visible on entering the gym. Bowen did a quick scan of the cardiovascular and stretching sections. There was no sign of Johnson. He went up to an exercise bike and deliberately didn't look over to the weights as he got on and adjusted the seat. It was only when he was sitting on the bike and had his phone in his hand that he glanced towards the far side. There were three men there, two standing either side of a bench and one lying on it, hands poised on a barbell that rested on a stand. Johnson wasn't either of the two whose faces Bowen could see, but he could be the man lying on the bench.

He turned away, not wanting to be seen staring, and began to pedal the bike, scanning the room without looking over towards the weights. A mirror in the opposite corner meant he could watch the men without it being obvious. His view wasn't perfect, but he would be able to see when the man on the bench sat up.

Bowen watched the weights go up and down several times. He had no idea how many kilos there were – probably more than his own body weight. He saw the man's hands come off the bar and the guy slide down the bench. Bowen turned to see Ryan Johnson sit up. He realised he had stopped pedalling, and started again. He was still staring. *Look away*. Shit. Johnson had seen him. He moved his gaze, but not before the prime suspect in their murder enquiry blew him a kiss and winked. As Bowen turned, he heard the other men laugh. With a slight tremble in his right hand, he typed out *He's here* and pressed 'send'. Had he blown it? Ryan Johnson had seen him, but he didn't know he was police. The wink and the kiss – that wasn't a suspect responding to undercover surveillance. That was a narcissistic homophobe who assumed he'd just caught a gay man checking him out. He had got that vibe off Ryan and his entourage before.

Bowen checked his heart rate on the display. 170. He attempted to look nonchalant watching the TV screen. His phone was ringing. Gadget. He answered and waited.

'Yes, OK, I'll come now. Do you think you might have left your keys at work?'

⚔ ⚔ ⚔

Doyle had told Morgan that she could go home a little while ago, but there were a few loose ends that she wanted to tie up before she left. She had Chloe's diary in the evidence bag. With the school caretaker standing over her, Morgan hadn't wanted to look through it when she had retrieved it from the teacher's desk. She had reasoned that a work diary was unlikely to unveil anything significant in the hunt for the woman's killer, so had given it a low priority. Now she wanted to give it a quick once-over before logging it into the exhibits store. With gloved hands she took it out and began to check each page methodically. The entries failed to reveal anything relevant. The note about parents' evening prompted the detective to scribble a reminder to check which pupils Chloe Kennedy had taught and see if any of the parents flashed up on a PNC check. She had waded through nearly the entire book when she came to some lined pages for notes at the back. On one line was written *fb* followed by ten seemingly random characters. They were carefully printed, the writing style different to the cursive script used in the rest of the book. Two lines below, *em* had been written, along with another ten characters. Another two lines down was *mob*, followed by six digits. Morgan brought up the Facebook login page on her laptop. Although they didn't have Chloe's mobile phone, Morgan had her number. She entered it in the login details, followed by the random characters Chloe had transcribed next to the letters *fb* in the password box. She clicked on the login button.

'Get in,' Morgan said rather more loudly than she intended as the dead woman's Facebook profile opened in front of her. They would have got it eventually through official channels, but this had saved a lot of time and some other poor bugger's effort.

'Got something, Anna?' Hales asked from opposite, where he was also peering at a computer.

'I've got into her Facebook. Last entry is from Friday evening – she posted a selfie of her and Dani. Just going into her Messenger.'

Hales came round and stood behind her.

'Jesus,' Morgan said as she read the first message.

'Liam,' Hales shouted. 'You might want to come and take a look at this.'

Morgan clicked on another message as Doyle came into the room.

'What you got?' the DCI asked.

'Anna's got into Chloe's Facebook. Have a read of these messages from Johnson,' Hales said.

'What an arsehole' was Doyle's verdict. Morgan couldn't disagree. 'I just had Gadget on the phone. Ryan Johnson was at the gym. Him and Bowen are on their way back. CID are poised to follow when Johnson leaves.'

'Don't you think we should bring him in? I mean, there's enough here to make him prime suspect if he wasn't already, and we could probably charge him with stalking or harassment or something,' Hales said.

Doyle looked as if he was considering this. 'You're right, to a point. But if we pick him up now, it will be gone midnight before a solicitor is found and we can have a crack at him. If we keep tabs on him tonight, he'll probably lead us to where he's been staying since Chloe gave him the elbow. We can bring him in first thing and give him a good going over when we're all fresher and we've had a chance to read all these messages. We can also get a team to search his digs at the same time.'

'You're putting a lot of faith in CID, aren't you? I wouldn't have thought they've got much experience in covert surveillance. And if they lose him, Mr Burns will go apoplectic.'

Morgan briefly caught Doyle's eye.

'What? What is it?' Hales asked.

'I decided to take out a bit of insurance. While Johnson was pumping iron, Gadget put a tracker on his car.'

'Jesus,' Hales said. Then he looked at Morgan 'And you knew about this too? Christ, Burns will go spare if he finds out.'

'It's not illegal. Besides, he's not going to find out. When we pick up Johnson, Gadget will retrieve it before his car goes off to forensics.'

'It's only not illegal if you've got a warrant. And that kind of electronic surveillance needs to be authorised from on high – you know that. Burns is a stickler for the rules.'

'Look, if it all comes out, I'll take the rap. You and Anna knew nothing about it, and Gadget was following my direct orders and assumed I had got permission. Besides, I was going to email the super about it, get him to sort out the legal bit. But you know my email's still not working.'

'So that was all bollocks what you said in the briefing? That I needed to be informed of every single detail?'

Doyle shrugged. Morgan thought Hales had a point. She got the impression that her two senior officers didn't yet trust each other, and hoped she wouldn't get stuck in the middle of any tension between them.

'Where the hell did you get it from?' Hales asked, sounding less irritated.

'I bought it ages ago; they're not expensive. It was for a job I was on where getting hold of one was proving a pain via official channels, but there were no such issues with Amazon Prime.'

An email alert flashed up on Morgan's screen. 'We've just got a message from the FLO. Chloe's parents have formally identified her body.'

Chapter 12

June 1996

'Fuck, Jay.'

The boy studied Michelle's face as she gazed at the scene in front of her. The smell had hit them before they had even reached the ginnel. It was the same smell he remembered from when he was little, in the garden the morning after his dad had done a bonfire.

'Fuck, that's fucking awesome,' Michelle said.

'Do you like it?' He turned away from her and took in the destruction. The pigeon loft was just a pile of burned-out timber and blackened, buckled wire mesh. Among the now sodden ruins, Jay could make out bits of charred skeleton, like tiny chicken bones. The fence that had separated the next-door garden was gone, a couple of concrete posts still standing defiantly.

He hadn't planned to do any serious damage to the house. He had only thrown the last of the petrol over the back door to stop anyone coming out and chasing him. But the kitchen, which protruded from the rest of the property, was a burned-out carcass missing its back door and windows. You could see where the flames had licked the brickwork, changing the colour from rust to charcoal.

'Shit – Toto, he sleeps in the kitchen.' Michelle's face changed from wonderment to horror.

'It's OK, he came out of the cat flap and ran off out the open gate,' Jay reassured her. 'He couldn't wait to get away. I bet he fiddles the dog too.'

Michelle winced. 'He's going to go spare. Those racing pigeons were his world. Good, fuck him. Fucking flying rats.'

'You like it, then?' the boy asked.

'Yeah, but fuck, Jay. This is wild. You could get some serious time for this.'

'I don't care.' He did. He hadn't thought he would get sent down, even if he did get caught. He'd only meant to burn the shed – and as for the birds, posh people ate pigeons. 'He needed to be taught a lesson for what he did. I wanted to show you I believe you.'

'Shit, Jay.' Michelle tugged at his sleeve. Jay looked up, to see a man in the upstairs window staring at them. Michelle was first to react, and gave him the finger.

'Fucking nonce,' the boy shouted, then threw a half brick towards the window. Then, for the second time in not many hours, he was running down the alleyway, this time following Michelle, his heart racing, and not just from the exercise. His head filled with a combustible mix of excitement, fear and elation, with the added catalysts of THC and CBD.

人 人 人

They hadn't been back to the children's home since. The pair had spent the day wandering around Fleetwood, finding secluded spots to skin up and have a smoke. They now found themselves sitting on the grass in a park, Michelle using three large Rizla papers to roll a joint.

'It's a shame you can't do a GCSE in that,' Jay said. 'You'd get an A star.'

'You're crazy, Jay,' Michelle replied, carefully crumbling hash into the papers.

'I mean, you've already done all the practical work a million times over, and I'm sure there aren't any questions that would come up in the exam that you wouldn't be able to answer.'

They giggled.

'You would get a U, though. You're shit at skinning up.' This was true, they both knew; his efforts always ended in a loosely packed reefer that dropped hot rocks all over their clothes.

'But I've got a year before my exams. I could get good in that time,' the boy responded as the girl sprinkled the tobacco from a Benson & Hedges into the Rizlas. 'Besides, I'm good at other things.'

'I think there is less chance of them giving out GCSEs for lighting fires than there is of them handing them out for rolling joints,' Michelle said.

They both started to giggle hysterically.

'When's your next exam?'

'Tomorrow morning. Maths. Only two more after that, then freedom.' She lit the joint and took a long pull on it.

The boy felt that he never wanted this moment to end. 'Will they really get you your own place after that?'

'That's what my social worker says.' She took another drag and then spoke as she exhaled. 'I'm a looked after child, priority for a council place when you turn sixteen. You'll get one too.' She passed the joint to the boy.

'I'm going to miss you. Place won't be the same without you.' He took a lungful of smoke and felt a knot of pain in his chest at the thought of Michelle leaving.

'Don't be silly, you can come round. We'll be able to have a smoke, listen to music loud. It'll be wild.'

'I've got you a housewarming present for when you move out.'

'You're sweet. What is it?'

'I can't say. It's a surprise.' He had found the video recorder in a skip and then spent days taking it apart, cleaning the parts and reassembling it. Now it was as good as new. He had even knocked on the door that had the skip outside and asked the owner if they still had the remote. 'Have you got a TV?'

'You haven't got me a telly, have you? Where did you nick that from?'

The boy took another long drag on the joint, then passed it back to Michelle.

'Shit, Jay. You're whiting out. Let's walk to the garage and get some food.'

It took them longer than expected to walk the half mile to the petrol station. The effects of a day smoking cannabis had taken its toll on Jay, and every so often he had to stop and sit on a garden wall or bus stop seat.

'You stay here,' Michelle told him. 'You look way too mashed to go in there.'

Jay sat down on a patch of grass and leaned against a fence. 'Get me some of those Space Invader crisps. And a can of Tizer or Irn-Bru.'

'Got it,' Michelle said, crossing the road towards the garage.

'Michelle,' he shouted out to her. 'Don't forget a Curly Wurly.'

She gave him a thumbs up for a reply.

It was only after she'd gone into the shop that he noticed the cameras covering the petrol station forecourt. He hadn't thought about them before. He hadn't supposed that the police would put much effort into investigating a burned-out shed, but the house had looked quite damaged too. What if they did investigate, and checked the footage? They would see him yesterday evening filling up two cans of petrol. They might not check, he told himself, and if they did, how would they know who he was? He doubted the pictures were very good quality. But then, this morning, the man had seen them from the upstairs window. He might not have known who Jay was, but he knew Michelle. Too well, in fact. Them being there didn't prove anything, though. He was just getting paranoid because he was stoned.

Two more hours passed before the pair drifted back to the children's home to face the inevitable bollocking from the staff. They had been out all day and not let anyone know where they were. The boy, although still quietly mellow, was feeling rather less wasted than before.

'Shit, Jay,' Michelle said, coming to an abrupt halt as she rounded the corner.

'What?' Then he saw it. The police car sitting outside the large house at the end of the road where they lived.

Instinctively they turned and marched back the way they had come. The boy half expected to hear shouts and a siren from behind.

'Don't run,' Michelle said. They walked briskly up the road and then up a ginnel.

'You think they're there for us?'

'For you, you mean. I didn't do anything.'

'Yes, sorry. What should we do?'

'I don't know. Fuck.'

He could see tears forming in the corner of her eyes. 'Look, you go back. You have an alibi for last night right. The staff will have seen you.' Jay sounded much more confident than he felt. 'It might be about something else. If it is, come back here and get me and I'll go in.'

'And what if it is about the fire? He saw me from the window, and he'll think I was involved too.' She was crying now.

'Tell them the truth: you were in all night, and I took you there to show you. Say that I said someone had told me about it, not that I did it. You can't get done for this. If it comes to it, I'll say it was all me.'

'It *was* all you, Jay. I didn't ask you to do it. I can't get done, not now.' She sobbed harder.

'I know. Look, if you're not back in ten minutes, I'll disappear. Say you haven't seen me since this morning if anyone asks.'

'OK.' She wiped her face on her sleeve. 'What will you do?

Where will you go without any things?'

'Can you meet me tomorrow after your exam?'

'Sure. Where?' she said, sounding a bit calmer.

'Bring anything you can get from my room, clothes and that, but don't let anyone see you. And you know where my parents are? Where we went at Christmas?'

Michelle nodded.

'Meet me there.'

'OK,' she said. 'Take this.' She gave him the B&H box containing the remaining cigarettes, a tiny amount of puff, some Rizlas and a lighter. 'Good luck,' she said and kissed his cheek. Then she went out of the alleyway into the street.

She'd kissed his cheek. She had actually kissed his cheek. Jay smiled.

Chapter 13

Day 2: Wednesday 14th June 2023

A burst of static.

Powell's voice crackly in the earpiece. 'We're burned, the target's clocked us. He's got the kid.'

Opening the car door. A blast of wind, cold on his cheeks.

'He's going down the back staircase. Heading for the car park.'

Pulling on the cloth police cap. His feet running as soon as they hit the tarmac.

The commander's voice. 'All units, we need to stop Campbell before he gets mobile.'

Hand in his jacket, the Glock released from its shoulder holster. Rounding the corner, Campbell disappearing down the car park ramp. Legs pumping harder, closing the gap. An electronic chirp, lights flashing on a BMW. The kid was held tight to Campbell's chest, knife against her throat.

'Armed police! Let go of the girl. Put the knife down.' Safety catch off. *Breathe.*

'Get the fuck back, or I'll kill her.'

'Armed police. Drop the knife.' *Breathe.*

'I mean it – I'll fucking kill her.'

Finger on the trigger. Aim at the head, don't miss. Breathe. Squeeze.

The report was deafening, echoing round the car park. A ringing, then silence. He could only see her scream.

Blood, lots of it. On the car. On Campbell. On the girl. Had he shot her? Her chest was moving up and down, tears on her cheeks. Campbell, lifeless. Entry wound on his forehead. He hadn't missed.

Breathe.

Scooping the child in his left arm. She clung to him. His right hand still held the gun. Up the ramp, out of the car park. Fresh air, daylight. A man standing on the pavement, aiming a phone at him.

人 人 人

Doyle woke with a start, sweating. He'd had the dream before, too many times. At least these days he seldom had the flashbacks when he was awake. He fumbled under the duvet, grabbing the dog tag that hung round his neck. Its twin was under the ground eight thousand miles away. He gripped the metal disc as he tried to bring his heart rate down. Why wouldn't his unconscious let him be free of this? The outcome had been as good as it could be – unless you were Jamal Campbell, of course. He looked at his phone: 5.45 a.m. and no missed calls. He could try and get another half hour's sleep to add to the three he'd had. Or get up now, quick shower, teeth and breakfast. Maybe a shave afterwards, if there was time. He turned on the light.

人 人 人

Liam Doyle wondered why Detective Superintendent Croucher had bothered to shut the door that separated the office from the incident room. If it was privacy that Mr Burns was looking for, then he might have been better not bellowing at the top of his voice.

'I can't believe you didn't bring him in yesterday! Those CID officers that spent all night in their cars twiddling their thumbs come out of our budget, you know.'

'Well, at least we now know where he lives. Chloe Kennedy wasn't murdered where she was found, or at her house.' Doyle knew he was wasting his breath, but he also knew Croucher's type: if he didn't reply, say something back, Croucher would ask why he didn't have anything to say for himself. You always had to play the game with these arseholes.

'That's not the most important thing, and you know it! Surely you, more than anyone, should be familiar with the risks of leaving a murder suspect out under surveillance?'

Doyle chose not to take the bait.

'Have you read the messages he sent to her? I mean, Christ, they are pretty damning.'

'It was me that got DI Hales to forward them to you.' Doyle kept his voice calm and measured – not because that's how he felt, but he suspected that it would piss off Mr Burns even more.

'Well, what do you intend to do about it?'

'I was about to go and bring him in when you showed up. Sir.'

The exchange was interrupted by a knock on the door. Hales stuck his head in. 'Sorry to interrupt. I thought you'd want to know. Johnson's on the move. In his car. CID are following.' Hales went to shut the door and duck out – understandably, Doyle thought – but Croucher had other ideas.

'Come in, Geoff. We might as well get your thoughts on all this too. Did you agree with the decision to put the suspect under surveillance rather than bring him in?'

That was how it was then, Doyle realised. Divide and rule. 'It was my decision alone. I felt as SIO on this case, it was my call to make. We'll pick him up shortly, have all day to go at him in the interview room while we search where he's been living, get forensics to go over that and his car. By the end of the day, we'll have a pretty good idea of whether or not he killed Chloe Kennedy.'

'Jesus Christ, Liam, from where I'm standing it seems bloody obvious that he did it. You need to bring him in, get the evidence and charge him.'

There was another knock on the door and Morgan entered.

'You might be right, sir, but I still have a nagging doubt,' Doyle replied. 'Those messages were filled with hurt, rage and all manner of emotion. The murder was organised, methodical and meticulously planned. Could it really be the same person?'

'Don't make this more complicated than it is!' the super yelled back.

'Sir,' Morgan said, addressing Doyle, though she could have been speaking to any of the three men in the room. 'Sorry to interrupt. It looks like Johnson's heading towards Wigan. It might be wise to get going now so we can pick him up shortly after he stops?'

'Good plan,' Doyle said, grateful for the interruption and the chance to escape from the incandescent Mr Burns. 'Let's get going.'

'Aren't you forgetting something?'

Doyle hesitated, not knowing what his boss was getting at.

'The press conference is at ten. You will be hard pushed to make it back in time.'

'What press conference?'

'What do you mean, what press conference? At the school. Don't you read your bloody emails?'

Doyle was about to reply that he hadn't been able to access his bloody emails when Hales cut in.

'Sir, if we're so sure that Johnson's our man, do we really need the press conference?'

'It's a fair point.' Doyle noticed how the super's tone softened when he addressed the DI. 'But if we get an eyewitness who saw Johnson, it would give us useful evidence.'

'I agree with that, sir. But I really would like to see Johnson's reaction when we arrest him. I find it can be quite telling,' Doyle said.

'That's as maybe, but you're the SIO, and I need you in the press conference.'

'OK.' Doyle turned to Morgan. 'Can you make the arrest? Make sure you take a uniform with you with a bodycam to capture it.'

'Will do, boss,' Morgan replied.

'In fact, now I think about it, just arrest him for the harassment and threatening emails. We can then arrest him for the murder later on.'

'Is this really necessary?' Burns queried.

'Please, sir, just trust me on this,' Doyle said.

There was another knock on the door, and Price the odious miniature PC appeared, smirking. 'Sorry to bother you. I just thought I'd better let you know straight away. CID just called in. They've lost Johnson.' Having thrown a hand grenade into the room, PC Price promptly disappeared.

'You'd better bloody well pray they find him soon, Liam.'

Doyle noticed a pulsating vein exposed by Croucher's receding hairline. It seemed to be building pressure as he roared, making him further resemble his namesake. 'If he goes on the run and we have to spend resources trying to catch him ...'

Doyle wondered, if the vein burst, whether the blood would hit the ceiling. It was quite a low ceiling.

'...then God help you.'

'DS Morgan.' Doyle addressed the sergeant, turning away from his raging senior officer. 'With your local knowledge, would you mind taking a look at where he might be heading?' Doyle looked at his watch. 'He's an electrician, and it's ten to eight. I suspect he hasn't gone on the run, and it's more likely that he's on his way to work. See what you can do, will you?'

'Will do, boss,' Morgan replied.

人 人 人

The tracker made it straightforward to locate Ryan Johnson's car, and Gadget could see on his laptop that it remained parked next to a building site close to where the surveillance team had lost him. It looked like the new DCI had been right, Morgan thought as she entered the freshly built office block. It appeared to be close to completion. A combination of CID and uniformed officers had the exits covered, along with a couple of officers from Greater Manchester Police, whose patch they were now on. Gadget had gone to locate Johnson's car to remove the little magnetic device he had placed under the wheel arch the previous evening.

Morgan had asked PC Bowen to accompany her to make the arrest, reasoning that he would recognise Johnson quicker than anyone. The building's reception area was empty, but the distinctive creaking of an aluminium stepladder was coming from a room next door. There they found a man threading cables from the ceiling void into an array of sturdy-looking racking.

Even from behind, Morgan could tell that this wasn't the bodybuilder Ryan Johnson. She spoke as the man turned to face them. 'I'm DS Morgan from Lancashire Police, and this is PC Bowen. Are you one of the electricians working here?'

The man climbed down from the ladder before answering. 'Not exactly. I'm doing all the data cabling and IT installation, but depending on what you want, I might be able to help.'

'I'm looking for Ryan Johnson – I believe he's an electrician working here. Do you know him and where I might find him?'

'They're all working on the first floor today. I think there is one called Ryan, but I'm not entirely sure. What's it all about?'

'It's confidential. But thanks for your help.' Despite Morgan's attempts to be discreet, she had no doubt that, with the press conference and the inevitable media frenzy, the reason they were arresting Ryan Johnson would soon become apparent. By the time he finished work, the man climbing back up the ladder would have a bit of gossip to tell his partner or mates in the pub.

Ryan Johnson was also up a stepladder on the first floor. Morgan contemplated waiting until he got down before introducing herself, then she remembered the messages she had read on Chloe's Facebook previous evening. Comfortable with the risk that startling Johnson might cause a leg-breaking fall, she approached him from behind. 'Ryan Johnson,' she said, more loudly than was strictly necessary. 'I'm Detective Sergeant Morgan from Lancashire Police.'

Johnson turned, looking her up and down as if she was an item in a shop window. This made Morgan feel disappointed that he hadn't fallen. She invited him to come down to floor level, reasoning that any injury he sustained after arrest would count as happening while he was in police custody.

'What can I do for you, darling?' he said.

'I'm arresting you on suspicion of sending threatening messages under Sections 1 and 2 of the Protection from Harassment Act 1997,' Morgan said. 'You do not have to say anything, but it may harm your defence if you do not mention when questioned something which you later rely on in court. Anything you do say may be given in evidence.'

'Bollocks. You're wasting your time. She will drop the charges.'

'Mr Johnson, you do understand what I have just told you?' Morgan asked. 'You may wish to know that PC Bowen here is wearing a body camera that is recording everything.'

Johnson turned to Bowen. 'You? You're a fucking fed? That's a joke.' He sneered at the PC.

'A fed?' Bowen replied. 'How old are you? Twelve?'

There were a few sniggers from the other tradesmen who had wandered over to see what was going on.

'Right, then, shall we get this over without any more ceremony, Mr Johnson?' Bowen said, brandishing a pair of handcuffs. 'Put your hands out in front of you, please.'

Morgan couldn't help being impressed by how Bowen handled the situation. She had considered taking more officers in with them, bearing in mind Johnson's physique and what he might be capable of, but she had wanted to keep the arrest as low-key as possible, in keeping with an arrest for harassment, rather than murder.

Chapter 14

As it turned out, Doyle's decision to visit the self-storage unit the previous day and pick up a clean suit, along with a bag of equipment containing the tracking device and the large cable ties, had been a good one. His choice to grab a second cup of coffee and croissant after his fry-up instead of going back to his room to shave now seemed less sensible.

The press conference was being held in the school hall. It felt like an intrusion to Doyle. Most of the staff had only been told about their colleague's murder that morning, and were now breaking the news to their pupils.

Doyle wasn't opposed to the media, unlike some officers, and he knew that press conferences could prove useful in bringing forward valuable witnesses. He just wasn't comfortable in front of a camera. Mr Burns, in contrast, seemed to relish the chance to be in the spotlight. This worked in Doyle's favour, as his superior officer was more than happy to do the majority of the talking. They sat at a long table facing an assortment of television, radio and print journalists and their technicians. Doyle sat to the superintendent's left; on his other side sat the force press liaison officer.

His mouth was dry, so Doyle attempted to silently pour himself a glass of water as Burns informed the assembled throng that the body found in Anglezarke yesterday morning was that of primary school teacher Chloe Kennedy. This, of course, was no surprise to anyone in the room, since the press officer had already informed the news outlets of the reason for the conference. It would come as a surprise to their readers, listeners and viewers, however: the murder of a young teacher was guaranteed to elicit shock, followed swiftly by outrage.

Doyle tried to take a few quiet sips of water, but his attempts to be discreet backfired as his hand shook and he spilled some water down his shirt and tie. If Mr Burns noticed, he didn't show it; he carried on addressing the cameras.

'And now I would like to hand over to Detective Chief Inspector Doyle, who is the Senior Investigating Officer on this case. He will outline how the public can be of assistance.'

'Thank you, sir,' Doyle said, conscious that his voice was croaky, but not wanting to risk another sip of water with the cameras on him. 'Chloe was last seen just after 1.20 a.m. on Saturday morning. She was in Cunliffe Street, just off Market Street in Chorley town centre. We would like to hear from anyone who has seen Chloe since this time.' Doyle was more aware of his London accent than usual, knowing this would primarily be broadcast on local news channels. 'She was wearing the red dress and blue denim jacket seen in the photograph.'

The media team had used the selfie Chloe Kennedy had taken the night she went missing to show at the press conference, having cropped it to remove Dani Wheeler.

'She was not wearing these clothes when her body was found in the woods at Anglezarke. Her clothes are missing, along with her phone and handbag.' Doyle paused. He had done enough of these things to know you couldn't rush through them – you had to let each part sink in.

'We'd like to hear from anyone who was in the area of Anglezarke on Sunday night. Chloe's body was thrown from the viewing point above the cliffs. But she was killed somewhere else, and we need to know where that was. We also need to know where she was kept from early Saturday morning to late Sunday night.' Doyle risked a sip of water, and was grateful that he didn't miss his mouth this time. 'I would ask anyone with any information, however small or seemingly irrelevant, to contact us on the incident room number.'

Doyle handed back to Croucher, who invited questions from the press, most of which he fielded himself until a voice spoke from the back of the room.

'Jayden Clark, *Lancashire Chronicle*.'

Doyle heard his boss sigh. What was the problem? Doyle wondered, making a mental note to ask the super about the journalist later.

'Are you new to the force, DCI Doyle? I've not seen you at one of these before.'

'I'm new to this force, but not to running murder investigations.'

'From your accent, I'm guessing you're from the Met – am I right?'

'This isn't about me. Do you have a question about the case, Mr Clark?'

'Do you have any suspects?' Clark asked.

'We are keeping an open mind at the moment and would urge anyone with any information, however small, to come forward.' The press would find out soon enough about Ryan Johnson, but Doyle couldn't give them this now.

'Do you think she knew her killer?' a journalist Doyle had seen on Granada asked.

'As I said, we're keeping an open mind, and are not going to rule anything in or out at this stage.'

Chapter 15

'*You fucking cunt, Chloe. I'm going to make you pay for what you did to me. Just you fucking wait,*' Morgan read out from the papers on the table in front of her. 'What did you mean by that, Ryan?'

'No comment,' Johnson replied from his seat next to his solicitor and opposite Doyle and Morgan in the interview room.

'*I'm going to make you pay,*' Morgan went on. 'That sounds pretty threatening to me. Do you agree, Ryan?'

'No comment.'

Doyle knew, of course, that Ryan's solicitor had advised him to give a 'no comment' interview – what else could she really suggest, unless he was going to say he hadn't sent the messages? But that could easily be checked. This was, however, just the preamble. Doyle was going to enjoy wiping the smug look off both their faces very soon.

'What about this one, Ryan?' Morgan said. '*I was watching you on Friday night. I didn't recognise you at first with your new haircut. I see it now, you've become a fucking dyke. That's why you wanted rid of me. No one treats me like that, Chloe. Let's see if your new girlfriend still wants you after you've had acid chucked in your face, you dirty fucking lesbo whore.*' Morgan paused. 'Did you send that, Ryan?'

'No comment.'

Doyle kept his eyes on the man's face. He wanted Johnson to feel them boring into him.

'I make that four criminal offences in one message,' Morgan continued. 'We've got homophobia, which is now a hate crime. You were watching Chloe, so that's stalking. There's clearly harassment and threats to kill. I think you'll do some time inside for this, Ryan.'

Johnson flashed a glance at his solicitor.

'Looking at her isn't going to save you,' Morgan said. 'These messages look like you were quite unhinged. You were controlling her life and couldn't take it when she decided she had had enough and kicked you out. You got so angry you just wanted to hurt her. I'm right, aren't I, Ryan?'

'No comment.'

'Is that why you killed her, Ryan?' Doyle spoke for the first time since confirming his name for the recording.

'What?' Johnson's face was a picture of confusion as he slipped from his two-word script.

'Excuse me…' His solicitor began to speak.

Doyle raised a hand to silence her. 'Ryan Johnson, I'm arresting you on suspicion of the murder of Chloe Kennedy. You do not have to say anything. And this next bit's key for you, Ryan, so listen carefully.' Doyle liked adding his own annotation to the formal wording. 'It may harm your defence if you do not mention when questioned something which you later rely on in court.' Doyle looked Johnson in the eyes. All the bravado had drained from the younger man's face. 'Anything you do say may be given in evidence.'

'This is outrageous.' The solicitor got in as soon as Doyle had finished the caution. 'We should have been told about this before. I need to consult with my client.'

'Chloe's actually dead?' Ryan said.

'Yes, she is, Ryan. She was murdered,' Morgan replied.

'Relax, Ms Finch. We will take a break in a moment, and you can consult with your client then.'

'I will be making a complaint about this.'

Doyle wondered if the solicitor practised her stern face by looking in a mirror.

'Do you think this is an acceptable way to inform someone that a partner they have recently split up from has died?'

'Have you not been paying attention? Did you nod off or something?' Doyle addressed the solicitor. 'He threatened to throw acid in her face. I hardly think I need to take him to a nice room, sit him down on a sofa and break it to him gently.'

Finch started to reply then stopped, apparently lost for words, which was exactly how Doyle liked solicitors.

'Now, Ryan, in a moment you and Ms Finch can go and have a little chat about what you want to do from here. But before you go, I'm going to be very generous and give you some free advice.' Doyle said. 'With those messages you sent, there is enough for the CPS to charge you with Chloe Kennedy's murder while we find the rest of the evidence to ensure you get convicted.'

'But…' Johnson tried to interrupt and was silenced by Doyle's raised index finger.

'Everyone thinks you did it, Ryan. But if by any chance you didn't, then the best thing you can do is to come back into this room and answer every single question Detective Sergeant Morgan and I ask you.'

Tears were rolling down Johnson's cheeks, but whether they were tears of remorse or grief Doyle couldn't tell, but there was a good blend of fear in there, he was sure of that. 'If you come back and start down the "no comment" route again, I'm going to stop the interview and have you charged with murder, and I very much doubt you will get bail. No one is going to believe any defence you come up with later. Do you understand?'

Johnson nodded.

'Those remand wings aren't very nice, Ryan. I'm not sure the other inmates will take too kindly to someone awaiting trial for the murder of a pretty young schoolteacher.'

'Detective Chief Inspector really,' Finch said. 'This is just intimidation.'

'No,' Doyle said. '*That's* intimidation.' He picked up the printout of the Facebook messages on the table. 'I'm just giving some friendly advice.'

Doyle stood up. He was aware that he had been seated when Johnson had entered the room. Hours spent at the gym had given the younger man a muscled upper body. Genetics had given the detective a frame that filled a doorway, and it didn't hurt to give Johnson a reminder, as he contemplated his fate, that there was always a bigger man out there.

'Is twenty minutes long enough for you, Ms Finch?'

In the end it was a full half hour before they met back in the interview room. Doyle studied Johnson's face while Morgan rattled off the legal preamble to the proceedings. The whites of Johnson's eyes were bloodshot and the skin around them reddened and puffy. These weren't the signs of a few crocodile tears designed to elicit sympathy; the man must have spent most of the intermission bawling.

'Shall we start?' Doyle asked when Morgan had finished. Johnson gave a nod. 'Can you speak for the recording, please, Ryan?'

'OK,' Johnson said, a shake to his voice.

'Did you kill Chloe Kennedy, Ryan?' Doyle said as calmly as if he was asking whether Johnson took milk and sugar in tea.

'No. No, I didn't. Please, you gotta believe me.'

'OK, Ryan. So, you are aware, right now forensics are going over your car and home. We have requested your phone and bank records, and that's just for starters,' Doyle said. 'If you did kill Chloe Kennedy, we will find out. Now is your chance to tell us why, and put across your side of the story.'

'But I didn't. I really didn't kill her,' Johnson pleaded. 'I know it looks bad with the messages and that, but I didn't kill her, I swear.'

'What was the last message you sent to her?' Morgan asked.

'It's that one you read out earlier.'

'The one where you threatened to throw acid in her face?' Doyle asked.

Johnson nodded.

'Speak up, Ryan.'

'Yes.'

'That was two weeks ago. What made you stop sending them?' Morgan asked.

'After that last message, Chloe contacted me. She had ignored most of the others.' Johnson wiped a sleeve across his face. 'She said she was blocking me and if I sent her any more messages, she would go to the police.'

'And you just stopped straight away just like that?' Doyle asked.

'Yes.' Johnson paused. 'I was really upset by the break-up. When she sent me the message saying she would go to you lot, I was angry at first.'

'Go on,' Morgan encouraged.

'I was in the pub with a mate when I got the message,' Johnson said. 'I tried to explain to him why I was so angry. I showed him the messages I had sent. He didn't get it.'

'What did he say?' Morgan asked.

'He said I was mental and I needed help. He said she was right, and if I carried on, I would find myself locked up.'

'What did you think about that, Ryan?' said Morgan.

'I was a bit pissed off at first. I thought he should be on my side. But deep down I knew he was right.'

'Some people might think that the reason you stopped sending the messages was not because you were worried that she would go to the police,' Doyle said. 'But because you had decided to take things further and kill her.'

'No!' Johnson's voice was raised.

'I mean, it stands to reason, doesn't it? If you had decided to go down that route and act, you would have stopped sending the messages then, wouldn't you. I bet you thought that after a couple of weeks of no contact she would have deleted all the previous ones and we'd never find out about them. That's what happened, isn't it, Ryan?'

'No. I told you I didn't kill her. I didn't even know she was dead until you said. Why would I?'

'That last message you sent,' Morgan said. 'You wrote that you thought Chloe had started a relationship with another woman. Although, obviously, you didn't put it quite like that. Who were you talking about?'

'Her friend, Dani Wheeler.'

'What led you to believe that?' Morgan asked.

'I had seen them together one Friday night. I didn't recognise Chloe at first because she had cut her hair short. Completely different to how it was.'

'You were stalking her then, Ryan?' Doyle asked.

'No, no, it wasn't like that,' Johnson pleaded. 'Well, not really…'

'What was it like then?' Morgan said.

'I mean, I was out for a drink with another friend that night. But it had been my idea to go to Chorley rather than somewhere else, as I knew we might bump into her.' Ryan took a sip from the plastic cup in front of him. 'We were sitting in that Mexican bar on Chapel Street by the window when they walked past. I noticed Dani at first. She's the type of girl you notice. She was with another woman, and when she turned around, I saw her face. I realised it was Chloe with a really short haircut.'

'What made you think they were together?' Morgan probed. 'Were they holding hands? Did you see them kissing?'

'No, it wasn't anything like that. At first it didn't occur to me that they might be together. But I was surprised by the dramatic change in Chloe's appearance.'

'So, what? You just thought because she had left you and cut her hair short, she must be gay?' Doyle asked.

'No,' Johnson protested. 'I couldn't stop thinking about her and about her change of look all weekend.'

'So, you mulled it over in your head and then decided that Chloe must be shagging Dani Wheeler then, because she had cut her hair short?' said Doyle.

'No. I was at work on the Monday morning and I got talking to this bloke. We were working in the same area. He was doing data and that, and I was cabling for power points in the server room. We often ended up taking smoking breaks together. He told me that an ex of his had strung him along then disappeared, and the next time he saw her she was with another woman – she had short hair, piercings in her face, a completely different look.'

'Oh, I understand now. Then you put two and two together and came up with a number much bigger than four,' Doyle said.

'Look, I was messed up by it all, I can see that now, but I didn't kill her. You've got to believe me. I didn't do it.'

'OK,' Morgan said. 'Let's move on. What we want from you now is to go through everything you did at the weekend, starting on Friday after work and going right through Saturday and Sunday up to Monday morning. Can you do that?'

'Yes,' Johnson said.

'Good,' said Doyle 'And we're going to need everything: everywhere you went, everyone you saw, everything you did. Don't leave anything out.'

'What did you do Friday evening?' Morgan asked. 'Did you go out?'

'Yeah, I went to that Mexican bar again.'

'Did you go with someone, meet people there?'

'I met a girl there – we had a date.'

'What's her name?'

'Kelly. Kelly Saunders.'

Chapter 16

'Where are we at with everything else?' Doyle asked Hales. It had taken a further two hours for him and Morgan to get every last detail they could about Ryan Johnson's movements at the weekend.

'The guys we've got from uniform are getting all the CCTV they can from around the town centre Friday night. Gadget is piecing it all together, paying particular attention to the bits around Cunliffe Street and routes in and out,' Hales replied.

'The phone records have come in for Chloe's mobile, boss,' Asif said. 'It was switched off on Saturday morning at 1.23 a.m. in the vicinity of Cunliffe Street, then turned on again a minute later and then off again a minute after that.'

'Might she have been having phone trouble?' Hales suggested.

'Maybe that's how the booking with the cab firm got cancelled. The app might have crashed on her phone,' Morgan said.

'When did it come back on after that?' Doyle asked.

'Not till Sunday afternoon at 14.11, boss,' Asif said. 'From somewhere in the vicinity of Chloe's house. There was a text sent to a number that we know is her mum's mobile at 14.15, and then a tiny amount of data usage, which would cover the WhatsApp messages. Then the phone went off at 14.32 and hasn't been back on since.'

Doyle's heart sank as he saw Mr Burns enter the incident room. He had hoped his boss would have buggered off back to headquarters by now. 'In that case, the killer knew or got hold of Chloe Kennedy's PIN for her mobile. And he knew that turning it on would give a rough location of where the phone was.'

'Are you suggesting he went to her house just to send the messages?' Hales asked.

'He wouldn't have needed to go to her house; he could have sat in a car round the corner, turned the phone on, waited until all the messages came through and then replied,' Doyle said.

'That would take some balls,' Hales said.

'It would – and some planning. I think whoever did this was hoping we wouldn't find the body so quickly, and that we would think she was killed after Sunday afternoon.'

'And then not look too closely at Friday night,' Morgan said.

'Exactly.'

'I agree,' Croucher said. He had joined the small group who were mostly perched on the edge of desks. 'And I think it is reasonable to assume that her ex-boyfriend would know her PIN. Is the plan to get him charged?'

'Where are we at with forensics? Has anything significant come back yet?' Doyle asked.

'Nothing concrete,' said Morgan, checking her phone. 'There is an email update from Jen Knight. Doesn't look like Chloe was killed at the flat in Skelmersdale where Johnson's been staying. They're giving his car a good going over, starting with the tyres and wheel arches, looking for mud and gravel from Anglezarke – it's quite specific, apparently. They're also checking the boot for any trace of Chloe Kennedy in there, or fibres from the tracksuit she was found wearing. Her prints and DNA found in the rest of the car will be easily explained as Johnson has had that car two years – she must have been in it dozens of times.'

'OK. While we're waiting on all that, let's concentrate on his alibi, starting with Friday night,' Doyle said. 'Shaima, this Kelly Saunders that he claims he had a date with – find out all you can about her. Specifically, any links between the two of them. We need to know if there's any way she and Johnson could have met before Friday.'

'On it, boss,' Asif replied and immediately started tapping away at her computer keyboard.

'Morgan, are you OK to go and see Kelly Saunders by yourself?'

'Of course, boss.'

'She might be more comfortable talking to a woman on her own about her night with Johnson. If her recollection is too perfect, knowing exactly where they were at every precise minute, or feels in any way rehearsed, then we will bring her in and interview her under caution.'

'I repeat. Are we going to charge him?' Croucher interrupted.

'I don't see that we need to decide right now, sir. Let him sweat in the cells and see what we can dig up. If we think it's useful, we can have another crack at him in the interview room. Not bringing him in until today means we've still got till tomorrow morning before we need to get an extension.' It was petty, but Doyle couldn't resist making this point to his boss.

'I don't think he did it,' Hales said.

'You've changed your tune since this morning, Geoff. He's got clear motive and he expressed violent intent towards her. You're getting seduced by the sob story.'

Doyle could sense that the vein on Mr Burns' head was going to start pulsating again.

'It's not that, sir. I was watching his face on the screen when Liam asked if he had killed Chloe, and he looked genuinely shocked to me. I don't think he knew she was dead before then.'

'Johnson's clearly an arsehole,' said Doyle. 'Of that there's no doubt. But whether he killed Chloe Kennedy is another matter. I have my doubts too. But I think either way we will have a much better idea by tomorrow morning, and we can make a decision on charging him then.'

⋏ ⋏ ⋏

With the team all busy following various lines of enquiry, Doyle took the opportunity to have a quiet word with Shaima Asif. The intelligence analyst had impressed him with how quickly she cottoned on to things and responded to what needed doing. He had just the task to discreetly put her way.

'Do you think that's likely?' she asked after Doyle had outlined what he wanted her to look into.

'I'm not sure how likely it is at this stage. But it's certainly possible. Work your way back year by year, and don't just look for the obvious links. Look at missing persons, suspicious deaths, rapes with similarities. I've got a feeling that whoever did this will have some history. It's too well orchestrated.'

'Leave it with me, boss, I'll do some digging,' Asif said.

Doyle's work mobile started ringing. He took it out and glanced at the number: it was someone at Force HQ. 'This better be those bastards from IT,' he said to no one in particular. Asif put her hand over her mouth to cover a giggle.

'DCI Doyle,' he answered, moving into his office.

'Liam, hope this isn't a bad time? I know you've been thrown in at the deep end. It's Tara Langley, Force HR Director.' Her voice had the gravelly tones of a twenty-a-day habit. 'I've just been watching you on the telly – very debonair, Detective Chief Inspector, I must say. Though next time, be a bit more careful with the water.'

'Oh shit, was it that obvious?'

'Only a touch, but we didn't employ you to be a chat show host so I'm not sure it matters. There were a couple of matters I did need to speak to you about, though.'

'OK.' This sounded ominous, Doyle thought.

'Right, the psychologist. I spoke to her today, as we agreed. She suggested doing six sessions with you, then she'll decide what's best from there. The first one is booked in for three thirty tomorrow.'

'Is there any way we could postpone that for a week? We're up against it here,' Doyle said.

'I'd like to, but it was a requirement laid out by occy health – a condition of you joining. Just covering our bases after what happened in London.'

'Yes, I get that, and I'm not trying to be awkward. It's just this is a busy week – and I was signed off by psychology at the Met.'

'Out of my hands, I'm afraid. There's another matter we need to discuss too. I had the IT manager in my office earlier today. He alleges that you left an answerphone message being abusive to his staff.'

'Ah, that … perhaps it didn't come out quite as intended. I was just desperate to get my email working ASAP. It's causing me problems not being able to access it.'

'Yes. I thought that might have been the case, and I've managed to stop him taking it further. Though he insisted on playing me the message, and you were quite … aggressive.'

'Yes, sorry about that.'

'Oh, you don't need to apologise to me. But I think it's probably best if we make sure Croucher doesn't find out about it. This may surprise you, but he's not known for being understanding.'

'Thank you.'

'No problem. I will buy them some comic books or something and make this go away. But in return you'd better make sure you are here tomorrow for your appointment.'

'Will do,' Doyle said.

'Good, and I'll make sure one of … how did you put it? Oh, that's right, I'll make sure one of the useless twats calls you with your email login details.'

Chapter 17

The thing that struck Morgan first about Kelly Saunders was that she bore more than a passing resemblance to Chloe Kennedy. The detective sergeant wondered how many images Ryan Johnson had swiped past on the dating app before he found a woman who looked like his ex-girlfriend.

Turning up unannounced at the small firm of accountants in Preston had certainly caught the young woman off guard, as had been Morgan's intention. She didn't want to humiliate Saunders by cornering her at work, but if she had agreed to provide a fake alibi for Johnson, approaching her this way was bound to unsettle her. Perhaps enough to cause her to trip up.

'What's this all about?' Saunders asked Morgan in the crowded reception area, with other staff members listening. She looked shocked, her face pale and her hands trembling.

'I need to question you about an incident you may have seen on Friday night. Shall we find somewhere private to talk?'

When they were seated in an air-conditioned office, which Morgan assumed was used for meeting clients, the detective decided to be more open about why she needed to speak to the other woman. 'I need to ask you about Friday night and Saturday morning. Specifically, who you were with and where you went.'

Saunders flushed, but Morgan didn't read too much into this. If Ryan Johnson had been telling the truth, it was understandable that the woman might be embarrassed. God, she cringed even now when she thought back to her first eighteen months at university, waking up in different beds with different people, with only hazy recollections of the night before.

'OK,' said Saunders. 'What is this all about? You mentioned an incident?'

'I will come to that in a minute. But would you mind telling me first, where you were between 9 p.m. on Friday and 11 a.m. on Saturday, and who you were with?'

'I went out in Chorley on Friday night to a bar/restaurant type place. The Cancun Casa on Chapel Street. But I didn't see anything, and I certainly haven't done anything. I think you might have the wrong person.'

'Who were you with, Kelly?'

'Oh.' Saunders stiffened, smoothing out an imaginary crease on her skirt. 'I was on a date with a man.'

'Go on.'

'I met him on the dating app God's Gift. I know, awful name, but some friends had used it and it seemed OK.'

'Can you tell me the man's name?'

'Yes, his name was Ryan. Ryan Johnson, or maybe Johnstone. I'd have to check on my phone.'

'And was this a first date? Had you ever met Ryan before or known him previously?'

'No, never. To be honest, he isn't the sort of guy I would normally go for. But he liked my profile and sent me a message and – well, we didn't have much in common, interests and that... But I saw his picture and...' Saunders looked down. 'He was very good-looking, so I thought why not? And I agreed to a date.'

'What time did Ryan arrive, and how long did you stay in the bar together?'

'He was there when I got there, which was just after nine o'clock,' Saunders said. 'We stayed until, I think, just after two, when they closed up and kicked us out.'

'Was Ryan with you the whole of that time? Did he go off anywhere or disappear for a bit, go out to make a phone call, that type of thing?'

'Other than brief trips to the bar and the bathroom, no,' Saunders said. 'What is this? Has he done something?'

'Look, there's no easy way to say this, but a former partner of Ryan's has been killed, and we need to establish his movements over the weekend.'

'What, Chloe?'

Morgan was taken aback by the other woman's response. 'You know her?'

'No, no, I don't and that's terrible. I know her name because Ryan must have mentioned her at least a hundred times on Friday, and that's no exaggeration. He clearly wasn't over her.'

'What happened after you left the bar?'

'We went back to my place. I don't normally do that, but we'd been drinking and then had some tequilas and I just thought…'

'It's OK, Kelly,' Morgan reassured her. 'I'm not judging you. Not that there is anything wrong with that, anyway. I just need to know about Ryan's movements so we can rule him in or out of our enquiries.' She gave what she hoped was a sympathetic smile, and was reassured to receive one in return. Morgan was inwardly grateful that that period of her life was firmly behind her now. 'How did you get from the bar to your house?'

'We walked. I think we both needed a bit of air. It isn't that far to my place.'

'How long did he stay?'

'He stayed the night. He left the next morning about half past ten, maybe a bit later.'

'Did you sleep in that time? Is it possible he could have left and come back again while you were sleeping?'

Saunders took a moment to consider this. 'I locked the door when we got in. I aways do that – my housemate goes crazy if I forget. I put the key back in my bag. I guess he could have left and come back, but I think I would have woken. I woke up, I think, about six, needing a wee, and he was still asleep in my bed.'

'I know this is quite embarrassing, Kelly. But I do need to ask you about what happened with you and Ryan – what you got up to.' Morgan tried to sound supportive. 'I'm sorry.'

'Like sex?' Saunders smoothed her skirt again and shifted in her seat. 'We did have sex, yes. Sorry, but how is that relevant?'

'I don't mean to pry. But what was it like? Was there anything ... how can I put this? Anything particularly unusual or adventurous, say, about the sex?' Morgan found herself avoiding eye contact with the other woman. 'Did he tie you up, or was he rough – hands around your throat, that type of thing?'

'Oh God, no, nothing like that.'

Morgan noticed a smile begin to appear on Saunders' face.

'Actually, it was shit. It was all rushed and fumbled and over very quickly. And then to top it all, afterwards he was full of regret about his ex and worried that she might be doing the same thing with someone else. Talk about how to make a girl feel wanted just after shagging them. I could see why she dumped him...' She paused. 'Oh God, poor girl. I didn't mean to sound, you know...'

'It's OK. And thanks for being so honest. I know it's not easy to talk to a stranger about these things.'

'Those questions about sex – you were asking them because she was raped, weren't you?'

'I can't go into details about the case.'

'Look, for what it's worth, I can't see Ryan killing her. Pestering her to death and begging her to come back, yes, but he didn't seem as if he could hurt her – or anyone.'

'He's a big lad. Did you ever get any feeling of menace from him? Did you feel scared?'

'No, not at all, quite the opposite. I felt safe walking home with him.' Saunders smiled. 'Shame he couldn't live up to expectations when we got there.'

'Kelly, if it's OK, I'm going to ask you to make a formal statement about this. Would you be happy to come down to Chorley police station to do that? I can make sure it's a female officer and you won't have to say too much about what you did, just where you were with Ryan and the times.'

'Yes, that's fine. Ryan won't get in any trouble for what I said, will he?'

'No. Unfortunately, being shit in bed isn't currently a criminal offence. But if that changes, I'll make sure his name gets added to what I'm sure will be a very long list of offenders.' Morgan smiled wryly. She had a few of her own to add.

Kelly's laugh was a little nervous.

⅄ ⅄ ⅄

Francis Bowen was delighted to find himself still seconded to the MIT. In truth, his first meeting with his boss could have gone better. Shouting at a senior officer and brandishing a baton in their direction hadn't been the best way to introduce himself. But the DCI hadn't seemed too narked about it, and at least recognising Ryan Johnson had earned him some brownie points, even if that had been sheer luck on his behalf. Detective Sergeant Morgan choosing him to make the arrest with her had boosted his confidence further. Now Bowen was determined to pay back the trust the team were showing in him and make the most of the opportunity to create a good impression. And that might lead on to other things. He had always wanted to be a detective; that was why he joined the police after leaving university. The reality had turned out to be different to what he had been hoping for, and he hadn't always got the best vibes from some of the CID guys he had worked with. They had seemed arrogant and looked down on uniformed officers, even when it was the uniforms that were helping them out.

Since Ryan Johnson's interview, Bowen had been tasked with helping Gadget to get as much CCTV evidence as they could to either support or cast doubt on Johnson's alibi. He had started at the Cancun Casa on Chapel Street. There wasn't much in the way of CCTV inside, but the entrance was well covered, and Bowen was able to review footage from the bar. The manager recognised Johnson and confirmed he was a regular. He was seen entering the premises at 20.58, according to the time stamp on the camera, and leaving at 02.05 on Saturday, with a woman who Bowen assumed was Kelly Saunders. He had fast-forwarded through the film in between those times and it didn't appear that Johnson could have left the bar via the front entrance. Bowen downloaded the footage to a memory stick anyway. There was also a fire exit that went into a garden, then a goods yard behind. The manager had said that in theory Johnson could have left and returned via this entrance, but he thought it was unlikely as this was next to the kitchen. If customers were spotted going in or out that way, security would be alerted. The manager also confirmed that he hadn't seen Johnson with the same woman before.

The goods yard behind the Cancun Casa had been Bowen's next port of call. The shops and restaurants on Chapel Street all had rear entrances that led to the goods yard via gardens. There was good coverage on the perimeter of the bargain goods shop it served, but not the whole yard. It was possible, Bowen reasoned, that Johnson could have come out of the fire exit and vaulted the six-foot wall without being seen, though his alibi was starting to withstand quite a lot of scrutiny.

Bowen had been a police officer for nearly six years, and four of these had been working out of Chorley police station. He had spent countless hours in all weathers patrolling the streets of the town centre. He knew it better than anywhere. Chloe Kennedy had last been seen alive on Cunliffe Street. This was at the southern end of the town centre, off Market Street. Chapel Street was also off Market Street, but towards the northern end.

If, and Bowen knew now it was a big if, Johnson had sneaked out the back entrance of the bar, he would either have had to travel up Market Street, being captured on several of the town centre CCTV cameras, or he would have gone along Victoria Street or Railway Street. Railway Street had yielded nothing from the cameras on the community centre on the corner or from the pub halfway down the road.

Bowen was even less optimistic of turning up anything useful in Victoria Street. It was a residential road consisting of small Victorian terraced houses. He doubted there would be any coverage along here, but thought he'd better check. He was halfway down the street when he spotted a small black camera positioned above a front door. It was pointing towards Cunliffe Street.

Bowen knocked on the front door – not the full-on policeman's knock that would rouse the dead, but loud enough so that it couldn't fail to be heard by the occupants – who, he thought, taking into account the style of net curtains on the street, may be of advanced years. He was just about to knock again when the door was opened by a man with a shock of wild grey hair, who looked like the crazy scientist from *Back to the Future*. So much so that Bowen was slightly taken aback by the man's local accent.

'What d'you want?'

'Hello, sir,' Bowen said, smiling. 'I'm from Chorley police station.' He showed his ID. 'I'm investigating an incident that happened over the weekend.'

'That murder? Saw it on telly. Awful business,' the man replied, seemingly keen not to waste precious words on full sentences.

'Yes, that's right. That camera up there, does it work?'

''Course it bloody works. Wouldn't be much point in wasting money on camera that didn't work, would there?'

'Could I look at the footage on it from Friday night, Mr...'

'It's Gray,' the man replied.

'I'm sorry, what's grey? The footage from the camera?'

'Christ, you'll not make detective. I'm Gray. Mr Gray. You asked me what me name was.'

'Yes. Sorry, Mr Gray. Would you mind if I came in and had a quick look, maybe took a copy?'

'Suit yourself.' Mr Gray turned and shuffled down the hall and into the front room, leaving the door open for Bowen to follow.

The front room wasn't set up as a lounge, as was usual in most houses Bowen had been in. There wasn't a sofa or comfy chair, just a dining table with one dining chair and shelves crammed with old-looking books and magazines, many about railways and local history. In the corner, on an occasional table, was a dated, boxy CRT monitor that displayed the image from the street outside the house. When Bowen had reviewed CCTV from the local businesses, it was clear it had all been set up professionally and only covered a limited area outside their properties, in order not to breach privacy laws. Mr Gray, however, had gone for a camera with a fisheye lens which gave a very good view of the pavement and road outside, albeit one that was slightly distorted by the wide angle. The monitor was plugged into a basic digital control unit that could support up to four cameras. This meant it was quite straightforward to operate.

'Am I OK to have a play around with this to get what I want?' Bowen asked.

'Do what you like, just don't mess it up so it stops recording,' Gray replied.

Bowen found the time and the date on the recording just before Chloe Kennedy was last seen. He checked the time on the system against that showing on his phone, and noted that it was one minute ahead. There was a streetlight on the other side of the road to Mr Gray's house. This meant that although the footage Bowen was looking at was taken during the night, the image from the CCTV was still relatively clear. Bowen

watched the film from 01.00 to 01.30 on fast forward at 6×
speed: fast enough that he didn't have to spend more than five
minutes kneeling on Mr Gray's carpet, which was in desperate
need of a vacuum. Not so fast, though, that he wouldn't spot
Ryan Johnson or anyone else walking down the street in either
direction. No one went past on foot, and just one vehicle drove
by. This was light-coloured and looked like a taxi; it certainly
wasn't Ryan Johnson's black Audi. When Bowen was satisfied
that he had seen all he needed, he copied the footage to a
memory stick.

'What made you instal the CCTV, My Gray?' Bowen
asked, attempting to be friendly as he returned the system to
its original live view of the street.

'Hanging baskets,' Gray replied, as if this was all that needed
to be said.

'What about hanging baskets?' Bowen ventured,
immediately wishing he had just accepted the first answer.

Mr Gray gave Bowen an incredulous look, obviously
stunned that the police officer hadn't understood from his
previous answer. 'Last summer, some little toerag ripped them
down off wall. One of your lot came round – fat lot of use he
was. Told me they couldn't do anything about it or track down
the culprit, because there wasn't any evidence.' The old man
made quotation marks with his fingers when he said the last
word. 'I went to that shop on Market Street, does second-hand
stuff, think it's a pawnbroker. I bought that little lot. If the
bastards come round again, I'll have your "evidence" and you
can lock them up.'

Bowen doubted that anyone had ever been locked up for
vandalising a hanging basket, but he agreed all the same.

Chapter 18

It was just past four in the afternoon and most of the team had drifted back to the incident room, having completed their various lines of enquiry. Most of these concerned scrutinising the alibi that Ryan Johnson had provided in his interview. Doyle was relieved to see that DI Hales had managed to get a few more bodies working on the case. There was another civilian analyst, a specialist in the Holmes 2 computer software used by all police forces in the UK for major investigations. She would be updating everything to that database so that the increasing volume of information could easily be cross-referenced and no tiny detail missed or line of enquiry not followed up. Sitting at the desk next to her was another civilian who had been assigned the role of exhibits officer. He was responsible for making sure every piece of physical evidence collected was correctly recorded and looked after in a way that ensured all procedures were rigorously followed. Any failure in this task could give a defence barrister an open goal further down the line. The EO was currently in conversation with Jen Knight, the crime scene manager. Doyle was glad she was there. Now was looking like the perfect time to review where the investigation had got to, and decide where they went from here.

'Right, let's get cracking,' Doyle said, once he had everyone gathered around the evidence board. 'Ryan Johnson – has anybody found any holes in his alibi or inconsistencies in his story?'

'Friday night seems to check out, boss,' Gadget said. 'Jim's been round getting bits of CCTV, and there's nothing to suggest he left the bar on Chapel Street all evening. I mean, it's possible, not everywhere is covered, but it looks unlikely.'

'Good work, you two.' Doyle nodded to Gadget and Bowen.

'That ties in with what Kelly Saunders told me,' Morgan added. 'She said, barring the odd trip to the bar and the gents, they had been together all evening.'

'I ran the usual checks on her,' said Asif. 'There's nothing dodgy in her background and I couldn't find anything that linked her to Johnson previously. I went back through schools, colleges, Facebook friends, friends of friends, there's nothing to suggest they had already met.'

'OK, anything else?' Doyle asked.

'Me and young PC Price here have been following up on the rest of the weekend,' Birdseye said.

Doyle thought that only DC Nelson would refer to Price as 'young'; the diminutive constable had to be pushing forty, and had a distinctive bald pate that made him look like a monk.

'Everything checks out there as far as it can. He was at the gym at roughly the times he said he was, and in that pub in Wigan on Saturday night. Obviously, there are times we can't corroborate when he wasn't with anyone, but as far as we can tell, it all checks out, boss.'

'Jen, anything from forensics that makes you think we should be keeping Johnson as our prime suspect?'

'Not really, I'm afraid. We've been over the boot of his car with our low-adhesive tape and the fibres we collected are being analysed, but it doesn't look like that's going to produce anything useful,' Knight explained. 'We've taken samples from the tyres and under the wheel arches, but there's nothing to suggest the car has been parked at the viewing spot in Anglezarke. It will all be checked out in more detail at the lab, but it will be a few days before we get that confirmation.'

'Thanks, Jen. Anything to add, Geoff?'

'He's not our guy,' Hales said. 'Didn't look like it was him from the moment he cracked in interview. He would have to be Harry Houdini to get out of that bar and back without anyone noticing and then put Chloe somewhere – the boot of a car or a local building, tied up and gagged or maybe drugged – then come back the next day and kill her.'

'He could have had an accomplice, boss,' Birdseye suggested.

'That's certainly something to consider, Derrick. We should look into all his acquaintances. But I agree with DI Hales: he doesn't strike me as the cool, calm, collected type, interacting normally with everyone while murdering his ex.'

'When you put it like that, boss, I see your point,' Birdseye conceded.

'Does that mean we're going to release him, guv?' one of the seconded CID officers asked.

'Are we bollocks,' replied Doyle. 'We don't have to let him go until tomorrow morning. I wouldn't want Johnson to miss out on the full custody experience by depriving the little shit of a night in the cells. Besides, we still have the charges for the threats and harassment to consider. Which brings me on to my next point. If Johnson didn't do it, then who did?'

The room went quiet for a moment. Everyone knew what Ryan Johnson being innocent meant.

'You know who gave me the creeps a bit yesterday?' Gadget said.

'Go on,' Doyle encouraged the young detective.

'The caretaker at the school.'

'What was it about him?' Doyle asked.

'It's hard to put my finger on it; there was just something that didn't sit right.'

'That's the Ian Huntley effect,' Hales said. 'Since what he did in Soham, all caretakers seem like murderers. It was lorry drivers when I was your age.'

'What's his name?' Asif asked.

Gadget checked his notebook 'Elliot Parker... One thing about him that did seem odd is that he must be in his late forties, but he didn't dress or act like that.'

Doyle and Hales, both in their forties, exchanged a look.

'And how are men in their forties meant to act and dress, then?' Doyle asked.

'Well. Imagine you came into work dressed like me.'

Doyle looked the younger detective up and down. Skinny jeans that didn't quite meet the ankle, plimsolls, no socks, a tightly fitted short-sleeved shirt that revealed tattooed arms with toned biceps.

'Well then, I would look like a twat,' Doyle replied.

'Exactly,' said Gadget, smiling.

Doyle could see he was pleased that his new boss had seen his point. 'So why do you do it, then?'

'Why do I do what, boss?' Gadget asked.

'Why do you dress like a twat?'

There were liberal sniggers from around the room at Gadget's expense.

'No...' The young man looked flustered. 'That's not what I meant. The way I dress is age-appropriate. I'm still young.'

'Oh, I see,' said Doyle. 'So, you're saying I'm old?'

'No, that's not what I ...'

'What do you look like in uniform, Detective Constable?'

'What?'

'Because if you call me old again, that's what you'll be wearing to work for the foreseeable future.' Doyle turned to PCs Bowen and Price who, like everyone else, were enjoying Gadget's predicament. 'No offence, lads.'

'Help me out here, Sarge?' the young DC pleaded to Morgan. 'You thought he was a bit of an oddball too.'

'I would, but I'm enjoying myself watching you digging a bigger hole,' Morgan replied. 'I just had Parker pegged as the midlife crisis type.'

'He's made several comments on Chloe Kennedy's Facebook posts and pictures,' Asif said. 'Seems a bit creepy to me, boss.'

'Thank you, Shaima,' Gadget said, regaining some composure. 'I've remembered something else. When he took us to Ms Kennedy's classroom, he had a big bunch of keys, but he didn't have to search for the right one to open her desk. He got it straight away. And that was where her diary was, which had her PIN and passwords in it. So, he might have been able to access her phone after she died.'

'OK, now we're getting somewhere,' Doyle said. 'Where does he live?'

'He lives in a house on site at the school,' Morgan said. 'Only a five-minute walk from where she went missing.'

'OK, so we've got possible means and opportunity. It needs following up. When we're done here,' Doyle said, addressing Gadget, 'You and Derrick get yourselves down there and question him as a witness. Try not to rattle him at this stage, but check his alibi. If things don't tie up, we'll bring him in. But stay low-key at first. Oh, and Gadget.'

'Yes, boss?'

'Remember you're not in the actual fashion police. I don't want you arresting him on a charge of impersonating a millennial...' Doyle smiled. 'OK,' he said, silencing the sniggers. 'Although DC Washington has come up with an interesting angle that warrants further investigation, at this stage it's no more than a stab in the dark. Let's go back to what we know – or at least think we know – and take it from there.'

He strolled over to the large map on the wall next to the evidence board. 'Chloe Kennedy was last seen here.' He pointed to where a map pin had been placed on the corner of Cunliffe Street and George Street. 'At 1.21 a.m. on Saturday. This is confirmed by the record of the time her friend Dani Wheeler was picked up by the taxi company, and by the dashcam in the driver's car. Although it was late at night, this is just off the town centre and there would have been other people about at the time.'

'That's right, sir,' PC Bowen said. 'I've patrolled that area countless times at weekends. Although it doesn't get as rowdy as the city centre, I think if she had screamed or there had been any sort of disturbance, people would have heard and someone would remember it.'

'Good. Thank you,' said Doyle. 'It's useful to have that level of local knowledge. There are no further sightings of her on any of the local authority CCTV cameras around the town. That includes a couple she would have passed if she had decided for some reason to walk home to Adlington.'

'I checked on her bank records, as I wondered if she had decided to cancel the cab and walk because she was short of funds,' Hales said. 'But there was plenty of money in her current account. The cab she took into town earlier in the evening had been debited from her account, but there was nothing for the journey home.'

'Great, thanks, Geoff. So, it seems likely that she either went into a house within the vicinity of these streets...' He indicated a small area on the map. 'Or, more likely, she left in a car. And this is where we have the discrepancy between what her friend is saying: that she had booked a cab from Alpha Cars. However, Alpha Cars say that they have no record of the booking.'

'Alpha Cars don't deny that there could have been a booking,' Morgan said. 'But if it was cancelled by the customer before they were picked up, it would be deleted from their system.'

'But why would she have cancelled the booking?' Birdseye asked.

'Exactly,' said Doyle.

'If someone she knew turned up, offering to give her a lift, she might have cancelled,' Morgan said.

'That would fit in with your caretaker theory, Gadget,' Hales said. 'According to her friend Stacy, she asked him to come round to her house when she was kicking out Johnson. So she must have trusted him. If he had showed up and offered her a lift, it's likely she would have accepted.'

'Don't forget her phone,' said Asif. 'That was turned off then on again then off again at 1.23 a.m.'

'Maybe she was having trouble with the app and was trying to reboot it,' said Gadget.

'Right,' said Doyle. Experience told him that, although it could be useful, this type of conjecture could go on for hours. 'These are all very good thoughts, but we need to get some more information. Anna, we'll go back to the cab office and dig a little deeper. Bowen, you and Half Price come with us.' Bowen smiled at the new nickname Doyle had coined for his colleague 'They might not have a record of her booking and which driver it was allocated to before it was cancelled, but they will have records of who was working that night and they'll be able to tell us who was on which job and where at that time. From that, we will be able to work out which drivers were free. That should help us to narrow it down a bit. Geoff, you and Shaima and the rest of the team here can go through the CCTV again and get the registration numbers of every car that came in and out of the area in that period. I'm guessing they will mostly be cabs, and we can check them off with the different companies against their bookings.'

'Will do,' Hales said.

'Oh, and have any witnesses come forward from the press conference yet?' Doyle asked.

'Not yet,' said Asif, checking her screen.

'A bit early yet. After it's been on the evening news and people have seen her picture, we should start to get some calls.' Hales added.

'No doubt there will be a load of cranks among them,' Doyle said.

'You can guarantee it,' Hales said. 'Including our regular, who we call Mystic Meg. Phones up every time without fail, claiming to be clairvoyant, knows what the person who did it looks like and where they're hiding out. You know something? She's never been even vaguely close.'

⁂

Doyle was about to get into Morgan's car when his personal mobile rang. He glanced at the number and hoped it would be good news. 'Sorry, got to take this. Will only be a minute,' he told the DS and answered.

'Hi Liam, it's Bea. Have you got a moment?' Her Scouse accent was almost melodic.

'Very briefly. Good news or bad?'

'It's no news, I'm afraid, on the property purchase. But something else has come up which I thought might suit you in the short term.'

'Go on,' said Doyle.

'As well as sales, we deal with residential lettings. A landlord of ours is very keen to get a vacant property let, even if it's only a short-term or rolling contract. Strictly between us, he's the owner of the house that was set on fire on Sunday night.'

'What house?' Doyle asked.

'Oh sorry, I thought you would know. They think it's arson. Kids, most probably, got into the garage and set it alight.'

Doyle did recall Jen Knight saying something about the SOCO teams being at an arson. 'Oh, OK, now you mention it, I think I did hear something. But not my area, though, unless someone died in the fire.' He realised that sounded far more callous than he had intended.

'God, no, thankfully. The property hadn't been let since the last tenants moved out three months ago. The owner lives and works in Dubai, but he has six properties that he rents out in the area.'

Doyle looked through the car window and held up a finger to Morgan to indicate he would be another minute. The DS acknowledged this and went back to tapping on her phone screen.

'Four of the houses have tenants, and obviously the one that caught fire will need work doing on it. The other one is a nice old cottage in Limbrick. He's desperate to get someone in there as he doesn't want the same thing to happen to this one. I thought, why not kill two birds with one stone? I'd get you a good deal and a rolling one-month contract. Got to be cheaper than staying in a hotel for weeks. What do you think?'

'That does sound like a sensible option. Where's Limbrick?'

'It's a semi-rural area between Chorley and Adlington. It's nice and quiet. I could show it to you this evening, if you like? What time do you finish?'

'God knows,' said Doyle. 'Could be any time.'

'If you finish by ten thirty, call me and I'll meet you at the property. I can't do later than that. If I'm not in bed by midnight, I turn into a pumpkin.'

'Are you sure you don't mind going out that late?'

'Like I said, the landlord is desperate to get someone in, and I feel bad about the problems that have come up with the place you're buying.'

'OK, great. I'm going to need to go, Bea. If I finish before half ten, I'll give you a call, but if you don't hear from me today it just means I'm up to my eyeballs. Do me a favour, call me back tomorrow.'

'Will do. I'll email the details and the address, so if you get a chance, you can take a look.'

'Great. Thanks.'

Chapter 19

'I owe you an apology,' Doyle said as Morgan pulled the Peugeot up outside Alpha Cars offices.

'Do you?'

'I shouldn't have put you in a difficult position with DI Hales. Keeping him in the dark about the tracker on Johnson's car and telling you.'

'True, but it worked out OK. Boss, I know it's not my place to say…'

'Go on.'

'Why do I get the impression you don't trust the DI?'

'Is it that obvious?'

'I don't think anybody else has picked up on it.'

'He applied for my role. I saw him when I came for my interview. And he seems tight with Croucher. I don't want my every move getting reported back to him. Croucher strikes me as the type of boss who's going to be a constant pain in my arse.'

'You're not wrong about Croucher. But Geoff's alright – he just wants an easy life, really.'

'Then why apply for a job with more stress and more responsibility?'

'Croucher talked him into it. Convinced him it was worth it for the increased pension. I think he was quietly relieved when he didn't get it. He's a good DI, though. And so long as he gets off in time to make last orders – and a bit earlier for darts on a Thursday – he's happy.'

'And what about you? I'm guessing you're a bit more active out of work than drinking and darts?'

'Mostly, yes... Oh, I meant to say while you were on the phone in the car park. I decided to do a little experiment. I signed up to the Alpha Cars app and booked a taxi. I cancelled it again just before we set off.'

'Smart thinking,' said Doyle. He had assumed she had been messaging her fiancé to say she would be late home from work again. He also noted that she had changed the subject when he asked her about her own life. 'That means we'll be able to see whether a record of the booking still exists on their system.'

'Exactly. I waited to make sure a driver had been allocated before cancelling, and took a screenshot of it. We can check on the system in his car too to see if any record exists there.'

'Great.' A screech of tyres came from behind them, and Doyle turned to see Price and Bowen pull up. 'Let's go,' he said, climbing out of the car.

'Back again,' Dawn Taylor said to Morgan as they entered the cab office. 'Who's this you've brought with you today?'

'I'm Detective Chief Inspector Doyle, and we need to ask you some more questions about your bookings on Friday night.'

'Chief Inspector, hey? So you're the boss? We are honoured. In that case, you better come through and you can take a look.'

On the other side of the Perspex screen was a desk made from a piece of kitchen worktop that ran the width of the room. On this was a bank of four computer monitors, each displaying different information. On the wall above the plastic partition was a TV mounted on a bracket. It was tuned to BBC1 and was showing a game show. The volume was set low enough that it was impossible for Doyle to hear what anyone was saying, yet it was audible enough to be irritating. Next to this was a monitor showing a picture from a camera covering the entrance. Currently it was depicting PCs Bowen and Price, looking like a pair of comedy bouncers: one six foot of skin and bone, the other short and rather round.

'OK, what do you want to know?' Dawn asked, seated at the desk, mouse at the ready.

'First, would you mind giving us a quick run-through of how the bookings and app work?' Doyle asked.

'Of course, lovey.' Dawn pulled an office chair closer to her. 'You plonk your arse down here,' she said, tapping the worn seat.

Doyle did as instructed, while Morgan fetched her own chair from the other side of the office.

'This screen here,' Dawn said, poking a chewed biro at her monitor, which displayed a map, 'shows us where all the drivers are that are currently working. They're the green and red dots. The green dots don't have a fare and the red dots have a booking and are unavailable.'

'Does this record? Can you tell where your drivers have been at all times?' Doyle asked.

'Not like this, it doesn't. Sorry. Every job they do is recorded, but not their general whereabouts at any one time. This is more a tool for the controllers to use live. When a job is booked via the app, it's automatically assigned to the closest available cab.'

'Would their dot go red on the map at that point?' Morgan asked.

'The drivers have a unit in their vehicles. Once they press the button to accept a job, then they will appear as red on the map. When someone phones in to book a cab, I fill in the details here.' Dawn indicated another screen showing text boxes that could be filled in. 'And then I allocate a driver from the map here.'

'And what if a fare gets cancelled after it has been booked?' asked Doyle.

'Then the driver will go back to green again on here and be ready for another job. Because the app allocates the nearest car, the drivers tend to go back to the busiest areas once they have dropped off. Before we used the app they would head back here instead. On this one' – Dawn indicated a third screen – 'are all the current bookings, with the most recent one at the top. The ones in bold are still live.' Dawn used the mouse to scroll down the screen. 'These ones here that are greyed out are completed jobs. If I click on one like that…' She pressed a button on the mouse and the screen changed. 'It will bring up all the details of that booking.'

Doyle studied the screen. It showed the driver's name and car details, the time the booking had been made, and the time the passenger was picked up and dropped off. It also showed the customer's name and a little map of the route taken. 'OK, thanks, that's very useful. Could you go back to the previous screen, please?'

Dawn did as Doyle asked, and clicked back on the booking page.

'When DS Morgan was here yesterday, you said that a cancelled booking disappears off your system and is not recorded. Is that correct?'

'Yes. If the customer cancels the booking, it gets deleted. That's quite a recent thing. The guy from the app company said they had made the change due to data protection – that GDP thingy. If we at the office or the driver cancels a booking, then a reason has to be entered and it doesn't get deleted.' Dawn scrolled down the page of bookings again. 'Look, this is a booking from last night that was cancelled by the driver.'

Although it was greyed out, the booking clearly said 'cancelled'. Dawn clicked to open the details of the booking. There was a dialogue box in which was entered 'Passenger drunk and abusive to driver'.

'That's really useful,' said Morgan. 'Could I see the bookings for around quarter to five today?'

Dawn did as asked. Both detectives studied the page, silently confirming that there was no record of Morgan's cancelled booking from before they left the police station.

'What customer records do you keep on your database?' Morgan asked.

'Well, you can search for the customer by name by clicking here,' Dawn said.

'OK, put my name in. Anna Morgan.'

'I didn't know you were one of our customers?' Dawn said, tapping the keyboard.

'I just signed up.'

'There you go. This tells me your name and that you live near Withnell. Very nice round there, but a bit quiet for me. There's your mobile number and I can see the last four digits of your bank card.'

'Does it show details of any bookings made?' Doyle asked.

'Well, it would do here, lovey.' Dawn pointed to a box on the screen. 'Except she hasn't made any.'

'Can any of this be deleted or changed at all?' asked Doyle.

'Not by us it can't. The administration is controlled by the app company. What we can do is add notes. Like for instance "customer has mobility issues, please help in and out of car", that kind of thing.'

'Right, so what we need now,' said Doyle, 'is the record for every driver that was working on Saturday morning between 1 and 2 a.m. and the details of all the jobs they did. That way, we can rule them out of our enquiries – and we might even find another witness among them.'

'That dashcam footage your driver gave us yesterday turned out to be really useful, by the way,' Morgan said.

⚐ ⚐ ⚐

It had barely been a day and a half since Detective Constable Zach Washington – Gadget to his colleagues – had been to Devonshire Road primary school. The scene that greeted him today was rather different to the one he had arrived at the previous morning. The railings outside the Victorian school were now liberally decorated with floral tributes, cards and pictures penned by little hands. A mother was helping a crying eight-year-old tie a teddy bear holding a love heart to a railing, joining the other homages to the murdered teacher. Parents and children stood in small groups talking in respectful, hushed tones. Journalists and photographers sat in cars or slouched against garden walls, waiting to capture any developments. Gadget spotted BBC and Sky News outside broadcast trucks parked down the road. There may have been others around the corner. He had to admit that Birdseye had been right to suggest they make the short journey from Chorley police station on foot. Parking would have been a nightmare.

'Nice little number that, getting a free house with your job,' Gadget said as he knocked on the front door of the cottage adjoining the school.

'Not sure I would like it, living at work. It would be like you're never off duty,' countered Birdseye.

'*We're* never off duty.'

'You've got a point there, young Gadget, right enough.'

'Who is it?' a shaky voice called from behind the door.

'It's the police, Mr Parker. Do you mind if we come in?' Birdseye called back.

The door was opened by Elliot Parker, who did not look like he had undergone an epiphany since the day before and decided to dress more appropriately. He was, however, looking dishevelled, with reddened eyes and untidy hair.

'Mr Parker, I'm DC Washington. We met yesterday. And this is my colleague DC Nelson.'

Both men showed their warrant cards, but the caretaker was looking over their shoulders up and down the road.

'Everything alright, Mr Parker?' Birdseye asked.

'Yes, sorry, I thought you were journalists; they keep coming. That bastard over there has knocked on my door three times.'

Gadget glanced over to where Parker was pointing. Even after his short time in the MIT he had come to recognise the ratty features of Jayden Clark from the *Lancashire Chronicle*.

The journalist smiled and doffed an imaginary cap to the detectives.

'Perhaps it would be best if we came in,' Birdseye said.

'Yes, right.' The caretaker stepped aside to allow the two detectives past him into the hall, closing the door immediately they were over the threshold.

'We just need a brief word with you, Mr Parker,' Gadget said.

'With me?' Parker frowned, and Gadget wondered if he really was perplexed by the request. 'Sure, no problem.' He held out an arm, inviting the two detectives into the living room.

It was sparsely furnished with what Gadget assumed were Parker's own items. These looked out of keeping with the general décor of the property. A battered futon, a beanbag and a gaming chair were the room's main seating.

'Can I get either of you a drink?'

'No, you're OK, thanks, Mr Parker. I shouldn't think we'll be stopping long,' Birdseye replied.

Gadget noticed the caretaker's shoulders drop, visibly relaxing at his colleague's comment, and he wondered why. 'We're speaking to everyone who knew Chloe, Mr Parker. It's important that we find out as much as we can about her and her last movements.'

'Please call me Elliot. You make me sound like a teacher otherwise.' Parker laughed at what he obviously thought was a comical quip. 'I'm afraid I didn't know Chloe very well. I mean, we got on at school and shared a laugh and a joke sometimes, but that was it. We didn't see each other out of school.'

'Did you spend much time with her during school? At breaks, that kind of thing?' Birdseye asked.

'A bit, but not too much, to be honest. At breaks and lunchtimes, I'm often needed to sort things out.'

'But you generally got on OK with her?' Gadget asked.

'Well, yes, she was someone you could have a bit of a laugh with. Not too serious, unlike some of the older teachers.'

'How old are you, Elliot?' Birdseye asked.

'I'm forty-seven. But what has that got to do with anything?'

Gadget noticed the caretaker's shoulders tense back up again.

'Nothing much, really. I was just curious because you said about the older teachers being serious and – well, I mean, you aren't as old as me, but you're not Chloe's age either. She was a good bit younger. I just thought you might have more in common with the older teachers here.'

'I take it you haven't met Mrs Edwards, the head?' Parker said. 'She must have been born middle-aged, and there are a few others here made from the same mould.'

Gadget had to concede that the man had a point. 'And you were friends with Chloe on social media?'

'Yes, but I am with a lot of people. It's what you do, isn't it?'

'Are you married, Elliot, or do you have a partner?' Birdseye asked.

'No, divorced. No partner, just me. My ex-wife lives in Preston with my daughter.'

'Sorry to hear that,' Birdseye said. 'How long ago did you split up?'

'It's been a couple of years now. It was why I took the job here; it came with this place.' Parker waved his hand around, indicating his surroundings 'I'm still paying the mortgage on the house in Preston, even though she's moved her new boyfriend in.'

The way Parker spat the words out left Gadget in no doubt that he was not best pleased with this arrangement. 'Do you drive?'

'Yes. What's that got to do with what happened to Chloe?'

'Just routine questions, Mr Parker,' Gadget said. 'We think whoever killed Chloe used a vehicle to abduct her and dispose of her body.'

'You think I killed Chloe?' Parker was up off the beanbag.

'Relax, Elliot,' Birdseye said. 'In any murder enquiry, everyone who knows the victim is a suspect to some degree, and we have to try to rule people out. Now, do you own a car or have access to a car?'

'No,' Parker said, sitting back down. 'That's another advantage of working here. A short commute.' This time his laugh at his own joke sounded nervous.

'Have you hired a vehicle recently for any reason?' Gadget asked.

'No, not since I moved here.'

'Well, that's good then, isn't it?' Birdseye said.

'And would you mind telling us what you did at the weekend, starting with Friday night?' Gadget asked.

'Well, on Friday night the last teacher left at seven thirty. That was Patricia Edwards. Typical of her – nothing better to do on a Friday night. After that, I locked up, set the alarm and went to the corner shop and bought a few beers. I ordered a Chinese when I got back and watched the TV.'

'Were you alone all night? Is there anyone who can verify this?'

'Yes, I was alone, but that's what happens most Friday nights.'

'What did you watch on the telly?' Birdseye asked.

'The cricket. The T20,' Parker said.

'Who was playing?' asked Birdseye.

'Derbyshire against Notts.'

'That must have finished about ten o'clock. What did you watch after that?'

'I watched the news, then a Euro 96 documentary and then a film. *The Exorcist*. I was falling asleep by the end and went to bed.'

'And what about the rest of the weekend? What did you do then?' Gadget asked.

'It was a rare weekend where nothing was going on at the school. No contractors working or anything like that. I was able to get the 10.06 train from Chorley to Preston and pick up my daughter. From there we went to Blackpool, spent the day there and got back about quarter to eight. Izzy spent the night here. I took her back to her mum's just after lunch on Sunday.'

'Was the school alarm set all weekend?' Gadget asked. 'Did you or anyone else go into the school during the weekend?'

'I didn't, and nor did anyone else, as far as I'm aware. The alarm was set when I got back on Saturday evening. I noticed that as there's a keypad in this house and I always check. I'm not convinced any of the other keyholders know how to set it. I mean, why take responsibility for something yourself when you can just make me hang around and do it for you?'

'Do you know how to access the alarm log so that we can check?'

'Sure. It will tell you when it was armed and unarmed, and whose fob was used,' Parker said. 'There's a separate alarm for this house, but my fob works on both. You can check that as well if you like.'

'Thanks, that will be useful,' Gadget said.

'Elliot, you said your relationship with Chloe was a work one and you never saw her outside work,' Birdseye said. 'Were there any times that you met her outside work at all?'

'I bumped into her a few times in town. Last time a couple of months ago in Morrisons.'

'We noticed, Mr Parker, that you don't have a criminal record. As we would expect for someone doing your job,' Gadget said. 'This, of course, means we don't have a copy of your fingerprints on file. Would you mind if we take a scan of them so we can eliminate them from the ones we found at Chloe's house?' Gadget noticed Parker's Adam's apple shift up and down as he swallowed hard. He thought he could see a bead of sweat appear on the man's forehead.

'I-I-I... well, I'm not sure. It seems a bit...'

'If you're worried about something else, some misdemeanour in the past perhaps,' Gadget suggested, 'then you needn't be. All we're concerned with is what happened to Chloe. We will take your prints, compare them to ones at her house and elsewhere, and, providing they don't show up, we will delete them from the system.'

'No, no, it's not that,' Parker said, rising to his feet again.

'What is it then, Elliot?' Birdseye encouraged him. 'You need to tell us. This is a murder investigation – you can't hold anything back.'

Parker sucked in his breath, obviously trying to regain his composure. He appeared to Gadget as if he was standing on top of a precipice trying to psyche himself up to bungee-jump off.

'You might find my fingerprints at Chloe's house,' Parker blurted out.

'Please sit back down, Elliot,' Birdseye said.

'If you would prefer, Mr Parker, we can all go back to the station and you can answer our next questions under caution with a solicitor present?'

'No, no, that won't be necessary.'

'Are you sure?' Birdseye said. 'It's best that you tell us everything, but if that has anything to do with Chloe Kennedy's killing, it would be better if you had a solicitor with you.'

'No, no, it's not like that. It's nothing to do with that.'

'What is it then, Mr Parker?' Gadget probed. 'Why might we find your prints at Chloe's house when you just told us that you never saw her outside work?'

'Was there something more to your relationship with Chloe?' Birdseye asked.

'No.'

'What then, Mr Parker? Did you want there to be?' Gadget asked.

'No. I mean, she is … was … a pretty young woman, and I liked her. I still can't believe what happened to her is real. But I'm not stupid, I know she's miles out of my league, but she was nice to me, and I tried to be kind to her.'

'In what way did you try to be kind to her?' Gadget asked.

'You make it sound seedy. It wasn't.'

'I noticed you liked a lot of her pictures and posts on

Facebook. A bit familiar, isn't it, for a work relationship?' Gadget said.

Sweat was running down Parker's forehead. 'No. I wasn't meaning to be. I was just being friendly.'

'Why did you go to Chloe's house, Elliot?' Birdseye asked.

'Oh, yes, right. Like I said, I was just trying to be kind to her.'

'Go on,' said Gadget.

'Chloe was breaking up with her boyfriend. Who was a bit of an arsehole, by all accounts.'

'And you thought you would see if you could get in there, be her shoulder to cry on? Hit on her on the rebound?' Gadget asked. He noticed Birdseye giving him one of his stern looks, and knew he was telling him to back off a bit.

'No.'

'Go on, Elliot,' the older detective said. 'Why were you there?'

'This won't get back to Mrs Edwards, will it?'

'No. Not unless it's significant, and then it's bound to end up in the public domain,' Birdseye said.

'OK. So, as I was saying, Chloe was splitting up from her boyfriend and wanted to kick him out one Saturday morning. It was her place, but he was living there. Dani had agreed to go round for moral support. Then she got worried in case he got nasty, and so she asked me if I would be there as well.'

'And that was the only time you went to Chloe's house, Mr Parker?' Birdseye asked.

'Yes, and to be honest I wasn't too pleased to be asked, but I felt sorry for Chloe and wanted to give her support.'

'Why were you not too pleased to be asked?' Gadget said.

'I was a bit worried that if he did get angry, I'd get the brunt of it. As it happened, he was shocked and upset. I almost felt sorry for him. He just threw a few things in a bag and then left. He tried not to look at me or Dani, but I could see he was holding back tears.'

'And when you were at her house, where did you go? Did

you go up to her bedroom?' Gadget asked.

'No, I stayed downstairs, stood around like a spare part, mostly. I went into the kitchen and made tea at one point.'

'Sorry, Elliot,' Birdseye said. 'But what has that got to do with Mrs Edwards? I seem to be missing something.'

'It was a Saturday morning and we had an IT contractor in. We had these flash new screens installed that the school had got some funding for. He was setting up the apps on them. When there are people working on site, I'm meant to be around at all times. If she finds out I went out while he was here, she'd kill me… Sorry, I didn't mean that. Bad choice of words, but you know what I mean. I would be in deep shit.'

'It's OK, Elliot,' Birdseye said.

'I didn't want to let Chloe down, but I could hardly kick out the contractor while I went over to help her. As it happens, we weren't gone for long, and Chloe gave me a lift back. We picked up bacon barms on the way. We sat and ate them in her classroom. We even got one for the IT guy to keep him sweet, so he didn't grass me up to Edwards for bunking off.'

'And there's nothing else you can think of that you might want to tell us about Chloe and your relationship with her?' Birdseye asked.

'No, nothing. I mean, Dani knew her much better than I did.'

'And there's nothing we're going to find out further down the line and wonder why you didn't tell us about it now?' Gadget asked.

'No. Honestly, there isn't anything.'

'Good. Can we have a look at the alarm log for here and the school now, please?' Gadget asked.

Chapter 20

Parker let Gadget and Birdseye out via the main school gate. The older detective had suggested it, and Gadget knew he was hoping that exiting that way would mean the waiting press wouldn't realise they had been to visit the caretaker.

They had only gone a half dozen paces when a figure appeared at their side.

'Is the caretaker a suspect then?' Jayden Clark asked.

'No, Mr Clark, we were just checking if any of the victim's belongings were still at the school,' Birdseye replied, picking up his pace.

Gadget was happy to let his colleague field the questions. The press frightened him more than any criminal he had come across. They could twist your words so tightly your career would snap, and the chief crime reporter on the *Lancashire Chronicle* was notorious for it.

'Is it right that you have a man in custody? The ex-boyfriend?'

How the hell do you know that? Gadget thought.

'I'm sure our press office will keep you updated on any developments in the case, Mr Clark,' Birdseye replied.

'Why has Detective Chief Inspector Doyle been brought in from the Met? Does this case have connections to London?'

'No, Mr Clark.'

'There's another reason for Doyle being here? Was he kicked out of the Met? Or is he up here to shake things up, dole out some of his instant justice?' The journalist made a gun shape with his hand and mimed shooting Birdseye.

Birdseye stopped and faced the reporter, and Gadget followed suit.

'Mr Clark.'

Gadget had only ever heard Birdseye raise his voice once before, and that had been to a particularly unpleasant sex offender.

'If you have any genuine enquiries, I'm sure you have the number for our press office. Now if you don't mind, we have work to do.'

Too late, Gadget noticed a photographer on the other side of the road shooting the exchange. Clark nodded towards him then winked at the detectives. 'Catch you later,' he said, crossing the road.

It was only after the detectives had walked several hundred yards up the street and both had checked over their shoulders to ensure the journalist wasn't following them that either man spoke again.

'What do you make of all that asking about the new guv?' Gadget said.

'I don't make anything of it – the man's a shit-stirrer. Looking for any angle he can to spread scandal and sell papers.'

'OK, and what do you make of the new boss, then?'

'I've seen a few DCIs come and go in my time. I reckon he'll be OK. Wouldn't want to get on the wrong side of him, though.'

'That's true. He didn't seem too put off by his run-in with Mr Burns this morning… D'you reckon he shot that guy in London deliberately?'

'Well, I don't think it was accidental.'

'You know what I mean. There was no CCTV in that car park. The guy had a knife, not a gun. Rumour has it the DCI shot him before any backup could get to the scene. Didn't try to talk him down.'

'Zach.' Gadget knew the older man was going to give him a dressing-down as he used his real name. 'He's been investigated by the IOPC. Had to give evidence in the coroner's court and God knows what else. If they didn't find anything untoward, then there wasn't anything to find. Besides, the guy he shot had killed his wife and was holding a knife to his stepdaughter's throat.'

'Don't you think it was a bit odd that he was armed? I mean, we don't carry guns up here.'

'We don't tend to get many cases where the prime suspect in a murder is also under surveillance by the drug squad. He must have been authorised from when he was in the flying squad.'

'I know, I was just asking what you made of it. That journo seems to want to make more out of it.'

'I'm sure he does. And the DCI is not stupid. He will know we all know what happened in London. That kind of thing follows you around. But don't go listening to rumours or reading nonsense on the internet. The last thing we need is the new boss thinking we're all gossiping behind his back.'

'OK, fair enough. What about Parker?'

'I never realised what a sneaky bugger you are.'

'What?' Gadget protested, but he knew what Birdseye was getting at.

'All that stuff about fingerprints at her house. You could just have asked him if he'd ever been there.'

'True, but I wanted to rattle him a bit, shake his cage and see what fell out. What did you think of him?'

'I think Morgan had it spot on, to be honest. Midlife crisis, and I doubt very much that he killed her. What do you think?'

'I think you're right. If his alibi with his daughter checks out, I can't see how he could have been looking after her and torturing and killing Chloe at the same time. Plus the alarm log backs that up. Sorry it was a bit of a waste of time. I just got a funny feeling from him yesterday.'

'Hey, Gadget, you can't think like that. It's not a waste of time. If you get an itch in this job, you've got to scratch it. And we'll get the CID boys to follow up on what he's told us. If he didn't have his daughter when he said, or it turns out he does have a car or something else that contradicts his account, then that will put him right back in the frame.'

⅄ ⅄ ⅄

There had been thirty-six drivers working for Alpha Cars during the early hours of Saturday morning. Twenty-eight of them either had passengers on board at the time Chloe was last seen alive or were en route to pick up a fare. Of the remaining eight, one had dropped a passenger off in the outskirts of Liverpool six minutes earlier and, even with the lack of traffic at that time of night, could not have been anywhere near the vicinity. Another had dropped off in Leyland, a couple of miles north of Chorley town centre, at 1.18: although this was three minutes before Dani Wheeler had been picked up, it was eleven minutes after her booking, and she had said that both she and Chloe had been allocated drivers within a minute of making the bookings. Doyle and Morgan reasoned that, for now, that driver could be discounted too.

This meant that any of the remaining six could have been allocated the fare. These were the drivers they wanted to speak to as a priority. Morgan was supervising Dawn Taylor emailing her all their details, when Doyle's phone rang. A glance at the screen told him it was DI Hales. He decided to go outside to answer, out of earshot of the cab controller, who was now getting to know a bit more about the investigation than Doyle would like.

'What have you got?' The car park was deserted apart from PCs Bowen and Price.

'We've picked something up on the town centre CCTV. Might be of use.'

'Go on.'

'We've got a Prius with Alpha Cars logos on it entering the south end of Market Street at 01.28. You can't see it on the next camera at the junction with Anderton Street, which means it either went down Cheapside or Cunliffe Street. It didn't turn round and come back the way it went in either.'

'That's great, Geoff. Can you see the reg in the footage?'

'Yes. It's Foxtrot Alpha—'

'Don't tell it to me, text it to me. I'll go back in and check it against the drivers they had working. I'll call you back in a minute.' Doyle ended the call and turned to the two uniformed PCs. 'Bowen, with me,' he barked before walking back into the cab office.

Doyle arrived inside just in time to see his own image on the TV, which had now been turned up to be audible.

'Here he is, the man of the moment,' Dawn exclaimed as he entered.

'Oh, for fuck's sake,' Doyle said, seeing that the spilled water on his shirt and tie was clearly visible. His phone chimed as the text with the vehicle reg came through. He showed it to Morgan. 'Is this the reg number of one of those six drivers?'

The DS checked it against the emails on her own phone, where the driver details had just been sent.

'It's him – Mohammed Khan.' Morgan showed the DCI her phone screen.

'Mo? What about him?' Dawn asked.

'What was his last drop-off before the time we're looking at?' Doyle asked Morgan, ignoring Dawn.

Morgan checked the details on the email. 'He dropped off a customer at 1.08 in Holmeswood – that's about twelve miles away from Chorley town centre. His next job was a pick-up in Chorley on Park Road – that's at the top end – at 1.44.'

'Right, what's his address? We need to have a word with Mr Khan straight away.'

'It's…' Morgan scrolled down her phone screen, looking for the details.

'He's working now,' Dawn interrupted. 'He's just about to drop a customer off in Euxton. Here.' She tapped the map screen with an unlit cigarette.

'Book him in for a pick-up from Chorley police station ASAP,' Doyle said.

'Where shall I say the fare is going?' Dawn asked.

'Tell him wherever you like, but he won't be going anywhere until we have had a chat with him,' Doyle said. 'We'll get back there now. I'll call Geoff on the way. Oh, and Dawn, don't you dare cancel that job or make any contact with him.'

'OK.' Dawn threw up her hands in mock surrender. 'But Mo won't have nothing to do with it. He's not the type.'

'We'll see about that soon enough. PC Bowen here will be keeping you company until we have him safely in our care.'

⁂

Doyle felt a vibration in his jacket as Morgan pulled the Peugeot up outside the front entrance to Chorley police station. He could see Hales waiting, alongside Birdseye and Gadget. He grabbed his personal mobile from his pocket, catching the caller ID on the screen. 'Oh shit,' he said under his breath before answering.

'Dad, I saw you on the telly. On *North-West Tonight*. Does that mean you've moved? Are you up here now?'

Mohammed Khan's white Prius stopped in front of them.

'We've got this,' Morgan whispered, putting her hand on Doyle's arm before getting out of the car as her colleagues approached the minicab.

'You never told me you'd moved, Dad. I want to see you. When can I see you?'

Hales had the passenger door open and was brandishing his warrant card at Mr Khan. Smart move, Doyle thought. If the man decided to drive off, he would take out his door on the lamp post.

'Sorry, Harry, I miss you too.'

Gadget was at the driver's door, reaching through the open window to turn off the ignition.

'And I've not moved up here yet. Not properly. I haven't got anywhere to live. I'm staying at a Premier Inn. I came up Sunday night.'

Morgan had joined Gadget as Khan opened the driver's door.

'When can I see you, Dad? Can I come and stay at the hotel too, at the weekend? Can we have a Premier Inn breakfast together?'

Khan was standing by the door of his taxi – a small man with a long grey beard and wearing a shalwar kameez.

'I don't like it at school, Dad. There's this boy called Conor and he always says nasty things to me. He says I talk funny. Can you come and arrest him?'

'I wish I could, Harry, but you know it doesn't work like that.'

'Could you come to school and put him in handcuffs?'

Doyle was pleased to see that Gadget hadn't felt the need to put Khan in handcuffs. It was hard to know whether to treat him as a suspect or a witness at this stage. But right now, he was all they had – if Ryan Johnson hadn't killed Chloe Kennedy.

'Harry, I'm kind of tied up at work at the moment. Got a big case. That's why you saw me on the TV.'

'Grandma said you've put on weight. Are you going to catch the bad guy, Daddy?'

'I sure am. And I'm going to look at a house tonight – just a temporary one. I'm going to be around a lot more now.'

'Will I still be able to stay at the hotel with you before you check out? Please?'

'I can't make any promises, but if work allows, you can stay a night at the weekend. But only if your mum agrees.'

Khan was being walked into the police station, flanked by Morgan and Gadget. A uniformed PC passed them on the way out and Hales pointed him towards the minicab, presumably telling him to keep an eye on it until it could be driven into the station car park, as it was a possible crime scene.

'When you catch the bad guy, are you going to arrest him or shoot him like you did last time?'

Doyle winced. If anyone else had said that, he would have lost his temper. But Harry had no filter; he said whatever was on his mind. Doyle wondered if he was just giving voice to what everyone else was thinking. 'I'm going to arrest him, Harry, and put him in jail. Look, son, I'm sorry, but I've got to go. I'll call you tomorrow or the day after, I promise. OK?'

'OK. Mum says she wants to speak to you.'

'OK.' Doyle's heart sank, but he knew it was coming.

'I love you, Dad.'

'I love you too, Harry.'

'I love you, Dad.' It always had to be said twice, keeping to the same script.

'I love you too, Harry.' There was a brief pause.

'Liam, what the bloody hell is going on? When were you planning on telling us you had moved up here?' Doyle's ex-wife's voice had none of the loving quality of that of his son.

'Things happened rather quicker than I expected. They wanted me here sooner, and the Met were more than happy to let me go. Before I knew it, I was here.' He knew his words sounded hollow, like he was making excuses.

'You can't treat him like that. It's not fair. Harry needs reliability and consistency in his life.'

Doyle closed his eyes.

'He shouldn't find out on the news that his dad's finally moved closer to him.'

'I know he shouldn't. But when you decided to move up here, you knew it would take time for me to get a transfer.' He took a deep breath. The last thing he needed was to be drawn into an argument.

'And you've only been up here five minutes and you're already putting your work before your family.'

Doyle stared hard at the back of the white Prius. He had a feeling that, by the time this conversation was over, he'd have memorised the number plate, and he would also be able to recall every chip and splash of mud on the paintwork.

'Look, Fiona, I didn't mean it to be like this. I'd just got up here when the case came in. I can't turn it down.'

'It's always the same – the job takes over. Why couldn't you have got a less operational role?'

He knew that she wasn't just talking about the hours. She blamed the incident in the underground car park in south London for the break-up of their marriage, but in truth the bullet he had fired wasn't the cause of their divorce. It was just the final straw.

'That's not me. I'm not the office paperwork type. Sitting at headquarters all day with the top brass, toeing the party line. Did you watch the bit on the news about the case?'

'I caught the end. Harry called me to come and see it; my parents had it on.'

'The woman who was murdered, she was a young primary school teacher like you used to be. With all her life ahead of her. Her parents are devastated. Their world has been turned upside down. I owe it to them and Chloe to catch whoever killed her.'

'That's very noble of you. But you owe it to Harry to be there for him. He needs you. He's struggling at school. We need to talk at some point. We need to see the school SENCO.'

'The what?'

'The Special Educational Needs Co-Ordinator. Harry needs more support, and we need to think about whether he's going to go to a mainstream secondary school or somewhere that might suit him better.'

'He's only in Year 4 – he's got two more years before all that.'

'Yes, but he's going to need an ECHP – you know, an education and healthcare plan – and that will take time to get, and then you have to apply for secondary schools in September of Year 6.'

'Do you really think he might need a special school?'

'I don't know. I just want him to be happy. Kids can be so cruel, especially if you're the odd one out.'

'OK. I'll make some time so we can talk this through and see the teacher, I promise, but please give me a week to get settled.'

'Can he at least stay with you one night this weekend? It would do him the world of good.'

'I'll do my best.'

The Prius's lights flashed and a white-suited figure wearing a mask and overshoes got in, presumably to drive it into the underground car park.

Chapter 21

Mohammed Khan's solicitor had questioned the validity of his arrest, which he said was based on 'pathetically flimsy' evidence. Doyle had reminded him that he wasn't required to tell him everything they had at this stage, though the truth was, other than the CCTV putting Khan near the scene when Chloe disappeared, they had absolutely sweet FA.

They could have taken the opportunity to interview Khan under caution, but by arresting him they had the chance to get forensics to go over his car. If he was responsible for Chloe Kennedy's murder, this would be their best chance of finding significant evidence. Doyle had been hesitant about this course of action, but having got a bollocking from Mr Burns that morning for not arresting Johnson the previous evening, he felt vindicated in the action he took now.

Thankfully, despite his protestations at the disclosure meeting, in the interview room it soon became apparent that the solicitor hadn't advised his client to respond with the old favourite, 'no comment'.

'According to the records we got from Alpha Cars, you dropped a customer off in Sandy Way in Holmeswood at 1.08 a.m. on Saturday. Do you remember that?' Morgan asked.

'Saturday?' Khan asked, his voice heavily accented.

'Very early on Saturday morning – or late Friday night to most people up at that time,' Morgan clarified.

'Oh yes, I do remember. Was out in the sticks,' Khan said.

'Could you tell me what you did after that? Where did you go, Mr Khan?' Morgan asked.

'I turned round in customer's drive. It is a slim lane and no streetlights. There is ditch – I was worried about reversing in it. The parking sensors, they don't pick that up. It was very muddy too. I started driving back towards Chorley. Was not more than a couple of minutes and my screen bleeped to say a job had come in. I pulled over to side of road. I always pull in, officers. I looked at screen, was pick-up. Lady in Cunliffe Street, Chorley, going to Adlington.'

A look passed between Doyle and Morgan. Khan had just admitted being assigned Chloe Kennedy's fare.

'It must have been busy night, as I would not get given this job when so far away normally. I pressed button to accept and carried driving back there.'

'What route did you take back to Chorley?' Morgan asked.

'The way the device told me to go. On A581 through Croston. I had just got to Euxton and screen beeped again. Said customer cancelled fare.'

'What did you do then, Mr Khan?'

'I carried on into Chorley town centre, as that is where most of our jobs come from at that time of night. If another job had come through, I would have taken it, but nothing came so I drove up to Cunliffe Street.'

'Why did you do that?' Doyle asked. 'If the customer had cancelled the job?'

'Last week, same thing happening to my friend. He was just round the corner when job was cancelled. He went there anyway. Lady there wanting cab, but problem with app, and job got cancelled by mistake. He got the fare, got her to ring office and book. He then took her home.'

'When was that?' Doyle asked.

'The weekend before – Friday or Saturday I think.'

'And who is your friend who this happened to?' Morgan asked.

'Amir.'

'Is that Amir Hussain?' Morgan asked.

'I think so – only know him through working. He is nice guy.'

'What route did you take to Cunliffe Street?'

'I went along Shepherds Way, then right at the roundabout then into Market Street. Then first right.'

'And what did you see when you turned into Cunliffe Street, Mr Khan?' Doyle asked.

'Nothing. There was nobody waiting so I assumed lady had cancelled on purpose, as screen had said.'

'Have you got a dashcam in your cab, Mr Khan?' Morgan asked.

'No, no, sorry.'

'Did you notice anyone else on the street? Any other cars there with their lights on or people in them?' Doyle asked.

'No, not that I saw. I was driving slowly, looking around, but I didn't see anyone.'

'OK, and what did you do after this, Mr Khan?' Morgan said.

'I turned down George Street and went back down Shepherds Way to the other end of town centre. There are more bars that end – we get more jobs there.'

人 人 人

It took a further hour for Khan to talk Doyle and Morgan through what he had done the rest of the weekend, which mainly consisted of sleeping and working. They would be able to check the details of when he was working against the log at the cab company, but even so, there would be gaps where he did not have passengers, and Doyle suspected that the information given would not conclusively rule him in or out.

Hales had been watching the interview on the monitor, and greeted the DCI and DS when they walked back into the incident room.

'I've sent Birdseye, Gadget, Shaima and the rest of the day shift home. Hope that's OK?'

'That's great. Thanks, Geoff.' Doyle looked at his watch. It was twenty past nine.

'I've told everyone to be back here at 7 a.m. for a briefing, but I can call round and change it if you like?' Hales said.

'No, that's perfect. It's going to be a busy day tomorrow.'

'What do we think of Khan? Could it really be him?' Hales asked.

'I'm doubtful, to be honest, but let's check out what we can of his story and see if forensics find anything in his car. If it's not him, then we have narrowed the time of Chloe Kennedy's disappearance that night to less than eight minutes between when Dani was picked up and when Khan got to Cunliffe Street. So that's progress,' Doyle said.

'I just can't see it being him,' Morgan said. 'He's too … I don't know, nice.'

'Nice!' Doyle said. 'I'm not sure that defence will hold up in court. *It can't have been my client that killed her, despite all the evidence to the contrary. Just look at the man – he's far too nice to do that.*'

Morgan and Hales laughed.

'Don't take the piss, boss, you know what I mean,' Morgan said.

'I do. But stranger things have happened. Have we had anything back from the press conference yet?'

'Only the usual cranks so far,' Hales said. 'Oh, and a woman called to say you had spilled water down the front of your shirt.'

Morgan was unable to suppress a giggle. 'It wasn't me, boss, honest,' she said.

Doyle smiled. 'Look, you two should get off home too. Have we got anyone from CID tonight to follow up on a few things?'

'We've got a couple. They start at ten and will be up as soon as they get here,' Hales said.

'Great. I'll stay and fill them in. See you two back here first thing.'

Doyle didn't have to wait long for the two CID officers to arrive; they were in the incident room by twenty to ten. He recognised them from the night before.

'Be with you in two minutes!' he called from his office as he fired off a text to Bea, the estate agent, to see if she could meet him at the property at quarter past ten. If he was lucky, he might even make it back to the hotel in time for a pint before they called last orders at the bar. The reply from Bea came back straight away.

See you then.

'Right,' Doyle said, walking over to the two CID officers. 'I've got a few bits for you to follow up on for me.'

'It doesn't involve sitting in a parked car all night again, does it, boss?' the bald one said. 'My back still feels stiff.'

'You're in luck – it doesn't. I've got a bit of detective work for you to do. Check out some leads and alibis.'

The officers seemed relieved. Doyle outlined what he wanted them to get on with. He had just finished when Inspector Phil Regan walked in.

'Hi, Liam. I've just got to do a custody review before I go off shift, and you've got two in the cells. I need to know the plans for them,' the inspector said.

'Johnson can be un-arrested for the murder, but he needs to be interviewed again for the harassment. I want him charged. He pretty much confessed to that earlier in the second half of the interview, but it's worth having another crack at him. In fact,' Doyle said, a pleasing thought springing to mind, 'you two could do that after you've checked all those bits with the cab firm. Don't worry how late it is. His solicitor, Ms Finch, is very professional. I'm sure she won't mind being disturbed at any time of night to support a client in an interview.'

The bearded CID man smiled. 'Oh, I know Ms Finch, sir. It will be a pleasure to drag her here in the middle of the night.'

'Good,' said Doyle. 'And make sure he gets charged with as much as the CPS will go for. He might not have killed his ex-girlfriend, but he's still a nasty bastard.'

'And what about the other chap, Khan?' Regan asked.

'Got to keep hold of him for now, I'm afraid, until we have checked what he told us, and forensics have finished with his car.'

人　人　人

The driver of the BMW in front of Doyle clearly saw his blue flashing lights in their mirror and dutifully pulled over to let him past. When he had rounded the corner into Long Lane, the DCI turned off the strobes. If he was going to be living here, he didn't want to arrive in a fanfare, with neighbours peering out between the curtains. Strictly speaking, this wasn't an emergency or police business, but the delay caused by Inspector Regan sticking to procedure meant he was running late. He didn't think it was fair to keep Bea waiting for him at this time of night.

Although it was dark with no street lighting, Doyle did notice an attractive-looking old-fashioned inn that looked familiar. He realised they had passed it the day before when Morgan had driven him to Anglezarke woods. The property Doyle was looking for was further up the hill, according to the satnav. That would make it good for a sobering walk on his way back from the pub.

He pulled up at the destination at twenty past ten and was relieved to see that Bea was not already waiting. Stepping out of the car, he gently shut the door, not wanting to disturb his potential new neighbours. The property sat in the middle of a terrace of six cottages. Doyle couldn't make out much detail in the dark, but he could tell that the cottage was old and stone-built. He had a fair idea of what it would be like inside from the brochure the estate agent had sent to his personal email.

A BMW pulled up behind his car and Bea got out. Apparently unconcerned about the local residents, she slammed her door then clicked over to him on her heels.

'So, it was you who was flashing me back down the road. If I'd known, I would have let you chase me,' she said, in a voice just loud enough that if any of the locals were still awake, Doyle was pretty sure they would have heard.

'Sorry. I got held up leaving work, then had to rush to get here.'

'I see you're making your mark already. What is it, two days since you've been up here, and you're already a local celebrity?'

'You saw it, then?'

'I did. After you.' Bea unlocked the door then invited Doyle to step through ahead of her. 'So you're the man in charge, Detective Chief Inspector?'

Doyle detected a playful note to her voice. 'Not quite. The other guy's the one in charge.'

'Oh, the one with that funny vein.' She motioned to her head. They were now standing in an empty living room. 'Shit, sorry, he's not a friend of yours, is he?'

'No, not at all. The man's an arsehole.'

'I thought that. You can just tell with some people. Anyway, here we are.' Bea motioned around the lounge. 'The redecoration was only just finished last week, which explains the painty smell. It's also why it's not furnished yet. But if you have your own furniture in storage, you could use that if you want, which might work out better for everyone. Save you a few bob, too.'

Doyle wandered through to the only other downstairs room, which was the kitchen. It was nicely done and pleasantly laid out, with patio doors leading out onto what according to the pictures in the brochure was a garden with scenic views over the surrounding countryside. Now it was just a sea of dark and shadows.

'I know it's a lot smaller than the house you're still – hopefully – going to buy. But the type of location is what you were looking for. As a temporary measure, it must be cheaper than staying in hotels.'

'Is there any more news about the other house?'

'I'm afraid not. I honestly couldn't say how it will go… Apparently someone gazumped them by twenty grand on the place they were buying.'

'It still amazes me that's allowed.'

'Don't get me started. You wouldn't catch our agency doing that at this late stage. That's why estate agents have such a bad name.'

'You should try being a police officer. Still, at least we're not solicitors.'

Bea smiled at Doyle. 'Best be grateful for small mercies.'

'Shall we go upstairs?' Doyle asked, immediately regretting his choice of words.

'Why, Detective Chief Inspector, you haven't even bought me dinner yet,' Bea teased 'Get your arse up there and I won't put in a complaint. And mind your—'

'Fuck,' Doyle said a moment after the solid thud of his head meeting the ceiling signalled his arrival on the top floor.

'Here, let me have a look at that,' Bea said, turning on a light in the front bedroom. 'Well, it's not bleeding, but you might get a bit of a lump. I think you'll live.'

'Thanks. Occupational hazard,' Doyle said, wandering into the empty double bedroom. 'When I was a young PC, I once had to have six stiches in my forehead when I forgot to duck when chasing a suspect through a fire exit door. I was lying on the floor with blood pouring from my head, my sergeant standing over me, bollocking me for letting him get away.'

'What had he done?'

'Stolen a video from Blockbusters.'

'You ever feel guilty that it might have been you that caused them to go bust?'

Doyle laughed.

'That young woman…' The jokey quality had gone from Bea's voice as she followed Doyle into the smaller back bedroom. 'The one that was murdered?'

Doyle opened and closed the built-in wardrobe doors – not because he was particularly interested in what was inside, but it just seemed like something you did on viewings.

'I think I recognised her from somewhere. But then I do meet a lot of people in my job. Do you think you will catch who did it?'

Doyle turned to face the estate agent. 'I really hope so. It was heartbreaking having to tell her parents.'

He crossed the landing to a tastefully decorated bathroom, complete with bath and shower that looked like it had never been used. Having seen all that was on offer on this level, Doyle made his way back to the stairs.

'Mind your head.' This time Bea's shouted warning came just in time.

'Thanks. I wonder if I will ever get used to that,' Doyle called back as he reached the ground floor.

'Sure you will. You will develop muscle memory or something after you've brained yourself a few times. Unless you're totally stupid, that is. On second thoughts, you might want to get one of those skull-cap thingies the rugby players wear... So, what do you think?'

'You've just called me stupid. Is that what you say to all your customers?'

'Not really. I normally wait until they're out of the door then call them a lot worse. But I like you, so I'll insult you to your face.'

'Thanks – I've never felt so honoured. How much will it set me back?'

'He was going to stick it on for £850 a month, but it's unfurnished and he's desperate to get someone in. He's paranoid about having another property burned down. I think he'll take £550 maybe, especially considering you're a police officer.'

Doyle did a quick calculation in his head. 'On a rolling one-month contract. I'll take that.'

'I'll speak to him tomorrow. If he agrees, I'll get contracts drawn up. I won't need anything from you other than a signature. I've got all your credentials, and you've been checked out already for the purchase on the other place.'

'Only one thing, though.' Doyle realised there was a potential pitfall. 'If he is desperate to get someone in here, I'm not sure when I'll have the time to physically move all my stuff in and get the furniture put together.'

'Where is the storage unit?'

'Just off the M65 near Preston.'

'No problem. I've got a man with a van. I mean, I don't actually have the man, he's not chained up in my basement. But anyway, I put loads of work his way, so he owes me a favour. I'll get him to move everything in for you and put it together, if you like? You'll have to pay him for his time, but I'll get him to fit it in urgently once we've got the contracts sorted.'

'That's perfect, thanks.'

'No problem at all. I'm very glad I'll be able to call your new landlord with some happy news. It wasn't pleasant phoning him to say that one of his houses had gone up in smoke.'

'I bet. I was going to ask you about that. What was that house like?'

'It was a good bit bigger than this. Not far away, but off the main road. Detached, newly refurbished. They think it was possibly kids that got in and set fire to the garage. The fire spread, and half of the downstairs was burned.'

'Can you do me a favour and send me the brochure for that one too? I'll take a quick look, make sure it's all been followed up properly.'

'Sure. Have you got a work email you want me to send it too?'

'You'd think so, wouldn't you, but best send it to my personal one. Our IT haven't sorted out my email yet.'

'Jesus, and I thought our IT department were useless.'

Chapter 22

June 1996

The boy's feet ached, and he was sure he had a couple of blisters. He had walked all the way from Fleetwood to Lytham the night before, not wanting to spend precious money on tram and bus fares, or risk being caught jibbing it. With the tide out he had been able to walk much of the way along the deserted beach, safely away from the gaze of any police officers who might be looking for him. It was past one in the morning when he arrived at the cemetery. The gate had been locked, but it had been no problem getting over the fence.

He was exhausted, and had slept like a baby on the bench opposite his parents' grave until the rising sun woke him up just before five o'clock. His thirst had been so bad that he had considered drinking the water from a vase on a well-tended plot just a few along from where his mum and dad lay. He had resisted this temptation and waited until just after seven to make his way into town, where he had treated himself to a bacon barm and a can of Coke. Blending in with the rest of the Monday morning pedestrians, he felt relaxed. This was his hometown. It had a familiar, almost comforting, feel – a reminder of better times. He'd walked past his old house, the place he had lived until he was nine years old.

He hadn't been worried that any of the neighbours would recognise him now. Even if they did, they would pretend not to. He knew his family would've been the subject of much gossip: entertainment for the curtain-twitchers. His mum had been screaming at the bailiffs as a policewoman ushered the two of them away: the start of their journey up the Fylde coast and down the social ladder. He had been happy there – until the night a police officer had knocked on their door to tell them that they had found his dad. The lifeboat crew had fished his lifeless body from the sea.

He looked in the cigarette packet. Just one left. He took it out and lit it, then looked at his watch. Twenty past two. Michelle would be here soon. Her exam must have finished a few hours ago. She would have fags; he was sure of that. He looked back at the headstone: the foster family had paid to have his mum's name carved into the granite below his dad's. He wanted to remember his mum as she was before. Before they left their home in Lytham St Anne's. Before the depression. Before the drinking. Before the men. Before the cancer. Before her hair fell out and the tumours invaded her brain, changing her into a nasty old witch.

She'd gone from the bedsit in Cleveleys into a hospice, and he'd gone to a foster family in Fleetwood. Until the social worker had turned up the day after the funeral and taken him to the children's home. He didn't protest, just packed up his things. They had been nice people: they had come with him and stood there, right in front of where he was now, on the day of the funeral. Afterwards he had sat in the garden at their house, stroking their little girl's rabbit. Gliding his hands across its soft brown fur … then watching its big round eyes as he squeezed its neck until its little legs stopped kicking. The girl – Tilly – had screamed the place down when she'd found Benjamin Bunny dead in his hutch the next day.

He hoped Michelle would be here soon, and in a good mood. He wanted to run through his plan with her. It was simple, really. He could hole up here until she got her flat. It would only be a few weeks at most. Then he could live there. He could help out with jobs in the house. Fix up discarded electronic bits and sell them on at boot fairs. In a few weeks the fire would be old news; no one would be looking for him any more. He knew she would go for it. She had to, after all he had done for her. He was on her side. Maybe then she would start to love him back.

Where was she? There was no sign of her, just a man and a woman walking along the path towards him. Maybe he could ask them for a cigarette. The woman looked familiar...

Fuck. It was the social worker. They must have followed Michelle here. He got up and turned to run, then he saw a policeman waiting at the other end of the path. He took off between the headstones. There were shouts. They called his name, but he didn't look back. Then his foot caught on a raised ledger stone and he was falling.

Then ... nothing.

Chapter 23

Day 3: Thursday 15th June 2023

Doyle had been pleased to see that the incident room was already a hive of activity when he arrived just after six thirty. He'd grabbed himself a coffee and had a brief catch-up with Hales and Morgan. Now he stood in front of the evidence board with the team, ready for the morning briefing.

He did notice one absentee: Detective Superintendent Croucher. Hopefully he was tied up at Force HQ and would remain so for some time. The big board was now adorned with many more photos and snippets of information than twenty-four hours earlier, including some photos of Chloe Kennedy from the post-mortem. Alongside this, a collection of pins protruded from the wall map.

'A quick recap of where we are,' Doyle said as the stragglers took their seats. 'Ryan Johnson, the ex-boyfriend. His alibi seems to check out, and you haven't found anything of interest on his car, have you, Jen?'

'We're still waiting on results from the tests on soil samples from the tyres and wheel arches, but it doesn't look like there will be anything to confirm it'd been driven to Anglezarke. We didn't find any obvious bits of the distinctive rock you get there. We did a thorough taping of the boot and didn't find any fibres that could have come from the tracksuit Chloe was found in, or the clothes she was wearing when she went missing.'

'Which means, for now at least, we don't consider Johnson a suspect,' Doyle went on. 'But don't worry – we're not going to let him walk out of here empty-handed. The CPS are currently deciding what they can charge him with, and he will be visiting a magistrate this morning.' There was a general mumble of approval. 'Was our friend Miss Finch able to attend when you interviewed him last night?' Doyle asked the two bleary-eyed DCs from the night shift.

'She was, sir, yes. With the other things taking priority, we weren't able to get on to it until half past three in t' morning, and unfortunately, she was none too pleased to be woken up at that time,' the one with the beard reported back, earning himself a few chuckles of approval. Clearly the solicitor was not well thought of.

'This guy. Elliot Parker.' Doyle pointed to a blown-up image on the board. 'The caretaker at the school Chloe worked at. Derrick, Gadget, want to let everyone know where we are with that?'

'Go on, young Gadget,' Birdseye said.

'We did wonder if he could be involved, as he had struck me as a bit odd when we visited the school on Tuesday. He had also been with Chloe when she kicked Johnson out of her house, but he didn't mention this to us. On top of that, he'd liked quite a lot of Chloe's social media posts and written the odd comment. It just felt a bit creepy for a man over twenty years older than her.'

'He doesn't have much of an alibi for the Friday night – told us he stayed in.' Birdseye picked up the thread. 'But on Saturday morning he went to Preston by train and picked up his daughter. They spent the day at Blackpool then she stayed the night at his house, which is attached to the school. I checked with his ex-wife last night, and she confirmed this.'

'Could he not have kept Chloe somewhere on the school

premises and killed her when the kid was watching a film or sleeping or something?' PC Price, who was still assigned to the team, asked.

'We checked the alarm log for the school. It had been set on the Friday and not unset until Monday morning,' Gadget said. 'Besides, he doesn't have access to a vehicle either, and if I'm honest, on chatting to him again, it just didn't strike me that he could've done it. I think DS Morgan was right yesterday when she said he was more midlife crisis than murderer.'

'Well, it was worth following up,' Doyle said. 'If you get a feeling about something – a hunch or whatever you like to call it – it needs checking out. And that goes for all of you. If something seems out of place, even if you can't put your finger on it, follow it up. Find out what that something is.' Doyle was pleased to see Gadget smile at his public vote of confidence. He didn't want any of his team, especially the younger members, being afraid to use their brains and explore ideas. Many a case had been cracked open on a hunch.

'This guy.' Doyle indicated Mohammed Khan's photo. 'Came into the frame yesterday evening. Geoff, do you want to fill everyone in?'

'Khan is a driver for Alpha Cars. He was seen on a CCTV camera here.' The Pearl jabbed at a pin among a cluster on the map. 'At 1.28 on Saturday morning. He was not then seen on the camera here, further along Market Street. This means he had to have turned off either down Cheapside or Cunliffe Street, where Chloe Kennedy was last seen at 1.21. He dropped off his last fare at 1.08 in Holmeswood. For those who don't know, that's twelve miles away, towards Southport. He picked up his next job on Park Road, at the other end of town, at 1.44.'

'He could easily have picked up Chloe and either gagged her or drugged her and stuck her in the boot in that time,' one of the local CID officers, who was just starting his morning shift said.

'That's what we figured, so we arrested him yesterday,' Hales went on. 'He was quite forthcoming in interview, and said he went there as Chloe Kennedy had been assigned to him and then the job got cancelled when he was en route. He said a similar thing had happened to another driver, Amir Hussain, the previous weekend, and the job had been cancelled by mistake.'

'Guys.' Doyle nodded at the two CID officers from the night shift, whose names he couldn't recall. He would check after the briefing and try to commit them to memory. He couldn't keep thinking of them as Baldy and Beardy. 'Do you want to explain what you uncovered last night?'

'Sure, boss,' Beardy said. 'What Khan told us – about Amir picking up a job the previous weekend that had been cancelled – is true. He got the customer to phone up the office and book it in, then took her home. The job was at roughly the same time and place: late Friday night, picking up from Cunliffe Street. And get this: the passenger was Chloe Kennedy.'

Eyebrows were raised and there were some gasps from those in the room who weren't privileged enough to already have this information.

'That's a hell of a coincidence, isn't it, boss?' Birdseye said.

'It certainly is,' Doyle said. 'And I believe in coincidences as much as I believe in that guy with a white beard and red suit who delivers presents at Christmas.'

'Harsh way to break the news about Santa to Gadget, boss. He'd already started writing his list,' Morgan said.

'I thought he was talking about Birdseye,' Gadget said. 'Though I always thought he was older than Father Christmas.'

There was some laughter, and Doyle saw Birdseye flick Gadget the Vs.

Baldy took up where Beardy had left off. 'When we checked the records, we found that Dani Wheeler had also booked a cab the previous week. She was picked up around five minutes before Hussain arrived.'

'When I got the dashcam footage from Hussain, I downloaded everything,' Gadget said. 'I can check and see if the previous week is still there.'

'Great, do that straight after this. Check everything – every parked car, every person on the street. There might have been an attempt to take her the previous week, or a dress rehearsal, even,' Doyle said.

'Isn't it a bit odd that when you two spoke with Amir on Tuesday, he didn't mention that he had this cancelled fare with Chloe Kennedy the week before?' Birdseye asked, looking at Morgan and Gadget.

'We did ask him about that,' Beardy said. 'He told us it didn't occur to him, as they were asking about the Friday just gone. He said he did mention to them that he had picked both girls up several times in the past.'

'That's true,' Morgan said.

'Although this confirms what Khan told us in interview yesterday, it doesn't rule him out,' Doyle said. 'How did you get on with following up his alibi?'

'We checked the cab firm records,' Baldy said. 'He worked that Friday night until 5.30 a.m. Saturday. Then he was back in at 7.30 p.m. Saturday and worked through to 5.45 a.m. Sunday. That night was rammed; there wasn't more than twenty minutes between jobs at any time.'

'We did wonder…' Beardy picked up the story. 'If it was Khan who did it, whether that's why the body wasn't dumped until the Sunday night, even though she died on Saturday. Perhaps he was driving round Saturday night with her in the boot, with the intention of disposing of her, but he was too busy with work. By the time he got free it would have been light. His shift on Sunday night was much quieter, and he would have had ample opportunity to get rid of her then.'

'Not possible,' said Jen Knight, getting up and walking to the evidence board. She pointed to a photograph taken in the morgue of Chloe Kennedy's lower legs and feet. 'To get this amount of livor mortis, Chloe would have had to hang with her feet and ankles as her lowest point for many hours after death – that's why the blood pooled here, leaving this deep colouration. There was no way she was in the boot of a car Saturday night.'

'Which raises the question, what was her killer doing with her for all that time?' Hales said.

'Could he have been fucking her after she was dead?' Price asked.

Doyle looked at him. The man was naturally crude, but he was only asking what several others in the room were thinking.

'Dr Gupta says it does not appear there had been any significant sexual assault post-mortem,' Doyle said.

'The reason for waiting so long could be more practical than to do with a sexual motive around the killing,' Knight said. 'We know from the PM that Chloe died at some point on Saturday – the level of lividity in her feet and ankles shows that. We assume that she was taken to the deposition site in a vehicle. It's June, so it doesn't get fully dark until just before ten o'clock, and it's light again by twenty to five. If Chloe was thrown over that cliff face in daylight, anyone driving or even walking or cycling past could have seen.'

'But why not do it in the early hours on Sunday morning?' Hales asked.

'Rigor mortis,' said Knight. 'Typically, it sets in within four hours of death and can last up to eight hours, depending on the temperature. Chloe was quite slight but she wouldn't have fitted in the boot of a car without being bent in half or her knees tucked up. Dr Gupta thinks she died at some point Saturday – most likely, in the afternoon. There is no way you would be folding her up into the boot of a car with rigor present. You would either have to wait till it passed or chop her up.'

An interesting point, Doyle thought, and he had to acknowledge he hadn't considered this. 'Which brings us back to Khan. If he is involved and, that is looking like a very big "if" at this stage, then Chloe would have been in the boot of his car at some point. Forensics are going over it now. Although we won't get any absolutes today, we will get a pretty good idea of whether they've found any fibres that could have come from Chloe's clothes. If not, we have to let him go, as we don't really have much on him. And if that does happen, then in terms of probable suspects we are left with the square root of fuck all.'

'Have we had anything back from the press conference?' Bowen asked.

'Good question, Jim,' Hales said. 'So far, nothing, but it's been all over the internet and has hit the printed media this morning. Most of the nationals have put a column in about it.'

'If Chloe Kennedy decided for whatever reason to walk home, then someone will have seen her,' Doyle said. 'If not, then she either left in a car or went into a property somewhere nearby. We need to focus on the area around Cunliffe Street. Gadget, you and Bowen go back over every piece of footage. Every car that went anywhere near there at the time needs to be traced, the driver checked out and contacted, in case they saw anything or have a dashcam. DS Morgan, can you take everyone not needed elsewhere? We need to check every building in the surrounding streets. Knock on every door. See who was there at the time. Check every business premises. Anyone who doesn't seem right, check them out. And all of you, remember: anything that comes up, however small, make sure you pass it on to DI Hales and Mandy over there so it can be put on the Holmes 2 database.'

Mandy half raised a hand so everyone could see who she was. Doyle hoped he had got her name right; it might be Sandy. Another name he'd have to check – and try to remember.

It was just after eight when the briefing finally finished and Doyle checked his personal email, which was still the only one he had access to. He was pleased to see that he had already received a message from Bea. She had sent the brochure of the house that had been set on fire. He rattled off a quick reply thanking her, before opening the attachment, briefly wondering whether he should put an 'x' at the end of his message, as she had done. He decided not to, as he never did that, and she probably did it all the time; it wasn't aimed specifically at him.

When he looked at the picture of the property, he rushed over to Knight, who was on her way out of the incident room.

'Jen, have a look at this,' Doyle said, showing her the phone. 'It's the estate agent's brochure of the house in the arson attack on Sunday night. Look at that...' He zoomed in on a photo that showed the inside of a garage.

'That's interesting. I wasn't on that job, as I was put on this one.'

'Shall we take a look?'

Chapter 24

The acrid smell in the garage was strong enough to penetrate the paper mask that Doyle wore, alongside the disposable onesie complete with hood, overshoes and gloves. The scene bore no resemblance to the photo of the home gym that adorned the estate agent's brochure. There were still the metal carcasses of workout benches and some blackened weights, but every bit of fabric had been burned beyond recognition. Doyle wondered if the pile of discoloured sand in one corner had been inside the punchbag in the photo. It wasn't in the centre of the room, where the hook it had hung on lay on the sodden floor. The timber beam it had been fixed to now presumably formed part of the ashes that had been spread around the room by the fire brigade's hoses. He made his way to the middle of the room, to the hook.

'See those cut-outs in the brickwork?' Knight pointed to each side of the room. 'They're what the ceiling beams would have run between. The hook would have been attached to one of them, at that height.'

Doyle noticed that some of the roof beams above had survived. 'According to the initial forensic report, the fire started here, on the floor. How tall are you?' he asked Knight.

'Five foot six.'

'And Chloe was five foot five. Do me a favour – hold your arms above your head like this.' Doyle held his own arms above his head, crossed at the wrists, and Knight copied without question. He looked between the brickwork where the beam would have sat and her raised arms. 'Taking into account that you're an inch taller and your feet are flat on the floor, it looks to me like this could be where Chloe was strung up, sexually assaulted and killed.' A shiver ran up Doyle's spine as the words left his mouth.

'I think you could be right,' Knight said.

'What did they get from the scene?' Doyle asked. 'Anything useful?'

'Not that I could see, from a brief scan of the report before we came up here. But they weren't looking for anything to link this place to a possible murder scene. The team here were looking at how and where the fire started. Once they established that it was probably arson, they looked for anything that might give them a clue to who did it.'

'We're going to need to go over it again, see if we uncover anything else.'

'We're pretty stretched at the moment, but I'll see if we can get more people in. I'll go through the forensic report again, and the exhibits list, and see if there's anything there that could be useful.'

Doyle stopped to think. The house was double-fronted, with the garage adjoining the left-hand side. The part of the house next to the garage was pretty badly damaged by the fire, but other than smoke damage, the other side was largely untouched. 'When the SOCOs were here the other day, would they have fingerprinted the whole house, or just around where the fire was, and where whoever lit it might have got in?'

'Honestly, I'm not sure. With a house this size and with no loss of life, they might just have concentrated on the potential entry. If other parts looked like they hadn't been disturbed, they would probably have left them. Resources are tight. A print found nowhere near the fire wouldn't prove anything, other than that person had been at the house at some point.

Everyone knows about fingerprints these days, and even a group of pyromaniac kids would know to wear gloves.'

'I want the whole house dusted, particularly the bits that aren't fire-damaged. All the obvious surfaces someone looking around might touch – door handles, cupboard door handles, light switches, that kind of thing,' Doyle said.

'OK, but do you really think that's necessary? It will take a while, and surely the killer will have known to wear gloves. There was no trace of his DNA or a clothing fibre or anything on Chloe's body.'

'Maybe, but this house was up to let, and if our killer decided to view it, it would be a bit odd if he turned up in summer wearing gloves, don't you think?'

⚔ ⚔ ⚔

Bea had been right, Doyle thought as he drove back up the narrow lane that linked the property to the main road fifty yards away. The house was remote – but it wasn't *that* remote. Locals might still have noticed something. From what Doyle knew of people living in quiet rural settings, they often paid a lot more attention to what was going on compared to those who lived cheek by jowl with neighbours in urban areas. Someone had seen the fire that night, after all, and called the fire brigade. If they hadn't, the whole house would have burned down. Perhaps if Chloe was murdered there, the killer had banked on the house being destroyed – and that it wouldn't be linked to the case. If so, this could well be the break they needed.

As he turned onto the main road, he called Bea's number.

'Well, good morning to you, Detective Chief Inspector.' Her cheery Liverpudlian voice rang out through the car's speakers. 'What can I do for you today? I see you got my email.'

'I did, and thank you for that. In fact, I'm just on my way back from there now and I could do with a bit more info. How long has it been on the market to let?'

'I'll have to check, but it must be around five or six weeks. The owner used to live there with his family before they moved to Dubai. It was rented until just after Christmas to some friends, and then after they left he decided to get it fully refurbished before letting it again. To be honest, we advised him against that. There's not a huge demand for renting those big family houses, and he would've been better off selling it and buying a couple of smaller places like the one you looked at last night.'

'I see.'

'I think it was his wife, to be honest. I don't know for sure, but call it a woman's intuition, I think she still had hopes that they would move back. Well, I guess that idea has gone up in smoke now. Literally.'

'Do you know if anyone viewed it?'

'There were a couple of viewings, but I didn't do them. We have someone else who deals with rental viewings… Wait, you don't think that it's somehow connected to the murder, do you? Is that why you're so interested in it?'

'I…' Doyle paused for just a fraction of a second too long. Normally, fobbing someone off was second nature to him. 'Honestly? I'm not sure, Bea.'

'Jesus. Do you think she was killed there? You said on the TV she was killed somewhere else, not where she was found. Is that what you're thinking? The poor girl was murdered there? It's been all over the press and social media this morning.'

'I don't know, but we need to check it out. If you could do me a massive favour, it would really help. Can you get the details of everyone who viewed the property, and the person who did the viewings? We'll need to speak to them today. But please don't tell anyone why we're interested. This is just about the fire, if anyone wants to know.'

'My lips are sealed. And it's Eve you need to speak to – she will have done the viewings, but she doesn't work Thursdays as she always works Saturdays. I'll send you her number, but she's notoriously hard to get hold of on her days off. I can dig out the details of anyone who viewed it.'

'Thanks, Bea, you're an absolute star.'

'You've given me the creeps. To think, he might have been here in our office…'

'Sorry – try not to think too much about it. If the house is connected, then the killer will be giving your offices a wide berth.'

'I guess I'll have to take your word for that.'

'I guess so, but if you're worried about anyone or anything, call me.'

⊥ ⊥ ⊥

A thought occurred to Bowen as he and Gadget were trawling through the CCTV footage from around the time Chloe had disappeared. They were noting down the number plates of any cars in the vicinity, and screenshotting people on the streets. All would have to be traced and checked, as they could hold vital information. The killer might even be among them.

'Have you looked through the footage from that old man's house on Victoria Street?' Bowen asked.

'No. I thought you said there was nothing useful on it?'

'That was when we were looking for Ryan Johnson going between the bar and Cunliffe Street. I was looking for Johnson on foot, or his car. But I'm pretty sure another car went past at the time – a taxi.'

'Let me find it,' Gadget said, searching through files on the computer. 'Is this it? Private CCTV, Mr Gray, Victoria Street?'

'That's the one.'

Gadget opened the file and the wide-angle image from Mr Gray's camera filled the screen.

'Start at one o'clock and run it through on times six until we see the car,' Bowen said. Gadget did as instructed. The pair watched the image silently for several minutes. Beams of headlights came into view, and Gadget slowed the playback in time to see a light-coloured car go past. He rewound the image and paused it, showing the rear view of the car. It was a Prius with an Alpha Cars sticker on the back.

'Did you check the time and date on the system when you were there?'

'I did it. It was one minute fast.'

'Right, so 1.21 a.m. The same time that Dani Wheeler was being driven off in Hussain's car, and two minutes before Chloe's phone is turned off.'

'That's Mohammed Khan's registration number.'

'Are you sure?'

'Yes, certain.'

'And he told us he went straight to Cunliffe Street from Market Street, where he was picked up on CCTV. He didn't mention this little detour a few minutes earlier. Boss!' Gadget shouted.

Bowen turned, expecting to see DI Hales, but DCI Doyle was also there, having just entered the incident room. Both men came rushing over.

'What have you got?' Doyle asked.

'This is Victoria Street. It runs parallel to Market Street.' Bowen was aware that his voice had gone up an octave. 'And look at the time and date.'

Doyle and Hales studied the image in the screen. It showed a Toyota Prius, with an Alpha Cars sticker next to the registration plate and a little dent next to the Toyota badge.

'That's Khan's registration number,' Doyle said.

'You had it memorised?' Hales said. 'I'm impressed.'

'I spent ten minutes on the phone yesterday when you guys arrested Khan, staring at the boot of his car. It's not that impressive.'

'This means Khan lied to us,' Gadget said. 'This has to be a breakthrough. He could have driven up to Cunliffe Street and picked up Chloe. Drugged her or knocked her out or something, then cancelled the job on the app on her phone and turned it off.'

'Seems plausible,' Hales said. 'But why would he have driven back round and down Market Street afterwards?'

'I don't know. Maybe—'

'Perhaps he was covering his tracks in case of witnesses.' Bowen interrupted.

'Go on,' said Doyle.

'Well, if anyone remembers seeing his car in the vicinity, being picked up on the Market Street camera after the job is cancelled gives him an innocent explanation for being there.'

'Maybe,' Hales said. 'Did Dr Gupta say when we were likely to get the toxicology results back? We should know if Chloe was drugged then.'

'Hopefully today or tomorrow latest,' Doyle said. 'That's great work, you two. It feels like we're getting close, but we're not quite there. Let's gather what more we can now, then get Khan in the interview room again later. If nothing else, we now have grounds to keep him longer. There's just something nagging at me, and I can't put my finger on what it is yet.'

'Sir.' It was one of the civilian staff addressing Doyle. 'Sorry to interrupt, but I've got a call for you from IT. They said it was urgent.'

'Thanks. Can you put IT through to my office?'

He answered the phone when he entered his temporary office off the incident room. 'DCI Doyle.'

'Hi, it's Mike from IT.' No surname and no accountability, Doyle noted. 'I hear you've been having problems logging into your email.'

'That's right,' Doyle said, having a quiet word with himself not to lose his temper. 'I've also had problems getting hold of you. I've left several messages on your voicemail.'

'Oh yeah, that's not checked.'

But someone *had* checked it, and complained about the abuse Doyle had left them.

174

'We say to email any problems you have, and that raises a job number.'

'Do you think there might be a tiny difficulty with that if your issue is that you can't access your email?'

'Yeah, maybe, I guess, but you could always phone us then.'

Doyle rubbed his head. He wondered if some of these IT people were actually human and not some kind of shit robots that hadn't been programmed properly before they left the factory. 'OK, I'm a bit pressed for time, so would you be able to give me my email login now, so I can get back to what I was doing?'

'Oh, I can't give it to you over the phone. Security and all that. I could email it to you.'

Doyle took a deep breath, his free hand balling into a fist 'Do you think there might be a little problem with that, Mike?'

There was a short pause. Doyle was happy to wait to see if this IT genius could work it out.

'Oh, yeah. I guess.'

'Do you have my work mobile number on your system?'

'Oh yes, it's here with all your details.'

'Great. Can you text me my login info then?'

'I guess so. Good idea. I'll do that.'

Doyle waited until he was sure that he'd hung up before he roared, in a voice that would have been heard across the incident room, 'Fucking bunch of useless dickheads!'

Chapter 25

There were many unpleasant tasks to be carried out over the course of a murder investigation, but the one Derrick 'Birdseye' Nelson found himself doing now wasn't one of them. After getting the call from the DCI, he had visited Mrs Walker, the woman who had called 999 on the night of the fire. She hadn't been able to tell him much, other than it was her dog barking that had woken her. She had gone downstairs to let him out, and seen the orange glow of the flames. She knew they had been coming from the empty house up the road.

After thanking Mrs Walker for all her help – and the tea and cake – Birdseye decided to walk around the small village of Limbrick, knock on a few doors, chat to a few people, and see what he could dig up.

The dry summer weather was still holding up, making it a very pleasant day for a stroll. Birdseye was walking along a small lane towards some houses when a collie came bounding towards him, tail wagging. He gave the dog a pat and a stroke while the owner, a man who looked to be around his own age, caught the dog up.

'Sorry about him, he's a bit over-friendly,' the man said.

'I used to have one just like him. Do you live round here?'

'Up there by the river. It's lovely and quiet, especially on a day like today. But not so far from civilisation that you feel cut off. Are you thinking of moving here?'

'Not exactly, sir, no,' Birdseye said, fishing in his pocket and producing his warrant card. 'I'm investigating the fire that happened on Sunday night. Did you hear about it?'

'Oh, yes. Something like that is big news round here. We were woken up by the fire engines. If you're investigating, I'm guessing you must think it is arson, then?'

'That's right, Mr ...'

'Downs, Kenneth Downs. Crikey. I thought it must have been accidental – that the new people moving in had left something on, or something.'

'New people, Mr Downs? What made you think someone had moved in there?'

'Well, I saw a car coming back from the house, down the lane. It was one of those electric jobbies – damn thing nearly ran me over. Didn't hear it coming.'

'When was this?'

'Let me see, it would have been Saturday morning. Quite early, about half past seven.'

'Are you sure of that? Saturday morning?'

'Yes, I was out walking Chester here. He needs a lot of walking, and I like to wear him out before breakfast. It must have been Saturday, as on Sundays I walk him up to church in Rivington instead. Hilary drives, and we stick him in the back of the car to sleep during the service.'

'You said the car was electric. Can you remember anything about it? What colour was it? The make or model?'

'Yes, it was white – one of those Toyota ones that has an engine and electric. It was some kind of taxi; it had logos on it. I assumed it was returning from dropping people off at the house.'

'Did you see the driver, or anyone else on board?'

'No, sorry. I don't think there was anyone else, and I didn't see the driver. He tore past once I had got out of the way. You know what these cab drivers are like, always dashing about like bloody lunatics.'

⅄ ⅄ ⅄

The energy in the incident room bumped up a level as the morning's developments were passed between team members. Everyone sensed that they were getting somewhere, and the pieces in the middle of the jigsaw were falling into place. But Doyle couldn't shake the nagging feeling that he was missing something. Maybe it was what Morgan had said after the interview last night, about Khan being too nice to be the killer. She certainly had a point. He had felt the same too, but the evidence was stacking up against him. It wasn't that, though. An image came into his mind, and he crossed the incident room to Gadget's desk. 'Pull up that still from Victoria Street with the back of the cab, will you?'

'Yes, boss,' Gadget said, operating the mouse to bring the CCTV images up on his screen.

'There.' Doyle pointed to the car's Toyota badge. 'That dent wasn't on Khan's car yesterday.'

'You sure, boss?' Gadget asked.

'Yes. I spent ten minutes staring at it while I was on the phone yesterday.'

'He must have had it repaired since Friday night, then. Forensics should be able to check the paint on that part of the boot and see how old it is.'

'Maybe. Is there another image of his car from Friday night from behind, so we can see the dent?'

'The one on Market Street is front on, but we did clock him on the approach to the Clifford Street roundabout. Give me one moment, boss, and I'll find it.'

As Gadget looked through the files, Morgan entered the incident room. She strode over. 'I hear we've made some good progress. Looks like I was wrong, and Khan is our man.'

'We've made progress, yes. But you might not have been wrong about Khan. I'll be able to tell you one way or another in about a minute.'

'Oh?'

'Got it, boss,' Gadget said as an image flashed up on his screen. The short bit of dual carriageway it depicted was empty, apart from a Toyota Prius.

'Zoom in,' Doyle commanded. 'There, look. No dent, and there's mud splattered on the back bumper. That wasn't on the other image. Khan must have had a hell of a seven minutes getting that dent repaired and then getting the back of his car covered in mud. How did he do it?'

After a few more mouse clicks, Gadget had the images side by side on the screen. From the dent on one car and the mud splatter on the other it was clear that, although the registration plates displayed the same number, they weren't the same car.

'Someone's masqueraded as Khan and picked up Chloe Kennedy before he could get there,' Morgan said.

'Exactly,' said Doyle. 'The question is, who?'

'Boss, look at this.' Gadget had pulled another clip up on the screen. 'This is the dashcam footage from the previous week, from Amir Hussain's car. We looked at it straight after the morning briefing, like you said, in case there had been an aborted attempt at taking Chloe, or a dress rehearsal.' Gadget moved the clip to the point he wanted, then played it at half speed. 'This is after he picked up Chloe Kennedy. Watch further up the road. That's Victoria Street.'

The young detective paused the image. There was the unmistakable shape of the front of a Toyota Prius protruding from the junction, waiting to turn right onto Cunliffe Street.

'We didn't think too much of it this morning. You don't see the full front of the car, so you can't get a registration number from it.'

'The footage from the private camera on Victoria Street — have you got it going back to that date too?' Doyle asked.

'Afraid not, but it might still be on his system. Jim only downloaded footage from the night she went missing.'

'Right' said Doyle. 'Bowen, get your arse over here.' His voice boomed across the room.

The young PC came scurrying, a look of panic on his face. 'Yes, sir?'

'You're going to introduce me to your friend on Victoria Street, and we're going to see if we can get some more footage from his CCTV,' Doyle said. 'And while we're gone, you two can bring everyone else up to speed.'

⅄ ⅄ ⅄

'I've seen you on the telly,' Mr Gray said. 'So, the monkey's brought the organ grinder round. It must be serious. Bet it's not about my hanging baskets, though.'

'Afraid not, Mr Gray. It was terrible what happened to your hanging baskets, though,' Doyle said. 'Some young people these days – they have no respect. Would you mind if we come in for a minute? See if we can get some more footage from your CCTV system.'

'Suit yourselves. The young man knows where it is and how to work it.' Gray turned and walked back into his house, leaving the officers to follow him. 'Are you a cockney?'

'Close enough,' Doyle said. Bowen went straight over to the CCTV equipment.

'You think you'll catch him then?'

'The killer?' Doyle asked.

'Yes, of course the bloody killer. I didn't mean the kids who smashed up my hanging baskets.'

Doyle saw Bowen smirk. 'I'm pretty hopeful we will, yes.'

'Here, take a look,' Bowen said.

The image was frozen. The date stamp showed 01.28, but on the previous Saturday morning. A Toyota Prius with a dent in the back, just as before. The number plate was different, though. Doyle checked it against the number he had scribbled on a sticky note before they left the police station. As he had thought, this time the car displayed Amir Hussain's registration plates.

'Great – get a copy of that. Thank you, Mr Gray. You have been most helpful. Thanks to you, we're a lot closer to catching the killer. But do us a favour.' Doyle tapped his nose. 'Don't mention to anyone that we got that footage.'

'No, no, of course not, Detective. Always happy to help.'

ᴧ ᴧ ᴧ

'OK. Thoughts?' Doyle addressed the team members seated around his desk. He had his own ideas and was developing a few hypotheses, but he wanted to hear what the others had to say first. He was aware that he was the boss, and a new one at that. If he came up with all the suggestions, it would be easy for the others just to agree. He wanted them to think about the problem, come up with their own ideas.

'Chloe was a definite target. We can now be reasonably certain of that,' Morgan said. 'And it looks like there was an attempt to take her the previous week.'

'Agreed,' Doyle said.

'Whoever killed her knew which car had been allocated to pick her up both times, and was able to change their plates to match the cab plates. So they had already had the plates made,' Hales said.

'Does this put Ryan Johnson back in the frame? He might have had the app on his phone linked to hers,' Gadget suggested. 'Is that possible?'

'Perhaps,' said Doyle. 'Let's look at everything else and see where it's taking us.'

'There are still some unknowns about this that don't make sense,' Morgan said.

'Go on,' Doyle encouraged.

'Assuming the person who did this had planned it in advance, he would know that for the last six weeks Chloe had been going out on Friday nights with Dani Wheeler. They left at the same time and waited for cabs together. How would the killer know that Dani's cab would arrive first? We saw how the app works. How would the killer know which woman would be left waiting? And no doubt a few times the cabs would turn up together.'

'Just a thought…' Bowen said.

'Go on, Jim.'

'They ended each night drinking in the Manhattan Project, which is a gay bar. Now, I know Chloe wasn't gay, but Dani is, and whoever did it could have assumed that Chloe was gay too. It might have been motivated by homophobia – or hatred of women. The killer might not have cared which woman he got, and just taken the one that was left on her own.'

'Could make sense,' Hales said.

'But what about the cars?' Morgan said. 'Not all the drivers use the same type of car. Would someone who planned things so meticulously in other ways have sat there every week waiting for one of the girls to be allocated a white Prius from Alpha Cars?'

'It does seem too random,' Hales agreed.

'What if there were two of them working together?' Birdseye suggested. 'You said that the controller also books cabs on the system. What if *they* were selecting the cabs that got sent to pick up Chloe? It wouldn't be such a random waiting game then.'

'That's a very good point, Derrick. I think you might be getting somewhere close with that,' Doyle said.

'It wouldn't necessarily have to be the controller,' Morgan said. 'In fact, it's more likely it would be someone who had hacked into the system – or had administration rights.'

'Should we get back to the cab firm with a warrant and go through their IT system, boss?' Gadget said.

Doyle took a moment to think. 'I don't know about anyone else, but I'm getting a bit of an uncomfortable feeling. We've been back and forward to Alpha Cars, each time getting more information. It's starting to look, to me, like whoever is responsible for Chloe's murder has a connection to them. If that is the case, every time we go back there, there is a possibility of them seeing how the case is progressing, what we're asking, and how close we're getting to them. If we go marching in there and seize their equipment, it will be days before we get all the information off it, possibly weeks, and our killer will know what we're thinking.'

'What about the app company?' Morgan said.

'Go on,' Doyle said.

'Well, Alpha Cars use an app developed by another company. When we were there on Tuesday, they told us they'd just had an engineer out to look into the cancelled bookings problem. Maybe we should be looking there?'

'A very good point. They should be able to clarify if what we have been told about the bookings is correct, if bookings can be overridden, and who has admin rights,' Doyle said.

'It's Dudley App Solutions Ltd,' Asif said, looking up from her computer. 'It might surprise you to know they're based in Birmingham, not Dudley.'

'Right. Morgan, you get down there. Take Gadget with you,' Doyle said. 'You two have got the best chance of understanding the IT geeks.'

'I'm not sure whether that's a compliment or an insult,' Morgan said.

'We'll phone ahead. Let them know you're coming, but not why,' said Doyle. 'We'll make sure you get to see the people at the top straight away. If we get any resistance whatsoever, we will get a warrant and shut down their whole operation until this is resolved.'

'There are two listed directors, boss,' Asif said. 'Looks like they're brothers. Edward Dudley is CEO and Charles Dudley is Technical Director.'

Chapter 26

With Morgan and Gadget heading down the M6. Doyle began to feel the first pangs of hunger. It was almost one in the afternoon, but his early start meant he'd missed the chance to gorge himself on the Premier Inn's 'all you can eat' breakfast buffet. He decided to take a walk around the town centre and find some lunch. It wouldn't hurt to get a feel for Chorley and its people. The detective felt his feet had hardly touched the ground since Tuesday. Dashing from place to place in cars, in and out of incident rooms and interview rooms, hardly gave him a sense of his new surroundings.

Then something occurred to Doyle. He wasn't just looking around a town that was the backdrop to a young woman's abduction and murder; he was looking around the town that would be the nearest to where he was about to call home. He hadn't given a lot of thought to the realities of moving north. He hadn't had the chance.

Since Fiona had decided to return to her roots after their separation, taking Harry with her, Doyle had spent every free weekend travelling up and down the country. He'd wanted to see as much of his son as he could, although it would have been easy to let things drift, put further time between visits – every other weekend becoming a few days at half-term, then a couple of weeks a year, ending up with him being a father figure rather than a parent. He had seen that happen countless times to others in his line of work; they'd struggled to balance a career and a broken family, and had finally let their family drift away. He couldn't let that happen. Harry needed him. Life was tough enough for his son without Doyle not being around. He had given serious consideration to jacking in the job, cutting his losses and doing something else. But what were his options? He didn't want to swap investigating murders and other serious crimes to work on divorce cases and insurance fraud as a private investigator. That wasn't him. Doyle liked his job, and he was good at it. But he had to find a way of stopping it getting in the way of the rest of his life.

It had been the obvious solution to move forces. He'd been thinking Greater Manchester Police. That would have been similar to the Met, or maybe even Merseyside. Then this job had come up. Detective Chief Inspector running one of Lancashire Constabulary's major investigation teams. He had the rank and the experience. It was where in the country he needed to be. He'd applied the same day. He was surprised to be asked to attend an interview the next week, and to receive a job offer the day after. He wasn't sure he was ready to be a country cop, and he wasn't sure the country cops would be ready for him, but he took the offer nonetheless. Lancashire sought references from his superiors. They were desperate for their new DCI to start. The Met couldn't wait to get rid of him, so the transfer happened far quicker than Doyle was expecting. The blood on his hands from the underground car park had washed off easily enough, but not, it seemed, the stain on his career – at least, as far as the Met was concerned.

As he looked around Chorley town centre, Doyle liked what he saw. It helped, of course, that the sun was shining for the third day in a row – which, judging from his previous experience, must be a record for Lancashire. Chorley didn't sit on the outskirts of a city or even feel like a town on the edge of a bigger town. It wasn't a suburb of Preston or Bolton or Blackburn or Wigan. It was a town of its own, nestled between countryside and moors. Only the police posters that adorned every shop window, appealing for witnesses, diminished the appeal of the place. Even those, Doyle thought, showed that the people cared and mourned the loss of one of their own.

'Are you following me, Detective Chief Inspector?'

The mocking voice made Doyle jump. 'Bea, what are you doing here?'

'I work here! I thought you might have realised that from the fact that our address is right underneath the signature on my emails. Are you sure you're a detective?'

'I never said I was a good one.'

'Are you looking for clues now?' Bea dropped her voice to a conspiratorial tone.

'No, sandwiches. I'm starving.'

'Well, in that case, I'm your girl. There's a great deli round the corner. I was just on the way there myself. Their minted lamb baguettes are divine. Why don't we get some food and pop back to my office to eat? You can sign the contracts on your house. I can also dig out all the details of the people who viewed the other property.'

人 人 人

Bea hadn't lied; the minted lamb was mouth-wateringly tasty. Doyle ate as the estate agent printed off the contracts, while eating her lunch.

Doyle noticed a newspaper on her desk. The back page of the *Lancashire Chronicle* was speculating about summer transfers for the county's football clubs. 'Is there anything in there about the murder?'

Bea tutted as she pulled the newspaper away and stuffed it in her desk drawer. 'You don't want to be reading that. All sensationalist tabloid stuff. It's a grotty rag. It's only there because we were looking at advertising in it.' She got up and crossed the room to the printer.

Doyle realised he was looking at her legs and glanced away just before she turned round, hoping she hadn't noticed.

'There you go.' Bea slapped two copies of the contract on the desk in front of him. 'You have a read and a sign of those while I look for the details of who viewed that property in Limbrick.'

Doyle had just finished scanning the documents when Bea spoke, looking at her screen.

'Only three lots of people have viewed the place since it was advertised. The most recent one was just last week, on Thursday. A Mr and Mrs Walker. On her notes Eve has written *Didn't seem too interested, looking for something a bit smaller. Retired couple wanting to downsize. Will let them know if something more suitable comes up.* The one before that was two weeks ago. A Dr Patel. Eve wrote *Just started looking for somewhere to rent, will want to buy eventually. Moving up from London for job in Manchester.* A bit like you, then. *Were looking at several more places over the weekend. Not sure if it would be too far for them to commute into Manchester.*' She paused. 'Didn't they think that Jack the Ripper might have been a doctor?'

'That's because he mutilated his victims and removed body parts. At least Chloe Kennedy wasn't violated like that.'

'Oh God, Liam, I'm sorry. I wasn't trying to make light of what happened to that poor girl. I don't want you to think I'm an evil, uncaring bitch.'

'It's OK, I don't, and you're being very helpful. You said there were three: what about the other one?'

'Monday 29th May. That's two and a bit weeks ago. A Mr Oswald. Eve wrote *Looking for somewhere for his wife and kids to live, a bit bigger than where they are now. Seemed to like the garage gym; less interested in the rest of the house. Said he had a few houses to look at, and might want another viewing with the family. Follow-up call on 5th June went straight to voicemail.*' She looked up. 'My money is on him.'

'Could be,' said Doyle.

'Oh my God, d'you really think so? You think Eve showed the killer round the property where that poor girl was killed?'

'I don't know yet. Chloe might not have been taken there, and it might be a complete red herring. But it is one area we need to look into. I – or someone from my team – will need to speak to Eve, as soon as possible, and I'll need all the contact details for everyone who has viewed the house.'

'I tried calling Eve after we spoke earlier, but she hasn't called me back. That's not unusual, though. In this weather, she's probably out walking somewhere. She'll be back in by nine tomorrow morning.'

'When someone wants to view a property, do you check their details? Check they are who they say they are?'

'Oh God. That's a bit of a bone of contention, to be honest. If someone wants to actually rent or buy somewhere, then we need to see all their details. But if they're just looking, we ask for a phone number, home address, email. We don't check them all, though; we don't have time. We'd never get any viewings done.'

'I understand. If you can get me the details you have, we'll check them out.'

'It frightens me a bit at times. It's mainly women who work here, and we go out on our own to viewings. Honestly, we haven't got a clue who anyone is, other than what they have told us. And of course, there was that Suzy Lamplugh in London, who disappeared after showing someone a property.'

'True, but that was a long time ago now. It might be worth asking to see a driving licence or similar when they get here, or, even better, ask them to send you a photo of it beforehand.'

'Now that's why you made Chief Inspector. Why hadn't I thought of that?'

Doyle smiled. 'Those notes about the viewings – do you always take them?'

'Yes, it's a good way of keeping track. If ten people see a property and say they didn't like it because they don't like the décor, for example, then we feed that back to the owner. Or if someone keeps viewing properties but never puts in an offer, we might think they're not serious about looking.'

'What did you write about me after the viewings I went on?'

'Now, that's confidential information. If you want to see that, you are going to need a warrant...'

'Shit,' Doyle said suddenly, looking at his watch.

'Somewhere you've got to be?'

'Afraid so.' He might just make it to his appointment if he could park close at Force HQ and didn't have to run halfway across the site.

人　人　人

Dudley App Solutions had their offices on the eighth floor of a plush glass-fronted building close to Birmingham city centre. When the lift doors opened, Morgan and Gadget found themselves walking into what appeared to be a games room with an American-style pool table, table tennis, and several consoles linked to huge TV screens. There was even a basketball hoop and half a court marked out in one corner.

'Nice,' Gadget said as the lift doors shut behind them.

'Are we in the right place?' Morgan said. She wasn't sure what she had been expecting, but this certainly wasn't it.

A man Morgan guessed to be in his mid-thirties, but dressed like a twelve-year-old skateboarder, wandered over. 'Are you the police dudes?' Skater Boy asked.

'I'm DS Morgan, and this is DC Washington.' Morgan held out her warrant card for an inspection, which didn't seem to be required.

'Cool,' Skater Boy said, using three syllables to pronounce the word. 'I'll take you to the Brain Zone to meet Ed and Chaz.'

He led the detectives through the company's offices, past people sitting and standing behind an assortment of quirky furniture, working on pristine white computers. Most were wearing headphones and one guy was dancing to a tune only he could hear, apparently oblivious to all else around him.

Morgan felt as if she had stepped out of the lift and into a parallel universe. By the time they reached the 'Brain Zone', she was almost disappointed to find that it was just a loudly painted office, albeit one with great views across the city.

'These are the police people you said were coming,' Skater Boy said to introduce them to the office's occupants.

'I'm DS Morgan, and this is DC Washington.'

'Welcome. I'm Eddie, and this is Charles,' one of the two men said. In comparison to Skater Boy, they looked relatively normal, in jeans and T-shirts, but Morgan had imagined the owners of a company that had made a profit of over £2 million the previous year to be dressed in pin-striped suits.

'Thank you, Joe. Can you shut the door on your way out?' Eddie said. 'Please take a seat.' He indicated a large oval table at one end of the room. 'I spoke to DI Hales on the phone. He wouldn't tell me what this was about. He just said it was serious and urgent, and you would explain when you got here.'

'That's right,' said Morgan, sitting in a plastic chair that was more comfortable than it looked. 'Sorry about the cloak and dagger. We are investigating a murder, and we hope that you might be able to help us with one of our lines of enquiry.'

Charles placed a jug of water and four glasses on the table. 'Murder, gosh. Sorry, before we start, would you like anything else? Tea or coffee, perhaps?'

'Just water's great, thanks,' Morgan answered for herself and Gadget. 'A young woman, a schoolteacher called Chloe Kennedy, was abducted last Friday night and then murdered.'

'I saw something about that online yesterday,' Eddie said.

'She regularly used a minicab company called Alpha Cars, booking each cab using the app designed by your company. But the night she was abducted, her booking was cancelled and has disappeared off Alpha Cars' system. Another car, with cloned registration plates the same as the cab that had been allocated to her, turned up and took her before the real cab could get there.'

'Sorry,' said Charles. 'Are you saying that the record of the booking disappeared from the system?'

'Yes. There is no record on the company database that any booking was made.' Morgan looked serious.

'That's not possible. Any booking, cancelled or otherwise, should remain on the system. If it's not there, then the cab was not booked. End of story.'

'Well, the driver said he received the booking in his car, and her friend, who was with her, also confirmed she booked a cab using the app,' Morgan said.

'That might be what they *said*, Detective Sergeant. But this is a computer program – it's fixed. It doesn't change. If a booking is made, it is recorded,' Charles said.

'Might it be possible that the woman didn't actually make the booking, she only *thought* she had? I mean, we have heard of that happening after people have had a few drinks,' Eddie said.

'It might, if this was the only incident of it happening, and it hadn't been confirmed by several people. But the same thing happened to this young woman the week before, with a different driver. He went and found her anyway, and the booking was manually added to the system. But there was no record of the original booking when we looked at Alpha Cars' system.'

'This is bizarre. It just doesn't make sense.'

'The manager at the cab company told me she had reported the problem of bookings being randomly cancelled, and one of your engineers had been out to look at it,' Morgan said.

'Ah, now, that wouldn't be one of our engineers, exactly,' Eddie said. 'We subcontract out all the physical support to other companies operating in the local area. Our software is used throughout the UK and Europe. It wouldn't be feasible for us to deal with that ourselves. Other companies instal it at the cab firms and in the vehicles, and deal with any issues. We just license it, issue updates and product support, that kind of thing.'

'And there was no record of any of these cancelled bookings on the system?' asked Charles. 'You are quite sure?'

'Yes. I tried it myself. I booked a cab, waited for the booking to be confirmed, then cancelled it. By the time we got to their offices, my booking wasn't on the system.'

'This is all very strange,' Charles said, punching numbers into his laptop. 'Bear with me and we will find out exactly what is going on. What did you say the name of the taxi company was?'

'Alpha Cars. In Chorley, Lancashire.'

'Got them. Right, we're in,' said Charles. 'What is the time and date of the first missing booking you're interested in?'

'Well, she was abducted on Saturday 10th June. Her friend booked her cab at 01.09.'

'OK, got that. Is her friend Dani Wheeler, pick-up in Cunliffe Street?'

'Yes, that's right.'

'Well, I can tell you that what the cab company is claiming is correct. There are no other bookings showing up at that time, or close to that location, on the operator pages,' Charles said. 'Now, I can go into the administrator pages and see if there's anything there. One moment… Shit.'

'What is it?' Morgan asked.

'Come here and I'll show you.'

Morgan, Gadget and Eddie Dudley scrambled round the desk so they could see Charles's computer screen.

'This shows me not only what the operators at the cab firm can see, but all admin activity. See here? At 00.50, administrator number 2476 logged on, and logged off at 01.52.'

'Someone was in the system playing around with it at that time?' Gadget asked. 'Can you see what they were doing?'

'I'm looking,' Charles said. 'There's nothing here to say they did anything. But if I check here… Got you.'

'What?' Morgan asked.

'Here.' Charles pointed to the screen. 'This shows all the deleted entries from that account. They're made by the administrator. Normally you wouldn't expect to find any – or, at most, one or two where a genuine mistake has been made.'

'Is this like looking in a recycle bin on Windows that hasn't been emptied?' Morgan asked.

'More or less,' said Charles. 'Except the administrator can't empty it themselves. Only we can. In fact, he probably doesn't know the bin exists. I added this to all our software so that if there was any malicious use, we'd be able to find it.'

Morgan detected a smug expression on the geek's face, which seemed aimed towards his brother. Charles, it appeared, was the programming genius in this outfit, and Eddie was the businessman. 'And what has been deleted?'

'Quite a lot. But I'm guessing this will be the most significant. At 01.09 Chloe Kennedy attempted to book a cab. The admin put that on pause. Then at 01.11 he restarted the booking, but manually assigned a cab driver who was at a location twelve miles away – Mohammed Khan. At 01.22, that booking is cancelled.'

'That's it, then,' said Morgan, getting up. 'That's him. Administrator 2476 is our man. Who is he?'

'Him, or someone who has got hold of their login details somehow,' Charles said. 'Even then, they'd need to know how to operate the system.'

'We need to know who that person is. Now,' Morgan said.

'OK. Come with me. We'll look up the subcontractor details,' Eddie said.

'Gadget, you stay with Charles. I want copies of all that information and everything else that might be useful,' Morgan said.

'See, dear brother,' Charles said, 'as I am always telling you, I am the brains behind this operation.'

Chapter 27

'Perhaps I should run through some general housekeeping bits while you get your breath back. I'm Dr Wade. You can call me Jackie. Can I call you Liam?'

'Sure.' *Christ, I'm unfit. I've still got a stitch.*

'I'm a clinical and forensic psychologist. I have spent much of my career working at Ashworth high-security psychiatric hospital. I'm semi-retired now and, among other things, I carry out psychotherapy and psychological assessment for police officers.'

'Which of those am I here for?'

'Good question. I suspect a bit of both.'

'So, you could sign me off as unfit to work?'

'Only if you are unfit to work. Perhaps you'd like some water?'

Can she see my hand shake as I pour the water? It's cold and satiating. I can't resist another glass.

'Now, I know you had psychological treatment in London, but I'm afraid your notes haven't made it up here yet. But I understand it was after you shot a man dead. Would you like to tell me what happened?'

No, but I'm going to have to, or risk being signed off work. 'I had no choice. He'd killed his partner and had a knife to her daughter's throat.'

'OK… Something I'm curious about: is it usual for homicide detectives in the Met to carry guns?'

'No, but this time was different.'

'Go on.'

'I was an authorised firearms officer from my previous role in the flying squad, and had kept that up to date after transferring to Major Investigations. We were called in to investigate the murder of a woman in Southwark, and it turned out it was her partner who had killed her. He had quite a record – dealing, gangs, violence. We were all set up to make the arrest, then I got a call from an assistant commissionaire telling us to hold off.'

'Why?'

'Good question. Apparently, he was part of a drug supply network and had been under surveillance for weeks when we turned up in the middle of their operation. They were expecting him to be making a big pick-up in the next couple of days, which would lead them to some bigger players in the network.'

'How did that make you feel?'

'I was furious. Murder trumps drug dealing, and we were ordered not to make an arrest. This guy was dangerous. I insisted that members of our team were involved from that point on, and because of the risk, anyone authorised was armed.'

'Why did you insist? Didn't you trust the surveillance team?'

'He had committed a murder while they were watching him. They either hadn't noticed or hadn't reported it.'

'And when you shot this chap, were you still furious then?'

Jesus, this is like being cross-examined in the witness box. 'No. I was doing my job. He had just killed someone and had a knife to a kid's throat. I shouted two warnings.'

'That must have been terrifying. Were you worried you would accidentally hit the girl?'

'No. He was standing, holding the girl at his waist. I aimed for his head.' *How many more times will I have to tell this lie? I can't change the story now, having said it in the original statement. I can't tell her he was holding the girl to his chest, just six inches below where the bullet hit. A sudden pain, centre of the chest. Just breathe, it will pass. Don't close your eyes or you'll see it all again – the blood, the panic. The moment that seemed to last for ever. Had I shot her? Breathe.*

'Did you get flashbacks afterwards?'

'At first. Yes.' *Give her something; she'll get your previous records eventually.*

'Not any more?'

'No – well, not really.'

'Oh?'

'Sometimes, when I dream.'

'Ever get panic attacks?

'No.'

'Really? You looked like you were going to have one a minute ago.'

'Maybe. I'm just fed up of talking about this.'

'I'm sure you are, but that doesn't mean you're over it… If you twist that necklace round in your hand much more, you'll break it.'

When did I grab that? 'It's not a necklace. It's a dog tag.' *Shit, shouldn't have admitted that.*

'Don't they normally come in a pair?'

'Yes. The other is buried in Port Stanley.'

'Oh, with your father?'

Doyle nodded.

'I'm sorry… the Falklands War?'

Doyle nodded again. 'Scots Guards.'

'You must have been quite young?'

'Three and a half.'

'You obviously still feel the hole he's left in your life.'

'I'm not really sure how I feel. It was so long ago, I don't remember much before that.'

'I'm afraid our time is up, Liam. Perhaps you can tell me more about that next time… You might also want to share what you've been holding back today. I sense an elephant in the room…'

'I'm not holding anything back.'

'It's OK. I don't expect you to tell me everything straight away. We have to build up a trust. I'm not against you; the enquiry is over. My role is to help you move on from the incident and ensure you're able to cope with the ongoing stresses of your work.'

We'll see. 'OK.'

'Shall we say, the same time in two weeks?'

'OK.'

'And Liam, don't be late next time.'

⋏ ⋏ ⋏

'Boss, you got a moment?' Asif asked Doyle as he walked into the incident room.

'Sure, what's up?'

'You know that stuff you asked me to look into yesterday? I think I might have found something.'

Doyle grabbed a chair and pulled it up next to the intelligence analyst, not wanting anyone else to overhear their conversation until he knew what Asif had uncovered.

'What have you got?'

'There's this.' Asif brought up the image of a young woman on her screen. She was white, had closely cropped brown hair, and her nose was pierced. 'This is Karolina Valanciunas. She was Lithuanian. She had been living in various places in and around Manchester since coming to the UK in 2016. Her body was found on Saddleworth Moor, hidden in bracken, in May 2020. She had been strangled with a ligature and had been there several weeks by the time she was found.'

'Similar cause of death, but ligature strangulation is not that uncommon.'

'No, but there's more.'

'Go on.'

'The country was in the middle of a Covid lockdown at the time. Although people were permitted to go out to take exercise, they weren't allowed to travel to do it. They think that's why she remained undiscovered for so long. She hadn't even been reported missing because people weren't seeing each other then, so no one noticed she was gone.'

'That makes sense. Is there more that might link her to our case? I mean, the short hair and the fact that a ligature was used are similarities, but they aren't unique.'

'I think so.' Asif brought up another picture on her screen. 'This is her in January 2020, just a few months before. Both pics are from her social media.'

The difference was striking. It was almost as if Doyle was looking at another person. In this picture Karolina had long flowing brunette hair and no nose ring. There was a definite similarity to the picture of Chloe that Doyle had seen two days earlier on her parents' sideboard.

'Friends say she cut her hair and changed her image after splitting up with her boyfriend. The team investigating had him as prime suspect, but by the time her body was found and they started looking for him, he had left the country and was back in Lithuania.'

'Did he ever show up there?'

'He did. Dead from an overdose. The authorities there couldn't confirm whether it was deliberate or accidental. He had mental health problems and drug and alcohol issues, by all accounts. But there's more, boss.'

'Go on,' Doyle encouraged.

'There's this.' Asif pulled up another image on her screen.

'What is it?' Doyle stared at the photo of the small metal object.

'It's called a gripple. It's used to join wire rope and make a loop at the end, which can then be tightened or loosened. The marks on the back of Karolina's neck were identified as coming from one of those. She was strangled with a wire rope and the killer used a gripple to prolong the process, tightening the ligature in stages, just like Chloe Kennedy's killer did with that giant cable tie.'

'Fuck,' said Doyle. 'Sorry, 'scuse my language.' The similarities were starting to look more than coincidental.

'It's OK. You think we might have something?'

'You know what, I think you might. Can you do me a favour? Pull up all the information you can on it and I'll go through it tonight after I finish work. Could you send the post-mortem report to Dr Gupta and ask her opinion about similarities and differences between the two killings? Also, send all the forensics to Jen and get her view on those.'

'Will do.'

'Oh, and Shaima, can you also check for any house or building fires around the time Karolina was killed? Near where they think she went missing, and near where the body was found. And when you've done that, keep looking.'

'What for?'

'For more. If the two are linked, then there could be three or four – or more. Keep going back and see what you find. Focus on the particular similarities. The recent haircut, the prolonged ligature strangulation, maybe even the recent break-up, and the ex being the most obvious suspect.'

'On it, boss.'

'Oh, and one more thing: this is strictly confidential, need-to-know only. For now, that's just me, you, Dr Gupta and Jen Knight. Until we know for sure whether the two are linked, we can't risk it getting out. There would be mass hysteria and the press would have a field day.' As Doyle walked across the incident room to his office, he could feel the hairs on the back of his neck stand to attention. Chloe's murder had always felt to him like the work of a calm, calculating killer, someone who had killed before. He wasn't certain that the victim Asif had unearthed had been murdered by the same hand, but it was looking like a distinct possibility.

Chapter 28

'What the bloody hell is this?'

Doyle resisted the temptation to reply that the item thrown down on the desk in front of him was a newspaper, deducing that this wasn't the answer his superior, Detective Superintendent Croucher, was looking for. Instead he picked up the tabloid and saw from the banner across the top that it was the *Lancashire Chronicle*. He noticed the reason for his boss's latest bad mood. The headline leapt off the page: *Chorley Murder – Police Get Killer Cop on the Case*. To compound the problem, there was a picture of Doyle. Not a photo taken from the press conference the day before. No, the *Lancashire Chronicle* had used an image shot by a member of the public twenty-one months ago in London. It wasn't the first time this picture had appeared in a newspaper; most of the national tabloids had run with it at the time. It showed Doyle emerging from the underground car park moments after shooting Jamal Campbell dead. He was dressed in bloodstained jeans and a lightweight jacket, with a cloth police cap on his head. In his right hand he held a handgun, and in his left arm he clutched a bloodied child. He even had blood smeared across his face.

At the time, the press had used the image to suggest a brutal murder by the police stemming from institutionalised racism. A story that – thankfully – changed when it emerged that Campbell had savagely murdered his partner and had been using his young stepdaughter as a human shield. The blood was Campbell's, and Doyle had been covered in it after pulling the terrified child from the dead man's clutches.

'Shit.'

'Shit indeed, Detective Chief Inspector. This isn't the image we are looking for in the Lancashire Constabulary.'

'With respect, sir.' Doyle tried to keep the irritation from his voice. 'I can hardly be held responsible for how the press report something. It's not as if you didn't know what happened down in London, and you were the one who wanted me at that press conference.'

'You are the Senior Investigating Officer – of course you should have been at the press conference. Or are you telling me you aren't up to the job of SIO?'

Doyle took a breath. It was less satisfying than punching the pompous arse in the face, but a considerably better career move. He opened the paper, to see the full story splashed across pages two and three: *The recruitment of tough crime-fighters like DCI Doyle shows that the force is gearing up to take the fight back to the criminals, shaking off the provincial village bobby image more suited to days long gone.* Doyle noticed the name of the hack who had written the piece. Jayden Clark, the reporter who had questioned him about his background at the press conference the day before. He also noticed a picture in the bottom corner of page three: it showed Birdseye and Gadget talking to the journalist. A caption read *Murder detectives didn't deny that DCI Doyle was sacked by the Met and brought in by the Lancashire force to shake things up.* He would have words with those two later.

At least the article explained why Bea had been keen for him not to see the paper in her office. What must she think of him after reading that and seeing the picture?

'Well?' Mr Burns said, apparently waiting for further explanation from Doyle.

'I fail to see how what the press write about me has any relevance to my ability to run an investigation. And, as I told you on the phone, it looks like we have had a significant breakthrough.'

'You better fill me in on that, then.'

Doyle stuck his head out of his office door and summoned Hales, Birdseye and Asif to join them before giving Mr Burns a full update – or, perhaps more accurately, the edited highlights of what he wanted him to know at this stage. He began with the progress they had made since Morgan had phoned from the software company in Birmingham with details of the subcontracted IT firm that had been servicing the app for Alpha Cars.

'The company is called James Fisher IT Ltd. Its only listed director is a James Martin Fisher,' Doyle said. 'Shaima, would you mind bringing us all up to speed with what you've uncovered about the company and Mr Fisher so far?'

'Sure, boss. They're up to date with their filing with Companies House and HM Revenue and Customs. Looks like Fisher is the only employee.'

'After this, I will send off the authorisation so we can get everything we need from HMRC and Companies House, as well as the company's bank account details,' Burns said. 'If they don't employ anyone else, this James Fisher has got to be our man.'

'Maybe – probably, even,' Doyle conceded. 'But they could have employed another sub-contractor to work for them. Go on, Shaima.'

'The company website is very professional and looks legit, but the registered address is an address used for lots of businesses, and the phone number goes through to a switchboard operated by the same people. We've checked. They just answer the phones, then email the company with the enquiry. They don't have any direct contact with James Fisher, or anyone else on the company's behalf,' Asif said.

'And what about Fisher himself?' Burns asked. 'What have you been able to dig up about him?'

'He's forty-two and has a background in IT. He works full-time for another company, though, so he must have set up this one as a sideline,' Asif said. 'Perhaps he was looking to build it up and then leave his full-time job.'

'Perhaps,' Hales said 'Or he had started it up as a cover, knowing what he was going to do. I've been on to the DVLA, and they're sending through his driving licence, which will have his picture on. It's three years old, but it should give us a good likeness for him now. I also discovered from them that there are two vehicles registered to James Fisher IT Ltd: a white Citroën Berlingo van and – this is the best bit – a white Toyota Prius.'

'Great work, Geoff,' Croucher said. 'He has to be our man.'

Doyle heard the excitement in his superior officer's voice, but his own internal voice was telling him not to get carried away.

'A technician from James Fisher was at the Alpha Cars office on Monday afternoon after they reported problems with the app,' Hales said. 'I have sent two uniforms down there to get images of him from the CCTV.'

'Good,' said Burns. 'And what do we know about this James Fisher's personal life?'

'He's got no previous – not so much as a speeding fine. He lives in Handforth in Cheshire, just south of Manchester,' Asif said, reading from her laptop screen. 'He's married to a Julie Fisher, née Hartley. They have two children, a boy of six and a girl aged three.'

'Jesus,' said Birdseye. 'Wife and kids at home, and he's out murdering young women.'

'Peter Sutcliffe had a wife at home too,' Hales said.

'OK, we're getting ahead of ourselves. We don't know for sure that this James Fisher did kill Chloe Kennedy. But he's certainly got some questions to answer,' Doyle said.

'How do you suggest we play it from here, Liam?' Burns asked. His tone had softened a touch, Doyle noticed.

The DCI looked at his watch. 'You're not going to like this, sir, but it's quarter to seven now. Morgan and Washington should be back from Birmingham in the next half hour. I suggest we ask Cheshire Police to help discreetly locate Fisher and keep tabs on him for now. We'll dig up all we can on him – vehicle movements, mobile phone records, etc. Then we'll pull him in first thing tomorrow and see what he has to say for himself. It will all come down to alibi. If we can put him anywhere close to Chorley at the relevant times, then we know it's him. If he can prove he was somewhere else, then we know it's not him. We aren't going to get anything useful by questioning him tonight.'

'OK. Point taken,' Burns conceded. 'I will get on to Cheshire Police and make the arrangements with them myself. I play golf with one of their ACCs – he should be able to ensure that we get full co-operation from on high. But I want James Fisher sitting in an interview room first thing tomorrow morning. It's Friday tomorrow. If we can get our act together, we can get him charged by the end of the day, less than a week after the murder. That will go down well with the press. And you can give the whole team the weekend off. Looks like they've done well.'

There was a knock on the door, interrupting Croucher's premature congratulations, and PCs Bowen and Price walked in.

'Great timing,' Hales said. 'Have you two got the CCTV of our prime suspect from the cab office?'

The two officers shared a slightly awkward look before Bowen answered. 'Well, we have, sir, yes. The thing is, it's not really very useful, sir.'

'What do you mean, not very useful?' Burns barked. 'It doesn't have to be in 4K high-definition; we just need a facial image that we can compare to his driving licence photo and confirm whether James Fisher is our man.'

'His face is obscured on the way in and the way out, sir,' Price tried to explain. 'They only have the one camera, over the door.' He held up a memory stick.

'Right, well, let's stick that in Shaima's laptop and we can all have a look.'

Doyle noticed a pained expression on Bowen's face as Price did as instructed. Everyone gathered round the computer. They watched a man of average height, his collar turned up and baseball cap pulled down over his face, pass the camera, his head bowed, revealing none of his features. The fact that he had managed to reveal nothing of himself other than his skin colour – white – and his height – average – made Doyle think that this was indeed their man. He was deliberately and skilfully avoiding his image being recorded.

'That's him on the way in,' said Price. Doyle resisted the urge to point out that everyone in the room had worked that out for themselves.

'And coming out?' Doyle thought it even less likely that the man's face would be revealed on the way out, the way the camera was pointing.

Another look flashed between Bowen and Price before the image played. Two familiar figures came into shot on the CCTV.

'That's...' Mr Burns said, clearly recognising them too.

Then a thick cloud of vape smoke appeared on the image, completely obscuring the face of the man leaving the cab firm as he walked past Detective Sergeant Morgan and Detective Constable Washington, who were clearly visible. All seven people in the room were momentarily frozen in silence.

'That's the man we now think killed Chloe Kennedy?' Burns asked rhetorically. 'Walking straight past two of the Major Investigation Team detectives who're trying to catch him?'

Doyle noticed the vein on Burns' head had begun to pulse again.

'We'd better hope that no one from the press gets hold of this little gem. The department will be a laughing-stock.'

'That might be the case, sir,' Doyle said. 'But Morgan and Washington could hardly have known at the time who he was.'

There was another knock at the door, and two figures looking very much like those that had just been on the screen appeared in the room, to silence and stares.

'What?' said Morgan, looking at her colleagues. 'Have I grown horns or something on the drive back from Birmingham?'

Chapter 29

December 1999

The windscreen had started to mist up, his breath condensing on the cold glass. He would have opened a window if it wasn't so fucking freezing. He could start the engine, then he would get the benefit of the vehicle's heater, but starting the ignition would draw attention, and he didn't want that. With his coat sleeve, he wiped the windscreen.

He could see what he assumed were the lounge and bathroom window of her apartment across the road. It was on the first floor. He'd been in to check, sliding in the communal door as someone came out. The lights were off; she wasn't home yet. His watch said it was only quarter past five, and it was already dark. Only one flat in the block appeared to have made any effort with Christmas decorations: a pathetic two-foot plastic tree sat on the windowsill, adorned with flashing multicoloured fairy lights that looked like they might flicker and die at any moment.

He'd left work early, saying he was feeling unwell. As soon as he'd found what he was looking for, he couldn't wait any longer. It had been three and a half years since he'd seen her. He'd been a boy then; he was a man now. He'd tried writing to her at least a dozen times from the young offender institution in Wetherby. He didn't have her address so had just written to her at the children's home, hoping they would forward the letters to her, but of course they didn't. If they had, she would have come.

Two and a half years locked up and just two visits – both from the fucking social worker who had helped put him in there. His lawyer had told him to plead guilty to criminal damage, so he had. 'Arson with intent to endanger life' was what he got convicted of. Pouring the petrol over the kitchen as well as the shed apparently demonstrated that, with three people sleeping above. It didn't matter that one of them was a paedophile – in fact, he couldn't even mention that, his lawyer had said. The dog hadn't helped his case. They'd found it in the bin, the wire still round its neck. A couple of women in the jury had gasped when they had been told that. The judge had called him 'a deeply disturbed young man on a dangerous spiral of destruction that had to be stopped', before handing him a five-year sentence. He'd served two and a half, including time on remand, then he'd been released for good behaviour eleven months ago.

He wiped the windscreen again with his now damp sleeve. A light came on in the living room. He could see a figure moving around inside, but couldn't make out if it was her. Then the bathroom light came on, and he saw a shadow at the window. His heart pounded. What should he do? The bathroom light was off again, and there was movement in the living room. He could ring the buzzer, but what would he tell her about how he had found her?

All those months of looking, checking up with people around Fleetwood who had known her. Then out of the blue that morning, an opportunity had just presented itself. The woman had not logged off her computer when he'd come to check it for Y2K compliance; it was one of the last to be done. He hadn't known her National Insurance number, but her full name and date of birth had been enough. Maybe he could tell her that. She would be pleased to see him after all this time, and probably impressed with how he had hacked the system to track her down. Evil genius, she used to call him.

He was out of the car. He was going to do it, going to press the buzzer. Then the lights went off in her flat. He waited by the van – a car, really, just without rear seats and windows. Over its roof, it was easy to watch who would come through the door. He had parked in the shadows, but streetlights lit the building's entrance. The door opened. It wasn't her. A different woman, in jeans, a leather jacket with lots of zips, a woollen hat. Not Michelle. Maybe she would be out in a moment. The woman lit a cigarette, the lighter giving her face a warm hue, picking out her features.

Shit. It *was* Michelle. What had she done to herself? The dark eye make-up, tufts of short hair poking out from under the hat. The turned-up jeans, leather biker jacket, and those fucking awful Dr Marten boots. It was as if she had been vandalised. Beautiful Michelle, the light that had shone through the gloom of the children's home.

She was walking down the street with purpose. Maybe running late, maybe just in a hurry to get out of the cold. He decided to follow, zipping his coat up to keep out the biting wind and pulling up his hood. He was pleased to find his gloves in his pocket. He didn't know Manchester well – or at all, in fact. Michelle ducked and weaved through the people and the traffic, and at times he worried he would lose her. He got a sense that they were heading towards the city centre: the streets became busier as they walked.

Christmas lights reflected in shop windows. People spilling into and out of bars. It was all alien to him. They weren't like the weekend revellers he saw in Blackpool. These people were different: young people, not families like those that went to see the illuminations. He saw two men walking together, holding hands. They stopped and kissed right there on the pavement by the canal. Michelle went into a bar. Perfect. He could wait a moment and then follow. Pretend he had bumped into her by accident.

He watched Michelle through the plate-glass window. Another girl approached her. She had cropped hair and was dressed like Michelle. The other girl flung her arms around Michelle's shoulders and kissed her. On the lips. Michelle didn't pull away. She kissed her back. They were snogging right there in the bar. Lit up in the big window. Michelle. His Michelle, kissing a girl. He felt like someone had plunged a knife into his chest.

人 人 人

It had been a cold night. He had kept out of Michelle's sight as she and the group she was with drank and laughed. They'd moved to another bar, where they drank more. He'd wanted to go up to her, but something about the people that she was with put him off. Much better to meet her when there was just the two of them. He followed Michelle and *that girl* back to her apartment. At one point they came close to seeing him, when they stopped to kiss. He kept walking past them, hood up, head down, before turning off and doubling back behind them.

It had been just after one in the morning when he'd got back to his van. He'd considered driving home, but he couldn't just leave. For three and a half years he hadn't stopped thinking about Michelle, and now he had found her, turning round and going home without making contact was unthinkable.

He had the sleeping bag in the back. That was why he had bought the Astra van and not a car: so he could camp in it. The van kept out the bitter wind, but not the cold. The sleeping bag was cheap, made for the summer. He hadn't got around to insulating the vehicle. He gave up trying to get any more sleep just after six in the morning, drove off and found a McDonald's, got some food and used the loo. He found a phone box too, and left a message on the work answer machine, saying he was still feeling too ill to come in.

The van's heater had felt like bliss, warming his cold bones. The lights in Michelle's apartment were still off when he parked in the same spot. It was just after eight when the bathroom light came on. Ten minutes later, that girl emerged from the entrance and trotted up the road, in the same clothes she'd worn the night before. No doubt she was late for work or college or whatever she did. There was no further movement until nearly ten o'clock. The lounge curtains were flung back, and there was Michelle in the window. No make-up, just that beautiful face. But her hair – even though he'd seen it the night before, it still shocked him. Cropped short with a fringe – why would she have done that to herself? It reminded him of his mum when she'd had cancer and all her hair fell out. When the tumours got into her brain and turned her poisonous. He shuddered.

That had been forty-five minutes ago. He'd seen no movement since from her apartment. People had come and gone through the communal door, but not Michelle. But wait – someone was coming out now. It was her. She set off in the same direction as she had the night before. He started the engine and, after giving her a head start, drove slowly up the road. She turned the corner and headed towards a zebra crossing. Perfect. He pulled up just as she was halfway across. He pressed the horn, harder than he had intended.

'Fuck off!' Michelle shouted without turning.

He struggled to wind the window down before she was out of earshot. 'Michelle, Michelle.'

She turned on his second shout. She looked confused, like she didn't recognise him.

'It's me, Jay.'

Her confusion changed to something else; he didn't know what. It wasn't the broad grin he had hoped for. He beckoned her towards him. She hesitated. A horn blasted behind him.

'Fuck off!' he and Michelle shouted at the same time. He pulled the van into the side of the road so the car could get past, then leaned across and wound down the passenger window.

'Jay, what the fuck are you doing here?'

'I was just passing, had to drop something off round the corner. I nearly didn't recognise you – you've changed. Where are you going?'

'Just to the library. I'm studying, trying to get into uni next year.'

'Get in. I'll give you a lift.'

'I don't know, Jay. I kind of like to walk.'

'Go on, Michelle, we can have a catch-up, remember old times. Besides, it's freezing out.'

She hesitated. What was she afraid of? he wondered. They were mates, weren't they? 'Come on, Michelle.'

'OK, OK.'

He pulled the catch on the door so she could get in. He waited until she had finished fiddling with her seatbelt before he pulled away. He didn't know where he was going. He didn't care.

'You live round here, then?'

'Yeah, not far.'

'It's good to see you, Michelle. It's been so long.'

'Thanks. When did you…'

'Get out?'

'Yes.'

'Eleven months ago. Was worth it, though.'

'Really?' She frowned.

'To pay him back for what he did to you.' He stopped at some lights. He was vaguely heading into town, he thought.

'You killed my dog, Jay.'

'That was an accident. I'm sorry. It came for me, and I found the wire and tried to put it on like a lead and tie it up. It must have strangled itself. You got to believe me, Michelle, I would never have done that on purpose. You know I didn't want to hurt you. What they said at the trial was lies.'

She turned away. 'Go left at the next lights. It's not far.'

'You believe me, don't you, Michelle?'

'I don't know what to believe. My sister was asleep in the back bedroom. She could have been killed.'

'But she wasn't. They made that sound worse in court too. It was a stitch-up. She was never in any danger.'

'I don't want to think about it any more. It's a time of my life I want to forget. Jay, you've missed the turning.'

'Michelle, it's been years. We were good friends. Surely you can spare a bit of time to go on a little drive now?' He offered her his cigarette packet; she took one and lit it using her own lighter. 'You were the only person who was nice to me back then. I just wanted to repay the favour. I never meant for it to get out of hand. I only wanted to burn down those pigeon sheds. You were pleased at the time.'

'OK. Please, let's not talk about that any more.'

'What are you studying, then?'

'A levels, at an adult education college. I want to do social work. What do you do?'

'I work in computers. I did some of that inside, and when I got out I started making them, breaking down old ones, putting in new parts, getting them working again.'

A hint of a smile finally appeared on Michelle's face. 'I've still got that video recorder you were going to give me. I nicked it from your room after you got arrested.'

'Does it still work?'

'It does, yeah. You do up old computers and sell them on?'

'I did, and I was signing on, obviously. I had an interview at the job centre and said I was into computers, so they sent me to do some tests and gave me a job working for them in a team going round doing millennium bug fixes. They were desperate for it. Pays much better than I could have got anywhere else, and tons of overtime.'

'Nice. Where are we going, Jay? I need to get some study done. I've got an essay due in before the Christmas holidays.'

'D'you still smoke?'

'As in smoke smoke?'

'Yes.'

'Sure.'

'Let's go and have a smoke together, for old times' sake.'

'It's not even lunchtime.'

'That never used to bother you.'

'We were kids then, with fuck all else to do. Besides, you're driving. You could lose your licence.'

'I haven't got a licence.'

Michelle laughed. 'Dickhead.' Despite the insult, there was still the hint of a smile.

'It will be a giggle. Let your hair down.'

'I haven't got any hair to let down now.'

'Yeah, what's with that?'

'I wanted a change, to be who I wanted to be. Not the girl that men wanted me to be. I've changed a lot. My life's changed a lot.'

'I've changed too.'

'Good. I hope you're happy. Where are we going, Jay? You're heading out of town.'

'When I was about eight or nine, my dad used to take me out to the moors. We would camp anywhere we fancied, not in a campsite. They were good times. One of the places we went is not far from here. We can go, have a quick smoke, then I'll drive you back.'

'It had better be quick, and you'd better not get us lost.'

Chapter 30

Day 4: Friday 16th June 2023

Even though it was nearly the longest day of the year, Doyle had been up for over an hour before the sun made an appearance. The briefing had started at 4 a.m. sharp in Wilmslow police station – a place that Doyle suspected organised rather fewer dawn raids than many other police stations up and down the country. If things had been left to Doyle, he would have been more than happy to turn up at the address with a handful of officers and detain Fisher himself. Mr Burns and his Assistant Chief Constable golf buddy, however, had other ideas. Officers from Cheshire Constabulary would be making the arrest and then handing Fisher to Doyle and his team to interview. Risk assessments had been carried out. As Fisher was wanted for murder, it was decided that they should force entry, with officers kitted out in body armour and riot helmets. Doyle didn't approve of this, considering there would also be two young children in the house, but it was all he could do to persuade those higher up that they didn't need armed officers too. With this small concession gained, he had reminded himself to pick his battles, reasoning that any fallout from this approach would land on the top brass, not him.

The target house was a 1930s semi in a leafy street, with driveways bursting with nearly new BMWs, Mercedes, Teslas and Range Rovers. Anyone opening their curtains to let in the rising sun would do a double take at the sight of the black-clad figures silently moving into position.

Doyle and his team lurked in the background, waiting for their cue to move in.

'Go. Go. Go.' The words sounded like a stage whisper in Doyle's ear. This was followed by the noise of splintering wood as the front door imploded. Despite the early hour, Doyle was still sharp enough to pull out his earpiece before he was deafened by the shouts of 'Police!' that sent birds scattering and curtains twitching.

When Doyle stepped over the threshold, past the broken front door, he could hear children crying and a woman – presumably Julie Fisher – screaming at the top of her voice. The pale shagpile was soft underfoot as the DCI went upstairs. He suspected that, up until two minutes ago, no footwear more substantial than a slipper had trodden this carpet. He found James Fisher sitting on the double bed in the master bedroom, his hands cuffed in front of him, looking dazed, as if he hadn't woken up yet and this was all part of a dream.

'He's not said anything, sir,' a helmeted figure informed Doyle. 'He just held his hands out as instructed while we cuffed him.'

Doyle reminded himself not to read too much into Fisher's reaction to his house being stormed at dawn. How were you supposed to act in those circumstances, whether or not you had killed someone?

'You fucking cunts, you've no right to come in here frightening the children.' Even from downstairs, the woman's voice was loud enough to cut through all the other noise. It would seem Mrs Fisher's reaction to being dragged out of bed was rather different to her husband's.

'She punched one of our guys in the nuts,' Helmet said.

'Proper connected as well. I'm hoping one of the bodycams has picked it up. I might make it my screensaver.'

Doyle smiled back. It was good to see that some people could enjoy their work at this ungodly hour.

⅄ ⅄ ⅄

Morgan had felt sympathetic towards Julie Fisher – or perhaps empathetic, she wasn't quite sure of the difference. But whatever her feelings towards the other woman's plight, they were fast drifting away and being replaced by a strong desire to punch her in the face. She'd vowed years ago not to let people push her around again: a principle that had been tested on many occasions since she'd joined the police, by suspects and colleagues.

The family interview room at Wilmslow police station was all soft furnishings and pictures of tranquil sunsets – no doubt designed by a committee of men in suits with the sole purpose of creating a calm, warm atmosphere. It hadn't worked – at least, as far as Mrs Fisher was concerned. She, understandably, just wanted to be taken to her children. Slightly less understandably, she had been yelling this at the top of her voice for ten minutes now, in among a lexicon of expletives that would have made the new DCI proud. Completely unreasonably, Morgan felt, Mrs Fisher had been shouting in her face: 'You better get out of my way, you fucking dyke bitch, or are you just hanging around so you can give me a full body cavity search?'

If Morgan was being bitchy, she might have thought that it wasn't just the dawn raid, her husband being arrested for murder, and being separated from her offspring that was upsetting Mrs Fisher, but the fact that the beautician had been denied the opportunity to do her hair and make-up before leaving the house.

'Mrs Fisher,' Birdseye's voice was soft. 'If you could just take a seat.'

'Oh, fuck me, it speaks. What are you going to tell me? I won't be getting any Christmas presents if I'm not a good girl?'

Morgan had to stifle a chuckle. Derrick Nelson had handed out the secret Santa gifts at the department Christmas party. He'd hired a red suit, but he'd not needed the white beard that came with the costume.

'Please,' Birdseye persisted. 'If we're making a big mistake here, you need to help us.'

'Why the fuck should I help you lot?'

'James has been arrested for murder. If you think he didn't do it, you need to help him.'

'Of course he hasn't murdered anyone. Have you seen him? He can't even get a fucking spider out of the bath.'

'Please, Mrs Fisher, take a seat.'

Morgan had to hand it to Birdseye. He could be a lazy arse at times and a bit dopey, but he did have a way of calming people down and getting them to open up. Perhaps it was his grandfatherly quality. Julie Fisher did as requested, choosing a seat opposite Birdseye. Morgan chose a soft chair next to her colleague. The fight seemed to drain out of the other woman as she sank into the lilac cushion.

'What is this all about? Who is he supposed to have murdered?'

Morgan kept quiet, thinking it was better to let Birdseye take the lead.

'A young woman.' The DC fished a photo out from a folder in front of him. 'Her name's Chloe Kennedy.' He handed the picture to Julie Fisher. 'She was a schoolteacher, aged twenty-six.'

'But James – he wouldn't have. He couldn't hurt a fly.'

Morgan noticed that Julie Fisher's flushed face was fast draining of colour, as tears began to form in her eyes.

'Do you know where James was Friday night and in the early hours of Saturday morning?'

'Well, yes, sort of.'

'What does "sort of" mean? Were you with him or not, Julie?' Morgan couldn't resist jumping in.

'No, I wasn't with him, but I know where he was. He was with his brother in Spain. They went on a golf weekend.'

'And you're sure about that? They couldn't have gone anywhere else?'

'No. His brother stayed at our house on Thursday night, and I drove them to Manchester Airport Friday morning.'

'Can I ask you about your husband's company, James Fisher IT Ltd? What do you know about that?'

'What? He hasn't got a company. He works for an insurance company in their IT department.'

'You're quite sure, Mrs Fisher?' Morgan asked. 'He doesn't use James Fisher IT Ltd for his own private work on the side?'

'No, he doesn't do any private work on the side. He's either with me and the kids or playing golf. The last thing James wants is to take on any more work.'

人 人 人

'My client has asked me to read out a prepared statement, after which he will answer any reasonable questions you may wish to ask.' Doyle had given Fisher's solicitor a brief outline of the case against him in the disclosure meeting. He was naturally cautious about giving away too much, but felt that laying out what needed to be answered straight away might be the best way to get answers. The man sitting opposite him and next to Fisher had spent a further forty-five minutes with his client before the interview could start.

'I had no involvement in the murder of Chloe Kennedy, and was not in the country at the time you have informed me that she was killed. I travelled to Spain with my brother Paul Fisher last Friday morning, and returned on Monday afternoon. This can easily be verified by several sources. I'm happy to give you flight numbers, accommodation details and anything else reasonable to help you with this,' the solicitor read.

Doyle looked across at Hales and caught his eye. This wasn't the sort of alibi that could be easily faked.

'Furthermore, I do not know anything about the company James Fisher IT Ltd – in fact, I was not aware of its existence until today. My name, date of birth and National Insurance number on this company's records are, however, correct: it would seem that my details have been fraudulently used in the registration of this company with Companies House. In 2016 I had a number of documents stolen while I was on holiday in Portugal, including my passport, driving licence and National Insurance card. I reported this to local police at the time, and the British consulate assisted me to obtain travel documentation to return home. It may be that the documents stolen then were used for this purpose.'

This was shaping up for being one almighty fuck-up, Doyle thought.

'I feel that the police have been extremely heavy-handed in the way they have dealt with me and my family this morning. I will be making a formal complaint and seeking damages. I will briefly answer any reasonable questions relating to this matter, but I insist that I am released without charge or delay, as my ongoing detention is a breach of my human rights.'

The solicitor placed the handwritten statement on the table between them and gave Doyle a satisfied smile that clearly conveyed that he believed his client.

Doyle took a moment to compose himself. If Fisher was telling the truth and he was merely a victim of identity theft, he needed to tread carefully. 'Thank you for your statement, Mr Fisher. I do have a few further questions, if I may, and then we will get everything verified as soon as we can. At the time when you had all these documents stolen, were you living at the same address as you are now?'

Fisher looked at his solicitor, who nodded.

'No, we lived in a flat in Stockport then. We moved from there to Handforth in March 2018.'

'And after you moved, did you put a redirect on your mail from that address to the new one?'

'Yes. Well, we did for the first year. You have to pay for it, and it runs out after a year, but we had changed everything by then so we didn't think it was worth renewing.'

'Did you own that property, Mr Fisher?'

'Yes.'

'And did you meet the people who moved in after you?'

'We met the people who bought it. They seemed nice. They were an older couple – said they were getting it as a buy-to-let to increase their income for retirement.'

Doyle considered this. James Fisher IT Ltd had been incorporated as a company in July 2019. Paperwork and bank confirmations would have been sent out, which would have alerted Mr Fisher had he still lived at his previous address or was still having his mail redirected. But by then the mail redirect would have ended. If Fisher's story checked out, they were at another dead end. Chloe Kennedy's killer was playing a very long and sophisticated game – and it looked like they still had absolutely no idea who he was.

⋏ ⋏ ⋏

'So his story checks out?' Morgan asked, getting into the passenger seat of Doyle's car. He had picked her up outside Chorley police station for their early-morning trip to Cheshire, and was now about to drive them back to the incident room.

'As alibis go, it's pretty foolproof. The CCTV at Manchester Airport confirms he got the flight, and there's a record of him coming back into the country on Monday. Nothing in between. Shaima's carrying out further checks to confirm this. I feel quite sorry for him, really.'

'So do I. His wife was horrible.'

Doyle laughed. 'That's not quite what I meant. I take it she gave you a hard time, then?'

'She was downright rude and insulting. And I know I shouldn't let her get under my skin. I dealt with far worse when I first joined up, working response.'

'Try and see it from her point of view. She gets woken up first thing in the morning by a bunch of burly coppers smashing her door in and frightening the life out of her and her children.'

'You know she hit an officer.'

'I did hear, yes.'

'We could charge her with that.'

'Given the circumstances, I think it's probably best not to.'

'I know… So, where do we go from here? It's like we're back to square one.'

'It certainly feels that way,' Doyle conceded. What were they missing? Every time they thought they were getting close to the killer, another layer was stripped away and then they were no nearer to finding out who or where he was. The leads had been good leads; some good detective work had taken them as far as they had got. But whoever it was, he was always one step ahead of them. It was like playing pass the parcel: every time one layer of wrapping paper was removed, there was another underneath. Harry didn't get the game. Doyle remembered that time at a friend's party when Harry had waited patiently for the music to stop, holding the present. He had been most disappointed to be cheated out of his prize, and simply ripped off the rest of the paper when the music started up again. The looks the other parents had given him as he'd coaxed him away from the game, then taken him home from the party in full meltdown, screaming and ripping off his own clothes. Poor little bugger. He couldn't have coped with the temptation even if he had understood the rules. Maybe he needed to be more like Harry, and find a way to rip through all the layers at once. But how could he do that?

'Penny for them?'

'Sorry. I was just wondering what we're missing.'

'It doesn't make sense. Whoever did this stole those documents in 2016, set up the company in 2019, then killed Chloe in 2023. She would only have been ... what? Nineteen in 2016. Could a teenage ex have held a grudge for all that time?'

'Or?'

'Or Chloe's not the only one he's killed? Shit.'

'That's what I've been thinking. He's too well organised for this to be his first murder. I asked Shaima to look back for other similar cases.'

'And?'

'She found one that has significant similarities, and she's still looking.'

Chapter 31

'Boss, boss, you got a minute?' Asif shouted across to Doyle the second he entered the incident room. He hoped she had found something useful, as they desperately needed a new lead.

'What have you got?' Doyle said, making his way over to her desk.

The intelligence analyst waited until he was close before she said in little more than a whisper, 'I think I've found another one.'

'Another victim?' Doyle blurted out his reply rather louder than he had intended, and was relieved to see that no one appeared to have heard.

'Yes, look.' Asif pulled up a picture on her screen of a young lady with cropped bleached blonde hair. 'This is Victoria Quinn as she looked a few weeks before she went missing in Leeds in April 2019. Her body was found in a shallow grave in the Forest of Bowland three weeks later.'

'She doesn't look like either Chloe Kennedy or Karolina Valanciunas. You said she was buried? No attempt had been made to bury the other two women,' Doyle said.

'That's true,' said Asif. 'But look at this picture.' Another image flashed up on the screen. 'This is her two years previously.'

Doyle slowly exhaled a long breath of air. The woman in the second picture bore a considerable resemblance to Chloe Kennedy, and could almost have been related to Karolina Valanciunas.

'She was strangled with a wire rope and had been sexually assaulted. Did you see the emails from Jen and Dr Gupta, by the way?'

'No – when did they come through?'

'Both within the last hour. Jen said that, according to the forensic report, a very similar type of wipe was used to clean Karolina and Chloe Kennedy post-mortem. They leave a residue, apparently. Dr Gupta said there were enough similarities between the killings to make her feel it's quite possible that they were carried out by the same person.'

'And what about Victoria Quinn? Was her body cleaned with wipes too?' Doyle asked.

'No, there are some differences there. But there were some strange marks on her skin that the pathologist said happened after she died. They think she was cleaned with a jet wash.'

'Fucking hell. Sorry, I didn't mean to—'

'It's OK, boss. It's pretty grim, jet-washing a body, isn't it?'

'It is.' Doyle paused for a moment as a thought took shape. 'Karolina Valanciunas was killed right at the start of the Covid pandemic in 2020. At that time, everyone was using wet wipes and such like. People were even wiping down their shopping before it came into the house. Maybe our killer got the idea to try that and found it a lot easier than using a jet wash to get rid of any traces of himself from a body.'

'He must have found it easier if he used it again on Chloe Kennedy.'

'Exactly.'

'But why would he bury Victoria and just dump the other two?'

'Good question. If I were to guess, I'd say you bury a body because you don't want it to be found. Correct?'

'Yes.'

'The reason you don't want it to be found is that it confirms that the person is dead and murdered, not just missing. But there might also be some evidence on that body that leads back to you. Every contact leaves a trace – that's the basics of forensic science that every copper in the world knows, but also pretty much every killer.'

'OK, but why change that?'

'Well, despite burying her, Victoria was found. It's not easy burying a body. No doubt he chose a quiet spot where he wouldn't be seen. But that's not guaranteed. He would have had to park somewhere while he dug the grave – someone could have seen the car. There are rocks and possibly tree roots, so the digging wouldn't have been easy. And even when you've done all that and put the earth back in, you're left with a big pile on top. It's obvious that someone has been digging there, and if people are looking, the body will be found. And then you've wasted all that time and effort and made it even more likely that you'd get caught, as someone might see you or your car when you're digging the grave.'

'I guess that makes sense.'

'If the body is somewhere inside, it would be a lot easier to thoroughly clean it and remove all traces of yourself, then get rid of it quickly. Somewhere that you can be in and out of before anyone sees you. I think this is why he keeps eluding us. We aren't dealing with a novice. Our man is experienced in what he does and is continually evolving his technique, making it harder for us to trace him.'

'Shit, boss, you really think these are all linked? All three women killed by the same person?'

'I do. Get all the info from both of these cases and keep looking for more. Mispers too – if he was burying them before, there might be some bodies that have never been found. And try to find any possible arson sites. I think it's likely he would have burned down the place where he killed Victoria Quinn too.'

Asif had done well, he thought, as he walked back to his office. The victims all recently cutting their hair was a puzzle, and an unusual link, but a link nonetheless. Added to the other similarities in the MO, it was almost impossible that the cases weren't all connected.

ᴸ ᴸ ᴸ

Doyle was sitting with a few of the team in the incident room having lunch when Jen Knight came in. She lobbed an evidence bag onto the desk in front of Doyle. He picked it up and examined the contents through the clear plastic. It contained a single key, of a type that would fit many a front door up and down the country. This key, however, did not look like it had just come out of a pocket or a handbag; its shiny metallic surface had been replaced by a veneer of black sludge.

'What's this?' Doyle asked Knight.

'A key,' she replied. 'Specifically, the key to Chloe Kennedy's flat.'

'Where did you find it?'

'Funnily enough, right here in the police station. It was among the exhibits taken from the original forensic examination of the house fire in Limbrick. One of the only things in the garage that was still identifiable in all the burned-out debris. If I had to guess, I'd say that Chloe's clothes, phone and other belongings were doused in petrol when the fire was started. They found a few buttons from a Levi's denim jacket too.'

'Brilliant, Jen. This pretty much proves that was where Chloe was killed.'

'I thought we'd proven that already, when Birdseye found the witness who saw a Prius coming from the house?' Gadget said from his seat opposite.

'That,' said Doyle between mouthfuls of baguette, 'is circumstantial. This.' He pointed to the exhibit bag with his free hand. 'Is proof. Evidence forensically linking Chloe Kennedy to the house fire.'

'The trouble is,' Hales piped up, 'we're still no nearer to working out who the bastard actually is.'

'True,' said Doyle. 'But in about ten minutes, Morgan and I are going to see the letting agent who showed people round the property. It's not unreasonable to hope that the killer might have viewed the place to have a quick recce.'

'Do you know how many viewed it?' Hales asked.

Doyle wiped his hands on a paper napkin and opened his notebook. 'There were only three viewings. One lot were a retired couple, so I think we can probably rule them out. Another was a Dr Rishi Patel.'

'Harold Shipman was a doctor,' Gadget said.

'True,' said Doyle. 'But his MO was rather different.'

'What about the other one?' Hales asked.

'A guy called Lee Oswald.'

'It will be him for sure,' Birdseye said, gesticulating with his homemade cheese and pickle sandwich.

'How can you be so sure?' asked Doyle.

'It's obvious, isn't it?' Birdseye replied, brushing crumbs out of his beard.

'Is it? How?' Hales asked.

'Well, President Kennedy was – conspiracy theories aside – killed by Lee Harvey Oswald,' Birdseye said. 'This guy's killed Chloe Kennedy, and he's used a made-up name of Lee Oswald. He's playing with us.'

'Fuck me, Derrick, you're a genius,' said Doyle. 'Why didn't I spot that?'

'Yeah, nice one, Del Boy,' Gadget said.

'Del Boy?' Doyle gave Gadget an incredulous look. 'Surely he's more Uncle Albert with that beard.'

人 人 人

'I got the impression he was a bit of a tyre kicker, not seriously looking,' Eve Frampton said.

Doyle and Morgan were questioning the letting agent in Bea's office on Market Street.

'What gave you that idea?' asked Morgan.

'He just seemed to be going through the motions. He wandered round from room to room, opening the odd cupboard door, not really looking. You get a sense for that. When people are imagining themselves living in a property, they look round more – open wardrobes, talk about where their stuff would go. But now I think about it, he was much more interested in the garage.'

'Interested how?' asked Morgan.

'It was done up like a home gym. He spent a lot of time looking in there. He seemed to like the punchbag hanging from the ceiling – he mentioned that. But it didn't strike me as odd. It's just men, isn't it? They're easily distracted by toys and gadgets.'

'They certainly are,' agreed Morgan, adding a, 'No offence, boss, I'm sure you're not like that' before Doyle had the chance to object.

'Did he ask many questions during the viewing?' Doyle said.

'No, not really, which was another thing that made me feel he wasn't seriously looking. He did ask what the security was like.'

'You've given us a pretty good description of him. How would you feel about working with one of our specialists to create a photofit impression? Doyle asked.

'That would be fine. Look, I don't mean to be rude, but I need to go soon. I've got another viewing in ten minutes.'

'That's OK. I think we've got all we need for now, Ms Frampton. We will be in touch to arrange a time for you to meet our artist, if that's OK.'

'Yes, sure. You've got my details.' Eve got up and left the room. Before Doyle and Morgan had gathered up their things, Bea entered.

'Great, do I get my office back now, Chief Inspector?' Bea said.

'Yes, sorry, we're just leaving.'

'Before you dash off, I wanted to run something by you.'

'Go on.'

'I've managed to get the man with the van booked for tomorrow afternoon. He will get all your stuff from the storage unit and take it to your new pad – you won't have to do anything.'

'That's great, thanks.'

'If you can meet me there sometime Sunday, I'll give you the keys and you can get moved in.'

'Thanks, but I might not be able to do it this weekend. I've got a feeling I'm going to be flat out at work.'

'Sorry, boss,' Morgan said. 'None of my business, I know. But you don't need to work all weekend. We can share the work between us. We are capable, you know.'

'Yes, I know that—'

'Good, that's settled then,' said Bea.

'I need to see my son too, at some point. I'm not sure I can fit everything in.'

'I'm happy to work all day Saturday if I can get Sunday morning off,' Morgan said. 'The weather's still going to be good, and I want to get out on my bike; I've not had a chance all week. Birdseye will be delighted to cover Sunday morning. His wife will drag him to church otherwise, and he's always looking for an excuse to get out of that.'

'God, I know how he feels,' said Bea. 'My mum used to make me go to mass every Sunday.'

'So, you can see your son and move house. And I promise one of us will call you if anything significant comes up.'

Doyle couldn't help feeling that his life was being arranged for him.

'That's that, then,' said Bea. 'And bring Harry to the house with you Sunday morning. I'm sure he'll be excited to see his new room.'

⚔ ⚔ ⚔

'How old's Harry?' Morgan asked as they strolled back to the police station.

'Nine, and he's had a rough time the last few years.'

'Is he the reason you moved up here?'

'Yep – there's only so much you can take of the M6 and M1 services, and I think I'd hit my limit.'

'Not to mention the roadworks.'

'So true. Have you got kids?'

'No. Shaima has – twin boys, they drive her round the bend.'

Was it his imagination, or did Morgan change the subject every time he asked her about her life? Doyle wondered. Maybe she was one of those people who liked to keep work and home life strictly separate. That was understandable in this job.

Chapter 32

'OK, listen up, everyone. What I'm about to tell you now does not leave this room. Understood?' The tapping of keyboards ceased, along with the chatter. Doyle felt everyone's eyes on him. In most offices, staff would be winding down for the weekend at this time on a Friday afternoon, but his team had been working flat out since he had joined it on Tuesday morning, and he needed them to keep going. 'Shaima, would you do the honours, please?'

The intelligence analyst stepped forward and pinned two A4 pictures to the evidence board.

'This young woman,' Doyle said, pointing to the photo of a woman with short dark hair, 'is Karolina Valanciunas. She was originally from Lithuania but lived in Manchester. Her body was found on Saddleworth Moor in May 2020. She had been there for several weeks, but despite decomposition, insects and other animals having a feed, the pathologist was able to determine that she was strangled with a ligature. They also found a chemical residue on what was left of her skin, that was found to have come from cleaning wipes.'

The only sound in the incident room was the whirring of the air conditioning as everyone processed this information.

'This woman is Victoria Quinn.' Doyle indicated the second image. 'She was from Leeds. Her body was found in a shallow grave in the Forest of Bowland in April 2019. She had also been strangled with a ligature. The pathologist who worked on her case thinks the killer made an attempt to clean the body with a jet wash post-mortem.'

'Jesus,' Birdseye said.

'You think they might be linked to Chloe, boss?' Gadget asked.

'The fact that all three were strangled with a ligature is a similarity, but not in itself remarkable. The fact that all were young women is just another similarity, and so is the attempt to clean the body in all cases. That the women all had short hair is stacking up the similarities. But what really makes me think we're past the point of believable coincidence is this. Shaima, would you put up the next two pictures?'

Asif once again stepped forward and pinned two more 8 × 10 prints below those she had just added. There was a hush as everyone studied the new images of the two long-haired women, taking in the similarities they had with the short-haired women in the photos directly above them. If thoughts had sounds, Doyle guessed he would be hearing something similar to a coin-pusher machine at the arcade paying out, and the clatter of many pennies dropping at once.

'Bloody hell,' Birdseye said, one hand massaging his beard.

'Bloody hell indeed, DC Nelson, though I think my expletives were somewhat stronger when Shaima brought this to my attention.'

'They definitely were, boss,' Asif confirmed, to no one's surprise.

'Like Chloe Kennedy, both these women cut their hair short not long before they were killed. I think you will agree that, although they look quite different with short hair, all three women looked alike before they had their hair cut.'

'You really think we're dealing with a serial killer here, boss?' Gadget asked. Doyle couldn't tell if the shake in his voice was from excitement or fear, or maybe a bit of both.

'With all these similarities, and especially the recent haircuts, I can't see how the three murders cannot be linked.'

'What else do we know about these two other victims?' Bowen asked.

'Karolina went missing sometime during the first lockdown. It is not known exactly when, as people weren't seeing each other then, so it wasn't reported. But her body had been lying there for at least four weeks when she was found. Greater Manchester Police thought the killer was her ex-boyfriend, but he had gone back to Lithuania before they were able to question him. By the time the authorities there had caught up with him, he had died of an overdose. We are obviously getting all the investigation files sent over, but I think the GMP thought the ex-boyfriend was guilty, so they stopped looking.'

'That's another coincidence, isn't it, boss?' Gadget asked. 'We initially had Ryan Johnson in the frame for Chloe. If he had turned up dead, we might still think it was him.'

'It's certainly worth bearing in mind, though I'm not sure where it gets us now.'

'What about the other one – Victoria?' Birdseye asked.

'Victoria Quinn, or Vicky, as she was known, went missing after a night out at a gay bar in Leeds. She was not seen alive after that. Some walkers became suspicious of a freshly dug piece of ground near Slaidburn and reported it. We are awaiting more information, but it doesn't look like the police ever had a credible suspect.'

'Chloe had been on a night out in a gay bar before she was taken. Do we think there might be a homophobic motive to this after all?' Birdseye asked.

'You've got a point there, Derrick,' Hales said. 'What do you think, Anna? Is there?'

'What you asking me for?' Morgan said.

Doyle noticed a frostiness to her reply.

'Oh, I wasn't. I didn't mean anything by it.' Hales was trying to hastily reverse out of a tight spot. 'It's just that, you know, you've got … well, more of a personal perspective on it, haven't you?'

'What, because I'm a woman?'

'Well, that and…'

'And because I'm gay?'

'Well, yes,' Hales replied, sighing with what looked like relief.

'But I'm not gay.'

'What?' said Gadget.

'Are you sure?' Birdseye asked. Doyle could see that the older man regretted it the second the words were out of his mouth.

'Of course I'm fucking sure. I'm thirty-three years old. I've managed to work out by now who I prefer to shag.'

'But your fiancée. I thought that was a woman,' Hales said, bemusement writ large on his face.

'His name's Sam. It's short for Samuel, not Samantha.'

'Oh. We never knew that,' Hales replied, looking like he had just learned a fascinating piece of trivia.

'So, for the last eight months while we've been working together, everyone has just assumed that I'm gay? Because, what? I have short hair and a partner called Sam?'

'You're quite into sport too,' Gadget added.

'And you each came to the conclusion, because of these three massive clues, that I must be gay? I don't think our serial killer has got much to worry about with you lot trying to catch him, has he?'

'To be fair,' Hales said. 'We didn't come to that conclusion on our own. We discussed it and we all agreed.'

'For fuck's sake,' said Doyle. 'When this case is wrapped up, you three are going on an equality and diversity course. I mean, I'm not surprised about those two old bastards.' He waved his hand towards Hales and Birdseye. 'But Gadget – I thought you younger generation were more on top of this kind of thing.'

'Well, I must say, DS Morgan,' said Bowen, 'I am very proud of you. It was very brave to come out as straight like that in front of your colleagues. And I for one won't judge you or treat you any differently because of it. Although I must admit I am a tiny bit disappointed; I thought you were on my team.'

'Good, that's settled. Now, does anyone mind awfully if we get back to the task in hand and try to catch this bastard?' Doyle said. 'Before we went off on this tangent about DS Morgan's sexual preferences, DC Nelson asked whether there might be a homophobic motive behind these killings. I now know that this might not be your strong point, but what does everyone think?'

'I don't,' Asif said.

'Go on,' said Doyle.

'The link isn't to do with being lesbian or bisexual or even just having short hair. The link is that they all had long brunette hair and then cut it. It's the changing of their appearance, the act of cutting their hair, that triggers them being chosen as a victim.'

'I think you've struck the nail on the head,' said Doyle. 'Anyone disagree?'

'Boss, just one question.'

Doyle was surprised to see Half Price speak up. He hoped he wasn't going to chip in with a vaguely homophobic point or a thinly disguised dig at Bowen.

'Now we know – or, at least, we think we know – that our killer has done this before, how will this help us to work out who he is, and catch him?'

'Good question,' Doyle admitted, rather than complimented. 'First, straight after this briefing I'm going to phone the Super and tell him that it appears we have two linked homicides. For a start, that should mean that we get allocated more resources. We will no doubt have to liaise with the teams that investigated the other two cases. More importantly, we can now view the cases together: this gives us a whole new lens through which to see things. Something that doesn't seem significant when taken on its own might become more apparent if it occurs in two or more of the cases. Maybe even the same person might pop up in each investigation. But for now, we have a lot more to look at, as well as examining all the new leads that are coming in from our current lines of enquiry.'

人 人 人

Mr Burns took the news rather better than Doyle had anticipated. He had half expected him to fly off the handle and accuse Doyle of overcomplicating matters and to concentrate on the Chloe Kennedy case. Croucher sounded reluctant when he conceded that they would be getting the extra resources Doyle had requested, stressing that this would not be happening till Monday at the earliest. After ending the call, Doyle ventured from his office into the incident room, where his mood was lifted further by the appearance of Bowen and Half Price loaded with pizza boxes. This elicited activity from all corners as team members moved in to claim their slice of the action. Bowen handed Doyle back his bank card along with the receipt; the DCI chose not to check how much this act of bribery was costing him. There wasn't much conversation as they all tucked in, other than murmurs of 'cheers, boss' and 'thanks, sir' between mouthfuls.

Doyle was on his second slice of pepperoni when he realised Hales was missing from the group. 'Where's Geoff?' he asked no one in particular. Clearly not wanting to stop eating, Birdseye mimed the act of smoking then pointed to the ceiling. Doyle had wondered how Hales, with his gout-plagued leg, managed to take such short cigarette breaks: it was quite a trek from the incident room down to the car park. The wily old bastard must have been nipping out the fire exit onto the roof. Sure enough, right on cue, Hales limped into the room. The packet of mints in his hand was swiftly returned to his pocket when he saw the pizza.

'Boss, when you're done, can I have a word?' Asif had her laptop in hand, clearly keen to show him something else.

Doyle contemplated another slice, but decided against it. He ushered Asif into his office, 'Don't tell me you've found another one?'

'Not exactly, boss.' She placed the computer on his desk and pulled a seat up next to him so they both could see the screen. There were two pictures of the same woman: one with flowing brunette hair and the other with a cropped cut with a fringe.

'This is Michelle McCarthy, a misper from back in December 1999. She's not shown up since. She was last seen in Manchester, where she was living, a couple of weeks before Christmas. She wasn't reported missing, though, until mid-January 2000. She had an on-off girlfriend, and apparently texted her to say she was going back to Fleetwood, where she was from, because there was some kind of emergency with her younger sister. It was only after the Christmas break when none of her friends could get hold of her that they started to become worried. Her sister had not contacted her about any emergency; her relations with her family were not good. She went into care when she was fourteen because she alleged that her stepdad was abusing her. He was never charged with anything, but social services must have thought there was something in it, to put her into a children's home.'

'In that picture of her with long hair, she bears a distinct resemblance to the other girls. But she went missing over twenty years ago,' Doyle said.

'There's something else, boss. The police spoke to all her friends, past and present, both in Manchester and around Fleetwood. But there was one person they couldn't get hold of – a friend of hers from when she was in the children's home. He had been around until recently, but neighbours said he upped and left after Christmas, saying he was going to Spain. The officers investigating even had a theory that she'd gone off with him.'

'That sounds possible. Young people do these things, especially if neither have a stable family background.'

'The thing is, though, this friend had served two and a half years for arson with intent and got out the winter before Michelle disappeared. He had burned down part of her family home and the attached pigeon loft to get revenge on her stepfather. He also strangled her pet dog … using a wire rope ligature.'

'Now, that sounds very interesting. Who is he?'

'His name's Jason Carter. He was fourteen in June 1996 when he committed the arson and eighteen in December 1999, when Michelle went missing. He would be forty-one now, and he'd fit the description of our suspect.'

'Did he ever resurface anywhere?'

'Not that I could find. Apparently he was only followed up for three months by probation after he got out.'

'That figures. Things weren't as tight back then, especially as he was a juvenile when he committed the offence.'

Chapter 33

Doyle knew he should be sleeping. He had even turned the lights out and tried, but it was no good. His mind was racing and he had just lain there in the dark, thinking about the case. After half an hour of trying to force his brain to switch off, he had given up and turned the lights back on. He had read all he could about the other cases that Shaima Asif had found, and he was even more convinced that they were linked. It was the one back in December 1999 that most intrigued him. Michelle McCarthy, another young woman who had vanished from Britain's streets, leaving those who cared for her still without answers years later. Karolina Valanciunas and Victoria Quinn could be linked to Chloe Kennedy by several similarities in the MO of the killer, but without a body or any indication what had happened to her, they couldn't compare their cases to Michelle's.

Two things were niggling in Doyle's brain, though. Michelle McCarthy, before having her hair cut short, bore a striking resemblance to all the other victims – or perhaps more correctly, they bore a striking resemblance to her. He wondered if she had been the first victim, and all the others had been chosen because they looked like her. The other thing that drew Doyle to her case was her friend, who the police had been unable to trace. It was suspicious enough that Jason Carter had been convicted of setting fire to her family home, and strangling her pet dog. Then he had vanished around the same time that Michelle had, and he had never resurfaced. He hadn't paid National Insurance, claimed benefits, renewed his passport or even been arrested. Like Michelle, it seemed he had just dropped off the face of the earth.

Carter had been convicted in the summer of 1996, and few details of his case could be found on any of the digital databases. But Doyle made a few urgent phone calls at the end of the day, and these had resulted in Doyle taking a short detour on the way back to his hotel to Force HQ in Hutton, where he collected three large box files that had been left for him at the front desk. These contained the paper records on Jason Carter and the offence that had earned him a spell in a young offender institution.

Doyle replaced the forensic report of the arson back in the box. He hadn't discovered anything particularly illuminating. Unleaded petrol had been the accelerant used, but that was the case in a great many malicious fires that were started. In his experience, the choice of fuel used to get things going was more often determined by availability than the arsonist's choice.

Then Doyle came across a Social Circumstances Report. This had been written for the court by the social worker who had Carter on her caseload at the time of his arrest. It started at the beginning of his life and summarised key events until the fourteen-year-old Carter found himself before the judge. There had been nothing remarkable about his early childhood, certainly until he had started school. In fact, his early life – in comparison to many others who ended up in a children's home – had been charmed. He had lived with both his parents in Lytham in an upmarket semi-detached house just a few hundred yards from the beach. His father had been a successful businessman running a small chain of video rental shops in Lytham St Annes and Blackpool. His mother was described in the report as a housewife.

At primary school, academically and developmentally, there was nothing that stood out about the boy. A couple of behavioural issues had been reported about his relationships with other pupils but, to Doyle's frustration, the report didn't elaborate on these.

He took a long drink from the glass of water by his bed and read on.

In March 1993, Roger Carter had been found drowned on a sandbank near Lytham St Anne's. The coroner recorded an open verdict, having not been able to conclude whether Mr Carter had intended to take his own life. He left behind his wife and a ten-year-old boy. Roger Carter, it transpired, had racked up mountains of dept, borrowing against the family home to try to rescue his floundering businesses. His modest chain of video stores hadn't been able to hold their own when the big boys moved into town. In July that year, Jason Carter and his mother were evicted when their house was repossessed. They found themselves living in a bedsit in Blackpool, then Cleveleys.

'Jesus,' Doyle said. It had gone from happy families to a messed-up childhood in one page of A4. He turned over.

Things didn't improve for the two remaining members of the Carter family. In January 1994, Marie Carter was diagnosed with breast cancer. This metastasised extensively and, in spring 1995, thirteen-year-old Jason went into foster care while his mother went to a hospice for the last few months of her life. Jason was moved from the foster family to a children's home in Fleetwood after the sudden death of the family rabbit, which Jason was blamed for. The report did not elaborate, but Doyle would be willing to bet a good amount of his weekly wage that the bunny had died from some form of strangulation.

During his time at the children's home, staff noted that Carter suffered from night-time enuresis. Something occurred to Doyle from a forensic psychology training course he had been on. What had the psychologist called it? That was it – 'the homicidal triad'. Cruelty to animals, fire-setting, and bed-wetting in children and adolescents. On their own these behaviours didn't mean much, but if they all happened together, they could be a red flag, warning of an individual's potential for committing murder in later life.

Carter had all three.

Doyle read on. At the children's home, Jason struck up a close friendship with Michelle McCarthy. The burning of part of the house and the pigeon loft was seen as an act of revenge against Michelle's stepfather, who she had alleged repeatedly abused her, although he was never charged. Carter was arrested for the offence, having been found sitting by his parents' grave in Lytham Park Cemetery. It was Michelle who had told the police where he could be found, after she'd found out about the death of her pet dog.

Doyle put down the report, processing the information it contained and what it meant. *Jason Carter, where are you now? I'm coming to find you.*

Chapter 34

December 1999

'See, Michelle, I told you it was beautiful here.'

They gazed through the windscreen at the rugged landscape in front of them. Islands of dark rock jutted up between patches of gorse and heather. The late morning sun was obscured by thick clouds, lurking ominously, poised to spill their contents.

'It's kind of spooky and mysterious. Not in a bad way, though. Like in *Wuthering Heights*,' Michelle said.

'What, that old song by what's-her-name?'

'Kate Bush.'

'Yeah, that's her.'

'No, I mean the book that the song's based on, by Emily Brontë. It's set in the moors not far from here. I've been doing A Level English.' Michelle exhaled a plume of smoke through the tiny opening in the van's window, then passed the joint back to Jay. 'You've got better at skinning up.'

'Thanks. It's wild up here. It's like you're a million miles from anywhere.'

'Yeah. We'd better not stay too long, though. If that snow starts to come down heavier, we might get stuck.'

'You ever heard about the Moors Murderers?'

'What, Myra Hindley and Liam Brady?'

'It's Ian Brady. Liam Brady was a footballer.'

'I thought you didn't like football, Jay?'

'I don't. That's not the point. Brady and Hindley buried their victims on these moors. Some of them were never found.' He passed the joint back to her.

'Fuck off, that's creepy. This snow's getting heavier. I think we should get going. You don't want to get too wrecked to drive down these roads when it's like this.'

The windscreen wipers swished, giving them a clear view of a wild, whitening landscape.

'We're a bit like them, me and you. Partners in crime.'

'Fuck off, Jay, they killed children! And we're not partners, in crime or otherwise.'

'We were like partners back then.'

'No, we weren't. You were just a kid who'd had a tough time. I felt sorry for you.'

'You liked me better than all those other boys back then.'

'Because you didn't harass me or try to fuck me or get me to suck you off.'

'We could've been partners, Michelle, me and you. We still could.'

'No, we couldn't, not back then and not now. Let's get going. I want to get back. I'm serious.' She threw the joint out of the tiny gap in the window.

'What you doing? There was plenty left on that.'

'I told you. I want to get going. You're freaking me out.'

The wipers swished the screen clear again.

'Why couldn't we be together, Michelle? I might've been a boy back then. But I'm a man now.'

'Don't. You've got your life and I've got mine. We've both moved on. Let's go.'

'I wouldn't be like all those other men in your past. I'd treat you right.'

'Fucking hell, Jay. I don't like men, OK? I like girls. It's not about you or any other guy. I just like women.'

'But you never used to.'

'Yes, I did. I always have. It's just not the kind of thing you brag about when you're a teenager in a children's home. I'm gay. That's who I am. This is the real me.' Michelle turned away and looked out of the window.

'Is she your girlfriend then?'

'What?' Michelle turned back.

'That girl with the bleached blonde buzz cut?'

'What the fuck? Have you been watching me?' There was fire in her eyes.

'No, no, it wasn't like that. I saw you in a bar. I was going to say hello, and then I saw you with her.'

'Jay, that's fucking weird. You were watching me – what the fuck? I want to go now. Take me back.'

'Michelle, don't be like that. Just stay and chat. Please.'

'No. Get me down from this hill or mountain or whatever the fuck this place is, back to civilisation. You're freaking me out.'

'I get why you feel like you do. But I'm not like other men. We never got the chance to be together. I would treat you right. Look after you.'

'I don't need looking after. I need you to start this van and take me back to Manchester. You need to move on from that time in the children's home. I have, and you need to.'

The wipers swiped another film of snow from the windscreen. The road was now more white than black.

'I did two and a half years inside for you, and you can't even stay and chat for half an hour? You owe me.'

'I don't owe you fuck all. I never asked you to do that; I didn't want that. I didn't want you to kill my dog or put my sister's life at risk. You need help. You're not right.' Michelle opened the door, letting in a blast of freezing air.

'What the fuck are you doing?'

'I'm going back. If you won't take me, then I'll walk.'

'Michelle, don't.'

The door slammed. He watched in the mirror as she walked away, leaving footprints on the road. Head bowed against the wind, she didn't look back.

'Fuck.' He smacked his hands on the steering wheel.

She was getting smaller in the mirror as she descended, approaching the bend. He crunched the van into gear and turned the vehicle round. The van slid as he pulled out of the layby onto the road. Michelle was round the corner now and out of sight. He braked before the bend, not wanting to go skidding off the tarmac. Even so, the van slid unnervingly sideways as he turned the steering wheel. He could see her again. He slowed down to pass her, and she didn't look up. *Christ, she'll freeze. How far are we from any houses?* He rounded another bend at a snail's pace and pulled in by a gated entrance to a track. He got out and felt the bite of the chill wind burning his cheeks. He went to the back of the van and lifted the boot, sitting down on the edge. He leaned into the vehicle, shielding himself from the breeze, as he lit a Silk Cut.

Then he saw Michelle. She stopped when she saw him. She held something in her hands; he couldn't tell what.

'Fucking hell.' He saw, rather than heard, the words come out of her mouth. She bowed her head again and kept walking.

'Michelle,' he called to her as she got close.

'Fuck off, Jay.'

'Don't be like that. Get back in the van. I'll drive you straight back.'

'I'll walk.'

'You'll freeze.'

'I'll get someone to pick me up as soon as I get a signal.'

'Do you even know where you are, where to get them to meet you?'

'I'll work it out.'

He got up and walked towards her. 'Get in the van.'

She didn't answer. He grabbed her wrist. She struggled and tried to pull free, but he was stronger now. He was a man now.

'What are you doing? Get off me!' She screamed the words into the wilderness. He put an arm around her and pulled her to him. She tried to get away, but her feet slipped on the snow.

'Get off me,' she screamed again.

He put his hand across her mouth to silence her. She bit his hand.

'You cunt.' He punched her in the stomach, winding her, and pulled her towards the open boot of the van before she could catch her breath. He pushed the top half of her body into the van but her legs held firm, pushing back against him.

He reached into the boot, grabbed a luggage strap and pulled it round her neck, feeding the soft end through the buckle. She tried to wriggle free, but he was right behind her, his groin against her arse as she pushed. She was writhing and grunting, trying to break his hold. He pulled the strap hard, and her hands came up to her throat, grasping at the strap, trying to get it away from her. He reached round and undid her belt and the top button on her jeans, yanking them down.

He felt her legs clamp together, keeping him out. He undid his own jeans and freed himself. He pulled the strap tighter around her neck and kicked her left leg sideways, opening her clamped thighs. He pushed and pushed, guiding himself with his free hand, until he managed to squeeze inside her. Despite the choking strap around her throat, she let out a yelp.

His left hand found its way up her top. Her flesh was warm against his icy hands. He pushed her bra up out of the way and cupped a breast in his hand. She yelped again. His right hand pulled, tightening the strap. He thrust in and out, squeezing her breast. She writhed against him, trying to free herself. He pulled the strap and kept going. Her efforts to resist became weaker as his got stronger. And then he felt the ecstasy of his release. It continued to pulse out of him, and he felt the pulse in her neck fading. He pulled harder on the strap, unable to stop.

'Oh, Michelle.' He said the words out loud, though he wasn't sure if she could still hear him. 'You see, we were meant to be together. And you ruined it. It's your fault it ended like this.' He pulled again on the strap, hard, then pulled out and away from her. Her body slumped into the boot of the van, lifeless.

⊥ ⊥ ⊥

An electronic chirp from behind him startled him out of his thoughts. It was a mobile phone. *Her* mobile phone. Michelle was still in the back, zipped into his sleeping bag. He had thought about dumping her on the moor. It felt fitting somehow, but he knew he couldn't. He had been caught before because he had been careless, not thought about the CCTV at the petrol station. He'd read about DNA, and he knew that his would be all over Michelle, inside and out. He needed to put her somewhere where she would never be found, and slip away before she was missed. He pulled over. He didn't know why he had driven back towards Manchester. Perhaps he had hoped that Michelle would come round, agree that it had all been a misunderstanding, and he could drop her home and move on. But that wouldn't happen; he knew she was dead. By the time he had stripped her clothes off in the back of the van, she was stone cold and getting stiff.

The phone chirped again. He reached into the back of the van and fished it from her coat pocket. He looked at the screen, which showed an envelope icon next to the name Zoe B. A text message, he realised, and opened it.

Hi Miche, thanks for last night. Shall we have a night in together tom? Save some money n not go out. We can have more fun just the 2 of us. Xxx

The phoned chirped again and another text message flashed up; they must have come into a good reception area. This message was from Mel Little Sis. It read

Hi Michelle, hope you're OK, missing you. R u going to come up and see me at Xmas? Mum and him away new year's eve, you could stay then and catch up. Love you xx

He didn't have a mobile phone and had never sent a text message. The two replies he wrote now might just be the most important texts he ever sent. He read back through a few texts on the phone, deciding what to write and seeing how Michelle would have written it, before settling on

Love to hun but need to take a rain check. Little sis having big problems at home. Need to get back there and support her. Should be back next week xxx

He sent that to Zoe B.

Sorry Mel, can't make New Year's Eve, lots of study 2 do. Well behind. Will see you in the new year though. Love you xx

He sent that to Mel Little Sis.

After a bleep told him the messages had been sent, he opened the back of the Nokia. The SIM card went into a rubbish bin, along with the battery. The phone went into a canal. He still needed to work out what to do with Michelle, but he hoped he had now bought himself some time.

Chapter 35

Day 5: Saturday 17th June 2023

'I'm not convinced,' Mr Burns said.

Doyle wondered why his superior officer had decided to attend the Saturday morning briefing. Judging by his attire, he was all ready to spend the day on the golf course. Doyle could just about understand the attraction of a round of golf, especially on a day as sunny as this one, but why did those who played have to wear such ridiculous clothes?

'This could all be irrelevant. We don't even know if that girl, Michelle McCarthy, is dead, let alone if this Jason Carter killed her,' the DS said. 'What the team here need to do is concentrate on Chloe Kennedy and not get sidetracked.'

Doyle had spent the first ten minutes of the meeting outlining to the team why, after all the reading he had done the previous night, he felt that Jason Carter was their man. He expected his theory to be picked apart, and was quite prepared for scrutiny, though to have his hypothesis dismissed out of hand by a man wearing a purple diamond-patterned tank top was disappointing. He took a deep breath before responding.

'I agree we should concentrate on what we have here – Chloe Kennedy. But that doesn't mean we shouldn't look at the bigger picture as well. Whoever the killer is, they have been one step ahead of us all the way. Do you at least agree that it's likely that the person who killed Chloe Kennedy also killed Karolina Valanciunas and Victoria Quinn?'

'I certainly think it's possible, which is why first thing Monday morning the SIOs on both those cases, from Manchester and Yorkshire, will be coming here. You can outline what we have then. If they agree they're linked, we will proceed accordingly. In the meantime, we really need to get a picture of the man we're looking for, whoever he may be. What's happening about that?'

'Eve Frampton, the estate agent, is with the specialist now working on an e-fit pic, sir,' Hales said. 'Once we've got that, we can take it to the cab firm and see if the people there think it's a good match to the guy who did their IT. If it is, we'll put it out over the media.'

'We really could do with an actual photo,' Mr Burns said. 'Those e-fit things never look much like the person once you catch them. Is there no—'

'Gadget,' Morgan shouted. 'Sorry for interrupting, sir. Did you get all the footage from Amir Hussain's dashcam, right up to when we met him at the minicab office?'

'Yes. I've got everything that was on there.'

'The mystery IT man, our killer, was walking out of the car park as Amir was driving in. Check it. There might be a picture of him on there that's not obscured by a cloud of vape smoke.'

The incident room fell silent as everyone crowded round Gadget's laptop. The young officer found what he wanted in under half a minute.

'Bingo,' Doyle said as a man walked into the frame, visible through the car windscreen.

Gadget slowly played the footage back and forth until the best view of the man was on screen, and zoomed in. It showed a figure in a Nike baseball cap. He had kept his head down, but he had looked up as the cab came into the car park. He could have been anything from mid-thirties to mid-forties, he had light brown hair and was average height. He fitted the description of the suspect they were looking for. But then again, so did a lot of people, thought Doyle.

'Great work, now do us a favour,' instructed Doyle. 'Get a screen grab of that and run downstairs and check with Eve if that looks like the guy she showed round the house where Chloe was killed.'

'I recognise him from somewhere,' Morgan said.

'Of course you do,' said Mr Burns. 'You practically walked into him when he was coming out of the minicab office.'

'No, from somewhere else,' Morgan said.

'Anyway, I'm off. Get that picture out there. Hopefully it won't be long before someone recognises him and we find out where he is.' With that, Croucher left the room. Doyle sensed the team relaxing.

'Boss, just a thought,' said Birdseye. 'If we brought in some kind of facial recognition expert, they might be able to compare the man here to photos of Jason Carter when he left the young offender institution. Age them up and see if it's the same person.'

'No need,' said Jen Knight, who had been silently working on her laptop. 'I've just had some results come back. One of the fingerprints lifted at the house in Limbrick, from a wardrobe handle, has returned a match for Jason Carter. Looks like your theory is correct, Liam.'

That was indeed good news. They now had a name and a photo for their suspect. It was just a shame it hadn't come in a few minutes earlier, so Doyle could have seen the conceited grin being wiped off Mr Burns' face.

'Did you say it was Lytham Park Cemetery where Jason Carter was arrested for the arson?' Birdseye asked.

'Yes, why?'

'Oh, nothing … but that's where R2-D2 was cremated.'

'What?' Doyle asked, thinking he must have misheard Birdseye.

'That little robot from *Star Wars*?' Hales asked.

'That's the one.'

'They're called droids,' Gadget said.

'Why would you cremate a robot?' Doyle felt compelled to ask.

'Well, not the robot itself, boss.'

'Droid,' Gadget corrected, irritation in his voice.

'The actor who played him – you know, the man inside,' Birdseye said.

'There was a man inside?' Gadget sounded disbelieving.

'It was the 1970s, son, there was a man inside everything,' Hales said.

'He was dead, like – the actor, Kenny Baker – before they cremated him.'

'Well, thank fuck for that,' Doyle said. 'It would have been pretty cruel if he was still alive.'

⊀ ⊀ ⊀

After the morning briefing, Doyle arranged to try and locate Carter. Now they had an actual photo of him, they sent this to the press office to be distributed across all forms of media. Someone, somewhere, must have seen him and know where he was living. If he tried to leave the country by conventional means, the odds were stacked against him. They might not have much detail on Carter, but now they had the bank statements for James Fisher IT Ltd, Morgan would go through them today to see if any transaction might give them a clue that would lead them to Carter.

Doyle had delegated the task of drawing up a weekend rota to DI Hales. He'd instructed him to try to keep everyone happy and make sure they all got some rest. To be fair to the Pearl, he had done a pretty good job. No one had moaned about the shifts they were booked on, though this might be due to all the overtime being welcome in a cost-of-living crisis, or to the desire to catch someone who would soon become a notorious killer. Doyle suspected for most of the team, it was a bit of both.

Not due back in work until the following lunchtime, Doyle went straight from the incident room to pick up Harry from his grandparents' house. The boy liked Doyle's car, and Doyle soon gave in to Harry's repeated requests to press the button to turn on the blue flashing lights. When Harry tried to turn them off, he had accidentally activated the sirens and startled himself with the noise. He screamed in the front seat, his hands clamped across his ears, for a good minute after Doyle had silenced the wailing.

The rest of the afternoon passed without incident. Harry hadn't said much as they went from a playpark to an ice-cream parlour and for a walk around a canal boat marina. Doyle knew that he would receive a bollocking from his ex-wife for giving Harry McDonald's for his evening meal, but the drive-through was on their way back to the hotel and he could hardly prepare a healthy, nutritious meal there.

Premier Inns were good for Harry. It didn't matter where you were in the country, the rooms were all more or less the same. Even though Doyle was staying there alone, he had booked a family room, knowing that when Harry came over, he would be able to relax in its comforting familiarity. Many things in life did not come easy to Harry, but the boy made short work of connecting his iPad to the hotel's Wi-Fi and was soon sitting on the double bed playing *Minecraft*. Doyle settled down next to him.

Now he finally had his work email up and running, it had taken huge amounts of restraint to resist checking it while he was out with Harry. He knew that if there were any significant developments someone would have called him – at least, he hoped they would have. Now with Harry settled and engaged in another world on the screen, he took out his phone and had a quick look. There were several messages. The toxicology results for Chloe Kennedy had finally come back; it was no surprise that traces of several sedatives had been found in her system. Doyle hoped that the dose she had been administered had been strong enough that she wouldn't have been aware of what was happening to her, but he guessed that her killer would have given her just enough to stop her putting up any meaningful resistance during her abduction. The drawn-out nature of the killing suggested that Carter got some perverse pleasure from the women's suffering.

Doyle put away his phone and turned the TV on. The north-west news was just starting on BBC1. Jason Carter's image came up on the screen, while the newsreader announced that Lancashire Police were looking for this man in connection with the murder of Chloe Kennedy. Wait till they find out about the other women, Doyle thought. The media would have a field day.

'Anyone with information about the whereabouts of this man, who may also be known as James Fisher, should call the incident room number displayed at the bottom of the screen,' the newsreader said. 'Carter is considered to be extremely dangerous. Members of the public are warned not to approach him, but to call the police immediately if they see him.'

Doyle was grateful that the number on the screen wasn't actually the incident room number, but the one for the telephone operators at Force HQ. Hopefully they would be able to filter out most of the inevitable crank calls before they reached his team.

'Are you going to catch the bad guy, Dad?'

Doyle was a little taken back by his son's question, as he had thought that Harry was absorbed in his game. At times, he felt that a bomb could go off down the road and Harry wouldn't notice, he was so wrapped up in what he was doing.

'It might not be me, but someone will catch him, Harry. And he will go to prison forever.'

'Do they have the internet in prison?'

Doyle had to stifle a laugh. 'No, and they aren't allowed iPads either.'

'I'm definitely never going to live in prison, then.'

'Do you know what we're going to do tomorrow morning after we've had breakfast?'

'Will it be the buffet breakfast, Dad?'

'Yes, Harry.'

'Will you put everything on my plate so that nothing is touching?'

'Yes, Harry.'

'And no squeaky mushrooms?'

'No squeaky mushrooms.'

'Promise?'

'Promise. And you know what we're going to do after that?'

'What?'

'We're going to go and see a house that I'm moving into. It's got a bedroom for you too.'

'Is Mum going to move in there as well?'

'Harry, it's—'

'Are we all going to live there?' Harry's face had lit up at this thought, and now Doyle was going to crush him all over again. They had had this conversation in various guises hundreds of times before, and every time he told the boy that they wouldn't be living together as a family it broke his heart once more.

'No, Harry. I'm sorry. But we will all be living much closer together, so you will see much more of me than you have done for the last nine months.'

Tears streamed down Harry's face, which had morphed into a picture of total sorrow. Doyle wondered how his expressions could change so instantly.

'I want to go back to London.' The words came out between sobs and sniffs.

'We can't. You know that. Your mum's got her job up here now, and I've moved my job up here. And you're at a new school.'

'I don't like my school. The boys aren't nice to me.'

Doyle put an arm around his son and pulled him in, so Harry's head rested on his chest, his tears soaking Doyle's T-shirt.

'We were all happy back in London in that house. All together as a family. I want to go back there. Everything was happy then.'

Doyle kissed the top of his son's head. 'I'm sorry, Harry. I really am.'

Chapter 36

Morgan was just finishing an email to Doyle and the rest of the team summarising the day's progress and what needed to be picked up the next day. She had been through the bank statements for James Fisher IT Ltd, highlighting any useful entries, and had left them on Doyle's desk.

A press release had been sent out along with Carter's photo, saying he was wanted in connection with Chloe Kennedy's murder. Doyle had wanted the link to the other murdered women to be mentioned too, but this had been blocked by Croucher until they had met the teams who had investigated the other cases. This decision had pissed Morgan off, as it would mean the story wouldn't make the main headlines nationally and was only likely to be featured prominently on local news, possibly giving Carter the chance to slip away unnoticed. A wanted serial killer would have been another matter; every network would have run it as their main story, with the photo of Jason Carter flashed across TV screens, social media and the printed press up and down the country. As it was, only those with nothing better to do on a Saturday night than watch the local news would see the story today, along with Carter, who Morgan knew would be following developments in the investigation closely.

She pressed 'send', noticing that it was almost 6 p.m. She would be home by half past. Sam would've cooked something nice; he always did when she had to work at a weekend. A little treat to look forward to at the end of the day. She would allow herself one glass of wine, but no more than that. Any more and she would feel the effects tomorrow: her resting heart rate would go up and her recovery time would increase, meaning no chance of getting a PB time on her ride.

The phone on her desk rang.

'Morgan,' she answered, trying hard to suppress a yawn.

'It's Kay from the front desk. There's a guy down here wanting to see you. Says he's got information about Chloe Kennedy's killer. He recognised the man on the TV.'

That was the other problem; all the cranks had nothing better to do on a Saturday night than watch the news. Morgan scanned the incident room, looking for someone to go downstairs and take a statement. She knew Half Price was working, and this was just the job for him.

'Did the man give you his name?' Morgan asked, playing for time, hoping the diminutive PC would walk back into the room before she had to go looking for him.

'Yes, it's Elliot Parker. He says he's the caretaker at the school where the murdered woman worked.'

Morgan's gaze moved from the incident room to the phone on her desk, as if the object itself might spew out what information the caretaker had.

'Can you tell Mr Parker I will be right down? Is there an interview room free?'

⋏ ⋏ ⋏

'He's done some work at the school. James Fisher, or whatever his real name is. I saw him on the news this evening.' Elliot Parker started talking before Morgan had managed to close the interview room door.

'OK, Elliot,' she said, sitting down on one side of the desk and gesturing for Parker to sit opposite. 'Let start at the beginning. When was he working at the school, and in what capacity?'

'It was recently – he finished about six weeks ago. He was installing new smart screens in all the Key Stage 2 classrooms. Mrs Edwards had got funding for the project, and James Fisher IT quoted for the work. The office would have checked him out before he started work. I'm not sure if he would have needed an enhanced DBS. But his company must be legit, they are very thorough.'

'Sorry, I'm not familiar with the terms. Did Chloe Kennedy have a Key Stage 2 classroom?'

'Yes, it's Years 3, 4, 5 and 6. Chloe taught Year 5.'

'And these screens, I assume, would have been fitted when the school was closed? Would Chloe have met Jason Carter or James Fisher, as he called himself? Did the teachers receive training in using the smart screens? Or was there some other way that their paths may have crossed?'

'That's the thing – normally they wouldn't have done. The training was all quite basic and covered on the app, and as you say, the screens were fitted when the school was closed.'

'But do you think they might have met?'

'I know they did.' Parker breathed out heavily. 'Oh God, I'm responsible. For them meeting, I mean. If it wasn't for me, Chloe would still be …'

'It's OK, Elliot. It's not your fault. Nobody knew who James Fisher really was, or what he was like.' Morgan gave him what she hoped was a sympathetic smile. 'Please go on. How did they come to meet?'

'It was on that Saturday – the one I told your colleagues about, the young one and the old one. I had gone to Chloe's house to give her some support when she kicked her ex-boyfriend out. James, or whatever his real name is, was working at the school that day, in Chloe's classroom, as it happens, installing the screen. I shouldn't have left the premises with him there. But … well … I explained the situation to him and gave him the spare keys for her room and went. I guess I came back about an hour and a half later. Chloe gave me a lift back, and Dani came along as well. I went straight to the classroom to check if everything was OK. Mrs Edwards sometimes turns up unannounced at the weekends, and she would have had my guts for garters if she found out I had left a contractor alone on the premises. I guess she'll find out now anyway. Not that that matters. Not really.'

'Did Chloe and Dani go with you to her classroom?'

'Yes. Dani suggested we stop at the café on the way back and we had picked up bacon barms for lunch. We ate them in there. Chloe and Dani were on quite a high after the morning's events, and I was just relieved I hadn't been caught out.'

'Was there any interaction between Chloe and Carter?'

'Well, yes, I picked up a barm cake for him to say thank you, like, for not dropping us in it. So he stopped working. It were quite funny really…'

'Funny in what way?'

'We were all sat round one of the tables together, on those little chairs, eating. Dani told him that Chloe had just got rid of her ex, who was a right bastard. He said that his sister had got rid of her husband about a year ago and completely changed her look – you know, for a fresh start. He said she'd cut her hair short, even dressed different, and she felt like she had a new lease of life. Dani joined in and said to Chloe that's what she should do.'

'It was Jason Carter who suggested to Chloe that she should cut her hair short?' Morgan asked, trying to keep the shock out of her voice. Carter hadn't just targeted a woman who looked like Michelle McCarthy and who had then cut her hair short. He had been the one to instigate it, turning her into a victim to meet his needs.

'Yes, and when I saw her on Monday, she'd done it. Dani also suggested they go out drinking in town to celebrate, but Chloe said she couldn't, as she had her car parked outside the school. Dani was quite insistent and told her to leave her car and get it the next day.' He stopped, looking shocked. 'Oh

God, I can't believe I didn't think of this before, when you last interviewed me.'

'What, Elliot? What is it?'

'Well, then James – sorry, Carter – gave Chloe and Dani business cards for a local cab firm. He told them to download the app to their phones. He said he did their IT, and that the company was very good and looked after its customers. Oh God, this is horrible. He was luring her in, wasn't he?'

'It would appear so,' said Morgan, a nagging thought playing on her mind. 'Those keys you left him with – the classroom ones. Did they include a key for Chloe's desk drawer?'

'Yes, they would have, and the store cupboard.'

'Did you get them back off him straight away, do you remember?'

'No, it completely slipped my mind at first, but he returned them by the end of the day, so he wouldn't have been able to get back in afterwards. They're not the kind of keys you can just get cut at your local hardware store.'

No, Morgan thought. But he would have had ample time to go through Chloe's desk after meeting her and find her diary – which contained the passwords to all her social media and email accounts, and the PIN for her phone.

Morgan still had that nagging thought in her mind. She knew she had seen Carter's face before, and she was pretty sure it hadn't been from the minicab company, when he'd been obscured by vape fumes. 'When did Carter finish working at the school?'

'The next day – the Sunday.'

'And has he been back since, that you're aware of?'

'No, not as far as I know, and it would most likely be me I would have dealt with if he had a reason to come back. All the screens have been working perfectly since then.'

If not the school, *where* had she seen him? She knew she had, and recently. She frowned and racked her brains.

Chapter 37

Day 6: Sunday 18th June 2023

'Good morning, Liam,' a cheery Scouse voice greeted Doyle as he got out of the car. 'And you must be Harry. I'm Bea,' she said, holding out her hand to the boy, who looked at it for a second before realising he was meant to shake it, which he did enthusiastically.

'How old are you now? No, wait, don't tell me – let me guess… Twelve?'

'I'm nine,' Harry replied, adding, 'that's an odd number.'

'It certainly is. Well now, you look very big for your age. You must take after your dad – either that or you've had one of those big Premier Inn breakfasts and suddenly shot up.'

The boy laughed. 'My dad ate loads – that's why his belly is getting so big.'

'Well, in that case it's a good job we're moving him out of there. We wouldn't want him turning into Mr Blobby, would we?'

'I am still here, you know,' Doyle said.

'Who's Mr Blobby?'

'Oh, sorry – before your time. A big fat pink thing that used to be on the telly. Would you like to see inside the house, Harry?'

The boy nodded. Bea grabbed his hand and led him up the gravel path to the front door. She leaned in close to him and said in a stage whisper, 'Don't tell your dad, but you've got the best room. It looks out onto the countryside.' Harry laughed as they went through the front door.

Inside, the house looked very different to when Doyle had seen it earlier in the week. In the lounge, his sofa sat by the window, facing the TV, which sat on a cabinet that had been assembled from the flat pack state it had been in in the storage unit. His rug had been rolled out across the laminate floor. In the corner were three neatly stacked cardboard boxes, all with 'living room' scrawled across them in his writing. Best of all, resting on the sofa was his guitar in its case. He would play that tonight when he got in from work: pour himself a drink and sit down and play. It had been far too long.

Going through to the kitchen, he saw that the table and chairs had been reassembled and more boxes adorned with the word 'kitchen' had been stacked neatly.

'Wow, Bea, this is great, thank you so much.'

'You're very welcome. They've put the beds together upstairs too, and moved the boxes and clothes up there. You shouldn't need to do anything but unpack.'

'Can I go and see my bedroom now?' Harry looked from Doyle to Bea, not sure who he should be asking.

'Sure,' Doyle replied. 'It's upstairs at the back.' Harry didn't wait for further instruction, and shot off up the stairs.

'Mind your head.' This time Bea's warning came before the detective injured himself as he ascended.

Upstairs Harry was rifling through all the stuff in his new room, like he was possessed. 'Dad, all my Lego's here. The stuff I couldn't take to Grandma and Grandad's.'

Doyle was relieved to see his son beaming from ear to ear. First impressions meant a lot to Harry, and if he hadn't liked the house from the start, it would have been a hard sell from there on in.

'All my other toys are here too – the ones I've been missing. This is amazing.'

'I think he likes it.'

Doyle turned to Bea, who had come up the stairs behind them. 'Thanks so much. I really appreciate this. He needs a place where he can be at home with me too.'

'Well, I'm glad I've been able to put a smile on someone's face this week. With that fire, the problems with your purchase, and another one that fell through, it seems like I've just been delivering bad news lately.'

'I know the feeling,' replied Doyle.

'Dad, can I get a new computer for here so I can play *Minecraft*?'

'You don't need a new computer to play *Minecraft*. You've got it on your iPad.'

'It's not the same on the iPad; you can do more things on the PC. And it helps me to relax when I'm stressed.'

'I'll think about it.'

'You know, you'll be saving a good bit of money not staying in the hotel and needing to have that storage unit,' Bea joined in.

'And it would be educational, Dad. I could do schoolwork on it.'

'That's true – you can't get far with homework these days without a computer.'

'OK, but you're not having it up here in your room, or I'd never see you.'

'Yes!' shouted Harry, then high-fived the hand Bea held up for him.

⚐ ⚐ ⚐

Morgan flicked the smaller paddle on the drop bars several times, moving the bike into a higher gear. The road plateaued out here then kicked up once more briefly to reach its highest point before it flowed downwards to the village of Belmont. She glanced at the bike computer on the handlebars and saw that her heart rate was 176. Not bad after two miles of solid uphill riding from the Anglezarke reservoir. She could feel the burn in the front of her thighs starting to wear off, just as her breathing began to steady. It was another beautiful day, and Morgan was grateful that the weather had held out until her day off so she could enjoy the West Pennine Moors in the sunshine. Not that she would have been put off by rain or wind or cold, though she might have chosen a different route. The steep descent she had negotiated before this climb, with the hairpin bend at the end, was treacherous in the wet, even though her latest pride and joy was blessed with hydraulic disc brakes.

She had thought about changing her route today, as it went right past the beauty spot from where Chloe Kennedy's body had been thrown almost a week ago. Part of her felt it was almost disrespectful to be enjoying that patch of countryside so soon afterwards. But this was one of her favourite routes: not particularly long at twenty-two miles, it had over eighteen hundred feet of climbing, testing both her legs and her cardiovascular system. Besides, she had reasoned to herself, people like Jason Carter did terrible things, but they shouldn't be allowed to taint the beauty of the places where they did them. Even so, she was relieved to see no reminders of the crime scene investigation when she rode past.

Morgan enjoyed several lungfuls of clean, cool air while she took in the scenery around her and approached the hill. Above her to the right was the true summit of Winter Hill, complete with the TV mast that could be seen for miles. To her left the landscape fell away and became a tapestry of greens and yellows, divided by drystone walls and sprinkled liberally with sheep. She was just about to power up the last short, steep section, hoping to record a good time on Strava, when she noticed a car parked at an odd angle in the layby ahead. And it wasn't just any car; it was a white Toyota Prius. As she got closer, she saw that it wasn't just any white Toyota Prius; this one had a dent on the back, next to the badge. Could this be the car that was used to abduct Chloe Kennedy? Had Carter dumped it here?

Morgan unclipped her feet from the pedals and pulled up behind the vehicle. She leaned her bike up against the wall, making sure she didn't knock the frame and that there was nothing on the ground to puncture her tyres. She removed her helmet and gloves and took her phone out of the pocket in the back of her cycling jersey. Snapping off a few pics, she approached the car. It was a strange place to abandon it if you didn't want it to be found. Perhaps Jason Carter had got spooked seeing his picture on the news last night, and had taken his car up here with a bike in the back, and had left it and cycled back down the hill.

Close to the boot, she crouched down, then opened her work email to find a picture of the CCTV image of the vehicle with the dent. They were identical. She pulled up the incident room number to phone it in and get the scene of crime people there. This could be major: the car's satnav might even lead them to where Carter was living. Before she had managed to press the call button, Morgan heard a scraping noise just behind her.

Turning, she saw boots and legs. She had no time to react. She sensed something moving through the air, and then an almighty force against her temple. Everything went black.

Chapter 38

Birdseye was the only officer in the incident room when Doyle arrived just before two on Sunday afternoon. The former had been only too willing to cover the Sunday morning and thus avoid the weekly struggle of trying not to nod off during the church sermon. Doyle had come into work after dropping Harry off with his grandparents. He was keen to go through everything to do with the case before officers from the Greater Manchester and West Yorkshire police forces descended on them on Monday morning. In his experience, there could be a lot of territorial rivalry between forces, and if there was something that hadn't been done or had been overlooked, someone was bound to be keen to point it out publicly. He hoped the fact that they already knew who the prime suspect was and had forensic evidence to back that up, would mean that even Mr Burns would not be minded to replace Doyle as SIO with a more senior officer, though he wouldn't put it past the man if he felt there was a sniff of glory to be had.

'Any updates, Derrick?'

'Nothing significant. I assume you got the email from DS Morgan last night about Carter doing some work at the school?'

'I did, thanks. And nothing about his whereabouts from the press conference and the release of his photo?'

'Nothing of any use so far. We've had our local Mystic Meg on – she says he will be hiding somewhere near a place of worship and a stream.'

'That narrows it down a bit.' Doyle laughed. 'Maybe you should have gone to church this morning after all.'

PC Bowen strolled into the incident room with an air of enthusiasm that was never seen in officers aged over thirty. By then they had always turned to the dark side and fully embraced suspicion and cynicism.

'Afternoon,' he said to both detectives, then turned to Doyle. 'Apparently, I'm yours until ten o'clock tonight if you want me?'

Doyle raised an eyebrow in response, and Birdseye tried to suppress a snigger.

'No, I meant…' the PC went on, his pale complexion rapidly becoming crimson. 'What I meant was that Inspector Regan said I could help with your investigation for the whole of the shift, if you need me?'

'Thank you, Francis. I'm sure we can make use of your skills.'

'It was my day off yesterday, but I heard on the radio that you're looking for someone called Jason Carter,' Bowen said, wandering over to the evidence board.

'That's right,' said Birdseye. 'You don't know him, do you?'

'No, but is that him?' Bowen said, pointing to Carter's picture on the board. 'I recognise that face – I've definitely seen him somewhere before.'

'Morgan said the same thing,' Birdseye said. 'It turns out he had been doing some IT work at Chloe Kennedy's school. You think you might have seen him there?'

'No … wait … Got it!' Bowen clicked his fingers. 'When DS Morgan and I went to arrest Ryan Johnson, Carter was there, working on the same site. We spoke to him as he was running some cables and we thought he might work for the same electrical company as Johnson, but he said he was doing

IT and claimed not to know him.'

'Did he now?' Doyle said. 'And you're quite sure that's him?'

'Yes, certain, one hundred per cent.'

The phone on Morgan's desk rang. As Doyle was standing right next to it, he was the one who picked it up. 'DCI Doyle.'

'Hi,' a male voice said. 'Can I speak to DS Morgan, please?'

'I'm afraid she's not back in work until tomorrow. Can I help, or would you like to leave a message?'

'Um, sorry, I don't want to waste your time. It's Sam, her boyfriend.'

'It's OK, Sam, what's up?' Doyle could detect real concern in the man's voice, which made him feel uneasy. The fact that just two days ago none of the team knew that Morgan's partner was a man suggested that he wasn't prone to phoning the office to track her down.

'Well, this might sound silly to you, like I'm worrying about nothing, but she went out on a bike ride just after half past nine this morning and she hasn't returned. I know which route she was going on, and I was expecting her back at around eleven. When she wasn't back by twelve, I called her mobile several times, but it went straight to voicemail. I drove round her route looking for her, in case she had had a crash or a mechanical problem and was out of signal, but I couldn't find her. There was no evidence of any accident either.'

'OK,' Doyle said slowly, processing what he had just been told. 'Is her car still outside the house?'

'Yes.'

'And her mobile she had with her – would that have been her work phone, or does she have another one?'

'It's her work phone.'

'You're not too far from Chorley, are you?'

'No. Withnell, only a couple of miles away.'

'Right, give me your postcode and I'll be straight round.'

As Sam told him, Doyle jotted it down on a sticky note. 'In the meantime, if you hear from her or get any news, call this number straight away.'

'What's happened?' Birdseye asked.

'It's Morgan. That was her partner – she should have been home from a bike ride hours ago, but she hasn't returned. Her car's still on the drive and her phone is going straight to voicemail.'

'She's not the type to just go off radar for a bit.'

'Those were exactly my thoughts, Derrick. I might be overreacting here, but taking into account that she's been investigating what has turned out to be a serial killer and Francis has just told us their paths crossed earlier in the week, I think we have to take this very seriously until she turns up safe and sound.'

'Shall I call round and get everyone in, boss?' Birdseye asked.

'Yes, and straight after that get on to the phone company and find out where her phone was last turned on. Stress it is very urgent. Bowen, get on to all the local hospitals and check whether she'd been admitted to any of them. There is a chance she's come off her bike and been injured. And get on to your colleagues downstairs. I want every bobby out on the street keeping their eyes peeled for any sight of her.'

⋏ ⋏ ⋏

The front door to Morgan's three-bed semi was thrown open as Doyle pulled up across the driveway. After a cursory wipe of his feet, he followed Sam's wiry figure into the house and through to the back, into an open-plan kitchen diner. Sam was only a few inches shorter than Doyle but easily a few stone lighter, and Doyle guessed he was about the same age as Morgan. The kitchen was beyond tidy, and a laptop and iPad were placed side by side on a granite breakfast bar that sparkled in the sun that shone through the glass roof.

'Sorry,' Sam said, turning to Doyle. 'I didn't introduce myself. I'm Sam, and you must be DCI Doyle.'

'No problem. Call me Liam.'

'I had these open to show you the route that Anna was riding.' He moved the trackpad on the laptop and the screen lit up, showing a map with a blue line marked on it. 'This is the Garmin app that she connects her bike computer to. The blue line shows the course she was taking this morning.'

'Is it possible that she took a different route, a longer course, maybe, and she's stuck somewhere else?'

'No, we always tell each other what our plans are when we're not riding together. In case of problems.'

'Was there a reason you didn't go with her this morning?'

'We don't always go together – it depends on our work schedules and training plans. I do triathlons and my calf was feeling tight after a long run yesterday, so I thought it best to rest it for a day.'

'Can you zoom in on the map so I can see the route more closely?' Doyle asked, and Sam did as requested.

'We're here.' He indicated a map pin at the top of the screen. 'She was going in this direction today, taking advantage of the dry weather to do this tricky descent here.'

Doyle noticed that where the younger man was pointing on the map was close to where Chloe Kennedy's body had been found. 'I don't know the area well, I'm afraid, but I have been there before.'

'It's where that girl was dumped, isn't it?'

'Yes. Do you think maybe she changed her mind? Took a different route, not wanting to be reminded of the case on her day off?'

'We spoke about that this morning; she was adamant that she wasn't going to let things that happen at work affect her life out of work. She didn't want to let bad people spoil beautiful places.'

'You don't think she might have got out on the road and changed her mind about that?'

'I understand you have only known her a week, but does

Anna strike you as the kind of person who would change her mind easily when she had decided on a course of action?'

'She hadn't struck me as that type, no. What's on the iPad?'

'That's got her Strava on it.'

'Her what?'

'Strava – it's a training app used by cyclists and runners.' Sam picked up the tablet and keyed in the code to bring it to life. 'Here,' he said, showing Doyle the screen. 'It shows each part of the route, broken down into sections, and the time she took to complete each section. This page is from the same ride she did last Saturday.'

'Wait, so does this record live?' asked Doyle, getting excited. 'Can we see how far she got today?'

'No, sadly not. I mean, I think you can get devices that can record live, but the one she has, you have to download after your ride.'

'Shame, that could have been very useful.'

'What you can see from this is all her times across each segment of the route. Look.'

Doyle looked at the screen, and saw that the sections appeared in a list. They didn't seem to be given conventional road names; instead, they were called things like 'son of b*stard hill' and 'Wilcocks to Sheephouse'.

'If I open each one in turn, you can see her quickest and average times over each section. Before you got here, I started writing down the approximate times she would have been on each section of road. I thought it might be useful.'

'It could help, yes. You're not a detective too, are you?'

'God, no. I work in IT.'

Doyle had a sudden concerning thought. 'Not in our IT at Force HQ?'

'No. Anna mentioned you had been having trouble with them. She said if I ever met you, not to mention what I did. She'll kill me.' Sam stopped talking and looked up at Doyle. 'What do you think has happened to her?'

'Honestly? I don't know.'

'You will find her, won't you?'

Doyle placed one of his big hands on the younger man's shoulder. 'I will do nothing else but look until we have found her.'

Sam touched the iPad screen again, bringing it back to life. As he did, he accidentally scrolled down to show a section titled Leaderboards.

'What's that?' Doyle asked.

'You can click on each of these subheadings and see who was fastest over each segment in each category.'

Doyle looked at the subheadings in turn. There was All-Time, followed by All-Time (Men), All-Time (Women), This Year, This Year (Men), This Year (Women) and then one for Today. 'Hang on, that section that says Today – will that show the fastest people who have ridden over each segment today?'

'It will show you everyone who has ridden over each segment today and downloaded their ride.'

'And do a lot of people use this Strava app?'

'It's by far the most popular app of its kind for cyclists – more people use this app than all the others combined.'

'And can you see what time all those people were on the road? And is there a way to contact any of them?'

'Most people use their real names but have their settings configured so that the part of the route within a mile of their house is not shown. Mainly to stop them being a target for bike thieves. But I wouldn't have thought it would be too difficult for you guys to work out who they are.'

Or for someone to work out what routes someone regularly took, and intercept them on a quiet bit of road. Doyle shook off the thought. 'OK, can you finish working out the times she should have been on each section, and which of these riders could have been there at the same time? I'm going to call the incident room and get people out searching the route she took.'

Chapter 39

When Doyle walked back into the incident room, it was a very different place to the one he had entered only an hour before. He was pleased to see that Birdseye had succeeded in getting everyone in at short notice on their days off. Asif was busy tapping away at her computer; Gadget, who, from the shorts he was wearing, looked like he had come straight from the gym, was talking on the phone; others were similarly occupied. What was noticeable was the total absence of any chit-chat, banter or laughter. Everyone had a task and was rigidly focused on it.

When he saw Doyle, Hales put down his notepad and crossed the room towards him faster than the DCI had ever seen him move.

'I've got uniform searching all around the route, with help from the local mountain rescue. I've taken the liberty of requesting a helicopter, but I'm not sure if there is one available. Of the thirty-three riders you have sent through from that Strava thingy, we have worked out who twenty-eight of them are so far, and are working on the others. We haven't been able to get phone numbers for quite a few of them, so PCs Bowen and Price are going round to each address to see if they saw anything, starting with the ones who rode the furthest on the same route as Morgan. Gadget's calling the ones we have numbers for. Inspector Regan's bringing in all the extra bodies he can get hold of.'

'That's great, Geoff. Sorry to pull you in on your day off.'

'There's literally nowhere more important for me to be.'

'I'm starting to get a really bad feeling about this,' Doyle confided.

'You don't think this is linked to the case, do you?' Hales asked in a hushed voice.

'That's what's worrying me. I can't think of any other reason for her to disappear.'

'I know what you mean, but how would Carter have known about her and where to find her?'

'He met her at that building site, when she went to bring in Ryan Johnson, and then she registered on the Alpha Cars app. He would have been able to see her name then search for her on Strava.'

'Shit… I guess you're right. But this must be a bit rushed? He'd planned Chloe's abduction for over six weeks.'

'But now he knows we're on to him. He will have seen that he can't access Alpha Cars' computer systems any more, and he'll have seen his face and name on the telly. What if, instead of deciding to run or go to ground, he thought he would have one more go while he can?'

'Fuck, Liam, you think so?'

'There's one other thing that doesn't make this any better. Think about Anna and how she looks: slim, short hair. She certainly fits the type he goes for.'

'Fucking hell.'

'She would have been due back about eleven this morning.' Doyle glanced at his watch. 'It's just gone three now.'

'How long do we think it was … you know, with Chloe?'

'We don't know for sure, but between ten and fifteen hours from when she went missing.'

'So, we've got about six hours to find her?'

'Maybe less.'

⋏ ⋏ ⋏

The woman who answered the door to PC Bowen was clearly shocked to see a police officer standing on her drive. A toddler clung to one leg and another child shouted from inside the house, 'Mummy, who is it?'

'Hello there, I'm PC Bowen from Chorley police station. I'm looking for Nathan Redman. Is he here?' Bowen smiled, hoping to put the woman at her ease.

'Yes?' The reply sounded more like a question.

'Would it be possible to come in and speak to him?'

'Mummy, is it Amazon with my game you promised?' The child's voice from inside came again.

'No, Josh,' the woman shouted back. 'Go and get Daddy from the garden.'

'It's nothing to worry about. We just think he might be a witness in a missing person investigation.'

The woman, presumably Mrs Redman, stood back and gestured for Bowen to come into the house.

'Go straight through to the back. Can I get you a drink?'

Bowen's reply to this question on such occasions was not based on his level of thirst but on two other factors: how clean the mug was likely to be, and whether the person making it was liable to spit – or worse – into said mug before serving it.

'A cup of tea, no sugar, would be great, thanks,' he replied, taking in the large kitchen, which was neat and clean above the reach of tiny hands. A lean man in shorts and flip-flops came though the French doors. If he was surprised to see a police officer in his house, he didn't show it.

'Hello,' he said, wiping his hand on a towel. 'I'm Nathan, how can I help?' Redman offered the officer a now dry hand.

'PC Bowen,' he said, shaking the man's hand. 'We are trying to find a woman: a cyclist who went missing this morning somewhere around Anglezarke and Winter Hill. We're looking for witnesses, and we understand you were cycling in the area this morning?'

'Yes, I was, but I don't recall seeing anything unusual. How did you know I was there?'

'You use an app called…' Bowen checked his pocketbook. 'Strava?'

'Oh, yes.'

'Well, according to that app, you were on Sheephouse Lane and Rivington Road about the same time as the person who has gone missing.' Bowen showed Redman a picture of Morgan. 'Do you remember seeing her, or seeing anything unusual at all on that part of your ride?'

'Not that I noticed,' said Redman, studying the picture. 'You said she was a cyclist?'

'Yes.'

'She would probably have had a helmet and sunglasses on, so I wouldn't have seen much of her face. Do you know what bike she was riding? I would know if I had seen that. I always look at what bikes people are riding.'

'He's bike-obsessed,' said Mrs Redman, placing a tea down in front of Bowen and a coffee by her husband. 'Normal men might have been looking at her arse, but not our Nath; he would have been looking at her bike.'

'And that's why you love me.'

'I haven't got any details of the bike, but I'm sure I could get some if you think it might help. Did you notice anything else unusual on that stretch of road?'

'No, not really.' Redman thought for a second. 'I mean, this isn't particularly unusual, but on the descent down into Belmont a car sped right past me, bloody close an' all.'

'Nath,' his wife hissed, nodding towards the children.

'Sorry. Anyway, he was driving recklessly and didn't slow down much for the bend. I thought if there were a cyclist coming up the hill the other way, he could take them right out.'

'Can you remember what type of car it was, what colour, anything else about it?'

'Yes – it were white. I think it was a local taxi. One of those

Toyota Prius ones. That made it even worse; it must have been going on electric because I barely heard it before it was past me.'

Bowen swallowed. 'That's really helpful. I don't suppose you can remember any of the registration number, can you?'

'No, but it would all be on my GoPro if you want to see for yourself.'

'You filmed your ride?'

'Yes, always do. I got knocked off a few year back and the driver sped off. I thought if it happens again, I'll get the bastard.'

'Nath, children.'

'Can you show me now?'

'Sure. Give us a minute to download it.'

⅄ ⅄ ⅄

'Boss!' Birdseye shouted across the incident room, putting down the phone. 'The search team have found her bike.'

'Where?' Doyle asked, making his way over to the large map on the wall.

'Just here.' Birdseye pointed. 'Off Sheephouse Lane. It's quite high up there. The lassie I spoke to said it was in the undergrowth, along with her helmet and gloves. It looked like it had been thrown over a wall from a layby. There was no evidence of damage, like she had been in a crash, other than a few scratches from the bracken. They're looking for her phone.'

'And Morgan's definitely not lying in the undergrowth somewhere near by?' Hales asked.

'They said not. They've searched everywhere within a few hundred feet of where they found the bike.'

Asif answered another ringing phone. 'Boss, it's PC Bowen. He says you're going to want to hear this.'

'Put him on speaker,' Doyle said.

'Sir?' Bowen's soft voice sounded a little tinny. 'I've just been with one of the cyclists. He recorded his ride on one of those GoPro cameras. At 10.17 this morning, as he was going down Winter Hill on Rivington Road towards Belmont...'

Birdseye helpfully pointed on the map at the point Bowen was talking about. It was just past where Morgan's bike had been found.

'He was overtaken by a white Toyota Prius travelling at a hell of a pace.'

'Fuck,' said Hales, voicing what they were all thinking.

'And get this,' Bowen continued. 'It had the same dent on the back as the car we were looking at on the CCTV the other day. It's the same car, sir. I'm sure of it.'

'Did you get the registration plates it's got on now?' Doyle asked.

'Yes, sir. Delta tango...'

Doyle turned and looked at the map as Asif wrote down the registration number. He then looked at his watch. Twenty past three. Five hours. He could have taken her almost anywhere in the country by now. 'Right,' he said loudly, to get everyone's attention 'We need every ANPR camera checked for that number. It's bound to be false, so find out who the real number belongs to and where they have been in the last few days so we can rule that out. I want every policeman in the country looking for that car. Birdseye.' Doyle faced the detective. 'Bowen said Carter was working at the same site in Wigan where we picked up Ryan Johnson. We need to get GMP round there to check whether he has taken her there, and we need to get on to whoever he was working for and find out if he worked at any other sites. He was probably going under the name of James Fisher IT, but he could have been using a different name or company name. Anywhere he might have had access to needs to be checked out.'

'Yes, boss.'

'We need to move the search off the hill to where he might have taken her. Gadget and Shaima, I want you to look for any empty properties that he could have used: start with where the car was last seen and work your way out. He took Chloe to a vacant rental property, but he had time to plan that. He could have taken Morgan almost anywhere that is not being used – old farm buildings, lock-ups. Get the search teams checking them all.'

'Burns has still not called us back, Liam,' Hales said.

'I'd better call the ACC then, let her know we think one of her officers has been abducted by a serial killer.' Doyle ran his hand through his hair. 'Fuck! We need to send someone to let her parents know what's going on too.'

'It's just her mum now, boss. She lives on the Isle of Man,' Asif said. 'It's where Anna's from.'

Chapter 40

Light. One thin horizontal band of light, just a bright yellow slit.

Pain. Her shoulders felt like her arms were being ripped out of their sockets. Something was stopping her moving her arms. *Shit, my head*, she thought, feeling a pounding at her temples. There was a dull ache behind her right ear.

Thirst. She swallowed. Her mouth was dry, so dry it felt like sandpaper. Something was stopping her from opening her mouth

Smell. Something sweet and acrid. Her own body? And something else. Something warm that reminded her of home. Not home now. Her childhood home. Her dad's garage.

Pins and needles. In her feet and knees. The tips of her toes were scraping on something hard.

Morgan blinked. The line of light went and came back again. She lifted her head, and the light disappeared from view. The pain caused by moving was too much. She had to close her eyes again.

人 人 人

The Assistant Chief Constable, who Doyle had only met at his job interview, turned out to be more useful and less confrontational than he expected Croucher would have been. She promised Doyle all the resources he needed until Morgan had been found, and said that she would liaise personally with other forces to enlist their help. ACC Reid also said she would ensure someone of senior rank on the Isle of Man force went to visit Anna's mother.

Doyle felt he should be out looking too – at least, he wanted to be out looking. But the reality was, every lead and possibility of where she could be was being followed up. It was just that there were so many of them. It wasn't like looking for a needle in a haystack; it was like looking for a needle in a thousand haystacks that were miles apart. Doyle needed to think. He needed to find a new angle, something they hadn't picked up before. Something to tell them where they should be looking to narrow down the search a bit. But what?

Copies of bank statements from James Fisher IT Ltd sat on Doyle's desk. A sticky note on the front read *I've been through these and highlighted what I think needs following up. Anna.*

Morgan had put a smiley face next to her name, which somehow served to galvanise Doyle. She was a good officer: he had known her less than a week, but he had worked that out on day one. Hell, she was a good person too, that was obvious. And she was his officer and he had to find her. No alternative could be considered. He had to find her, and find her fast.

Doyle turned over the cover page of the statements to see the first page of transactions. They had been ordered in reverse, so Doyle saw the most recent entries at the bottom of the first sheet. They knew from the accounts filed with Companies House that the business had a relatively small turnover of just over £75,000 a year. It hadn't been registered for VAT, leaving a very limited audit trail for them to follow. But Doyle supposed, with low overheads and presumably Carter doing all the work himself, that could have generated a very decent living. Morgan had annotated some of the entries in pencil. As Doyle read up from the bottom of the page, the first note he came across was next to an outgoing direct debit entry for £321.25. It read *Lease on the Prius. I've checked this.* The next comment was by an incoming amount for £3,500 which just had a six-digit number as the reference. Morgan had written next to it: *This is payment from Dudley App Solutions. I checked with them, and the number is the invoice number. All incoming amounts are referenced like that.*

I bet they are, thought Doyle. Makes it bloody hard to see who he had been working for. Near the top of the page another of Morgan's annotations piqued Doyle's interest. It was alongside an outgoing amount for £3,200. Anna had written: *This comes out every month on the 22nd, and has done since January 2020. Looks like it could be the rental on a property/ premises. Have tried checking. No joy so far, but can follow up with the bank on Monday.*

Doyle flicked through the other pages and saw that this transaction was highlighted throughout, with a second transaction for the same amount just before the first one in January 2020. Morgan might have been right, he thought. You would get a decent-sized industrial unit for that amount each month up here. But why would Carter need a decent-sized unit if his work was all IT-based? That didn't require lots of tools or industrial plant machinery. Another thing occurred to him: most commercial property was paid for quarterly in advance, but these transactions were coming out every month. The one payment of the same amount just before was exactly like a deposit on a house. 'Yes,' he said, rising from his seat behind the desk. Carter must have rented a house somewhere. But where?

The rent was £3,200 per month. Christ, that would be a lot of money down in London, let alone here. Maybe that was it. Was he heading down to London, taking Morgan with him? Somehow Doyle didn't think so. Flicking through the statements again, he saw that by far the biggest source of income was from transactions highlighted by Morgan as coming from Dudley IT Solutions, with some smaller ones from unknown places – one would be the school Chloe Kennedy had worked at, and another the site where they had picked up Ryan

Johnson. There was nothing to suggest that Carter had any connection with anywhere in the south, where most of these astronomical rents got charged. There was another thing, and this that sent a tingle down Doyle's spine. All the other victims they knew about had been taken from towns no more than fifty miles away from Chorley.

Then another thought occurred to him. Something Harry had said the day before, when he was upset. *We were all happy back in London in that house. All together as a family. I want to go back there.*

Doyle went over to the boxes containing the old files relating to Jason Carter. He rifled through them until he found what he was looking for: the Social Circumstances Report written by the social worker prior to Carter's trial for arson.

There was a knock, and his office door opened. 'We've found the car, Liam,' Hales informed him.

'Where?'

'Here,' the DI said, showing Doyle the map screen on his iPad. 'It's a car park, used mostly by walkers and mountain bikers. My guess is, he switched to another vehicle. Someone might have seen something or remember what kind of cars were parked there. Scene of Crime are on their way there now to give the car a good going over.'

'Geoff, I don't mean to state the obvious, but have they checked already? Anna isn't in the boot?'

'I asked the same myself. No luck, I'm afraid. But look, the car was here, near Tockholes – that's north of where Morgan was taken. It links up with the motorway here,' He moved the map screen with a nicotine-stained finger. 'Our man Carter is from Fleetwood way. He could have been heading back there. I've got Shaima looking for possible buildings around there.'

'Thanks, Geoff.' Doyle thought about mentioning his hunch, then thought better of it. The team were following up leads and logical lines of enquiry, and he needed them to keep going with that. Doyle could dig a little deeper himself.

Chapter 41

That band of light was daylight, she was sure of that now. That was a good thing, wasn't it? It meant it was still the same day. Or was it the next day? Had she been unconscious for so long, it was now Monday morning? She didn't think so; she wasn't sure why. The smell was two stroke oil; Morgan was sure of that too. She needed to stay awake try to block out the pounding pain, and think. Would they be looking for her by now? When she hadn't come home, Sam would have tried calling her, then he'd have looked for her, then called the police. But what if he had called the central switchboard and they had dismissed it, saying it was too early to report an adult misper who could have gone off on their own? Lovely as Sam was, he wasn't confrontational. Would he have accepted that and waited for her to come home, or reported her again the next day? This was her fault. She had tried to be professional, keep her work life and home life separate. Sam had never even met her colleagues. Perhaps if he had, he would have called the incident room. No, she wasn't giving him enough credit; he would have known something wasn't right and insisted that they look for her. Doyle was working this afternoon. When he heard, he would realise what must have happened. He said he didn't believe in coincidences, after all. He would have known that Carter had taken her. Wouldn't he?

Carter had taken her, she realised that now. Carter, the man who had killed Chloe Kennedy, and before her Karolina

Valanciunas, and before that Vicki Quinn. And way back in 1999, she was sure he had killed Michelle McCarthy too, and God knows how many others in between. He had told his neighbour then that he was leaving and going to Spain; there could be many more there, perhaps scattered across Europe, never found, or never linked to the same killer. And now he was going to kill her. It dawned on her slowly, like an emotion bubbling up the pit of her stomach and rising to her head. She was going to die.

Morgan didn't feel frightened – at least, she didn't feel what she knew as fear. She felt sad, so very sad. She wasn't ready for everything to end now. There was so much she hadn't done, places she hadn't seen, people she would never see again, and children she would never have. It was all going to end here, wherever 'here' was.

Stop it! she shouted inside her head. *You have to think. Give yourself the best chance to live.* She sniffed and blinked away the tears. More shapes were appearing as her eyes adjusted to the dark. It was a garage door ahead of her; the light was coming from underneath it. She was in a garage, that was what the smell was. This wasn't an abandoned garage smelling damp and musty; someone used this. Morgan listened to the hum of a petrol lawnmower: not far away, someone was cutting the grass. It was due to start raining in the early evening: a thunderstorm was forecast, coming in from the south-west. She knew, because she had checked her weather app before going out on the bike. It was still afternoon, then. Despite the pain, she turned her head to the right as far as she could before her arm, trussed above her head, stopped her. She could make out what looked like a workbench. As she stared, things came more into focus in the dark. It was a bench, with cables and tools on top of it. She could make out wire cutters and screwdrivers – and was that an angle grinder? Morgan shuddered. This was Carter's workshop. He had taken her to his own place, not some empty building.

She had left the bank statements on Doyle's desk. Hopefully he would have looked at them, and they would be trying to trace his workshop. That lawnmower was going on a Sunday afternoon. She must be somewhere residential. This must be a domestic garage. Would that mean they would be looking in the wrong place? Looking for an industrial unit? That other noise, the squawking – it was seagulls, she was sure of that. Where was she? Not many houses in the north of England commanded a rent of £3,200 a month. Was she on the south coast, maybe? She thought not; the weather was coming in from that direction, and in the time it would have taken Carter to get her there it would be raining, and no one would be out cutting their grass.

A light went on, temporarily blinding Morgan, as her night vision disappeared. Footsteps behind, walking towards her. This wasn't her saviour; there would be more urgency in their steps.

'Hello, Detective Sergeant Morgan. You might not remember, but we've met before.'

The accent was from somewhere in Lancashire; she couldn't place it, or the voice. She lifted her head. Vision restored, she saw the man's face. The face they had put out to the media yesterday, a face she had seen before in person. Now she knew where and when: on a building site when she'd been looking for Ryan Johnson.

'It looks like you've made me famous. Don't worry, I'll be happy to return the favour. Everyone will know your name soon enough. They will probably show scenes from your funeral on the national news.'

He was behind her now. There was movement. Hard plastic pressing on her neck and the clicking of the cable tie ratcheting as it closed around her throat. Her stomach churned; sweat dripped down her forehead. Was this it? Was she going to die now? She felt it squeeze around her then stop. She was still able to breathe, just. Morgan wasn't sad now. She was terrified: pure unadulterated fear. If it wasn't for the gaffer tape covering her mouth, she would have screamed from the bottom of her soul.

Chapter 42

In one hand Doyle held the Social Circumstances Report on the teenage Jason Carter, and in the other he held his phone, pressed against his ear. Harry wanted to go back to where he had been happiest: would Carter want the same?

'I didn't expect to be hearing from you again so soon.'

'Bea, I need your help. It's urgent.'

'OK,' Bea replied, sounding serious. 'What's up?'

Fuck it, thought Doyle, it would be all over the news soon. 'It's my detective sergeant, Anna Morgan.'

'The one who came into the office with you the other day?'

'Yes. She's been abducted, by the man who killed Chloe Kennedy. I need to find her fast.

'Oh dear God, no… But what…'

'Is there any way on Rightmove or one of those other sites that I can find property that has previously been listed for rent? A couple of years ago – it would have been let in January 2020.'

'It's not easy. If it was a property that had sold, then it would be straightforward.'

'Could you tell me the fastest ways to search? I know the amount it was let for, and when, and I think I know the area too.'

'If you can share those details with me, I will look for you and get on to anyone I know who might have records from that time.'

'OK. As I said, it would have been in January 2020. I think a house, probably with a garage or outbuilding. There was an initial payment of £3,200, which I think must have been the deposit, and then monthly payments of the same amount ever since.'

'Jesus, that's a lot. Not many properties would go for that much round here. Whereabouts is it?'

'Lytham St Anne's. If not right on the sea front, then not far off.'

'Ah, that would do it then. Even so, there will only be a few places that went for that. Leave it with me. I'll call a few people and get straight back to you.'

'Thanks.'

人 人 人

Doyle had already cleared the M6 and was hurtling along the M55, blue lights flashing and sirens wailing, when Bea rang back. He killed the racket to hear her better.

'Have you had any joy?' It came out more abruptly than he wanted.

'I've spoken to all the letting agents that cover the area, bar one, who I couldn't get hold of. There are only five of them. One I spoke to didn't have access to any records, but was going to get someone to go into the office. The other three have all come back to me. Out of those, there's only one property that ticks all the boxes. Let in January 2020 for £3,200 per month and very close to the sea – one street back, in fact.'

Doyle had already brought up the map screen on the car's display. He blasted his horn at the hatchback in front of him, which seemed oblivious to the SUV flashing like a Christmas tree approaching fast from behind.

'Move, twat!' he yelled, waving an arm for them to get out of his way. 'Sorry, bloody Sunday drivers.'

'You want to pull over to take down the address?'

B.D. Spargo

'No, just give us the postcode.' He punched it into the touch screen as Bea read it out. 'Orchard Drive?'

'That's the one.'

'What number?'

'Number seven.'

'Great, Bea, you are a superstar.'

'Thanks, I've been called worse.'

'Can you just hold on one minute?' Doyle was coming off the motorway, and needed to negotiate the slip road and roundabout. He put the sirens back on and managed to carve his way through the traffic back onto a clear stretch of road.

'Sorry, back. Are you there?'

'Jesus, you might want to warn me when you turn those things on – you damn near blasted my eardrums out.'

'Sorry, didn't think.'

'I'll forgive you. I got the letting agent to email me the details of the property. I've just sent them to you in case they're useful. There are pics and floor plans.'

'That's great, thanks.' Doyle swung the car out into the opposite lane to overtake a few cars in front. The gap was small; he hoped the Skoda's kickdown would be enough. He floored the accelerator, bringing a satisfying increase in engine noise as the automatic box selected a lower gear and the car lurched forward. The gap was tighter than he had thought. For a moment, Doyle feared he had overestimated it. Then he saw the front of the BMW that was coming towards him dip down sharply and he knew its terrified driver must have stamped on the brakes, giving him just enough room to pull in in front of the line of cars he was overtaking, who were also reducing their speed, clearly sensing peril.

'Never in doubt,' he said when he was safely back in his own lane.

'Sorry, what was that?'

'Oh sorry, was just getting through some traffic.'

'Shall I keep chasing those other two agents, in case this

isn't the right place?'

'If you don't mind, that would be great.'

'No problem. Look, Liam, I really hope you find her.'

'Thanks. Sorry, I'd better go, it's getting trafficky again. I really appreciate all you've done.'

'OK, bye. Take care, Liam.'

Doyle was on the outskirts of the town when his phone rang again. He groaned when he saw the name of the caller on the car's screen. 'Sir,' he said, pressing the button on the steering wheel to take the call.

'I've just spoken to Geoff. He's filled me in. You're on your way to Lytham, I understand.' Mr Burns' voice bellowed from the car's speakers.

'Yes, sir. I've got a possible address to check out.'

'Do you want me to get some backup round there? Maybe an armed response vehicle, if you think Morgan might be there.'

'I'm just following up a hunch at this stage. There might be nothing to it, and I don't want to take anyone away from the rest of the search. I'll check it out, see what I think, and if there's a possibility that Morgan's there, I'll call in the cavalry.'

'Makes sense. I'm not far from there myself. I was playing golf and didn't hear my phone – must have gone to silent by mistake.'

Or you didn't want to be disturbed until you had finished playing, Doyle thought.

'Give me the address and I'll meet you there. If it's not the right place, we can work out our next steps.'

Doyle read out the postcode Bea had given him, along with the door number.

'OK, thanks. And Liam, just take a look. If you think she's in there, call for backup. Don't do anything rash on your own.'

'Yes, sir.'

Chapter 43

Doyle had killed the sirens and flashing lights several streets back, not wanting to announce his arrival. He drove slowly past the property; he hoped, not so slowly that it would arouse suspicion in anyone looking out of the window. Just another car searching for somewhere to park. There was nothing remarkable about the house: a large, well-maintained Victorian semi with a drive and a garage off to the side. The Citroën Berlingo van in front of the garage was out of keeping with the other vehicles parked in the street, which mostly comprised upmarket family cars and SUVs. There were no other vans on the road that Doyle could see.

He parked his own vehicle outside a similar house further along the street. Before getting out, Doyle looked at the email Bea had sent him. From the photos, the interior of the house looked contemporary and stylish, as you would expect if you were paying that much in rent. That wasn't what interested him. He could see in one of the pictures that there was a gate between the garage and the house, and the floor plan showed that, as well as the roller shutter at the front, there was a door from the garage leading to the garden. Carter could have moved Morgan from the boot of the Prius into the little Citroën van and then taken her straight out of the back of the van and into the garage. It was unlikely that anyone passing would have noticed, considering how far back the garage was set from the road. Or it could be that the person who lived there had a van they used for whatever innocent purpose they chose, and this whole thing was a wild-goose chase.

He took the airwaves radio out of the glove box, just in case he needed to summon backup quickly, turning it on but making sure the volume was muted. Doyle walked back up the street to the house. The houses to either side had key safes next to the front doors, with combination locks on them. Holiday lets, he guessed, meaning no regular neighbours who might have seen Carter's face on telly. Number seven didn't have a key safe, but it did have a video doorbell. No chance Doyle would be pressing that. The street was empty, and Doyle walked up to the van on the drive. The bonnet was cool and there was no telltale clicking from the radiator to suggest it had recently been used. That didn't tell him anything either way. It had been hours since Morgan had been taken. He looked through the side window. There was a packet of large cable ties on the passenger seat. Plenty of people used cable ties, he reminded himself. There was what looked like an invoice underneath them on yellow paper, the type you got from wholesale places. Doyle tilted his head but couldn't read what it said. The top, where the company name would be, was obscured by the cable tie packet. He just wanted something concrete either way: was he in the right place? Should he be summoning backup? He went to the back of the van. It was parked right up against the shutter, which he noticed had a tiny gap underneath it. It was still bright outside, and Doyle couldn't tell if there was a light on inside. He needed those black clouds that were gathering ominously to the west, over the sea, to roll in.

Maybe he should wait for Mr Burns to get here, run things by him and let him decide whether there were sufficient grounds to get an armed unit to force entry. That would be the sensible, professional thing to do, but there was one problem with that. Morgan's life was at stake. Did he really trust Burns' judgement enough when the stakes were so high? Maybe there was a window in the back door or a bigger gap underneath the door – some way that he could see inside the garage.

The garden gate looked strong enough to take his weight if it was deadlocked and he needed to climb over. As it happened, there was just a bolt at the top and a ring latch keeping it closed. The hinges creaked as he pushed the gate open. Doyle winced and stood frozen for a second, waiting to see if someone would call out – or, worse, if a dog would come rushing towards him. There was neither. He made his way along the passage between garage and house, and saw a garden bench on a patio. There was a motorbike propped up on its kickstand next to it. It was an off-road bike with chunky tyres and a helmet hung on the handlebars. It appeared odd that it was out on the patio; surely it would normally be kept in the garage. Unless you suddenly needed more space in the garage for some reason... *Stop it, you're getting carried away. There could be any number of reasons why the bike would be there on a Sunday afternoon.*

When he entered the garden, the back entrance to the garage was just on his left. The door was panelled wood – not as solid as a fire door, but hefty enough. There wasn't a useful window that allowed him to see inside, or even a big enough gap underneath. From its hinges Doyle could see that the door opened outwards. It would take some force to get through, but would be easier than the roller shutter. He looked up and, to his horror, saw a CCTV camera tucked away behind a drainpipe. It was trained right on him. He didn't know if it was recording, or even if it was real, but he had a feeling that he was being watched. That was it. Fuck it, he decided. He would call for backup and get an armed unit to go in. If it turned out to be the wrong decision, he would take responsibility for it. He took the radio out of his back pocket and made for the gate.

人 人 人

Morgan knew Carter was in the room with her. She couldn't see him or even hear him, but she could sense his presence behind her. Not so close that she could feel his breath on her skin, like she had when he had fastened the cable tie around her neck, but not far away either. The light still came in under the shutter, and there was another artificial light from behind. Morgan had no illusions about what was coming; she had studied Dr Gupta's post-mortem report on Chloe Kennedy. She wondered if the fact that Carter was now back in the garage meant that her time was coming soon. Maybe her colleagues had already located her, and right now there was a team of black-clad armed officers standing by the entrance, waiting for the 'Go. Go. Go' in their earpieces, ready to force their way in and rescue her. She hoped that was the case, but somehow she doubted it.

The tips of her toes scraped on the floor. She had pins and needles in her legs and her arms felt like they were being ripped from her sockets, suspended as she was. She needed to think straight. Everyone must be looking for her, she was sure of that. Sam would have got through to someone and her team weren't stupid; they would work it out. What Morgan needed to do was wait until someone realised where she was. But what if they didn't work it out in time? Was she really going to suffer like Chloe had? Knowing what was coming and not putting up a fight? Was she fuck.

She had good core strength. Hell, she had worked hard enough on it. Maybe if she could just find a bit of energy in her arms to pull at the same time as scrunching up her abs, she could get her feet up and get herself swinging and maybe even kick Carter? She might not be able to get away or even stop him, but at least she might be able to hurt the bastard. At least there would be satisfaction in that.

She thought of him facing Doyle in the interview room, his face bloodied and missing some front teeth. And Doyle knowing she had done that to him. The DCI would be proud of her for having hurt him before she died. Why did that matter? Why did she want Doyle's approval? She had known him less than a week. She wasn't sure.

Focus, Morgan told herself. *Keep your breathing steady. When you think it's time, give it everything. Summon every ounce of strength you have left.*

She felt Carter moving. Was it time already? Had she missed her chance? He stood in front of her. He had an iPad in his hand. He turned the screen so she could see it.

There was Doyle, coming through a garden gate. He stopped for a second and looked like he was listening. Was this picture on the screen here and now? Was Doyle just outside? Carter didn't look concerned, if he was. The screen flashed to a view from another angle. Doyle was standing looking at a door. It could be the door behind her that Carter had come in and out of. She wanted to scream, but the gag stopped her. Then Doyle was leaving. The image switched to the other camera view. She could see him walking away; he didn't know she was in here.

NOW! she screamed in her head, and summoned all her energy. Her feet were up, and she swung and kicked her legs hard towards Carter. She felt her feet connect with him and he staggered backwards, dropping the tablet on the floor. He clattered into the garage shutter.

'You cunt,' he hissed at her, staggering to his feet.

Morgan writhed and twisted and tried to swing as he came back towards her. A second swing and kick missed its target, and then Carter had grabbed her. He pulled hard on the cable tie around her neck, cutting off Morgan's oxygen supply.

Chapter 44

The noise behind him was unmistakable: the sound of something hitting something metallic, and the resultant tinny rattle. The slats of the roller shutter were vibrating. Was someone trying to get out? Was there some kind of struggle going on in there? Doyle knew he had to get into the garage, and fast. He pressed the emergency button on the airwaves radio, which would summon help to his location, before sticking it back in his pocket. The back door had to be the best way in. He tried the handle. No luck; the door was locked. Doyle thought of trying to kick the door in, but he didn't fancy his chances. Then he saw the garden bench: it was a heavy-looking thing, maybe teak. That would have to do. It certainly felt solid in his arms; he needed it to be, for what he wanted. He took a deep breath, then ran and planted the bench like a medieval battering ram in the centre of the wooden door, all his weight behind it. There was a loud splintering noise, like a tree falling in a forest, then all the door's resistance was gone. Doyle hurtled into the garage after the bench, and landed awkwardly on the armrest of the garden bench.

Winded, Doyle tried to take in the scene. Morgan was in front of him, hanging by her arms from a roof beam, her legs kicking frantically. Doyle spotted the cable tie biting into her neck, and knew she was suffocating. He had no time to check the shadows and corners of the room, as had been drummed into him on his firearms training. Morgan was dying in front of him, and he had to get that ligature off her neck fast. He struggled to his feet; the pain in his ribs screamed at him to lie back down. There was a workbench with tools. He grabbed a pair of wire cutters and seized Morgan around the waist with one arm to keep her still. The cable tie was so tight on her neck that he couldn't get any part of the tool's jaws underneath it to cut. He picked a point on the side of her neck where he hoped there weren't any major blood vessels close to the surface and started cutting, the blades tearing at her skin as he went, even though he tried to be careful.

'Sorry, Anna.' There was a reassuring release of tension as the tie pinged off, and Doyle heard a sharp sniffing as Morgan's nostrils tried to fulfil her body's desperate need for oxygen. He ripped at the duct tape covering her mouth, removing that and a layer of skin from her face. She gasped and her body jerked involuntarily.

Too late, Doyle heard the noise behind him: someone moving, and a high-pitched whining. He turned just in time to get his left hand up to fend off the angle grinder that was heading for his face. The disc ripped into the flesh on his bare arm before Doyle was able to kick out at his assailant, sending him backwards just enough to stop the tool biting into him. Sensing that Carter was off balance, he went forward, landing a punch on his jaw and knocking the man off his feet. The grinder dropped from his hand, tool and battery parting company as they hit the concrete floor.

Carter was on the floor, trying to get up. If it wasn't for his desperate need to get back to Morgan and cut her down to give her first aid, Doyle might have taken a more conventional approach to restraining Carter. But in the circumstances, he decided on a hard kick to the midriff with as much of his eighteen stone behind it as he could. This brought a groan from Carter, who was lying on the garage floor.

He turned his attention back to his stricken colleague and found that Morgan was still gasping, rather than breathing normally. Her eyes were open, but they had rolled upwards. He picked the cutters up from the floor where he had dropped them and, taking Morgan's weight, started to shear through the nylon rope binding her hands to the garage ceiling. He heard a motor turning and a clicking, and for an awful moment thought that Carter was coming back at him with some other mechanical device. He turned towards the noise and saw that the roller shutter was coming up, flooding the garage with light and temporarily blinding Doyle. Carter must have opened it with a remote control. Doyle looked back to where he had last seen the man, clutching his stomach. He wasn't there. Had he slunk further back into the shadows? Doyle was sure he would have seen him go past. Maybe he opened the shutter as a distraction, then went out the back door.

He kept cutting until the rope gave, and Morgan slumped against Doyle. He held her with his heavily bleeding left arm, relieved that he was able to break her fall. Carefully he lowered her to the concrete floor without banging her head. *Airway, breathing, circulation,* he reminded himself as he laid her down.

'Doyle!' It was Mr Burns, shouting and running through the open shutter.

'Where's Carter, did you see him?' Doyle roared.

'No… Shit, is she alive?'

'Just about.'

'Backup and an ambulance are on their way. Your arm's bleeding badly – you need something on it. There's a first aid kit in the boot of my car. I'll take care of Morgan.'

'OK,' Doyle said, getting to his feet. 'You need to get her airway open, check her breathing.' He staggered out onto the driveway. He could hear sirens coming from all directions. Croucher's BMW was across the drive. As Doyle moved towards it, he was acutely aware of the pain in his chest and the stinging in his arm. He moved a set of golf clubs in the boot to remove the panel containing a first aid kit. Unzipping the pouch, he found a dressing which he hoped would be big enough to cover the wound on his arm. The sirens were getting louder, and there was another noise: an engine revving. Doyle planted the pad of the dressing on his arm, then used his mouth and right hand to tie it tightly in place. He looked back towards the house and garage. Burns was kneeling beside Morgan. He wasn't pumping her chest – was that a good sign? Did that mean her breathing had become more regular?

Then more revving. The motorbike was coming through the garden gate, Carter on it. Doyle looked back into the boot of the car. He pulled a club from Croucher's golf bag and swung it towards Carter as he drove onto the pavement. He missed the man's body but hit the motorbike hard, bending the golf club. For a moment Doyle thought he had him as the bike toppled sideways, but Carter got a foothold on the ground, righting himself, and with the back wheel regaining grip he pulled away and out onto the road.

Doyle was torn. Should he go after Carter or help with Morgan? But what could he do for her that Burns couldn't? And he still had a chance to catch the killer. His feet seemed to have made the decision independently; they carried him along the street after the fleeing motorbike and towards his own parked car. He was grateful that the automatic gearbox in the Skoda meant that he wouldn't need to use his left arm. He jumped in and roared up the street in pursuit of his prey. Rounding the corner and coming out onto the main road, he had to take evasive action to avoid a patrol car coming the other way. He could see the bike up ahead, weaving between cars as it sped away. He had the blue lights on, but kept the sirens off with the window open so that he could hear the bike. He knew he should get on to Control, call it in, a give a running commentary of the pursuit so that other units could join in, but the airwaves radio had gone from his pocket. It must have come out when he crashed into the garage. He tried to phone, but he couldn't get the number on the car's screen and concentrate on driving with only one working arm. Besides, if he called it in, they might call him off the chase for safety reasons. *Fuck that.* He had come too far now to let Carter slip away. He owed it to Chloe Kennedy and the other girls to catch him – but more than that, he owed it to Morgan.

The bike was getting further away. Periodically he saw it up ahead as it weaved between cars. Doyle was doing the same, but with less success in the bigger vehicle. Then Carter pulled out between the two lanes of traffic. There was an island in the middle of the road ahead, with a pedestrian crossing beyond that. There wasn't enough space for Carter to go round it. Doyle thought he would wipe out on the barriers, but before he got there the bike whipped between two oncoming cars and shot into a right turn. Doyle moved out into the middle lane and blasted the sirens, willing the oncoming cars to stop and let him through. As Doyle followed Carter into the side road, he noticed a sign that read 'Lytham Park Cemetery'. This was where Carter's parents were buried, Doyle remembered, and where the police had apprehended him after the arson.

Maybe Jason Carter wasn't looking to escape. Maybe he wanted a showdown.

Chapter 45

Doyle lost sight of the motorbike as it raced down the long, wide street, but he could hear it up ahead. The cemetery gates, which marked the end of the road, were closed when he got there. Carter's bike was leaning against the low wall to the right of the entrance. Despite the pain in his chest and the throbbing in his left arm, Doyle was able to step up onto the bike's seat, then vault the iron railings on top of the wall. A road ran from the gates to the chapel, dividing the graveyard in two. Doyle had no idea where the grave he was looking for was located. He chose the right side. He tried to run but his ribs wouldn't let him, so instead he settled into a fast walk with the occasional trot. He scanned the headstones as he went, looking for graves from the early 1990s. Somewhere there would be one containing the bodies of Carter's family. Would he find Jason Carter there, sitting by it, waiting? The dark clouds were closer now, obscuring more of the late afternoon sun. He was getting towards the far end of the graveyard, but he couldn't see anyone. He saw a bench under an oak tree. In the report of the juvenile Carter's arrest, he had read that the police had seen him sitting on a bench by his parents' grave before they picked him up. He approached with caution, berating himself for not having the foresight to retrieve his telescopic baton from the pocket in his car door. He hadn't called in and told Control where he was either. This worried Doyle less; after the police chase in broad daylight, it wouldn't take them long to work out where he had ended up, and the Skoda would have a tracker in it. He could call them now, but he wanted to keep his one functioning arm free to defend himself, not clutching a phone.

No one was sitting on the bench, or anywhere close by it. He had to be in the right area: the graves around here were all from the late 1980s and early 1990s. Although there were plenty of headstones, none were big enough to conceal Carter behind them. Doyle changed direction, stepping across several graves as he went, but keeping the bench and oak tree in his sight at all times. Approaching this way meant that if Carter was hiding behind the tree, Doyle would see him before he got there. With a couple more changes of angle he was at the bench, but Carter was nowhere to be seen. Doyle wondered if this was the right place: after all, benches and trees were all over the graveyard. Then he turned and saw that he was standing ten feet away from a headstone on which was inscribed Roger and Marie Carter's names. Crucially, from Doyle's perspective, one member of the family was missing from the scene. Jason Carter. *Where the fuck are you?*

By way of reply, there was a flash of lightning, casting everything in a blue hue.

It was possible that Carter had not entered the cemetery at all. He could have left the motorbike there and doubled back. He might even have left a car by the gates and switched into that, but Doyle didn't think so. He hadn't seen a car coming the other way as he had raced to the entrance gates; plus, that would have taken planning. Carter hadn't known he would be tracked to his house so soon, otherwise he wouldn't have been there. He had been surprised by Doyle showing up, and his getaway had been improvised. He had come here because of his emotional connection to the place, and he would still be here now. The rumble of thunder was to the west of the cemetery and still a way off, but it wouldn't be long before the rain came. There was another sound: the unmistakable *whap-whap* of helicopter blades tearing through the air. The police helicopter had a thermal imaging camera that would find Carter, and if the helicopter was here, then other officers on the ground wouldn't be far behind.

Out of the corner of his eye Doyle caught a flash of movement. He turned towards the far end of the cemetery, where a low wooden fence separated the burial ground from the fields behind. He couldn't see anyone. He set off in that direction. If Carter had gone to ground, the helicopter would find him – hopefully its presence would be enough to convince the killer that his game was up. Doyle picked his way through the graves rather than take the longer footpath. As he got closer to the fence, he noticed the dates on the headstones were getting more recent: the people buried here all seemed to have taken their final breaths in the late 1990s.

The helicopter was louder now, almost overhead. Doyle looked up, but he didn't see the dark blue livery of the National Police Air Service. Instead he saw the bright yellow North West Air Ambulance. Was it coming for Morgan? If it was, what did that mean? She must be alive, but she must be in a very bad way. More to the point, it meant that Doyle didn't have the aerial support and associated backup he had expected to be arriving imminently.

He heard a footstep on gravel to his right, and turned towards the sound. He was just in time to throw his damaged left arm up to fend off the motorbike helmet that Carter was swinging towards his head. Pain jolted up his arm to his shoulder. Doyle staggered back, losing his footing and landing on the ground. Carter stood over him, just feet away. He'd thrown down the helmet but he now held a hunting knife. Not letting Carter or the blade out of his sight, Doyle wriggled backwards, trying to get as far away from the weapon as he could. He felt the cold marble of a headstone against his left forearm, stopping any further retreat. He scrabbled around with his good hand, feeling for anything he could use to defend himself with, hoping for a flower vase or similar. All he got was a handful of soil.

'You might want to put the knife down, Jason. It won't be long until this place is flooded with police.' This wasn't the first time that Doyle had been confronted by someone brandishing a blade, but a scared fourteen-year-old, when Doyle was wearing a stab vest and had a canister of CS spray in one hand and a baton in the other, was a different prospect to having Carter, a man who had killed at least four people, standing over him. 'If you go now, you might have a chance to get away before they get here.'

'That's bollocks and you know it. There's nowhere left for me to run.'

'So why are we here?' Doyle could see Carter thinking. He had planned so much, but this wasn't part of his plan. 'You could've given yourself up back at the house.'

'All the people I've ever loved are here; it was the only place to come. How did you find me?'

'I followed you here.'

'No, I don't mean that. I meant, how did you know I'd done it, and where to find me? I saw you on the TV with water spilled down your shirt, and thought you had no chance.'

'Maybe I got lucky.' *Keep him talking. He wants to know. It matters to him how he got caught; it bothers him that he made a mistake.*

'You didn't get lucky. There wasn't any connection between me and that teacher, nothing that you could have traced back to me.'

'Her name was Chloe, Jason. And like you said, you had no connection to her. But I still found myself sitting in her parents' front room, telling them their daughter had been murdered. And for what? Some sort of weird, twisted gratification?'

'You should know. You've killed too. I've read about you in the paper.'

'I did it because I had to, not because I got a kick from it.'

'Are you racked with guilt for taking a man's life?'

'No. I'm just relieved I hit him and not the little girl.'

Carter wiped sweat from his forehead with his free hand. 'When your Sergeant Morgan arrested Ryan, I actually thought you might make something stick with him.' Carter laughed. 'I don't even smoke any more, but when I picked up that little comms room installation job where he worked, I made sure I always took a fag break whenever he did. He was easy to provoke – wind him up and watch him go. I shared a cell with a guy just like him in Wetherby. Ryan showed me some of the messages he sent her. He's just as twisted as me, in a way.'

'He isn't though, is he? He was angry, hurt and jealous. He'll be punished for the threats and the harassment, maybe do some time. But he never killed anyone. How many have you killed, Jason?'

Doyle saw the other man's eyes narrow. 'What?'

'I know about Chloe, obviously, but before her there were Karolina Valanciunas and Victoria Quinn, weren't there?'

Carter gave a shrug. It looked petulant to Doyle, as if he was saying 'It doesn't matter. They don't matter'.

'We couldn't find any more after that, even though we kept looking back. But then you went to Spain sometime around the millennium, didn't you? About the same time as Michelle McCarthy went missing.'

Carter inhaled sharply. The name had hit home with him, Doyle thought.

'Her body has never been found. But there were similarities between her and your other victims. Our analyst spotted the links.'

Doyle caught the inscription of a headstone just behind Carter, and something registered with him. 'And then we found your partial thumbprint on a wardrobe door handle in the house where you murdered Chloe. And we found her front door key; it hadn't burned in the fire. There were a few other prints, to be fair; lots of people had opened those doors while looking round the house. It's what you do, isn't it? But then, how many of those people had committed arson as some twisted gesture of love for a missing girl who looked like all the other dead women? Just you.'

Another shrug. 'One print? Is that it?'

'That's what it *was*. It's a bit more now. One thing I'm still wondering, though, is why here?'

'What do you mean? You followed me here. It's where my parents are buried, I said that.' Carter's speech was becoming faster.

Doyle had to be careful. Carter was getting agitated, and he still held a bloody big knife.

'No. All the people you've ever loved are here, you said. Yet your family's plot is back behind me. Which makes me wonder why we are *here* precisely. And you're bobbing around in front of me. Are you deciding when to strike and plunge that blade into me, or are you guarding something behind you? I didn't see the name on the headstone – not that it would have told me anything. But I did see the date.'

'That's enough. Stop talking now. I fucking mean it.' Carter took a step towards Doyle.

'They died on the 5th of December 1999. Eleven days before Michelle McCarthy was last seen alive. The person in there was probably buried within a day or two of Michelle going missing. So… is Michelle in there too?'

'Shut up. Leave her alone.'

Doyle knew he should try to de-escalate the situation. Carter was becoming enraged, yet he heard himself probing further. 'Was the freshly laid earth easy to dig through? You must have gone quite deep to prevent the foxes trying to get to her.'

Another flash of lightning.

'Perfect place to hide a body, among so many others. But it's hard work digging, I imagine, at night with the ground near frozen, but Michelle was worth it, wasn't she? She wasn't like the others.'

Carter changed his grip on the knife. Doyle had pushed too far. Carter's arm rose, ready to strike.

Another clash of thunder, closer now. Carter turned his head to the noise. As he turned back towards Doyle, Doyle flung the soil he'd been holding into Carter's face. Carter wiped at his eyes and blinked, trying to get rid of the soil. This gave Doyle enough time to kick out hard with both legs, sending his assailant toppling over backwards. In a flash Doyle was on his feet. leaning over Carter. He brought his size twelve boot down hard on Carter's right arm, and smiled when he heard the satisfying sound of bone splintering. Carter screamed and released his grip on the knife.

There were rotors overhead again. This time it was the police helicopter. In the distance, Doyle saw several black-clad figures running in his direction. He probably didn't need to add to Carter's misery by giving him a swift kick in the bollocks for the purposes of detaining him, but he did it anyway.

It had been a hard week, Doyle thought. You had to take job satisfaction where you could.

Chapter 46

Day 7: Monday 19th June 2023

He woke suddenly, disorientated. Where was he? Instinctively his right hand groped for the dog tag around his neck. Then the pain from his ribs and left arm brought back his memory of what had happened and where he was. He opened his eyes. The clock on the wall opposite said seven fifteen. There were voices from beyond the curtain. Doyle had no idea what time he had finally dozed off. He'd had X-rays of his chest, confirming he had two fractured ribs, but thankfully they didn't affect his lung function and required nothing more than painkillers and following the doctor's advice, which was 'I'd try not to laugh too much, if I were you.' His left arm, which had made close acquaintances with an angle grinder, was a different story, but even there Doyle felt he had got off lightly, considering he'd seen the builder at his last house use the same tool to cut channels into brick walls. The two deep gashes caused by the cutting disc had been thoroughly cleaned before being stitched. Doyle had tried his best not to scream during the process, but even though he'd been liberally dosed with medication beforehand, he had lasted no more than twenty seconds, as anyone in the A&E of the Royal Blackburn Hospital that night would be able to attest. The doctor had told him afterwards that he didn't appear to have any significant nerve damage and, other than some rather impressive scars, Doyle's arm should make a full recovery. He had gone on to comment, 'It's a good job you haven't got any tattoos.'

'Why's that?' Doyle had asked in his addled state, expecting some kind of interesting medical fact in return.

'They're an absolute bugger to get back together so the picture lines up. Your arm would have ended up looking like a Picasso painting.'

Doyle had wondered why the doctor had told him to avoid laughter and had then decided to make him giggle. He'd been right. It hurt.

His own health was not Doyle's primary concern, however. Morgan was on his mind. The ambulance crew had managed to get an update on her before they left the cemetery with Doyle. She was in a critical condition and was being airlifted to Blackburn. It hadn't taken much persuasion to get them to take him to the same hospital rather than the nearer Blackpool or Preston hospitals. He now had to find her and, more importantly, see how she was. Doyle decided to get up. There was nothing stopping him – apart from his own pain, he realised when he tried to sit up. He still wore his jeans, socks and shoes from the day before, complete with mud from the graveyard. His top half, however, was bare. It didn't take him long to locate his T-shirt, which someone had neatly folded and left on the cabinet next to the bed. Putting the thing on with a damaged arm and broken ribs was problematic, and he tried his best to keep his monologue of profanities under his breath.

He pulled back the curtain around his bed. He found himself to be in a much bigger room than he remembered, with several curtained-off bays, presumably filled with other unfortunates whose weekends had ended on a low note. Several people in scrubs were moving with purpose on a variety of missions.

'Leaving us, Chief Inspector?' It was the doctor from the

night before.

'I want to find my colleague. She was brought in by helicopter yesterday in a pretty bad way. Do you know where she'll be?'

'She's probably in intensive care. It's on the floor above.'

'Thanks. I take it I'm alright to go up there?'

'Sure, but they might not let you in. If you've got your warrant card on you, that might help. Can you make sure you're back here by half eight? The day shift will be on then, and if the consultant agrees, you can go home. But I want to send you away with something for the pain and a course of antibiotics for your arm, to prevent infection.'

人 人 人

The first floor of the hospital was considerably calmer at this time of day than the A&E department Doyle had come from. The corridor to the intensive care unit was deserted, then a short Asian woman came out of the ICU doors. It took a moment to Doyle to register that the woman was Dr Gupta. And then another realisation: Dr Gupta was the Home Office Forensic Pathologist. Her patients were all dead, many of them killed. And she had just come out of the ICU unit where Morgan was. *Fuck, no, it can't be!* Doyle broke into a run, his pain suppressed by emotion.

Dr Gupta saw him, and stopped and raised her hands. 'Liam, Liam, it's OK.'

He arrived in front of her. 'What's happened? Anna, is she—'

'She's alive, Liam.'

'Oh… I saw you and I thought that…'

'I'm sorry, I didn't mean to give you a fright. I heard about what happened yesterday, so I came to see how she was doing before starting work. I was just on my way down to A&E to see how you were.'

'Oh.' Of course, Dr Gupta worked in this hospital. 'And how is she?'

The pathologist knocked on the door to a side room, then opened it and led Doyle inside. He sat on the sofa, and she took the armchair opposite.

'She's been sedated – put into a medically induced coma. That's normal in these situations: it protects the brain and gives it a chance to recover.'

'She will recover, then?'

'They don't know for sure just yet, but there is every reason to be optimistic. She had an MRI last night, and that didn't show anything of concern. As you know, when the brain is starved of oxygen it doesn't take long before damage is done, but hopefully you got there just in time to prevent this. How are your injuries? You look a bit worse for wear.'

'Considering the state of some of your patients, that's quite a concerning comment, Dr Gupta.'

She laughed. 'That's true. Well, you don't look like you'll be making an appearance on my slab any time soon, if that's any consolation. Just as well, too – your feet would hang over the end. What have the doctors said about your injuries?'

'I think I got away pretty well, considering. The cuts on my arm are deep, but don't seem to have done any nerve damage, and they said my ribs should heal on their own in a few weeks.'

'Good. You need to rest, though, give your body time to heal. Don't overdo things.'

'Yes, Doctor. What about Anna? What will happen?'

'Well, I spoke to the consultant, and she said they will look to withdraw the sedation slowly today and take her off the ventilator. They put her on that as a precaution, to take the strain off her body. She was breathing for herself when the paramedics arrived. As the sedation wears off, they will know more about whether there is any brain damage, but they are optimistic.'

'And what about... Did he, did he...'

'I was worried about that too, and asked the consultant. She doesn't think so. There were no obvious signs of bruising around the area. But more importantly, she was still in her cycling shorts when you found her; they cut them off at the hospital. Because they have braces that go over her shoulders, there's no way he could have removed them with her hands tied above her head without cutting them off. I think it was very unlikely that he raped her.'

'Thank Christ for that.'

'Indeed.'

'Do you think she'll remember much about what happened? Did Carter give her the same sedatives as he used on Chloe?'

'Good question. I'm not sure. It will be hard to find out if he gave her anything, with all the other medication in her system now.' Dr Gupta took a moment to think. 'She might remember some things, and some things might be hazy. Of course, the lack of oxygen might also cause some amnesia.'

'I hope she doesn't remember too much.'

'Me too.'

'It's probably not the right time to tell you, but I might've found you another patient.'

'I had heard that too. In the cemetery at Lytham?'

'Yes, afraid so. She will have been there since December 1999.'

'Well, if that turns out to be the case, I will examine the poor girl's remains – not that we will be able to tell much, from a forensic point of view, after so long. But we will be able to ID her and be able to give some answers to her family.' She shifted in her seat. 'I assume Chloe Kennedy's parents will know you've caught her killer by now?'

'The family liaison officer would have told them ahead of any media briefing. I'll go and see them today, give them a chance to ask any questions.'

'Good. Well, you've had quite a first week in the job.'

人 人 人

Morgan was in a side room in the intensive care unit. The lights were low, and the only sounds were the rhythmic pumping of the ventilator and the quiet footsteps of the nurse, who busied herself around the bed. As well as a breathing tube going into her mouth, there was also a line into her nose, several going into her arms, and others disappearing under the bed sheets. A catheter bag hung on the side of the bed. A screen on a trolley beside the bed displayed all her vital signs. Sam was dozing in a chair next to the bed when Doyle entered. Slowly, Sam opened his eyes. Doyle could tell he hadn't been sleeping, just resting while he waited for more news.

He rose from the chair. 'I think it looks worse than it is. I hope so, anyway. They've got her under sedation'

'I've just seen Dr Gupta – she explained it all to me. Is there anything you need, Sam?'

'I don't think so. They've been looking after me well. It's just a waiting game now. How are you? I'm sorry you got hurt.'

'I'm fine, it's nothing.' Doyle meant it: his pain was nothing compared to Morgan's situation. 'I'm sorry I didn't find her in time and get her out of there sooner.'

'It's not your fault. I know you did all you could. Her mum's getting the ferry over this morning. Do you think you might be able to meet her, explain it all?'

'Of course, and if there's anything you or she needs, let me know.' Doyle took a business card from his wallet and gave it to the younger man. 'And can you do me a favour? If there are any developments, let me know.'

'Sure.' Sam thumbed the card into his wallet.

'If you need anything, anything at all, call me. Any time.'

Chapter 47

The incident room was subdued when Doyle entered it later that morning. He had taken a taxi from the hospital to his new home, showered and got changed – both activities causing him significant discomfort – then he'd gone to work. Normally incident rooms would be buzzing after such a major arrest, but with Morgan critically ill in hospital there were no such feelings of elation. When people saw him, the quiet room fell silent. Gadget pulled out a chair for his boss, which he gratefully sank into.

'How are you, Liam?' Hales voiced the question on everyone's lips.

'I'm alright. Really, you should see the other guy.' Doyle was at least rewarded with some muted laughter. 'Actually, how is he? I've not heard.'

'He's in hospital, under armed guard,' Hales said. 'He's going to need an operation to mend his arm, but my favourite bit? The doctor said he has extensive bruising of his testicles.'

'Good work, boss,' Gadget said.

'We should be able to interview him by the end of the week,' Hales added.

'Good, we can do that together.'

'Derrick?' Doyle said, turning to Birdseye.

'Yes, guv?'

'I've got a few things to do now, but in about an hour, can you come with me to see Mr and Mrs Kennedy?'

'No problem. I expect you'll want me to drive, with your arm as it is?'

'I guess so,' Doyle replied, unable to come up with an alternative.

'Anything you want me to do, boss? Gadget asked.

'There is something, actually, though strictly speaking it's not work.'

'What? I don't mind.'

'Can you find me a good deal on a computer for my son? He wants it to play *Minecraft* and probably some other games too.'

'Sure.' Gadget's eyes had lit up. 'He'll be wanting one with a—'

'Don't bore me with the details, Gadget, just find me one that does all that and won't cost me an arm and a leg or be obsolete in eighteen months.'

人 人 人

Chorley looked rather different in the rain. People moved with purpose from shop to shop, keeping out of the deluge. His phone rang, and he ducked under a baker's canopy to take the call.

'Liam, it's Tara Langley. Force HR Director. How are you?'

A question Doyle was getting bored of hearing, but he updated her on his condition anyway.

'Two things,' she said. 'First, we've had an update from the hospital, and I thought you would want to know straight away. Anna is off the ventilator and has been responding well. She's still very drowsy apparently, which is to be expected, but she has given the doctors a thumbs-up and been able to raise and lower her legs on command. It's good news – everything indicates that she'll be OK.'

'That's fantastic. Thanks for letting me know.'

'You're welcome. And well done.'

'Thanks.'

'Oh, there was one other thing.'

'Go on.'

'I'd advise you to avoid Croucher for a few days.'

'What? Even he can't be pissed off with me now.'

'You'd think that, wouldn't you? But the golf club of his that you used to try and stop your suspect? You broke it, and apparently it cost over £800.'

'What? How much are you paying him that he can spend that much on a golf club?'

'Well, quite. It's a Ping one, and apparently they are very expensive.'

'Funny – it made a *ping* sound when it hit the petrol tank of the motorbike.'

人 人 人

Doyle felt slightly awkward walking into the estate agent's office with a bottle of champagne in his hand, but at the same time he was relieved he hadn't gone for flowers. He was also glad to find that Bea was there and not busy with another client, which meant he was shown straight into her office.

'Wow, look at you. You look like you've been dragged through a hedge backwards.'

'Thanks.'

'Are you OK, though?'

'Yes, I'll be fine, thanks.'

'And your colleague – I saw on the news she was in a bad way.'

'She is, but she's improving. It looks like she will be OK.'

'Well, that is a big relief. It's been on my mind ever since you called me yesterday.'

'She was at that house you found. Without your help, we wouldn't have got to her in time.'

'Wow, maybe I should be a detective too.'

'I wouldn't recommend it; the hours are terrible. Here, I got you this to say thanks.' Doyle handed over the champagne.

'Bollinger – very classy, but I was hoping you'd take me out for dinner.'

'Friday night?'

'It's a date – deal, I meant deal.'

Doyle smiled. 'You pick the restaurant and I'll pay. I've only just moved here, you know, and I don't know the best places.'

'Ah yes. How was your first night in your new home?'

'I'll let you know tomorrow; I spent all night at the hospital.'

'Oh well, I'm glad to see you're more or less in one piece.'

'Thanks. Look, I'd better get back. But I'll see you Friday.'

'I'll call you when I've made a booking.'

人 人 人

As Doyle walked up the steps to the front entrance to Chorley police station, Bowen emerged from inside. When he saw Doyle, he rushed to greet him.

'Have you heard the news, sir, about DS Morgan? Looks like she's going to be OK.'

'I just got a call to that effect. I take it everyone's got that news?'

'Must have, if it filtered down to us. Such a relief.'

'You're back on normal duties now, Francis?'

'Afraid so – just off to see someone who's made a complaint about a neighbour smoking weed in the back garden. Quite a comedown from a murder investigation.'

'I can see that. You'd make a good detective. If an opportunity arises, you should go for it.'

'Detective Chief Inspector Doyle.'

Doyle turned to the other man now standing on the steps. It took him a moment to place him as Jayden Clark, the hack from the *Lancashire Chronicle*.

'I hear you've caught your man? In fact, not just caught him, but put him in hospital.'

'Well, you can't believe everything you hear, Mr Clark.'

'I've got my finger on the pulse.'

'And your tongue in someone's arsehole too, no doubt. I must say, I'm surprised to see you here. I thought you'd be at Force HQ for the press conference.'

'Press conference?'

Doyle looked at his watch. 'Starts in fifteen minutes. Didn't you get an invite?'

'I… er…' Clark looked towards Bowen, who nodded, as if to confirm what Doyle had said. The journalist then turned and headed down the steps, no doubt making for his car.

'Mr Clark,' Doyle shouted after him. 'Drive carefully, won't you? I've put up a £500 bonus for any officer that can nick you for speeding – or any other traffic offence.' He lowered his voice and smiled at Bowen. 'I wonder how far he'll get before he realises I was winding him up and there is no press conference?'

Chapter 48

Day 11: Friday 23rd June 2023

Jason Carter had been discharged from hospital on the Thursday evening into the care of Lancashire Constabulary, who were detaining him at Preston police station. Even without a formal interview there was enough evidence to charge him with the murder of Chloe Kennedy and the abduction and attempted murder of DS Anna Morgan. As expected, human remains discovered buried above another body at Lytham Park Cemetery had been identified by dental records as those of Michelle McCarthy. There was a decent amount of circumstantial evidence to link Carter to her murder. Detectives from Greater Manchester and West Yorkshire police would be interviewing Carter about the murders of Karolina Valanciunas and Victoria Quinn when Doyle's team had finished with him.

It didn't matter whether Carter said anything in the interviews. With what they had already, Doyle couldn't see him walking away from a trial with anything other than a whole life tariff. But Doyle wanted to know why. Why had Carter killed these women? He knew deep down that even if Carter did answer all their questions, it would never make sense.

Doyle had decided to let Birdseye and Gadget have the first crack at Carter. DC Nelson had a way with people, and was the most likely to get him talking. Carter had used technology extensively in Chloe's murder, and Gadget understood this better than anyone on the team. Doyle had briefed the young detective to ask questions along these lines, admiring the killer's work and feeding his ego. Doyle watched on a screen with Hales as the DCs warmed their prisoner up, before it was their turn.

'How's your arm?' Carter asked as Doyle entered the interview room.

'Not so bad. Yours?' Unlike Doyle, Carter was still wearing a sling with his forearm in a cast.

'Painful. But I'll live.'

'And you haven't changed your mind about not wanting a solicitor?' Hales asked.

'Can't see the point.'

'Fair enough,' said Doyle, making an effort not to let Carter see the amount of pain his ribs caused him as he sat down.

After Hales had done the legal preamble for the recording, Doyle got started on the questioning. 'You told our colleagues in detail earlier about how you were able to set up the company using James Fisher's details and trade as him. But there's something puzzling me about that.'

'What?'

'You stole his documents in the summer of 2016 and set up the company in 2019. Had you really been planning this for that long?'

Carter gave a half laugh. 'No, I didn't take them for that reason.'

'Why, then?'

'I'd been living in Spain and Portugal since 2000. I didn't have any real ID, just a made-up name. It wasn't really a problem. I did work for other people fixing computers and that for cash. Mostly ex-pats. I did alright.'

'And something changed?'

'The Brexit vote. There were lots of rumours then that Brits would have to register to keep living there, all kinds of things. Nobody knew what was going on. I could see there being a problem for me down the line, and I needed a way to get back. I kept a look-out for British tourists – anyone who looked a bit like me. I saw this guy go into a restaurant with his family. He had one of those man bags slung across his shoulder, and he put it on the floor when he sat down. I walked past him and hooked the strap with my foot. It had a passport, driving licence, National Insurance card, the lot.'

'Is that when you came back here?'

'That night, I chucked everything I could in the car and drove to Calais. It was so busy at the ferry port, they hardly looked at the passport. I don't think they even opened it.'

'We found Michelle's remains in the cemetery. Was she the first?'

Carter swallowed, and his expression changed. Doyle's sudden change of tack had caught him off guard.

Doyle let the question hang in the air, not wanting to fill the silence.

'She wasn't like the others. I loved her.'

'Why, then?'

'It was an accident. I'd waited so long to see her again after I got sent down. Thinking about her kept me going. She'd ruined herself: short hair, grungy clothes. She was still pretty but she looked a mess. She wasn't the same Michelle either. It was horrible.'

'How did it make you feel, Jason? What did seeing her like that make you feel? How did seeing her short hair make you feel?'

Carter had brought his knees up to his chest, his good arm wrapped around them. 'She reminded me of my mum. My mum when she was dying of cancer, with just little tufts of hair on her head. The disease had got to her brain, turned her nasty.'

'How did you feel after you killed Michelle?'

'Numb at first. Then relieved.'

'Relieved?'

'The new Michelle was gone, and I could grieve for the old one and move on. Like I did with my mum and dad when they died.'

'Then why did you carry on killing?'

'I didn't, at first. Not for another seven years. I tried to live normally, put it behind me. There was this Spanish girl who worked in a bar I used to go to. She was pretty and friendly, but I didn't really know her. Then one day I went into the bar and she'd shaved off all her lovely hair. It was in support of a friend who was having chemo.' Carter put his feet back on the floor. 'That kind of woke something up inside me. I started to fantasise about her.'

'Sexual fantasies?' Doyle asked.

'Killing fantasies. I started to keep tabs on her. Follow her after work, see where she went. All the time I was thinking how I could do it, and where. It was exhilarating. I planned it all out, but it was still just something in my head. And then I did it.'

'You killed her?'

'It was the biggest rush ever. I couldn't describe it. I was buzzing for ages afterwards. I wasn't worried I would get caught. I buried her body up on a hill where nobody would find it.'

'Then you had to do it again?'

Carter nodded. 'When I was in the Young Offenders, I shared a cell with a crackhead. He told me about the rush. Not just taking the drug, but the build-up from the minute he told himself he was going to do it. He used to rob people, and all the time he was doing it he was excited, knowing it would end up with his fix. It was the same for me: the planning, building up to it, ending in a climax when they took their final breath.'

Carter smiled. It was the most sinister thing Doyle had ever seen. His fists were balled up under the table, and he wanted to jump up and smash the life out of Jason Carter – for Chloe, Michelle and all the others, but mostly for Anna Morgan and what he had put her through. But he wouldn't; he was civilised. The best thing he could do for all Carter's victims, for all their families, was keep him talking and get answers.

'Why did you stop burying your victims, and just dump them?'

Carter shrugged. 'It's hard work digging a hole deep enough that they won't get dug back up by some animal and found. I didn't enjoy that bit. If anything, it distracted me from the buzz. Then that one got found anyway and I thought, what's the point? Just clean yourself off them and get rid. And it worked – you never found any traces of me on the bodies.'

Doyle shook his head. *And yet you're sitting here. If Chloe hadn't been found, she would have been just another misper like Michelle.*

⅄ ⅄ ⅄

Morgan raised a hand off the bed in a greeting to Doyle.

'Good to see you back in the land of the living.'

'Thanks.' Her voice was croaky, barely above a whisper. 'Has he been charged?'

'For Chloe Kennedy's murder and those of Karolina Valanciunas and Victoria Quinn. Items of jewellery belonging to all three women were found at his house. He has confessed to killing Michelle McCarthy, and will be charged for that too.'

Morgan raised her head slightly to take a sip of water. Doyle wasn't sure if he should help her, but opted not to.

'Good.'

'We will also be charging him for your kidnap and attempted murder, once you're ready to give a statement.'

'How's your arm and ribs?'

'Sore, but on the mend.'

'Glad to hear it. I owe you one, boss.'

'You can pay me back now, if you like.'

'How?'

'What nickname have the team got for me?'

'I don't think there's one.'

'You're still a rubbish liar, Morgan. What is it?'

Morgan took another sip of water. 'The BFG.'

'Not bad. Stands for Big Friendly Giant, right?'

'Nearly. Big Fuck-off Guvnor.'

Epilogue

October 2023

Doyle pulled his car up behind one that he recognised as belonging to Dr Gupta. Summer had drifted into autumn and leaves blew around in the damp sea air. He checked his black tie in the rear-view mirror.

'Shall we?' he said to the woman in the passenger seat.

'OK,' Asif said.

When they got out of their car, Dr Gupta got out of her own vehicle. Greetings completed, the three of them began the short walk towards the chapel of remembrance.

'Tell me, Liam, how is Anna doing? Really, I mean. I know she has been back at work a few weeks?'

'OK, I think, all things considered. Who knows, though? You don't go through what she did and not have some heavy scars.'

'Take great care of her. She's bright and tough, but this must have rocked her to her core.'

'I know. We'll do our best.'

'I've had some enquiries from a pathologist in Spain, you know.'

'I thought you might. How many have they found?'

'Three, so far, from the information Carter gave about where they were buried, and one who was found soon after she died, but her boyfriend was convicted for it.'

'Have you read the reports?'

'Not yet. They're being translated and then they'll be sent over. I'll let you know.'

'Thanks.'

They had reached the crematorium entrance. A woman who looked familiar was walking towards them, with a man in a black suit a few paces behind.

'Chief Inspector Doyle?' the woman asked, holding out a hand. 'I'm Melanie, Michelle's sister. We spoke on the phone.'

'Yes,' Doyle said, shaking her hand. 'Please call me Liam. This is Dr Gupta, the pathologist, and Shaima, our intelligence analyst. She found the link to Michelle.'

The women exchanged handshakes, and Melanie introduced the man behind her as her husband Gregg.

'I can't tell you what this means to me. Since she disappeared, I've spent my whole life wondering. Did something happen to her, or did she run away to start a new life, wanting to leave everything behind, including me? The first hurt so much because she was my big sister – growing up, I idolised her, and I just wanted her to be OK. And the second hurt because I hated to think that she could leave me and never get in touch.'

'I hope knowing the truth hasn't made things worse,' Doyle said.

'No, no, it hasn't.' Melanie looked Doyle in the eye. He could see that she resembled an older Michelle, as well as Chloe Kennedy. 'Now I know. I know she didn't leave me, and I can grieve her loss and love her again, knowing she didn't abandon me.'

'How did your mum take the news?' Doyle asked.

Melanie sighed, and Gregg placed an arm round her. 'She never believed Michelle when she told her what my dad did to her. Said she was lying, making it up to get attention. But I knew that she was telling the truth. I saw the way he looked at her, and heard her protest when he went in her room while Mum was out. When I told Mum she was dead, that she'd been murdered, you know what she said? *Good riddance.* I'd hardly spoken to her in years, anyway. I won't be speaking to her again.'

'I'm sorry,' Doyle said.

'Don't be. You found her and brought her back to me, and now at least I can love my big sister again.'

'I think those people over there may be her friends from college,' Gregg said, gesturing to a small group of people in their forties standing at the other side of the crematorium entrance.

'That's another sad thing,' Melanie said. 'It's just us and them here to mourn Michelle's death. Twenty-three years later, everyone else has moved on. I could never leave Fleetwood when she was gone – I wanted to stay close to where we lived in case she ever came back, so she could find me.' Melanie wiped tears from her eyes. 'I'd better go and say hello to her Manchester friends. Thanks so much for coming.' She walked off, Gregg a few paces behind.

Doyle turned to Asif. 'It's not a happy story, but at least now, thanks to you finding the connection, that poor woman has some closure.'

ACKNOWLEDGEMENTS

I am very grateful to a great many people without whom this book would not have made it to publication. In particular I would like to thank the following people who contributed their skills, knowledge and expertise alongside their unwavering encouragement. Rebecca Spargo, Hannah Chivers, Val Spargo, Christine Barnes, Jane Hammett, Tracy Pemberton, Ken Dawson and Kate Coe. I would also like to thank my two children for keeping me grounded in reality throughout the whole process and in life in general.

TO YOU THE READER

As well as the people mentioned above, I would also like to thank you the reader. When you choose to read a book, you decide to invest not only money but your precious time too. I hope you enjoyed the book and were left wanting to read more about Doyle, Morgan and the rest of the team in future books in the series. I would be very grateful if you would consider leaving a review and or rating where you purchased the book. This not only helps me, but also other readers like you to find the kind of books they like to read.

For more information about BD Spargo and further instalments of the DCI Doyle series visit: bdspargo.com

To sign up to the DCI Doyle Reader's Club and receive exclusive bonus content, regular newsletters and be the first to hear the latest news visit:

bdspargo.com/readers-club

ABOUT THE AUTHOR

Fast approaching fifty; without enough money for a sports car, BD Spargo decided to express his mid-life crises by turning to crime …

Thankfully for pretty much everyone this meant writing crime fiction rather than anything more nefarious. Originally from London, he spent his early career working in television and theatre including on the *Ruth Rendall Mysteries* broadcast on ITV.

A life changing accident necessitated retraining and a change of direction going on to work in mental health services. This culminated in ten years managing a groundbreaking forensic psychiatric service. He now lives in Lancashire with his family and is getting acclimatised to the rain.